FORGING THE WEAPON

BY

FRANK ROCKLAND

Copyright © 2014 Francesco Rocca
www.sambiasebooks.ca

Designer: Jonathan Relph
Copyeditor: Jennifer McKnight
Proofeading Editor: Allister Thompson

Library and Archives Canada Cataloguing in Publication
Rockland, Frank, 1956-, author
  Forging the weapon / Frank Rockland.

Issued in print and electronic formats.
ISBN 978-0-9917050-3-0 (pbk.).--ISBN 978-0-9917050-2-3 (epub)

1. Canada. Canadian Army. Canadian Expeditionary Force--
Fiction. 2. World War, 1914-1918--Canada--Fiction. I. Title.

PS8635.O33F67 2015   C813›.6   **C2015-902092-1**
                                                C2015-902093-X

Other Books by Frank Rockland

Fire on the Hill

What really happened on the night of February 3, 1916, when a fire destroyed the Centre Block of the Canadian Parliament buildings?

Inspector Andrew MacNutt of the Dominion Police's Secret Service, his wife Katherine, and Count Jaggi know, since they were there in the reading room when the fire started.

Ever since the war began, MacNutt has been struggling to secure Canada's borders against acts of sabotage organized by German military attachés based in New York City. The good news is that the Americans have finally ordered them back to Germany. The bad news is that Berlin has sent one of their best operatives, Count Jaggi, to replace them.

Using his cover as a Belgian Relief representative, Count Jaggi visits Ottawa, where he meets and is attracted to Katherine, who is helping him organize a local fundraiser.

Unaware that Inspector MacNutt has intercepted his secret messages and is hot on his trail, Count Jaggi takes a final trip to Ottawa to see Katherine, with tragic consequences.

Author's Note

Forging the Weapon is a work of fiction. All incidents, dialogue, and characters, with the exception of historical and public figures, are products of the author's imagination and are not to be construed as real.

Where real-life historical or public figures appear, the situations, incidents, and dialogue concerning the person are fictional.

In all aspects, any resemblance to the living or the dead is entirely coincidental.

CHAPTER 1

What a miserable Dominion Day, thought Captain James Llewellyn as he checked on his two horses before he hit the sack. They were tied with a dozen or so others at the picket line. His riding steed raised his head and cocked an ear. He liked the slight chill and the drizzling rain. His pal, the pack animal, was not as happy. His tail was swishing — not a good sign.

"Easy boy. Easy," he murmured as he softly stroked the animal's neck. The packhorse had spent most of the day tied to the picket line, which he didn't enjoy. He might be fine for the night, but tomorrow he'd have to find something for him to do. The rain should end by morning, so he might be in a better mood.

Llewellyn gave the packhorse a last reassuring pat before he headed to his bell tent. He had only taken a few steps when he spotted the sentry huddled under a tree trying to stay dry. Not for the first time he was glad he brought his own oilskin rather than the government-issue crap. But the youngster didn't have much of a choice. In fact, he was probably grateful that he had any kind of rain gear.

With 2,500 cadets and a hundred instructors descending on Niagara-on-the-Lake's military reserve for a week's training, the quartermasters were quickly overwhelmed when the weather turned bad. When some of the young men were told that they had to return home for the evening until they sorted things out, they refused. Llewellyn was pleased when he heard that. He liked their enthusiasm.

He was tempted to sneak up on the boy and yell boo, but he thought better of it. He'd speak with the boy's commanding officer in the morning.

When he reached his tent, he removed his coat and then bent slightly to enter. Inside it was rather cramped, with two saddles and packs set at the foot of the canvas cots. Resting on the packs were two Ross rifles. The stocky man of medium height lying on one of the beds made the small tent even smaller. Lieutenant Simon Rawlings was reading a newspaper by the light provided by an oil lamp hanging from the shelter's centre pole.

1

He peered over the top of the paper. "The horses are okay?"

"A little wet, but they'll be fine for my patrol," Llewellyn said as he unbuckled his waist belt, which contained his .455 Colt revolver in a holster, and laid it on one of the packs, which contained his week's supply of rations.

"I'm a bit surprised you volunteered to teach the cadets."

"Just scouting for talent," replied the captain.

Rawlings snorted in derision at the pun. Llewellyn was a Corps of Guides officer, the Canadian militia's scouting and intelligence unit. "Don't you have to be an officer and gentleman?" he remarked.

"We can't be all officers. Someone has to do the actual work," he replied. The cot creaked when he sat down. Sadly, Rawlings's attitude was common in the militia. The Corps was an amusing afterthought since mainly officers staffed it. When the Corps was created in 1903, its first commanding officer held the belief that only one guide per town was needed in wartime, but it was not necessary in peacetime. The CO felt that for a proper officer, with the correct frame of mind, training wasn't necessary.

Llewellyn was determined, as were a significant number of other Corps members, to remedy the situation. Convincing Ottawa was an uphill battle. In the last several years they'd managed to run a few programs to help train intelligence personnel.

"Found any prospects?"

"A few," he replied tersely. "They're enthusiastic about the idea of patrolling and scouting." One of the roles of the scouts was to locate and gather as much intelligence on the enemy forces as possible. They were then to relay the information such as the composition, numbers, their movements, strengths, and weaknesses to Canadian commanders.

"They want to be Mounties," Rawlings surmised with a grin.

Llewellyn snorted sourly. "They're young kids. Their idea of war comes from dime novels and Kipling. I lose them when I tell them that I spend most of my time surveying and mapping." The captain was a surveyor by trade. Canada was still a young country, and the maps currently available were not detailed enough for military use. What was needed were topographical maps of the terrain so commanders would know the best defensive positions where they could block an enemy force. This would buy time for the militia to mobilize and repel the attackers. Detailed assessments of the roads, train tracks, pastures for cavalry horses to feed, and telegraph lines were needed for the swift movement of Canadian forces.

Rawlings chuckled. "You're way too honest. You need to learn how to fib a bit."

Llewellyn sighed as he rubbed his neck. "I know. Anything interesting in the paper?"

"All of the officers of the London Field Battery resigned," the lieutenant answered in disgust.

The captain stopped rubbing his neck. "All of them?"

"Yep. They were pissed that their tents were searched without a warrant. Especially after they gave their word that they had no beer," replied Rawlings.

"What would you expect when beer bottles were found in the battery's line at Petawawa?" The camp near the Ottawa River was the main training facility for Eastern Canada, nearly 200 miles northeast of Niagara-on-the-Lake. "Everyone knows Hughes' attitude toward alcohol," the Corps of Guides officer pointed out.

"I don't know if I can trust a soldier that doesn't drink."

Llewellyn chuckled. "Have to give Hughes some credit for trying to bring the militia up to snuff. Nearly everyone in the reserve has attended a training camp this year." Colonel Hughes, the minister of Militia and Defence, had ordered that all men fit for duty were to attend one of the ten-day training sessions held in the first weeks of June at the Ontario Petawawa and Niagara-on-the-Lake facilities. The current cadet camp was the last for the season.

"Send him a gram and ask for an increase to the Guides' budget."

"Yeah, right! Ottawa's stingy with the defence budget."

"Stingy! I would call it something else."

Changing the subject, Llewellyn asked, "Anything else?"

"Nothing much," the lieutenant replied as he turned a page. He paused and then said, "There is a story here about some duke that was assassinated in Sarajevo."

"Archduke Franz Ferdinand?" Llewellyn asked sharply.

"You've heard of him?" asked Rawlings as he looked up from the paper.

"He happens to be the heir apparent to the Austria-Hungary Empire. When was he killed?"

Rawlings squinted at the tiny print. "It says June 28. He and his wife were gunned down on a state visit."

When Llewellyn said, "Ouch!" Rawlings looked at his friend quizzically, who then explained. "The political situation between the Empire and Serbia have been rather tense since the Austrians annexed Bosnia and Herzegovina six years ago. If the Serbian government was involved, there could be hell to pay."

"How do you know all this?"

Llewellyn grinned. "I'm an officer in the Corps of Guides, and I read."

Rawlings laughed. "I heard everything. An intelligence officer who actually reads."

When Llewellyn gave him a give-me-a-break look, Rawlings put the paper aside. "Well, it has nothing to do with us. So what devious training scheme does the captain have in store for our young naive cadets?"

As the rain began to beat more heavily on the tent, Captain Llewellyn outlined what he intended for the next day's session.

JULY 2, 1914
WESTMOUNT, MONTREAL

Paul Ryan slowly opened and closed the door to his house on Sherbrooke Street. He winced when the lock clicked shut rather loudly. He listened intently to determine if the noise had wakened the darkened house's residents. The servant's quarters were in the back, while his parents', brother's, and sister's rooms were on the second floor of the two-storey mansion. He hoped that he could get to his room without anyone noticing.

He froze when he saw a thin ray of light emanating from his father's study. The white-panelled door was slightly ajar. He was tempted to remove his shoes before he tried the stairs that were ten feet away. He decided the tan floral runner on the floor would be enough to muffle his steps.

He only took two when a voice called out from the study. "Is that you, son?"

Paul cursed silently. He didn't want to speak with his father, but he didn't have much choice. "Yes, Father," he replied in a normal tone with a hint of cheeriness he didn't feel.

"Come into my study. I want to have a word," his father ordered.

4

Paul's shoulders slumped slightly at the prospect. Then he straightened as he opened the door to face the music.

When he entered the study, he found his father scrutinizing an accounting ledger with a frown. One couldn't tell from his father's slumped shoulders that he was a tall man, slightly over six feet, his broad chest covered by a white cotton shirt with the sleeves rolled to his elbows. A slight paunch, encased in black slacks, pressed against the walnut desk's edge.

Not for the first time, he noticed that his father was beginning to age. He was in his mid-forties, and grey hair was starting to creep into his sideburns. His hair, parted in the middle, was dishevelled from his habit of running his hand through the brown hair when he was deep in thought.

His father's brow didn't change when he raised his eyes toward him. Everyone told Paul that he took after his mother. He was shorter by two inches, and he had a thin but wiry frame. His hair was a sandy shade of brown and his eyes had a hazel tinge. Unlike his father, he wore a moustache, a rather thin one, but it passed for one, barely.

"Where have you been?" he demanded.

"I went out to see Sir Arthur Conan Doyle at the Ritz-Carleton," he replied.

His father grunted in slight disgust. "So did he give you any writing tips?"

"No, he didn't," Paul answered. It was a bone of contention between himself, the oldest son, and his father. While Paul was very strong in math, he'd rather be a writer. His father, being a practical man, as he was so fond of saying, was of the opinion that being a writer was all fine and good as a hobby, not as a career where one would be able to provide for one's family. He wanted Paul to be an engineer or an accountant. He was not happy that Paul's mother was encouraging him to be a so-called artist. He was somewhat irritated that Sir Doyle was in Montreal trying to prove him wrong.

His father knew that he greatly admired the British author. He had all of the Sherlock Holmes novels, some in this study's bookcases. He pored over the books, trying to imitate the same Arthur Conan Doyle style in his own detective stories. Paul was ecstatic when he learned that the Canadian government had invited the author to visit and to help promote the new Jasper Park in Alberta. He followed the tour avidly, reading every news story that mentioned it. Sir Arthur Conan Doyle had arrived in Montreal nearly a week after he had landed in New York City, on May 27, 1914. When they announced his itinerary, they had scheduled a speech at the Montreal Canadian Club on June 3rd.

Paul could barely contain himself when his father, a member of the club, obtained tickets for him. The main hall, as well as the adjoining rooms at the Windsor Hotel, was packed. He couldn't get a seat near the main stage, but he was still able to get a glimpse of the great man from the back of the room. He wasn't disappointed when Sir Doyle stated that great Canadian literature would come in due course. It would be best if Canadians focused on developing Canada, making her economically strong. His father agreed with Doyle, and he used it against Paul on several occasions.

The next day, Sir Arthur Conan Doyle and Lady Doyle left Montreal via a great lake steamer and private railway cars to Jasper Park. From the reports, the British couple were impressed with what they saw, and they enjoyed their stay at Jasper. The author even threw the opening pitch at the first baseball game ever held at the park.

"He did say that he was somewhat surprised that he didn't see a lot of Canadian flags celebrating Dominion Day," Paul said.

"If he had visited downtown, he would have seen them," his father replied.

"Did he have anything else to say?"

"Not much. He and his wife were only here for the day. They took a private train car to Ottawa. He's to give a speech at a Canadian Club meeting at the Château Laurier in Ottawa before he goes back to England."

"I'm surprised that you didn't follow him," said his father, knowing full well he would have kicked his ass if he did such a thing. He was nearly eighteen, his birth date was on August 5, but since he lived with his parents he had to follow their rules.

"Me and my friends stayed downtown, but most of the bars were closed today." His father nodded. With the Temperance League gathering strength in Quebec, the provincial government had enacted regulations that the sale of alcohol be prohibited on public holidays.

"I know some of the workers at the factory wanted to get a beer at lunch, but they couldn't," said his father. He owned a textile plant in Montreal's east side. Even though it was a holiday, he had orders that needed to be filled. He expected Paul to join the business after he had completed his schooling. Paul was to attend McGill University in the fall.

6

"It would have been nice to have let your mother know," his father said pointedly. "She's been worried sick."

A mulish look appeared on Paul's face. "Sorry, Dad, I forgot." He didn't want to get into an argument about his mother's smothering.

"Don't let it happen again. You know her health is not the best, and I don't want to upset her."

Paul sighed. He couldn't wait to go to McGill and escape the cage that he was in. Even though McGill was in Montreal, he was planning to stay in the university's student residence. As yet he hadn't informed his parents of his decision.

"Good. Start packing tomorrow. We're going to St. Agathe for a couple of weeks' vacation."

"Aw, Dad. Do I have to? I want to stay here."

"And do what?"

"Things!"

"What things?"

"My friends and I have plans."

"Right," replied his father. Paul watched his father's eyes narrow in speculation. "Wait a minute, aren't most of your friends attending the cadet training camp in Trois-Rivières next week?"

Paul reluctantly acknowledged by inclining his head. Nearly 1,500 cadets were attending a summer militia camp, where they would be conducting infantry training and physical exercises. The cadets would be a mixture of English- and French-speaking units. Most of his friends were attending. He wanted desperately to go. Not so much for the military training, but rather, going to their summer cottage at Ste. Agathe was boring. There was nothing to do for two weeks.

"Definitely not! This will be your last summer before you're off to university. And you know what your mother thinks about the army."

"I have to grow up sometime," he retorted.

"Trying telling that to your mother," replied his father. "No! So go up to your room and get some sleep. It's going to be a busy day before we take the train on Saturday."

Paul glared at his father and then turned and jerked the door open. "Don't slam the door!"

Paul was tempted to do that exactly that. Then he reconsidered. Who did he want more upset at him, his mother or his father? It was no contest. He slowly and quietly closed the study door.

JULY 15, 1914
TORONTO GENERAL HOSPITAL, TORONTO

Samantha caught the man's hand before he could reach its intended target. "Now, now! None of that, Mr. Parsons," she admonished. The patient, a fifty-year-old with a broken leg, gave her a toothless grin. His teeth, he was fond of saying, were lost when a fight turned into a hockey game.

In the private patient wing of the Toronto General Hospital, Mr. Parsons was known to be handsy. The matrons were careful in the nurses that were assigned to deal with him. They tried to select the less pretty ones and those who were able to handle Mr. Parsons' wandering hands without offending him. Parsons was a wealthy man, and he had donated a substantial amount of the $2.2 million that it cost to build the hospital complex that sat on nine acres on the corner of College Street and University Avenue in downtown Toronto. The hospital had beds for 670 patients and could handle 500 outpatients a day.

It was natural that the hospital's administration kept a watchful eye on the young nurse trainees to ensure that there wasn't any kind of scandal.

Samantha was of medium height in her sensible low-heeled nurse's shoes, which were barely visible below her ankle-length white skirt. Her chest was hidden from view by a starched apron over a cotton blouse buttoned all the way up to her chin. Her sandy blond hair was tied in a coil hidden by a nurse's veil. A thin black line in the veil indicated that she was in her final year of the hospital's three-year training program.

Parsons looked startled by the young girl's strength as she returned his hand to rest on his amble belly covered by hospital linen. His grin lost its lustre. It was a good thing he was going to be released the next day. The patient had a mean streak. He would try to get back at her in one form or another.

When she was sure that he was safely tucked away, she made a note in the chart hanging on the door. She headed down the hall to the nurse's station. The station was a small wooden desk set in the middle of the floor, where they could keep an eye on the patients' comings and goings.

"So how was the patient?" asked Nurse Fields, who was starting her shift.

"He's all right. I took care of him."

"I see," replied Fields with a cocked eyebrow. Parsons' hands were not restricted to just Samantha.

"I hope that you have a quieter shift," Samantha said. Fields gave her a half smile in reply.

Samantha was glad to see her, since she had been on the floor for sixteen hours and she was reaching the breaking point. After she had briefed Fields on the patients' statuses, she took the stairs down three floors to the ground level and took the back exit. As she crossed the alley, she glanced at the traffic that rumbled by on Christopher Street. She then entered the nurses' residence building's rear door.

She heard some laughter in the reception area. Curious, she took a peek to see who was in. Several of the senior student nurses were entertaining their beaus. They were on the love seat that was beside a bookcase. Between the ladies and the men there was a gleaming solid wood table. This was as far as the men were allowed in; they were restricted to the reception hall. A steely-eyed matron kept a close watch on the men and women.

Samantha pulled her head back and headed up the stairs to her room. Her room was small, with a large white panel window that faced the courtyard. The rumbling of cars and horse carriages was louder than usual since the window was opened a crack. What wind there was caused a subtle wave in the heavy brown cotton blinds. She took off her nurse's veil, which she tossed on the bright, daisy-patterned blanket on the single steel-framed bed that dominated the room. Her uniform followed suit. From the pile of fresh laundry on the solid but uncomfortable-looking straight-back chair, she pulled out and put on her yellow pyjamas. She took the dress and the veil off her bed and wondered if she could get one more wearing before she had to send them to the laundry. She decided to put it in the wooden closet where she stored the rest of her clothes.

She was about to reach for the *Maclean's* that was lying on top of the magazines on the end table beside her bed when there was a knock at her door. A loud voice asked, "Are you decent?"

"Yes, come in," Samantha shouted.

The door opened, and her best friend, Irene Abbott, came in carrying her favourite drink: a steaming cup of Earl Grey with a thin slice of lemon on top for flavouring. She sighed contentedly after the first sip as she leaned back against the bed's headboard. Her thick pillow cushioned her back from the thin metal bars.

9

"Thanks, Irene. I needed that," she said.

Irene was twenty-four years old, with a very pretty oval face on a slightly stout body, currently hidden by the pinkish bathrobe she was wearing. Most men found her figure more attractive than Samantha's thinner frame. They had first met in anatomy class, and they both somehow managed to make it through their final year.

"Did you hear anything yet?" Irene asked as she sat beside Samantha on the bed.

Samantha shook her head as she peered over her cup. "No, not yet."

"I don't see why they wouldn't keep you," she replied. Samantha loved Irene to death, but she had a blind spot. Irene came from a well-to-do family, or at least better off than Samantha's. Samantha had to work, while Irene was only working to keep busy until she found a husband.

"Matron Hazel doesn't like me very much," answered Samantha.

"If they don't offer a permanent job, what next?"

"I don't know. I can always go back to Sudbury. They need nurses. The pay isn't that great, but at least I won't starve."

"There's plenty of husky miners there," mused Irene.

Samantha snorted. "The last thing that I need right now is a man. Sudbury is so boring! I want a little excitement before I settle down."

"Come to the dance tomorrow night. There will be plenty of young doctors."

"I suppose. They might be better than the Sudbury miners," Samantha replied, rolling her eyes.

"That's the spirit," Irene said as she rose from the bed to leave.

JULY 29, 1914
ROYAL MUSKOKA HOTEL AND GOLF COURSE, LAKE ROSSEAU

"Damn," swore Sir Robert Borden as he watched in dismay as his golf ball sliced gracefully to the right. He winced when he heard it rattle among the trees.

"Language, dear," scolded Laura, his wife, who was standing slightly behind him on the tee box of the sixth hole of the Royal Muskoka Golf Course.

"We should be able to find it," remarked Hugh MacLaren sympathetically. He was standing beside Laura, Millie, and the two caddies who were carrying their golf bags.

"I certainly hope so. It was a brand new ball. I paid fifty cents for it," replied Borden as he took a couple of swings, trying to find the flaw that caused the ball to land in a less than desirable location. He handed the driver to his caddie as he stepped off the tee.

His wife gave him a slight grin as she walked to the women's tee about forty yards in front of the men's. From the sandbox, she took a cup, upended it on the tee box, and then put her ball on top. She was careful not to get dirt on her ankle-length tan skirt. She wore a matching jacket, with a white blouse underneath. A feather hat that was more decoration than protection from the sun topped it.

He watched as she took her stance and then whacked the ball 180 yards down the centre of the fairway to rest near MacLaren's ball. They had been married for twenty-five years, their anniversary was coming up in September, and he needed to find an appropriate gift. They met at St. Paul's Anglican Church, where she played the organ. He soon discovered, besides her love of music and the theatre, that she enjoyed playing tennis, water sports, and golf. They played many rounds together while they were courting under the watchful eye of chaperones.

After Millie, her playing partner, hit her ball, they marched off to find Sir Robert's ball hiding in the trees.

"It's a beautiful day," said MacLaren.

"A perfect day. I'm glad that you invited Laura and me. I needed to get away from Ottawa's humidity."

"My pleasure. Was everything to your satisfaction when you arrived?"

"Laura and I were very impressed with the service we have received," answered Borden. MacLaren was the owner of the Royal Muskoka Hotel on Lake Rosseau. The 321-room hotel was one of the most prestigious and luxurious in the Muskoka's. The bulk of his wealth came from his printing operation. It was one of the largest in Canada, and he did a fair amount of business with the federal government. The hotel was a sideline for him, but it was doing well since it attracted visitors from all over the world. Even Woodrow Wilson, the president of the United States, had liked the region so much that he bought a nearby cottage after his stay at the resort.

As they searched for the lost ball, MacLaren said, "I've been following that mess in Europe. Do you think there will be war?"

Borden gave his playing partner a sour look. "I certainly hope not.

But there are members of my cabinet who are looking forward to it."

When MacLaren nodded in acknowledgement, Borden knew he had heard that Hughes was chomping at the bit for another war.

It was MacLaren who spotted a ball among the dead leaves. He yelled, "I found it. I think."

The prime minister came over and peered at the ball. "It's mine."

He frowned as he calculated that the odds of getting the ball on the green were not good.

"You could take a stroke and penalty," suggested the hotelier.

Borden shook his head. He didn't want to lose the stroke. He called to his caddie, "Bring me my niblick."

The caddie pulled an iron from the leather golf bag and handed it to the prime minister. He set up carefully so as to not disturb the ball, or he would incur a penalty stroke. He then gouged the ball out into the fairway through an alley he found through the trees.

The pin was set up on the left-hand side of the green. He took a couple of practice swings and was about to hit the ball into the centre when he heard panting and footsteps behind him. Since he had already started his downswing, he couldn't stop. He shanked the ball into the green side bunker.

He turned and glared at the interloper. The young messenger's face paled in horror. "Sorry … sorry," he stammered.

"Yes, what is it?" snapped Borden.

"I have an urgent telegram for you, Prime Minister. I was told to bring it right away."

"Give it here," he ordered as he snatched the offending paper from the boy's hand.

He tore it open and then removed a pair of spectacles from his waist jacket. When he finished reading the message, his frown deepened.

"Bad news?" asked McLaren.

"I'm afraid so. It doesn't look good in Europe. I need to get back to Ottawa."

"Right now?" asked Laura.

"Unfortunately, yes."

"I'll go back with you," Laura said.

Borden shook his head. "I'll be only gone a couple of days. Stay here and enjoy your vacation. I'll be back soon." He turned to MacLaren and asked, "When is the next boat leaving?"

"I own the boat. It'll leave when I say it does," he replied.

"Good. I'll catch it then the Grand Trunk train back to Ottawa," replied Borden as he headed toward the white-painted hotel with a brown roof. "It means that I can't make our game at the Beaumaris golf course tomorrow. I'll send a note extending my apologies."

"Of course, Prime Minister. I'll walk you in."

Borden waved him back. "Finish the game. I'll be fine."

CHAPTER 2

When Borden entered the Privy Council Chamber, he could feel the tension from the men who occupied the three quarters of the brown-black chairs at the large round oak table. Rodolphe Boudreau, his clerk of the Privy Council, had taken his usual seat against the wall behind his chair.

He took a head count and was satisfied that his key ministers had managed to be in attendance. When Parliament was prorogued in June, most of his cabinet either took vacations or went back to their ridings to take care of constituents and personal business affairs. Being an MP was a part-time job, since they essentially only worked while Parliament was in session. Being a minister required some additional time, but the departments essentially ran themselves.

Telegrams had been sent out requesting that the ministers return to Ottawa as soon as possible, which explained the tiredness Borden saw. Sitting from his left were William White, Finance; Charles Doherty, Justice; George Foster, Trade and Commerce; and Sam Hughes, Militia and Defence. Sitting on his right were Francis Cochrane, Railways and Canals, with Douglas Hazen, Naval Service, and Robert Rogers, Public Works.

"Thank you for attending this morning's meeting. We'll begin shortly. We are waiting for His Excellency to arrive."

"What the hell for?" demanded Hughes.

The rest of his ministers had the same question, but they would not have asked as bluntly as Hughes had. It was extremely unusual for the governor general to attend. It was at Privy Council meetings that government policy was discussed. Minutes of the discussions were not kept, but decisions were recorded and published as Orders-in-Council. Since the governor general represented the Crown, by tradition, he was not privy to the private discussions of his ministers.

"I've invited His Excellency, since he has a wealth of military experience and knowledge," replied Borden tersely. Which was true, since Prince Arthur, the Duke of Connaught, had served in the British Army from 1868, when he entered the Royal Military College, to 1907, when he became the commander-in-chief of all British forces in the Mediterranean.

Borden knew that he was going to have a problem with Hughes. There was considerable friction between his minister and the governor general, but the events in Europe were beyond anyone's experience — at least in this room.

He was interrupted before he could order Hughes to be civil when the governor general entered the room, dressed in a khaki uniform with his campaign ribbons on his left chest.

All of the men in the room rose to their feet.

"Please have a seat here," indicated Borden to the empty chair beside his at the round table.

Borden saw the slight hesitation when the duke saw that he was not being seated at the head of the table. Which was what he wanted. The governor general was under the impression that since he was technically the ranking military officer in Canada, he was in charge. Borden was trying to send a message to his Royal Highness that he would welcome the duke's suggestions, but it was he who would make the decisions.

"Thank you," the Duke of Connaught said. Only after he sat did the ministers take their seats.

"Gentlemen, it seems that a war is on the horizon. It's my reverent hope that the differences among the European powers can be peacefully resolved. However, matters don't look good at the moment," said Borden.

Borden could feel Hughes' excitement that his moment had finally come.

He continued, "Since war appears to be imminent, we need to ensure that Canada is prepared. Every department will need to provide support. However, the heaviest burden will fall on the Militia and Defence, the Naval department, Justice, Finance, Customs, and Public Works.

"First, let us start with the navy," said Borden, looking at John Douglas Hazen, one of his more reliable ministers. That was the main reason that he had assigned the Marine and Fisheries and Naval Department to Hazen's care.

John Hazen said unhappily, "I've asked Admiral Kingsmill to recall what sailors he could and prepare the *Niobe* and the *Rainbow* for sea. But it may take a week or so. And we may have only one ship. For the last several years, they have been tied to the docks. The boilers may have been lit once in a while to see if they work. Our previous policy was that if a seaman quit or retired, we didn't replace him. At the moment, we are focusing on the *Niobe* at Esquimalt, getting her ready for sea. They have about 235 seamen. Thirty-five to forty men from the *Rainbow* are on the train to Esquimalt to supplement her crew. Plus we activated one hundred men from the naval reserves. If the German battleship *Leipzig* is in the Pacific and she decides to attack British Columbia, there is very little that we can do to stop her."

"Won't the Royal Navy send us some ships?" asked Borden.

Hazen shook his head. "They have two ships in the Pacific, but they are sloops and the *Leipzig* out guns them. The Admiralty indicated that we may need to send the *Rainbow* to escort them."

The governor general jumped in. "They don't have the capacity at the moment. Most of the ships have been recalled to England. The navy needs them to blockade the German fleet in her ports."

"Damn Liberals," muttered Hughes.

Borden heard him and gave him a glare. He didn't need Hughes to stir the pot. After he won the election, he had put a stop to Laurier's naval program and replaced it with a plan of his own. The battle concerning his naval bill had been brutal, not only with the Liberals but with his own party. One of his own ministers had resigned in protest. His plans had been frustrated by the Liberal-dominated Senate, which had killed the bill.

"I thought that is what they were there for," Borden stated. He wasn't happy with the implications. One of the reasons he had sent George Perley to London as the acting Canadian High Commissioner was to discuss with the Admiralty the government providing $35 million to the Royal Navy for three dreadnoughts. One of the conditions would have been to make the ships available to Canada in time of need. He also hoped that by financing the ships he would get invited to take a seat at the Imperial cabinet, where these decisions were being made.

Borden was now worried about the country's ports, if there was no naval protection. "And our harbour defences?"

"The B.C. defences are not in very good shape. We had plans to upgrade them, but we didn't have the budget. Halifax's defences are better. Orders have been sent out to have the coastal forts and batteries manned," replied Hazen.

Borden stated, "So we're essentially on our own!"

"I'm afraid that is the case," replied the duke.

"What about the Americans?" someone asked.

16

"No, I don't want them to do us any favours," Hughes said flatly before Borden could say anything.

"I agree. We don't want them to give them an excuse to invoke their Monroe Doctrine," said Foster. The Monroe Doctrine was American foreign policy that stated that if European countries attempted to colonize, interfere, or meddle in North and South America, the United States would view it as an act of aggression and intervene. It generally didn't apply to Canada, but these were unusual circumstances.

Borden shook his head. "I doubt that the Americans want to get involved. We have to deal with any German threats on our own."

Hazen, seeing Borden was concerned, informed him, "We've activated militia units to protect our key canals, locks, and waterways to ensure secure shipping of food and ores across the Great Lakes water system. Especially the Welland Canal, through which most of our western grain is shipped."

George Foster, his trade minister, nodded in agreement. "I'm glad to hear that. We don't want any disruption in our grain shipments. Europe is one of our major markets."

"We can't very well ship grain to Germany, now can we?" said Hughes dryly.

"Of course not," snapped Forster, offended. "However, we could offer England some of the wheat that we have in storage."

"That's a good suggestion," replied Borden.

"I just hope that recruiting for the militia will not impact the upcoming harvest."

"I don't think that 25,000 men will have much of an impact," Hughes stated confidently.

Borden raised an eyebrow in surprise when the governor general nodded in agreement with Hughes. "Most of the men will be infantry, supplemented with cavalry and artillery. And we will be assembling them at Petawawa."

"I have decided to change the assembly point," interrupted Hughes.

Borden could see that the governor general was taken aback by Hughes' statement. It was obvious that Hughes had not consulted with the duke. For that matter, Hughes had not run it past Borden either prior to the cabinet meeting.

"You can't just change the plans at this late stage!" the duke blurted. "It has been published in the war book. All the units' mobilization plans have been predicated on the Petawawa base," he argued.

17

"Well, I have," replied Hughes.

"Why?" asked Borden.

Hughes shrugged. "I feel that men need to be as close as possible to a port so that we can embark them quickly for England. Petawawa, as far as I know, is nowhere near a port. We need to transport them there by rail and then put them on another train to the nearest port, which would be Montreal."

The governor general was still not mollified. "Do you have a different location in mind?" he demanded.

"I have not made that decision yet. I have officials in my department looking at various locations. Once one has been found, I'll inform the cabinet and, of course, your office," Hughes said as he tried to stare down the duke.

To prevent the governor general and Hughes from getting into a more heated discussion, Borden interjected. "Once Minister Hughes has a list of bases, we could then have a detailed discussion on their suitability." Borden turned to his finance minister. "So we will be able to finance and maintain a force of 25,000 men?"

White grimaced. "Up to this point, the economy has been in a slight depression. Our revenues have been down. We are going to have to borrow money. I was thinking maybe twenty to thirty million, if the war lasts six months. If it lasts longer, we may need to raise excise taxes to help pay for expenses. That is not going to be popular with the electorate."

"Tell me something that I don't know," said Borden. "We have to consider the election next year as well."

"If we still are at war, will we have an election next year?" asked White.

"I don't know. If, as Will said, the war will last only six months, it might be moot," replied Borden.

"What about the German immigrants? I heard that some are German reservists," stated Foster.

Borden spoke firmly. "If the German immigrants are peaceful, they are not to be harassed. However, if they attempt to leave Canada for Germany, they are to be prevented from doing so."

Borden took the silence in the room as agreement. "Now, we have a lot to do. One item I wanted to discuss is how we can expedite our response. Any other suggestions?"

Many of the ministers in the room adjusted their seats to become more comfortable. It was going to be a long meeting.

AUGUST 4, 1914
MINISTER OF MILITIA AND DEFENCE OFFICE,
WOODS BUILDING, OTTAWA

Colonel Sam Hughes rose from his desk and slammed his fist onto the newspaper he was reading. "They are going to skunk it!" he shouted furiously. "They are going to skunk it!"

His secretary poked his head into his office. "Problem, Minister?"

"Yes, there's a goddamn problem. London is going to skunk it!" he repeated as he picked up the newspaper and waved it at his private secretary, Kevin Pratt. "They are sitting on their asses while France burns."

"Yes, Minister," he replied.

"Damn," Hughes muttered as he retook his seat. "Did you get the latest reports on our readiness?"

"They're in my office. Give me a moment, I'll go get them," Pratt said as he turned toward the open door.

"Don't bother! I can read them later. Just give me the gist," Hughes demanded.

"Of course. Ever since we received the telegram from the War Office, we have undertaken the various measures prescribed in our war book."

The war book detailed the military units to be activated and the missions they were to undertake when a "precautionary warning" telegram was received. On July 28th, the British government had transmitted such a message to all the colonies that war was imminent in Europe.

Prior to January, the Canadian government didn't have a war book, despite the urgent appeals by various military officials, the latest being the army chief of staff, Colonel Gwatkin, and the director of Naval Services, Admiral Kingsmill, to their respective ministers. It was only after the urging of London that the key departments, Militia and Defence, the Naval Service, and Customs, were authorized to prepare one. The latest draft, currently waiting Hughes' approval, was finally completed in July.

"Everything appears to have gone smoothly, Minister. Guards have been placed at all wireless stations, telephone, and cable landings on both coasts to prevent sabotage. The Royal Canadian Regiment has been activated. The fortresses at Halifax, Quebec City, and Esquimalt are fully manned and are on high alert. The infantry and the non-permanent active militia have been called up, and they have been given their assignments and they should be on the move as we speak."

"Good! Very good!" Hughes was pleased by the news. Ever since he had become Minister of Militia and Defence, he had worked hard to increase the department's budget. One of the things he was most satisfied to see was that the near doubling of the number of men who attended the annual militia training camps from 33,000 to an all time high of 55,000 this year. Also, he was pushing through his plan to modernize the artillery. While the contracts had been let, they only received half of the requested artillery pieces they had ordered.

"The navy?" he asked. The navy didn't report to Hughes, since it was a separate department.

"As far as I'm aware, Admiral Kingsmill has recalled his sailors back to their ships and are preparing the *Niobe* and the *Rainbow* for sea operations. They are waiting on orders from the Admiralty. I can confirm with the Naval Department if you would like."

"There's no need," Hughes said as he returned to his desk. "Prepare a draft order-in-council that as of today my department will take control of all telegram cable offices in the country. And we will impose strict censorship on all communication traffic for the time being."

"Do you want a draft for today's cabinet meeting?"

Hughes rubbed the grey stubble on his head. "I'll mention it when we meet. We'll send a draft over later to the prime minister's office. I'll need a letter for the press to tell them that I would appreciate it if they wouldn't publicize any of our military and naval activities."

"Yes, Minister. I'll inform the Naval Department. I suspect that they would like to do the same thing for wireless."

"I'm not looking forward to today's cabinet meeting," said Hughes sourly.

"You don't think that the cabinet will authorize offering Britain troops?" asked Pratt in surprise.

"They better. Two members of the cabinet have already resigned over getting involved in Europe. The cowards! The key will be Borden. I shouldn't have any problems convincing him," Hughes said with a snort.

Pratt had been his private secretary long enough to know that Hughes believed that Borden was soft and easily intimidated. He didn't share that view with his boss. Borden put up with Hughes because he was a stalwart of the Orange Lodge in Ontario and could be counted on in bringing out the Tory vote. However, if Hughes overstepped himself, Borden might not have any choice but to cut the minister adrift.

"If Britain declares war, Borden will not have a choice. Canada would be at war as well," Pratt pointed out.

"I know," replied Hughes. "Unless they skunk it!"

"Do I inform Colonel Gwatkin to activate our mobilization plan?" asked Pratt.

Hughes frowned. He wasn't enamoured of Colonel Gwatkin, but then he wasn't enamoured of British Army professional soldiers on principle, since he felt they had robbed him of two Victoria Crosses for his service during the Boer War. "No, not at the moment. I need to think about it."

The secretary kept his face impassive. He wondered if he should give the colonel a head's up that the minister might change his mind.

Hughes picked up the newspaper on his desk, and then he turned his blue eyes on Pratt. "Lower the Union Jack on the building to half mast," he ordered.

"Minister! Who died?" asked Pratt in surprise. The flag was only lowered to half-mast when a personage of note had passed away.

"British honour! I will be ashamed to be a subject of the empire if England doesn't help France in her time of need!"

AUGUST 4, 1914
RIDEAU HALL, OTTAWA

The governor general, the Duke of Connaught, was in his office reading a report when Henry, his private telegraph operator, knocked and entered.

"Yes, Henry? Have we received another missive from London?" he asked with a brief smile. The duke had been called back from his western vacation, and he had just returned via his private train car in time for the cabinet meeting that Borden had convened yesterday morning.

"Yes, Your Excellency. I just received this from the Colonial Office," he answered as he handed the duke the typed version of the telegram.

The duke took the paper and read it then slowly dropped it onto his desk. The message was terse, only eleven words. It read, "See Preface Defence Scheme, war has broken out with Germany. HARCOURT."

He looked up at Henry then said, "It was to be expected. Have copies made for the prime minister and the appropriate departments."

"Yes, Your Excellency. I will get the messengers to deliver them." Henry knew the list by heart. Copies were to be forwarded to clerk of the Privy Council, the minster of Militia and Defence, the minister of the Naval Service, the Marine and Fisheries minister, the Customs' minister, the Dominion Police, and the Under Secretary of State of Canada.

"I believe that the prime minister is still in council, so he needs to know immediately. Also, inform my valet to lay out my field marshall uniform. I will don it in the morning."

"Of course, Your Excellency."

AUGUST 4, 1914
PRIVY COUNCIL OFFICE, EAST BLOCK,
PARLIAMENT HILL

Borden rubbed his eyes as he slumped slightly in his chair. This was the third time today he and his ministers were meeting to discuss his government's response to the crisis in Europe.

At the 11:00 a.m. meeting, he, the Duke of Connaught, and his ministers had discussed Perley's pessimistic message from London that war was imminent and that the government should offer Britain one to two million barrels of flour. A close friend and confidant, George Perley had been one of his ministers without portfolio until Borden had appointed him as the Acting Canadian High Commissioner to London in early June. Perley had instructions to reform and improve the commission's efficiency, which was found wanting. Also, he was to liaison with the British Imperial Government concerning changes to the *BNA Act* and to select a new building to house the Canadian High Commission.

When they had reconvened at four o'clock, the governor general read the telegram he had received from the king expressing his appreciation for the spontaneous support the colonies were displaying. They also discussed the deployment of militia units to Sydney, Canso, Glace Bay, and St. John to guard and protect government facilities.

"So can we do it?" Borden directed the question to Douglas Hazen, the minister of the Naval Service and the minister of Marine and Fisheries. This 8:30 p.m. meeting was being held to discuss how to best transfer the CGS *Canada* and the CGS *Margaret* to the Naval Service. Hazen had sent a briefing note concerning the two ships. Borden liked to have the facts at his fingertips. Launched in 1901, the Canadian Government Ship *Canada* was the flagship of the Fisheries Protective Services

Department. The vessel was 200 feet long, had a 557-ton displacement, and was armed with four Maxim machine guns. She and her crew were tasked to patrol and detain vessels fishing illegally within the Canadian twelve-mile limit. The Canadian Government Ship *Margaret* belonged to the Customs Department. The 182-foot long and 756-ton vessel was a coastal cruiser belonging to the Customs Protective Service. It was armed with two 6-pounder guns.

"I've discussed the matter with John here," indicated Hazen, "and according to the *Naval Service Act*, we can transfer the ships to the Naval Service from Fisheries and Customs."

Borden turned to Reid and asked, "You don't have a problem with the transfer?"

Reid gave a slight shrug. "Under the circumstances, I don't have much of a choice. The *Margaret's* a brand-new ship. We've only had her since April. We have to do the paperwork to transfer them so we can offer them to the Royal Navy. Also, we need to move the crews as well. The question will be how many will go over and what their pay scale will be, their current rates or the navy rates?"

"How many men are talking about?" asked Borden.

"About 120 or so. I'm not exactly sure," replied Hazen. "My staff also suggested that *Canada's* Maxims be replaced with two 6-pounders to give her extra firepower."

Borden frowned. He was about to speak about the cost when Blount, the clerk of the Privy Council, entered the chamber with a singled folded note.

"Yes?" asked Borden as he took the note. He unfolded it and read the message. When a shadow flickered across Borden's face, the other men knew it was not good news.

"Gentlemen," Borden formally announced, "Britain is now at war with Germany."

There was a moment of silence and then Reid asked, "So what do we do now?"

"The first thing we have to do is call back Parliament as soon as possible. We can only go so far with Orders-in-Council. Parliament will have to pass legislation that will allow us to prosecute the war," answered Borden.

"Agreed," replied Hazen. "But we'll need to get organized and the pieces of legislation ready. And we need to recall all of the MPs."

"That will take least a week or two," Reid pointed out.

Borden closed his eyes to think. "Let's call Parliament back for the 18th of August. I hope that will give us enough time to at least get the major pieces of legislation ready. As well …"

Cheering from the Parliament Hill lawn just outside the Privy Council Chamber's window interrupted him. A crowd had gathered there when they received the news that Canada was at war. Then he heard their voices start singing "The Maple Leaf Forever."

AUGUST 4, 1914
OFFICERS' MESS HALL, CARTIER DRILL HALL

The narrow officer's mess that the Governor General's Foot Guards shared with the Cameron Highlanders was buzzing with the nearly forty guard officers and their invited guests. The Foot Guard officers were easy to identify in their scarlet mess uniforms. They had changed into them from their ceremonial parade dress of red serge tunics, with a single row of double brass buttons, a white leather belt cinched by a brass belt buckle, dark blue pants with red striping on the outside seam, and black beaver bushies.

At 8:15, led by the regiment's band, 350 men and officers, sans the two officers and six guardsmen that were on duty at Rideau Hall, exited the red brick Gothic-style militia drill hall in downtown Ottawa. Since the route was well publicized, there was a fairly large crowd of spectators and well-wishers as they marched down Laurier, Metcalfe, Somerset, Bank, Parliament Hill, and Elgin.

Lieutenant-Colonel Woods took a glass from the silver tray that the white-coated orderly carried. "It was very good weather for the parade," he said, directing the comment to Hughes. Sam Hughes was dressed in a similar scarlet mess uniform. On his left breast were his miniature medals, which, if asked, he would point out that some medals were missing. His buttons and lapels followed the 45th Victoria Regiment's pattern, the last regiment that he had actively commanded.

"It was very good weather this evening. Very good marching weather," Hughes said enthusiastically. He had changed from his ceremonial uniform of the 45th as well since he had decided to join the Foot Guards on their parade. The crowds along the route seemed to have energized the minister.

Woods was well aware of the flag incidence at the militia's headquarters and decided to stick to small talk to avoid dampening the minister's good mood. The Foot Guards were under the command of the adjutant-general, since the regiment was frequently called upon on short notice to provide troops for ceremonial duties for various visiting dignitaries and guests.

He was about to make another witty weather comment when an orderly arrived with an envelope.

"Minister, an urgent message," said the orderly.

"Thank you," replied Hughes as he took it. Woods saw the minister's face light up when he tore it open and read the content.

Woods was perplexed as Hughes turned, grabbed the nearest chair that leaned against the wood panelled wainscoting, and placed it in front of him. He then stood on the chair. Using his drill voice, he called for the room's attention. "Gentlemen! Gentlemen!"

Slowly the noise died down.

"I need to read you this message that I have just been given. 'Preface previous defence scheme, war has broken out with Germany.'"

The officers broke out in cheers and applause. When Hughes stepped down from the chair, Lieutenant-Colonel Woods offered Hughes his hand and said, "The regiment is at your service wherever you require us."

AUGUST 4, 1914
TRAIL ISLAND, VANCOUVER ISLAND, B.C.

As the full moon cast shadows among the ships that dotted the Seattle harbour, an American submarine cast off her mooring lines. Her electric engines hummed softly as she navigated through the port. Once in a while a deckhand from one of the freighters turned his head toward the sub when he heard the sound of her propellers. Satisfied that the vessel was not sailing to close to his ship, he returned to his regular duties. If they were curious as to why the underwater craft was sailing out of the harbour at ten o'clock at night, they had learned long ago not to ask questions.

An hour later, her sister slipped her moorings at the Seattle Construction & Drydock. She took a different route out of the harbour. Again, no one made a remark. They assumed it was another shakedown cruise for the newly built H-class submarine.

When the city's lights disappeared behind the lead submarine's stern, she paused as she waited for the second boat. James Venn Paterson climbed up into the conning tower to scan the sea. Following him was Captain Logan, a surveyor from the London Salvage Association.

They were tense as they swept the horizon for approaching vessels. When they finally spotted the familiar conning tower, they expelled a sigh of relief. "Okay. We're far enough out. Switch to the diesels," ordered Paterson in a thick Scottish accent.

Paterson, originally from Glasgow, was the president of the Seattle Construction & Drydock Co. It was his company that built the two military crafts.

"Course, Captain Logan?"

The B.C. government representative replied, "I already provided it to your navigator. It's Trail Islands."

"I see," the Scot replied. Trail Islands was a group of islands near Victoria.

"When we arrive there tomorrow morning. My ship, the *Salvor*, will meet us for the inspection," stated Logan. "If the US Navy doesn't get wise."

"I hope not," replied Paterson as his eyes examined the horizon. The grey-painted hulls were nearly invisible at this time of night. He knew that he was contracted by the Chilean government to build the two subs based on a General Electric design. A couple of weeks ago he was in Victoria, where he was dining with potential clients at the Victoria Union Club. During the meal, he was complaining about the dispute he was having with the Chileans over deficiencies and their refusal to pay.

One of the members perked up at the news and asked if he was willing to sell the boats to Canada. "Sure, if the price is right," he had replied.

When he got back to Seattle, he received a message from Frank McBride, the premier of British Columbia, about the subs. He stated that he was sending Captain Logan down to negotiate a deal. With his recent experience with the Chileans, he decided to tack an extra $100,000 onto the price of the subs and demand that it be cash on delivery.

He knew that he had McBride over a barrel with the war brewing in Europe. B.C. was defenceless against German cruisers in the Pacific. The deal had to be done before war was declared or otherwise the US Navy would block the sale.

He and McBride agreed that if the boats passed Logan and the chief engineer's inspections, they would hand over a cheque of $1.1 million.

Paterson took a final look at the night sky and then ordered, "Full speed ahead."

CHAPTER 3

It was nearly ten o'clock, and Samantha was getting dressed for her evening shift. She was assigned to the day clinic on the University Avenue side of the hospital. The ward had a capacity of 500 patients a day and dealt with mostly simple cases. That is, if they had come in early enough. Since it cost money to get care, many of the patients held off until their situation became almost desperate. The only good thing about being assigned to the clinic was that she would get plenty of experience treating a wide variety of ailments.

"Damn," she muttered as she tugged a newly washed nurse's uniform out of the closet. The dress had got tangled on the hanger when she tried to jerk it off the wire. It took a couple of more pulls before it came free. The hanger jumped from the rod and ricocheted off the closet door into the recesses of the closet among the boxes of shoes that were stacked at the bottom.

"Argh!" Samantha yelled in frustration. "The hell with it. I'll get it later."

She tossed the uniform on the bed and had started to undress when Irene burst into the room without knocking. She stood in the doorway, panting.

Glad for the distraction, Samantha gave Irene an impish smile. "Take it easy. Catch your breath. If you faint, I'll be the one that will have to take care of you. Do you really want that?"

Irene shook her head. "No, I've seen how you take care of the patients," she replied in between breaths. She put her hand theatrically on her forehead. "I may not survive your gentle ministration."

Samantha laughed. "So why were you running up the stairs?"

"I had to tell you the news!" she shouted excitedly.

"What news?"

"We're at war. England has declared war on Germany. Isn't that exciting!" she blurted. When Samantha didn't react as expected, she asked, "What's wrong?"

"I had a meeting with Matron Hazel this morning," Samantha

replied sourly. The matron was the head nurse for the Toronto General Hospital.

"How did it go?" Irene asked with a touch of concern.

"I've been sacked," replied Samantha tersely.

"What do you mean, you've been sacked? You're the best third-year nurse that I know."

"Thanks, Irene," Samantha replied with a thin smile. "I'll be able to finish the year and graduate, but the matron said that it would be best that I find a new position. She said that I was not suitable."

"Did she explain why?"

Samantha shook her head. "I asked, but she wouldn't tell me."

"She never liked you," Irene said.

"Well, there is that, but I did get good evaluations from the doctors and other matrons."

"There's got to be more to it than that."

"It would be great if I could find out what. Maybe I can fix it," Samantha said as she sat on her bed.

"So what are you going to do now?"

"Well, I have some money saved. It isn't much, but I won't starve. At least not right away. I have to start looking for a new job. Where I'm going to find the time? I have no idea."

"At least the hospital could provide you with a letter of reference," said Irene.

"I certainly hope so," said Samantha. Without a letter of reference it would be difficult to get a high-paying job.

"Well, you can always join the army," Irene suggested.

"As what?" Samantha said as she wiped a touch of moisture from her right eye. She refused to feel sorry for herself.

"As a nurse, silly. They are going to need qualified nursing sisters. My second … or is it my third cousin …" Irene paused as to tried to remember which one. "Never mind. I can never get it straight. She served as a nurse in the Boer War."

"She did? You never told me that."

"Well, we never talked about it since our families didn't get along. The nice thing about the army is that they pay you, and you get to travel for free. Plus the room and board."

"Hmm," Samantha said thoughtfully. "Let me think about it."

Irene glanced at the table clock. "Isn't your shift starting in five minutes?"

"Oh my God! I'm going to be late!" Samantha shrieked as she jumped from the bed. Irene watched in amusement as Samantha buttoned up her uniform and rushed out of the room.

AUGUST 6, 1914
IMPERIAL THEATRE, MONTREAL

Paul offered Marie-Claude his hand as she stepped off the streetcar that stopped in front of the Imperial Theatre on Bleury Street.

"Do you see them?"

She scanned the crowd in front of the two-storey greystone movie theatre. She indicated "no" with a shake of her head. "Did we miss them?" she asked as she adjusted the pearl-coloured hat with an ostrich feather set at a rakish angle. It was perched on her short, curly brown hair.

"We're supposed to meet them in front of the theatre," he replied.

"They might have gone in and got their tickets," she suggested as she allowed Paul to lead her to the telephone pole in front of the building.

"If you hadn't …" Paul was about to continue until he saw the look on her face. He had been dating Marie-Claude for nearly a year. They both attended Westmount High School. He had just completed his final year in June, and she had another year to go. It was her amber eyes set in a delicate oval face that had attracted him when she first joined the school's book club. He knew if he continued on that tack, he would pay for it. Catching himself, he said instead, "They wouldn't do that. We always meet them here first."

"Oh, there they are," she exclaimed, waving at the two couples, part of their school clique, who appeared when the clanging streetcar rumbled away.

As they ran across the street, dodging traffic, Paul was surprised by the couples' attire. Not by the two young ladies, as they were appropriately dressed for their station. The blond waif, Lea, wore a summerwashed, sky-coloured pleated dress, while the taller brunette, Nicole, wore a tan, fancy-flowered checked dress. What surprised him was that Denis and Martin wore their military uniforms, complete with forge caps. Paul noticed the glances of approval people gave his two best friends.

"Sorry we're late. We missed the first tram," said Lea, trying to catch her breath from the brief run. She was holding Denis's hand.

"Oh yes, and then we couldn't get on the second car because it was packed," said Nicole as she hooked her left arm with Martin's right.

"*Oui*, everyone seems to be out this evening," said Marie-Claude.

Paul, bursting with curiosity, finally asked, "What's with the uniforms?"

Denis grinned as he straightened his frame. "Our units have been called up. We're on duty tonight at the wharf."

Martin, similar in height as Denis, but with a wrestler's build, bobbed his head in agreement. His cap was set slightly at an angle, revealing more of his slick black hair. "We have to report to the lieutenant with our rifles. We're on midnight guard duty."

"You two? You both have two left feet," said Paul.

"They're our heroes," one of the two ladies said in a giggling defence as they wrapped an arm around their boyfriends.

"You both look very handsome in your uniforms," Marie-Claude said as she ran a hand over Denis's jacket. She eyed Paul and asked with a mischievous smile, "When are you going to get one?"

"He has to volunteer first," Denis said.

"If his mother lets him," interjected Martin, winking at Marie-Claude.

Paul felt his face flush as his friends chuckled at Martin's zinger. Through clinched teeth he said, "Why don't we go in and get our tickets." He ignored his girlfriend's look that implied he was being rude to their friends.

What added insult to injury was he had to pay twenty cents to get to see the movie. Denis and Martin were let in for free. The ticket booth girl waved them through, saying, "Nothing is too good for our boys in uniform."

CHAPTER 4

Colonel Gwatkin was feeling tired when he entered his minister's office. He and his staff had worked late the previous evening reviewing the returns of the various units, determining their readiness for mobilization. He had felt a certain satisfaction that all the work that had been done for the war book was finally paying off.

"Good, Colonel. You're finally here," Hughes said brusquely. "Take a seat." He pointed to one of the two chairs in front of his desk.

Gwatkin sat ramrod straight as he waited for the minister to finish reading a report. He could tell from its cover that it was one of his. He suspected as much when Hughes had called him to his office. He had thought that he and his staff had done a good job preparing it. The minister's views on various topics were well known. Hughes had made that abundantly clear when he fired Gwatkin's boss, Major-General Mackenzie, shortly after he had been appointed as minister of Militia and Defence. When the War Office had made suggestions for replacement, Hughes simply appointed Gwatkin as the chief of staff's replacement. Gwatkin was well aware that it was more a case of a devil you know rather than simply his professionalism and efficiency. He had been recruited by General Lake in 1905 as his director of operations to help mould the Canadian militia into a genuine army. He had been tasked to develop strategies to defend against an attack from the United States, which he considered remote. And plans to send a division to Europe, which was a more likely prospect.

"I've read your report. I've decided to make some changes," Hughes said as he dropped it on his desk.

"What kind of changes?" Gwatkin asked. He had heard from several private sources that the minister was planning to change the assembly point. Whatever unease he felt in the pit of his stomach, he had plenty of practice not displaying them in front of the minister.

"No member of the permanent force will be allowed to join the expeditionary force. Only volunteers from the militia will be accepted."

Gwatkin felt his lips tighten slightly. "Minister, the plans were that the permanent force would be the core of the division, supplemented by the appropriate militia units to form a balanced division of infantry, cavalry, and artillery."

It was the wrong thing to say.

"Damn the plan," exploded Hughes. "I only want militia in the expeditionary force. Do I make myself clear?"

"Yes, Minister," replied Gwatkin. At least he had tried to get the minister to consider including some of the 3,000 men of the permanent force. They had been trained to British military standards, but that was the problem. Hughes did not have a high opinion of British military professionals.

"Also, I've decided that Valcartier will be the assembly point for the volunteers."

"But Minister, we don't have a camp at Valcartier!" Gwatkin protested. This was no small change that he was requesting.

"We've been acquiring land around Valcartier for the last several years to build central training camps for the Quebec militia units. I've decided to accelerate that plan."

From the stubborn look on Hughes' face, Gwatkin knew that he had already decided, but he felt that it was his duty to inform the minister of the ramifications of his decision.

"Minister, there are no facilities or infrastructure there. We'll have to build everything from the ground up. At Petawawa we have sufficient camp grounds, barracks, railway links, and supply contracts to accommodate the 25,000 volunteers you are planning to call," Gwatkin stated.

He felt that he didn't need to get into exact details, as he had to with other Canadian politicians, that an army marched on its stomach. The average soldier needed about 3,500 calories per day to maintain proper health and to perform his assigned duties. During training and combat operations, the calorie intake would jump to 5,000 calories. That meant that an average division required approximately twenty tons of food and water every day. This didn't include the horses for the cavalry and the artillery units. The average horse ate 25,000 to 33,000 calories daily. Since the division would have about 7,000 horses, it would need nearly thirty-five tons or more of hay, oats, and other feed.

All this needed to be transported by wagon, by truck, or by train. Ideally, he would like the supplies to be delivered by rail so that the provisions could be delivered cheaply, on time, and in sufficient quantities. This didn't include the tons of tents, bedding, uniforms, rifles, artillery guns, ammunition, and thousands of other items that an army needed in the field.

Hughes waved his objections away. "I'm ordering the construction workers at the Connaught Rifle Range to proceed to Quebec City to begin construction immediately. As well, I will be announcing to the newspapers that we will be calling for volunteers, and they will assemble at Valcartier."

Seeing that the minister would not change his mind, the only thing that Gwatkin could do was say, "Yes, Minister."

"Very well," replied Hughes.

Knowing that he was dismissed, Gwatkin rose stiffly to his feet. He allowed the door to close behind him.

AUGUST 7, 1914
FUSILIERS' ARMOURY, RICHMOND HILL

Llewellyn rode slowly up to the armoury at the corner of Hasting and Birch Streets. His horse's pace was a bit sluggish, indicating that the animal was getting tired. The captain wasn't surprised since they had been riding for three days. He suspected that he was more tired than his horse.

"We're almost home," he said as the horse slightly picked up the pace, heading toward the fortress-like building. While it had a martial, imposing look, he knew it was designed for sheltering the Richmond Fusiliers rather than as an unassailable defensive structure.

The one thing that he did notice was the unusual amount activity for a Thursday morning. Usually it was busy during the twice-weekly drill nights and the weekend manoeuvres. Only a skeleton staff was there during the daytime. Something was going on. He rode his horse to the back of the building where the stables were located. Lieutenant Rawlings was waiting for him.

"So how did it go, Jim?" he asked.

"It went fine, Simon," Captain Llewellyn said as he unsaddled his horse and put the saddle on a nearby rack. Rawlings was aware of the mission that Llewellyn had been tasked to do by the Dominion Police's Secret Service. They had requested that someone take a look at the various staging areas along the border for any unusual activity. "Everything was pretty quiet. Things seem to be hopping here," he continued as he then led the horse into an empty stall beside the white charger, which was the lieutenant-colonel's favourite mount.

"I'll say."

"Get a bucket of fresh water please?" When Lieutenant Rawlings handed him the bucket, Llewellyn hung it on the hook on the wall. He gently rubbed the horse as it drank noisily. It felt cool to the touch, which was a good sign.

"So we're at war then."

"I'm afraid so."

"Shit," Llewellyn muttered. It was not a surprise. He was expecting the news.

"The colonel wants to see you."

"Any particular reason?"

Rawlings shrugged.

"What's his mood like?"

Another shrug.

Llewellyn gave his horse a final gentle tap then said, "Can you get him some hay? Once he's done, give him a bag of oats. He deserves it. I'll go in and see the colonel."

"No problem, and good luck."

"Right," he replied as he brushed what dust he could off his uniform. He straightened his cap as he entered the drill hall. The armoury was relatively new. When Hughes became the minister of Militia and Defence, he managed, via some arm-twisting, to increase the militia's defence budget. A large amount of the expenditures went into the armouries building program. Every sizeable town in the country got a drill hall where the weekend soldier could train and socialize, especially in winter.

The echo of his Strathcona riding boots on the concrete floor were drowned out by the sergeant-major who was drilling a platoon of thirty men at the far end of the cavernous open space. The hall was seventy-five feet by one hundred feet and was surrounded by two floors of offices. He took the stairs to the second floor and headed for the lieutenant-colonel's command post. He glanced over at the Union Jack, the Red Ensign, and the Fusiliers' pennants that were hanging from the ceiling.

When he entered, the duty orderly was replacing the phone back on the hook. "Go right in. He's been waiting for you."

He acknowledged the sergeant with a slight grin. He removed his cap, placing it under his left arm, and then entered the inner office. The

35

first thing that the lieutenant-colonel said was, "Where the devil have you been?"

Llewellyn paused to consider his reply then stated, "I was asked by the Secret Service to scout the staging areas where German reservists may gather in the US." While the captain got along reasonably well with the Fusiliers' senior officer, he was not one of Topham's favourites. Llewellyn was a Liberal, while the lieutenant-colonel was a Conservative. It was an unfortunate fact of life that if you wanted a promotion in the Canadian militia, you needed to be aligned with the party in power, which meant that while Topham couldn't fire Llewellyn, he could still make his life so miserable that he would quit.

Lieutenant-Colonel Topham was in his late fifties with a stomach that rolled over his belt. Topham had made his fortune running a chain of nickel and dime stores in southern Ontario. Llewellyn knew the main reason he was involved in the militia was that it enhanced his business interests. He did look impressive in scarlet, which he wore as often as possible at parades and social events. Topham was particularly in love with his white charger, even though white was not a colour recommended for a cavalry horse. The horse was too visible on the battlefield. Snipers were known to fix on a target, making the horse a liability. However, the lieutenant-colonel had illusions that he was leading the charge of the light brigade.

"I've being trying to reach you for several days, Captain," the lieutenant-colonel remarked. The chair creaked when he leaned back. Behind him on the wall was a large photograph of Sam Hughes. It was framed by Union Jack and Red Ensign flags.

Llewellyn kept his face impassive. He had tried to explain operational security a number of times previously. "I never received any messages."

"Well. We are at war."

"With the Germans?"

"Of course with the Germans!"

"So are we being activated?"

Topham's shoulders were tense with frustration. "Damned if I know. I've been sending telegrams to Ottawa for clarification. I have not been able to get a bloody straight answer."

"The instructions were clearly written in the war book," remarked the captain. In May and June he had worked with the lieutenant-colonel in developing the war plans for the militia units in this district. They submitted the final drafts in June, and they had been waiting for requests for revisions by Ottawa. The one thing that Llewellyn knew was that there were always revisions. No matter if they made sense or not.

"Yes, I know. But, it seems that Ottawa has a different opinion. They've been pestering my senior officers and goddamn anyone else in the Fusiliers with telegrams and phone calls demanding nominal lists. They want to know when we will start recruiting. None of them are going through this office."

Llewellyn finally knew what was irritating the lieutenant-colonel. Military protocol required that requests for information be sent to the regiment's HQ before being cascaded down to the appropriate level. If they were received directly by the officers, depending on who was doing the asking and what they wanted, copies were to be sent to the commanding officer to determine if he needed to be involved. If it did, it would reflect the regiment's opinion with the senior officer's stamp of approval. He wondered if any were waiting for him in his office.

"So what exactly is going on in Ottawa?" asked Llewellyn. The photo of Hughes gave him a fairly good idea of what might be happening.

"Hughes decided to throw out the war book and create his own, from what I have been able to gather from my friends in Ottawa. He didn't like the plans that were drawn up."

"Great," remarked Llewellyn, frowning. "So what are you going to do?"

"I have no idea. Hughes has publicly stated that he wants twenty to 25,000 volunteers for an expeditionary force. So I don't know if the entire regiment is being sent or if we are simply a recruiting station for those who want to go."

"If we do recruit men, where do we send them? The plans called for assembling at Petawawa."

The lieutenant-colonel shook his grey hair. "The latest rumours are that Hughes wants to assemble them near a major port. It's either Montreal, Quebec City, or Halifax."

"So what do you want to do then?"

The lieutenant-colonel stared at him and said, "I've already assigned the other senior officers to prepare for the mobilization of the entire regiment on the assumption that we will all be going. I want you to look after the recruiting of new volunteers."

The captain hoped that his face did not display his true feelings. He was not keen on babysitting, again. "Yes, sir," he replied stiffly.

"Good," replied the colonel.

For some strange reason Llewellyn felt that Hughes' steel-grey eyes seemed to glare at him for his insolence. He turned his back on the photo and left the office.

AUGUST 8, 1914
THE ST. JAMES'S CLUB, MONTREAL

When Paul entered the St. James's Club's dining room, he scanned the seated patrons. He was searching for his father, whom he knew had lunch here every day. The club was located on the corner of Dorchester and Union, minutes away from his dad's office building.

A tuxedoed waiter approached him and asked, "May I help you, sir?"

"I'm just looking for my father," he said as he rose to his toes to get a better view. He was quite familiar with the crowded room, since his father dragged him here often. Nearly all of the round and square tables covered with white linen tablecloths and sterling silverware were occupied. A few of the brass-tacked black-brown leather dining chairs, embossed with the club's logo, were empty. Brass electric light chandeliers hanged from the low ceilings. Near the centre of the dining area there was a four-level condiment and dessert station. The St. James's Club was one of the oldest and most prestigious private clubs in Montreal, and there was a long waiting list. What made it difficult for Paul to find his father was nearly all of the men were dressed in dark-coloured business suits, and they were near his father's age or older.

He finally spotted him when a diner at a table moved slightly. He was sitting with two other men at the square table near the window.

For a moment he was torn as to whether or not he should speak with him now or at home this evening. However, when his father, laughing with his dinner guests, turned his head and locked eyes with him, he didn't have much of a choice. Especially when a frown appeared on his father's lined face. Their relationship was still rocky, and the news he was about to impart was not going to help. As he manoeuvred between the tables he overheard snatches of conversation about the latest war news.

"Grab a seat, son," his father ordered, pointing to the empty chair beside him. "You know Michael and Thomas."

"Yes, pleasure to see you again sir," Paul answered as he politely shook hands with the two men. His father insisted that he attend various club functions where he could develop his social and business contacts, which he would need when he took over his business affairs. Michael O'Hara, with the grey-black chin whiskers, was on the Canadian Pacific Railways' board of directors. Thomas Côte, with the mutton chop sideburns, was a director at the Bank of Montreal, the largest bank in Canada. These two gentlemen, along with the other men in this dining room, as well as the members of the rival Royal Mount Club, controlled over half the wealth in Canada.

"No problems at the office, I hope?" His father looked at his guests and said proudly, "Paul is working with me at the office this summer."

"Learning the business! Very good," said Thomas.

"Thank you, sir. Dad, can I have a word with you?" Paul asked.

"What is it? Out with it."

Paul was torn between demanding a private meeting and what his father's reaction would be. He couldn't help himself and blurted, "I volunteered today."

The two guests broke out in smiles and Thomas said, "Well done, lad! Well done!"

"Yes, if I was young I would join in a heartbeat," Michael joined in.

When Paul returned his gaze back to his father, he saw a frozen smile appear. "Yes, I'm very proud of my son."

Thomas said, "This calls for a celebratory drink."

"Of course. Order my usual. I just want to have a word with my son in private, " replied his father as he rose for his chair.

Paul followed him as they exited a door framed in a Grecian motif casement. When his father looked into the men's sitting room and saw that it was empty, he entered. "Close the door," he ordered. Paul stepped inside and closed the painted door behind him. The large glass panel painted with intricate geometric pattern rattled when it slammed shut.

"What the hell is this. You volunteered?" demanded his father.

Paul faced him and said, "Yes. I did volunteer this morning for the army. I thought you would be pleased."

"No, I'm not. For a number of reasons," answered his father. "The first is that you consider how this will affect your mother. She will not be pleased. You know your mother's health is delicate. She doesn't need the additional stress."

Paul felt his lips tighten.

"The second reason I don't want you to volunteer at this time is because I don't think that you thought it through properly. I don't want you to throw your bright future away."

"But Dad, everyone says that the war will be over by Christmas," he protested.

His father waved his statement away. "They're wrong, son. This is not some weekend where your friends Denis and Martin go off and play at war. A lot of men are going to die. Thousands, maybe hundreds of thousands. It will last for years."

Paul still wanted to protest, but his father put up his hand. "I heard the same thing during the Boer War. How long did that war last? And that was against the Boers, who were farmers. How long do you think a war will last against the industrial might of Germany and Austria? It's going to be a long and bloody war. Mark my words. I'm just asking you to wait."

"I can't, Dad," replied Paul as he looked down at his shoes. "I've already signed the papers."

His father, resigned, asked, "What regiment?"

"The 65th Artillery," replied Paul.

"Well, that's at least better than the infantry, but not by much," muttered his father. "Have you told your mother yet?"

"No. I wanted to let you know first," answered Paul, still looking at his feet.

"So, you wanted me to tell your mother," said his father with a knowing nod. "It's time you fight your own battles." He grimaced at the poor choice of words. "You'll have to sit down with your mother and explain it to her."

Paul sighed in resignation. "Yes, Dad."

"If you change your mind, let me know. I can use my connections to get you out. Or at the very least keep you here in Canada." His father must have seen the look of disgust on Paul's face. "Just think about it."

"Yes, Dad."

"Good," his father said as he opened the sitting room door. "Now let's go back to our table. I need a drink."

AUGUST 8, 1914
FUSILIERS' RECRUITING OFFICE, MAPLE STREET,
RICHMOND HILL

Llewellyn glared up at the man standing in front of him, who was waving his arms in the air.

"What do you mean I can't sign on?" he demanded. His dark eyes were beginning to bulge, and spittle was forming on his lips.

"Like I already told you, sir, we are only recruiting single men and married men without children. Married men with children are low on the priority list," the captain said patiently, even though knew that his explanation was a waste of time with this man.

"That was a fine how-de-do. Listen here," the man said, poking the table with his forefinger. "I have a mind to volunteer, and volunteer I will."

"Who will take care of your three children?"

"That's why I want to sign up. To get away from their bloody noise," he shouted.

The captain's face hardened as his patience wore thin. "I'm afraid that you are not a suitable candidate for the Fusiliers." He looked at the sergeant-major near the door. "Next!"

"Fuck you and the horse you came on," the man yelled as he jammed on his hat and stormed out of the Fusiliers' storefront.

"Good riddance," said Lieutenant Rawlings, who had half risen from his seat in case he needed to intervene.

"We're not that desperate for men," Llewellyn said as he looked out of the store window to the line of men that stretched for about a block. He, Lieutenant Rawlings, and Sergeant-Major Evans had been at it since eight this morning, and they had signed up eighty men already. They still had another five hours to go before they closed up shop for the day. The line didn't seem to get any shorter.

"Let the next one in," he ordered.

Evans opened the door. As the man entered, he glanced at the white chalk marks strategically placed on the dark oak doorframe. The regulations required that the minimum height for the infantry was five foot three and a soldier had to have a thirty-three-inch chest. Engineers needed to be an inch taller, while artillery gunners needed to be five foot seven. Llewellyn was pleased that the man exceeded the mark by at least six inches.

He could tell from the way he put his hat under his left arm, his stride, and the stance he took when he stopped before his table that he had seen service before, probably with the Imperial forces.

"Name?" asked Rawlings.

"Michael Curtis Booth," the man replied in a steady voice.

"Present address?"

"Five Maple Avenue. Flat 10b."

"Where were you born?"

"London."

The captain looked up at him and asked, "Ontario?"

A brief smile tugged at his lips. "England."

"A long way from home," Llewellyn remarked.

"Yes, sir, it is," was his simple reply. The way he answered pleased the captain. He liked him.

"Next of kin," continued Rawlings.

"Angela Booth."

"Wife?" asked Rawlings cautiously.

"Yes."

His answer caused a frown to appear on Llewellyn's face. He asked, "You are aware that we prefer single men?"

"Yes, but I have ten years of service with the 20th Imperial Yeomanry that you may find useful."

Llewellyn nodded to himself. He was right about the man having military experience. "What rank did you have before you mustered out?"

"Sergeant."

"Hmm, no children?" asked Rawlings.

Booth turned to Rawlings then said, "No, sir. The missus can't have them."

"Sorry to hear that," replied Rawlings.

"So is the missus."

"Okay then," continued Rawlings after a slight pause. "You need to agree to be vaccinated, and you understand that the service is for the length of the war."

"Understood, sir. Where do I sign?" he asked as he leaned forward toward the table.

"Before you sign on the dotted line, I need to ask if you offered your services to any other regiments, and if they rejected you," Rawlings said, holding his pen in the air for a moment.

"This is the first regiment that I tried."

"Good! Good! Sign here," Rawlings indicated on the attestation form. "It states that you have answered all of the questions truthfully, and you agree to serve for the length of the war."

"Now, raise you right hand and swear the oath," said the captain.

Booth raised his hand and said, "I, Michael Curtis Booth, do sincerely promise and swear that I will be faithful and bear true allegiance to His Majesty."

Llewellyn reviewed the signed papers and then said, "You'll need to pass a medical, and we'll need you to swear again in front of the justice of the peace. I don't think that will be a problem."

Rawlings nodded. "You're all set. Report to the armoury tomorrow morning."

Booth hesitated for a moment before asking, "Is there a chance that I may get an advance on my pay?" He looked down at his feet. "I hate to ask. I've been out of work for the last three months. It's for the missus."

The captain glanced at Rawlings, who gave him a slight affirmative nod. He was worth the risk. "We'll be mobilizing in a week or two. I think we can advance funds to you from the regiment's coffers and deduct them from your next pay."

Llewellyn wrote a note on a slip of paper and handed it to Booth. "Show the pay sergeant at the Fusiliers' armoury this note. He'll fix you up."

"Thank you, Captain," said a grateful Booth. He folded the note carefully then placed it in a battered black wallet. He then gave both men a snappy salute, turned on his heel, and marched out of the store.

"Looks like we got a good one," remarked Rawlings.

"We did, didn't we," replied a satisfied Llewellyn. When he saw the next candidate that Sergeant-Major Evans let in, he whispered, "Trouble's coming."

A grin appeared on Rawlings's face, which quickly disappeared. "I think you may be right."

"How can I help you, son?" asked Llewellyn. The man, boy, actually, looked like he was barely sixteen. There were various reasons why men volunteered, such as a sense of duty, trying to escape from a bad situation, adventure, and from peer pressure. This one he suspected was a mixture of adventure and peer pressure. If all his friends were going, he didn't want to be left behind.

"I would like to volunteer," he said, his voice trembling. A facial muscle twitched due to his nervousness.

"Very good," the captain said with a friendly smile.

"Name?" asked Rawlings, pen posed on the attestation paper.

"Andrew Gilchrist, sir."

"Date of birth?"

Instead of stating his date of birth, Gilchrist handed him a birth certificate. Rawlings glanced at it and then handed it to the captain. Llewellyn looked at the date on the birth certificate and did a quick calculation.

"I'm sorry, son. It seems that you are six months short of your eighteenth birthday." The look of dismay that crossed that young man's face caused him to feel a touch of sympathy for the boy. The boy was nowhere near eighteen. He had made a mistake when he doctored the birth certificate.

"I'm afraid that without your mother's consent I cannot sign you up," he said gently.

"She's all for me signing up! Honest!" he blurted.

Llewellyn shook his head regretfully. "Regulations, son." To give him some dignity, he said, "I think that you will make an outstanding recruit. If you bring your mom down, and if she gives her permission, I will gladly sign you up."

The boy's shoulders slumped in disappointment. It was unlikely that the boy's mother would agree. "Yes, sir," he said as he took back the birth certificate. Llewellyn watched as he gloomily walked out.

"You do know that he's going to try the Queen's Own next," remarked Rawlings.

"I know." Normally he would have applauded that boy's enthusiasm and pluck, but not today. He suspected that this war would be long and bloody. He wanted to give the lad some time to grow up first. He hoped that he was wrong and that they would really be back by Christmas.

AUGUST 10, 1914
OUTPATIENT CLINIC, TORONTO GENERAL HOSPITAL

"Ouch, that hurts," groaned the patient, who was sitting on the bed, bare-chested.

"Sorry," Samantha said. She had been a little rough with the patient when she was taking his vital signs. She didn't mean to be. She was upset that she had to work. She really wanted to attend the nursing association meeting being held that evening. The session had been arranged to provide the nurses who were interested with information on volunteering for the militia. Matron Hazel had, as far as Samantha was concerned, deliberately scheduled her for the night shift to prevent it.

It didn't help when Doctor Moore entered, with several interns in tow, to take a look at the patient. He demanded, "Chart!"

"Of course, Doctor," she said as she handed him the clipboard. She wondered what had agitated him. It seemed he was in the same foul mood as she was. The pudgy doctor was normally slow-moving and even-tempered. The doctor checked the chart and then handed it to one of the interns. "What is your opinion?"

Dr. Addison, with what Samantha thought was a pretentious moustache, grimaced then flipped the pages. "There seems to be nothing wrong with him that a good meal would not take care of," he stated as he handed the chart back to the older man.

The pudgy doctor stared at the young man, who looked rather thin and emaciated. He kept glancing at Samantha as he bit his lip. Moore tapped his lips with a pen then sighed as he signed the chart with his typical flourish. "You're cleared, my boy."

"Thank you, Doctor," the man said with relief.

"Humph," the doctor snorted. "Don't thank me yet. Thank me in six months when the militia puts some weight on your bones. Now put on your clothes and get out of here."

Samantha followed the doctor and the interns out into the hall as they left the young man to dress.

Dr. Moore surveyed the crowd in the outpatients' clinic lobby. Nearly all of them were young men waiting to be examined.

"Damned inconvenient," muttered the doctor. "And I'm not going to do it," he continued as he stared at Dr. Addison.

"Your decision, Doctor," he replied stiffly. "I have some patients I need to check on."

When the intern disappeared down the hall, Moore turned to Samantha and saw her confusion. "Sorry, Miss Lonsdale, I'm a bit put out with our young man. It seems that he has been giving medical clearances to some men who were questionable when he shouldn't have."

Samantha winced. Dr. Moore was well known for being a stickler. "What are you going to do?"

"I don't know at the moment," he replied with a touch of frustration. "And I unfortunately don't have much time."

"You're leaving, doctor?" Samantha asked in surprise. The doctor was a fixture at the hospital.

The familiar lopsided grin appeared. "Oh yes. My unit is being called up for active service. I'm the chief medical officer for the Richmond Fusiliers. All my patients will be transferred to a new doctor when they can find a replacement."

Samantha's eyes widened when she heard that he was in the militia. Still, she couldn't imagine the doctor in a uniform. She didn't want to appear too eager, so she asked, "What about Dr. Nuborg?" Nuborg was Dr. Moore's friend and colleague on staff at the hospital.

"Didn't you hear?"

"No," replied Samantha.

"He was in Paris at a medical conference when the war broke out. He can't get passage back because the cabins on the liners are all booked. He's trapped there. He doesn't know when he's going to be back."

"Will he be all right?" asked Samantha with a touch of concern.

"I hope so."

She hesitated a moment. She hated asking for favours, but she finally said, "Will you be needing nurses?"

"Of course. Not in the field ambulances, too dangerous, but in the general hospitals." He cocked his head to the side. "You're considering volunteering?"

Samantha nodded.

"What about your position here?"

Samantha responded with a shrug, which caused a look of consternation to cross the good doctor's jowls. "Why aren't you attending the nursing info session?" he asked.

She gave another half-hearted shrug. "I was thinking of sending in my application ..."

"And you wanted to know if I can give you a reference?"

"If you can make your way ..."

He put up his hand. "Speak no more. I'm quite willing to give you a reference."

"You would?"

"Of course," he replied. "You're a damn good nurse. Type up your application. I'll be glad to take a look before you submit it." He winked at her. "I know Colonel Dawson at Kingston, who has been assigned to review the applications with Matron Macdonald. Come to my office and I'll give you the address. I can't promise anything, but it may help."

"Thank you, Doctor Moore. I greatly appreciate it," Samantha said as she dodged a medical cart in the hallway as she followed the doctor.

A small smile appeared on her face as she thought how wonderful it would be that in spite of Matron Hazel's efforts she would be able to join the militia.

CHAPTER 5

AUGUST 18, 1914
HOUSE OF COMMONS, CENTRE BLOCK,
PARLIAMENT HILL, OTTAWA

It seemed appropriate that the light cast by the green chamber's stained glass windows seemed muted today. Normally the sunlight would stream through, enhancing the beauty of the marble arches in front of the spectators' galleries. Today, due to the overcast August skies, the chamber was dependent on the electric lights that hung from the ceilings and the desk lamps clamped to the tops of the wooden desks to provide illumination.

To thunderous applause, Sir Robert Borden took his regular seat in the middle of the front row after he made his announcement that the governor general's term had been extended indefinitely. As Borden scanned the House of Commons, he wasn't surprised by what he saw. Nearly every MP was in his seat. No member wanted to say that they were not in attendance on this momentous day. The spectator's galleries were standing room only. The reporters were practically falling out of the reporter's gallery above the speaker's chair on his left.

He knew that he would get complaints when they found out that only one reporter would be allowed to accompany the Canadian Expeditionary Force when they finally were sent to Europe. Hughes was going to make it clear that volunteering then claiming that they were war correspondents when they arrived in France was a non-starter.

When Borden thought about Hughes, he sighed. Yesterday the governor general had complained to him that Hughes had been disrespectful. He had to have a word with his minister about his behaviour. He wasn't hopeful that Hughes would listen. He suspected seeing the governor general wearing his field marshal uniform had set him off. Hughes was only a colonel, and he had been pestering him for quite some time for a promotion.

He did have concerns about the governor general wearing his uniform. While the Duke of Connaught was, under the *BNA Act*, the commander-in-chief of the militia and naval service, the title was mainly symbolic, and that was exactly the way Borden wanted to keep it. The governor general's term was to end on October 20. The telegrams from

London made it clear that the king thought that it unwise to replace the governor general under the current circumstances. The duke was not happy about it. It would make his life a little bit easier if Hughes and Prince Arthur got along. Since the men detested each other, that was unlikely. If they just were more respectful to each other, he would settle for that.

Borden listened with half an ear as Donald Sutherland, his MP for the Ontario riding of Oxford South, moved that the throne speech be accepted, declaring that, "Present is the time for united action." David L'Espérance, who represented the Conservatives in Montmagny, Quebec, seconded the motion by adding, "all party differences should be laid aside in face of the national danger." The Hansard clerks, sitting at the long table in front of him, were writing furiously as they transcribed the speeches verbatim.

Borden found himself nodding in agreement as he made notes in the margins of the speech that he was preparing. He always found writing the afternoon's peroration difficult. He was planning to deliver it after Laurier delivered his remarks to the Commons concerning Borden's war efforts to date and the important pieces of legislation that were to be passed.

His mind drifted off for a moment. He wondered how the Canadian golfers were doing in Chicago at the US Open. Francis Ouimet was the favourite, since he was the current title holder. Borden pinched his nose to regain his focus. He hadn't slept well the previous night. After his meeting with Sir Wilfrid, where he gave him a copy of the throne speech and the four pieces of legislation, the *War Measures Act*, the *War Appropriation Act*, the *Finance Act*, and the *Canadian Patriotic Fund Act* that his government was tabling today, he had worked to 1:00 a.m. before going to sleep. Last Friday, when he arrived home at six, he was so exhausted he fell asleep at 6:30 and didn't wake until 3:30 in the morning. Maybe he could get a round of golf in at the Royal Ottawa on Saturday afternoon after the morning's cabinet meeting. He suspected that he'd need a few hours of exercise. It amazed him how much time was wasted by his bickering cabinet ministers. Hughes, again, and William White, his finance minister, got into a heated discussion yesterday morning, which he had to smooth over.

When the chamber suddenly quieted, Borden lifted his head and saw Laurier, who sat directly across from him, rise to his feet. As usual, Laurier was impeccably dressed in a black jacket with a high-collared white shirt. The silk cravat held in place by a dark-coloured pin matched the seriousness of the occasion. Borden was somewhat apprehensive of what his political adversary would say. When they met yesterday, Laurier had assured him that he and the Liberals would support the government in this time of crisis. Sir Wilfrid did hint that he may have some trouble with members of his caucus, but he would deal with it. There were rumours that Laurier would spring the idea that the families of the CEF would be provided for while the troops were in Europe. He had warned Sutherland about that and to mention it in his opening speech.

Borden relaxed when Laurier started with, "We may differ as to methods. We have our differences and disagreements, but here and now, I give the assurance that in what has been done and what remains to be done, we shall take no exceptions and offer no criticism so long as there is danger at the front. We propose to tell the friends and the foes of Britain that a united Canada stands for the mother country."

The crowds interrupted Laurier with cheers and clapping. It was especially loud when he declared that when Great Britain was at war, Canada was at war. When Laurier took his seat, Borden rose and began clapping. He could hear the chairs behind him as the members of his party and the members of the opposition rose to their feet to join him. Laurier had given, as was expected, an eloquent speech.

When the applause died down, Borden glanced up to the spectator's gallery, where he saw Laura sitting beside Laurier's wife, Zoé. Laurier was a tough act to follow. He smoothed out the papers on his desk, took a deep breath, and then began.

"It is not fitting that I should prolong this debate. In the awful dawn of the greatest war the world has ever known, in the hour when peril confronts us such as this Empire has not faced for a hundred years, every vain unnecessary word seems a discord …"

AUGUST 20, 1914
FUSILIERS' ARMOURY, RICHMOND HILL

Llewellyn glanced at Lieutenant-Colonel Topham sitting at the head of a long dining table in the Richmond Fusiliers officer's mess. On the table were the remains of a four course meal that the battalion's HQ staff and senior officers had to endure.

Endure might be too strong a word. The captain found the meal was excellent. It had begun with oysters, thin carrot and spinach soup, and a crisp fried chicken appetizer, followed by beef Wellington with whipped mashed potatoes, English truffles, and green beans. The dessert was a deep-dish Macintosh apple pie with a thick slice of cheddar. Each course was accompanied by the appropriate imported French and Italian wines.

Under most circumstances, Llewellyn would have enjoyed the evening immensely. But with war being declared, there were numerous tasks that needed to be accomplished to ensure that the battalion was ready when the official marching orders arrived.

Even with the news that the British Expeditionary Force had landed in France several days before, the Lieutenant-Colonel had insisted that the monthly officers mess dinner had to go ahead as planned, since it could be the last one for some time in such easy and friendly environments. The Fusiliers mess hall was adorned with a long solid oak table that allowed for the seating of nearly twenty but could be expanded to accommodate twice that number. The room's walls were wainscoted with dark pine panels etched with flora designs. On the pale blue-painted plaster walls were portraits of the previous battalion commanders. At the end of the room was a copy of Wolfe dying on the Plains of Abraham. At the other was a large map of Canada.

All of the officers seated at the table were dressed in regulation summer dress uniforms. They wore white dress coats, black cummerbunds, black pants, and spit-polished black footwear. Miniature medals hung on the left breast of each officer. Like Llewellyn, most had service medals. Two of the senior officers had a Fenian Raids campaign medal and the North-West Rebellion service medal. A few others, such as captains Joseph Percival and Gavin Lime, had served in South Africa.

When the orderly poured the port into the glass of a young lieutenant, the captain noticed that the mess orderly gave a baby-faced lieutenant a subtle nudge to remind him that he was required to make the toast. The young lieutenant rose to his feet then said firmly and loudly, "To the king!"

Everyone rose to their feet and echoed, "To the king!"

Then they downed their port.

"Well, gentlemen, you have read our orders that Ottawa has sent to us," said Lieutenant-Colonel Topham. The officers nodded.

"We have been ordered to supply Ottawa with a list of suitable men by August 22th," Topham said.

"Does that mean that the battalion will not be activated?" blurted the lieutenant. Captain Llewellyn gave the officer a stare. Abashed, the lieutenant tried to disappear.

"While we have been authorized for 1,100 men, we are currently under strength. We need to recruit another 200 or so. Captain Llewellyn is seeing to that task."

The captain noticed the slight tone of disapproval in the colonel's tone. The colonel felt that he was being too picky with the volunteers. "Will the adverts be in the *Star* and the *Globe* for tomorrow?" Topham asked Llewellyn.

"They should be. I sent them in myself," he replied. "The major issue is getting the volunteers equipped."

He turned to Major Case, the senior quartermaster officer. "Major, how are we with supplies?"

Case frowned. "Not good, Captain. We are short on everything from ammunition to uniforms, rifles, and horses."

The colonel sighed. "The battalion had barely adequate equipment for a long time. Okay. You have to start ordering in supplies."

"Yes. But what do I do for money?" he asked.

"What did Ottawa say?"

"I've sent telegrams to Ottawa, but they haven't replied," he stated sourly.

"Buy what you need on my authorization. I'll dip into my personal funds, if necessary, and hope that Ottawa reimburses. Just keep receipts. You know how picky Ottawa can be without the proper paperwork."

"What about the rifles and ammunition? We have been issued with the Ross Mk IIs. We are slated to receive the Mk IIIs, but that will not be until next year. At least that was the schedule."

The colonel frowned. "Issue the Mk IIs for now. I hope that once we get mobilized that we be equipped with Mk IIIs."

"And ammunition?"

"We can equip each of the men with eighty-five rounds, but 3,000 rounds in the carts."

"Do we have enough carts?" Llewellyn asked, which got him an irritated look from Case.

"For Pete's sake. We don't have enough of those either?" demanded Topham. Case answered with a shrug.

He turned to his senior medical officer, Dr. Moore. "I hope that you have better news. Have all the men been inoculated? We have to be sure that the men are free from the most common ailments."

"I'm going through the medical records to ensure that they are all up to date. Captain Llewellyn has been keeping me busy with the new volunteers. I am hoping to be ready in time for our mobilization. Do we have an exact date yet?"

"I've contacted the Grand Trunk and the Canadian Pacific to see about train transport," replied Major Case. "They are under heavy demand, so they are trying to schedule us in."

"Are we heading for Petawawa?" asked the young lieutenant.

Case replied, "Ottawa has changed it from Petawawa to Valcartier."

"Where the hell is Valcartier?" demanded the lieutenant. When all the officers at the table looked at him, his face went white and he realized he had overstepped his bounds.

Llewellyn stared at the map of Canada, which didn't help, since it wasn't on this particular map. "We'll find out when we get there," he said. "Let's hope the GTR and the CPR know where it is."

"I certainly hope so," replied Topham, who actually cracked a thin smile. "In the meantime, we have our orders. This regiment is going to war, and I want us to be prepared."

CHAPTER 6

AUGUST 24, 1914
TRAIN STATION, QUEBEC CITY

Samantha kept shifting in her seat as the blue patches of the Saint-Charles River filtered through the trees. She straightened and leaned against the window as the outskirts of Quebec City appeared. She glanced at the two women sitting on the bench across from her. One of them had her auburn head buried in *Carrel's Illustrated Guide & Map of Quebec*. Samantha had bought the book before she left Toronto. She hoped that, if she had time, she could visit some of the sights. The other woman was curled in her seat, napping.

She checked her purse, where she kept the telegram that she had received from the Department of Militia and Defence, ordering her to report to Valcartier. Samantha was rather dazed by the rapid change of events. She had sent her application to Kingston with faint hope. Thousands of nurses were volunteering. She had shrieked in delight when she received the message that she was to report for duty by August 24th. It didn't give her much time for her to say her tearful goodbyes to Irene, the other nurses, and doctors she liked. She was touched when a group of patients gave her a bouquet of flowers as a going away gift.

A few days before she was to report, she had received instructions that her orders had been changed. She was to report to the immigration hospital in Quebec City. There was no explanation as to why the change was made.

She rubbed her left arm. It was still sore from all of the shots that she had been required to take. She wondered if Irene would be joining the contingent of nurses that the Toronto General was planning to send. She had been tempted to wait, but once she found out who the matron was she, was glad that she hadn't.

On the train she had spotted the nursing pins the two women wore and had introduced herself. She was glad that she did, since they too were volunteers. They had commandeered the two benches and had swivelled them around so that they had their private little alcove in economy.

"It looks like we've arrived," said Claire as she closed the book. She handed it back to Samantha then rose to get her luggage from the rack above her head. The loose light grey dress hid, somewhat, her slightly plump figure. She had ten years experience in nursing from Vancouver, and Samantha found her to be a bit on the terse side, but they seemed to get along well.

"Are we there yet?" asked Emily Richardson. She rubbed sleep from her eyes as she sat up.

"Did you get enough rest?" asked Samantha with a teasing smile.

"The train always makes me sleepy," she replied as she stretched her arms, causing the pale green bodice to tighten, enhancing her breasts. She scowled at a man when she spotted him staring at them. She seemed somewhat airy, but Samantha suspected some depth behind the child-like behaviour. "Where are we exactly?"

Samantha turned her head to the left and saw a two-storey stone building about 400 feet long, with a telephone pole every fifty feet or so, some of which were twisted out of shape.

"Louise Basin. It's our final stop," stated Claire as she put on a black hat and pinned it in place. Louise Basin was the key immigration point of entry to Canada. The wharf was capable of handling nearly 3,000 passengers a day.

The brakes squealed as the train gently jerked to a stop, and then they climbed down onto the platform, helping each other with their luggage. A woman, dressed in a dark blue uniform, was scanning the passengers as they stepped onto the platform. It took a moment for Samantha to place the face, but when she did she exclaimed, "Rita!"

Dropping her valise, she hugged her friend. "I shouldn't have done that," said Samantha as she released Rita and gave her what she thought was a salute.

Rita Newman's cheeks dimpled in amusement. "I'll let the hug pass just this once. But the salute is terrible."

"What are you doing here? You're looking well," blurted Samantha as she looked admiringly at her friend, who she hadn't seen since they graduated from Sudbury High. Two rows of brass buttons sparkled on her bodice. A belt buckle cinched her waist. The long skirt fell to a pair of gleaming black ankle boots. For a dash of colour there were scarlet cuffs and a high-neck collar. The two brass serpent medical insignias on her collar matched the badge on her black hat. The hat's colour matched Rita's hair.

"I'm doing fine. To answer your question, I'm here to meet you. I'm going to be your matron."

Samantha's eyes widened. "Oh my God!" Then she realized that she had forgotten her friends. "This is Claire and Emily. They volunteered as well."

"Pleasure," said Rita as she shook their hands. "Do we have everything?"

When they gave an affirmative nod, Newman took them directly through the immigration building so fast that Samantha barely had a glimpse of the cavernous hall with a long wooden counter, money-exchange wickets, and what seemed like a dining hall at the far end. Samantha's stomach growled. She hadn't eaten on the train.

Waiting for them was a Ford truck. The driver, a boy barely eighteen dressed in a khaki uniform, jumped out. "Sam, please help the ladies," ordered Rita.

"Yes, ma'am." He took the luggage and tossed it into the back. He then helped the ladies step up so they could take their seats on the two wooden benches.

When everyone was seated, Rita banged on the roof of the truck's cab. The motor sputtered then revved. Emily squealed in fright then grabbed her hat with one hand and the truck's rail with her other when the clutch engaged.

Samantha turned her attention to Rita. "It's so good to see you. It's been five years."

"Closer to seven, but who's counting."

Samantha chuckled. Rita always was a stickler for details. "When did you volunteer?"

"Seven years ago," answered Rita with a grin. Samantha blinked in surprise. She never did find out exactly why she left Sudbury. She was unable to get a clear answer from the man Rita was supposed to marry.

"I was in the militia for three years. Then I became a member of the permanent force four years ago. I'm based out of Ottawa. I've just been promoted to acting matron, and I've been assigned to start your training for military nursing. You're joining the first group of volunteers."

"How many are there?" asked Claire. Her knuckles where white, holding on to the wooden bench as the truck bounced on the potholes.

"About two dozen at the moment. You're going to be our first group. We're hoping to get the second group in a few weeks as Matron Macdonald reviews and completes the selection process." Samantha recognized the name. Matron Macdonald was the senior commanding officer of the Canadian nursing sisters. "By the way, I nearly died when I saw your application."

"Thanks, Rita. I appreciate it," replied Samantha as her cheeks blushed. She turned her head and saw what she thought was the Château Frontenac slowly recede.

"Where are we going?" asked Claire as it became obvious that they were heading toward the city's outskirts.

"The Immigration Detention Hospital at Parc Savard. We'll have to cross over the Saint-Charles to get to the other side."

"Why are we not going to Valcartier?" asked Emily as she finally gave up on holding her hat. She removed it and placed it in her lap.

Rita shook her head. "The camp is not quite ready for us. At least that is what Colonel Williams has indicated. We'll be there in a few weeks' time."

"We are such delicate flowers," muttered Emily, which brought a chuckle from the group.

It took about a half hour or so before the truck turned onto a dirt road that led to a spacious park. At the end of the road it drove up to a two-storey red brick building with a flat-top roof. At the top of the structure there was a sign with black lettering that read IMMIGRA- TION HOSPITAL — HOPITAL de l'IMMIGRATION. When Samantha jumped out of the vehicle she saw a number of square tents in the grass field next to the hospital. Sitting in front of them were several groups of men of various ages with their families. Small children clutched at their mother's skirts. From the snatches of conversation she could hear they were not speaking English or French.

"Coming?" asked Rita.

"Who are those people?" asked Claire.

"Immigrants," replied Rita as she climbed the stairs to the first floor veranda. "The hospital checks them to ensure that they are in good health before allowing them to enter the country. This is probably the last group, considering the situation in Europe. The hospital is normally closed during the winter when the ice shuts the harbour.

"Come in. I'll show to your quarters," said Rita as she opened the door and marched through. "On the first floor there is a general office, a doctor's office, an eye infirmary, lab, operating room, pharmacy, and a men's infirmary. I'll give you a complete tour later. We've taken over the women's infirmary on the second floor," Rita continued as she took the stairs to the floor above.

The women's infirmary was a large room lit by skylights and ten-foot-high windows. White-painted steel-framed beds and end tables were positioned along the industrial grey paint that covered half the wall, acting as a wainscoting. The top portion matched the colour of the bed frames and end tables.

"You've each been assigned a bed. Freshen up first then we'll meet in the cafeteria so we can explain your duties."

Claire raised her arm to ask a question. "Will we be getting a uniform like yours?"

Rita looked down at her dress uniform. "Not quite like mine, but yes. A $100 clothing allowance for a nursing sister's uniform. As a lieutenant in the Canadian militia you will also receive $2 a day pay. Copies of the rules and regulations of the Canadian Army Medical Service are available. Study them well, as you will be tested.

"Reveille will be at six. Make your beds and complete morning ablutions by seven. Breakfast will close at eight o'clock sharp. At eight fifteen report to the front entrance for morning exercises, which will be a three-mile route march followed by a hour of drill. The rest of the day will be filled various lectures, such as military etiquette. Officers get a bit prickly if you get their rank wrong. Other lectures will be on such topics as military hygiene and medical procedures.

"If you have any further questions, hold them for our meeting this afternoon. Dinner is at five. Don't be late," Rita stated. She then turned on her heel and headed for her room.

Samantha tossed her valise on the nearest bed and looked at the two women. "This is going to be fun." Claire and Emily looked at her as if she had lost her mind.

AUGUST 27, 1914
MINISTER OF FINANCE'S OFFICE, EAST BLOCK,
PARLIAMENT HILL, OTTAWA

Deputy Minister T. Cooper Bolville was frowning as he stroked his moustache. He glanced at Henry Ross, his assistant deputy minister, who was recording the decisions that were being made during the course of the meeting mandated by the prime minister. He knew that Borden would be reading them with interest. He was fairly certain the prime minister was using them as a spear point in reorganizing and modernizing the civil service, bypassing the opposition of such changes by various members of the cabinet. Especially those who liked to have a say how contracts were allocated.

"To recap." He still had an Irish accent, even though his family moved to Canada when he was fourteen in 1874. He had joined Finance in 1883 and he became its deputy minister in 1906. He was chairing the meeting, since the *War Appropriations Act* fell under his department. "We have agreed that as much as possible that all construction, purchases of materials and supplies should go to public tender."

"Yes, Cooper, that is correct," stated Eugène Fiset as he removed his eyeglasses and cleaned them with a white handkerchief. He adjusted the black cord that was attached to the right lens so that it sat more comfortably on his uniform's collar. Bolville gazed at the colonel tabs on Eugène's shoulders before moving to the service ribbons above his left breast pocket. The man from Rimouski was wearing the Queen's Medal, with four bars, and the Distinguished Service Order for his services as a doctor during the Boer War. "But only those that exceed $5,000."

Bolville looked over his glasses at Fiset. "We don't want to hinder your department's efficiency." He wasn't concerned about Eugène Fiset. He was not only the surgeon-general for the Militia and Defence Department but he was its deputy minister. Like him, since 1906. He was more concerned with Fist's minister, Sam Hughes, who had a forcible personality, to say the least. "But any contracts above that amount need to be submitted to the cabinet for their approval before they are released for tender."

"With the appropriate documentation," suggested John Fraser, who was sitting beside Fiset at the small table in Finance Minister White's office in the East Block. Bolville turned his attention to his former chief financial clerk. Having the auditor-general attend such a meeting was unusual, since audits were normally conducted after the money spent not prior. There had been some concern when he was appointed, in 1905, as whether or not he would be able to assume the independence that was needed for the office.

"Of course, John," Bolville replied with a smile. It didn't hurt to be on the man's good side. Especially when Borden had requested that Fraser attend. This was not lost on the deputy ministers sitting at the table.

"A reminder that all that the monies spent that fall under the *War Appropriations Act* need to be kept in their own accounts and should be separate from your normal department's operating funds," stated Bolville.

"Any payments should be made via cheques and should be applied against the letters of credits as proscribed in the act," added Ross.

"Good point," said Bolville.

"I just want to clarify how the pay and allowances for the force will be accounted for," requested John W. Borden, who was sitting on the general's left in civilian clothes. As the accountant and paymaster general for the militia department, he was responsible for ensuring that the men of the force were properly paid. He also happened to be the younger brother of the prime minister. When he first came to Ottawa in 1897, he had joined the department as its chief accountant, and he was recently appointed its paymaster general.

"The minister put out a call for 25,000 men, and from the reports that I have been receiving, we may exceed that number. Do the order in councils from August 6th to August 14th give the authority to continue the pay scales that we have determined to be suitable?"

Bolville nodded. "It does. They give you the authority for the current men and horses that are being mobilized."

"The latest figure that I have is 6,000 horses," replied Borden. "We have issued instructions that local regiments are to source the horses locally and then transport them to Valcartier."

"The orders include their forage, their transport to Quebec, as well as abroad, and their return," Bolville continued. "However, they are to be used only for the troops currently at Valcartier. A separate order-in-council will be needed for any troops being mobilized for Halifax, Quebec City, and B.C. The August orders also cover the purchases of the two submarines by the McBride government, and that were subsequently transferred to the naval department."

"For that I thank you," replied George Desbarats, the deputy minister for the Naval Department, as he stroked his salt and pepper beard. "Paying for them out of my current budget would have been a bit of problem."

"I know. You had a lot on your plate before this happened." Bolville was referring to the transfer of the Fisheries Branch from the Marine and Fisheries Department to the Naval Department that was mandated last June. Also, the Naval Department moved its offices from the West Block to the Rae Building on Mackenzie Avenue.

"It is going to get busier. Depending how long the war will last, we may need to build new wireless stations, acquire aircraft to supplement our fleet, and we may need buy new ships to ensure that our coasts are properly protected."

Bolville gave his counterpart a slight shrug. "You will still need to submit them to the cabinet and get their approval."

"That's understood," replied Desbarats. "I hate losing the *Niobe* and the *Rainbow*, but we're reviewing what we can do to enhance security. My people are examining it as we speak."

"So have I covered everything?" asked Bolville as he looked around the table.

Ross looked at his notes and then said, "I think so. We covered that amounts for guard troops, and their transport, will be covered under the *Militia Act*. If a second contingent will be needed, it would require the governor general to sign off on it. The expenditure for censorship have been covered by the August 2nd order-in-council. If funds are needed by the secret service, it would require consultation with the opposition, as per the agreement that was struck several years ago." He mumbled as he flipped various papers. He then looked up. "I can't read my notes. There was a questions concerning officers working in a dual capacity?"

Fiset nodded. "We have a number of officers assigned to censorship. They are on special duty, and they have dual roles. We will need to set up a special rate of remuneration for them."

"Hmm …" said Borden. "Let me talk with my staff, and we'll come up with the appropriate pay scale."

"Sounds good," Fiset agreed.

"I do have a concern about civil servants who are willing to volunteer. Will they be receiving their current salary on top of their militia pay?" asked Borden.

Bolville frowned. "We'll have to bring it up with the minister. As it stands now, if a deputy minister gives his permission for the employee to volunteer, he will be entitled to both his civil service pay as well as his military pay."

"There is a concern with morale when it gets out that they are being paid double," said Fiset.

"I'll make a note of it," remarked Ross.

"It looks like we are done for now. Any more questions?" asked Bolville a final time. "If not, we'll prepare a memorandum and circulate it."

A slight cough from John Fraser caused everyone to turn toward him. "I just want to add that I'm well aware of the extraordinary circumstances that we are all labouring under. I'm satisfied that if your departments follow the appropriate auditing procedures and that all expenditures are properly documented, my office will be quite satisfied."

"Thank you, John. That is much appreciated," answered Bolville. Everyone at the table beamed. It would make their life easier if the auditor general was happy. Unfortunately, the memo would come back to haunt them.

CHAPTER 7

Llewellyn checked the straps of his saddle to make sure that it was comfortably snug for his horse. Sometimes the horse found it amusing to enlarge his stomach an inch or so and snicker when the saddle would slide down as the rider put a foot into the stirrups.

"Ready?" shouted an echoing command.

The captain put a foot into the stirrup and hoisted himself onto his steed.

"Sabres!" He pulled the sabre out of the scabbard tied to his saddle. He made a salute then sharply put the blade at the rest position on his shoulder.

"Band!" The regimental band at the front of the column in the militia hall took a few moments to ready their instruments. Then they began to play.

"March!" came the command.

The huge doors at the front of the drill hall opened, and the column of nearly a thousand men plus their senior officers began their three-mile march to the train station.

The route that they had chosen was at least a mile longer than the regular one. However, the colonel wanted the parade to go through the centre of town, as did the city council. They all wanted a rousing sendoff for the men.

The men looked splendid in their khaki uniforms. The black boots and brass buttons gleamed in the sunlight. The temperature was going to be hot. They were predicting eighty-two degrees at noon. Their Ross rifles, with fixed bayonets, gleamed as the men marched with feet and arms syncing. It was no mean feat, since half of the troops were new recruits. The sergeants had drilled them mercilessly in the proper drill so that they looked somewhat like soldiers. They would be totally useless in a fight. That was what the training at Valcartier and in England would be for.

There was a large crowd that lined the streets as practically the entire town came to see them off. Many in the crowd waved Union Jack flags.

Groups of small boys mimicked the soldiers' march for a block or two until their mothers called them back.

When they got to the train station, the battalion arranged themselves in a square in front of a podium that had been set up for the mayor and the city council.

Topham dismounted from his horse and marched to the podium. The mayor, a tall, lean man with the silver chains of the mayor's office around his neck, rose and with his hands waved the crowd to shush.

"I'm going to keep my speech short," he announced.

"That would be a first," shouted someone from a crowd of civilians, which caused amused chuckles. He heard few behind him from the troops. He didn't turn his head, but he felt the glare of the sergeants bear down on the men who dared to laugh while on parade. A few of the men would be put on report and the appropriate punishment tolled out.

"I would simply say that this is a glorious sight. All of these fine, upstanding men are here to do their duty for king and country. I'm proud to be a British subject, but even more, I'm proud to be a Canadian," he said in a flourish. Then the crowd erupted into a thunderous applause. "Now I'll let the commanding officer of our troops say a word," he said as he relinquished the podium to the lieutenant-colonel.

Topham was in his element. He stood at the podium and looked into the admiring gaze of the crowd. He had worked for hours on his speech. He wanted it to be remembered so that when he came back from the war he would have a better opportunity to run for political office. He had even tested the speech on the Fusiliers' captains to get their reaction. Llewellyn tried to politely decline. It was not a good idea to offend his commanding officer. Well, at least not any more than he already had. At least he didn't pull out his speech and put it on the podium.

"Today, good citizens, we are off to fight to preserve the honour of England. In her time of need, her sons and daughters have responded to the call of duty. The sun never sets on the British Empire, and it will never will. Once we have trashed the bastards, we will be forever remembered in the annals of war. We are well trained and well equipped. And we will be back for the new year," he said with conviction.

"God save the king!" he yelled with a salute.

"God save the king!" the crowd shouted.

Then the men were led into the train station. Once inside, the soldiers relaxed. Each platoon was assigned a car for the duration of the trip. Llewellyn led his horse by the reins to the stock car at the rear of the train and walked him up the ramp to the stall that was assigned to him. He unsaddled him and placed a blanket on his back to help keep him warm. He then gave him water and bag of oats. Once he was satisfied that the horse was going to be okay, he made his way to his assigned car to look after his men.

AUGUST 29, 1914
TRAIN STATION, VALCARTIER CAMP

When Paul jumped down from the train car, he stumbled on some of the rail bed's loose gravel. His heavy kit bag flew off his shoulder. His eyes widened in horror as it slammed into the man in front of him.

"What the fuck are you doing, McGill?" growled Hank Enright as he rubbed his lower back where Paul's canvas sack had hit him. He was small, nearly five four, but he met the requirements for the artillery brigade's horse drivers.

"My foot slipped on the loose gravel," retorted Paul. "Quit calling me McGill."

"Yeah, right," Enright sneered as he glared at Paul. "Keep it up, McGill, and my foot will slip up your ass."

Paul sighed. He had inadvertently mentioned that he was planning to go to McGill University, one of the premier universities in Canada, and ever since he'd been stuck with the nickname. The more he tried to get them to stop, the more they teased him. Hank Enright was the worst of the twenty volunteers in his section of the 65th Horse Artillery.

From what he could tell, unlike the infantry regiments, the artillery brigades were nearly at full strength. The artillery was the most prestigious of the militia arms. The volunteers that the brigade selected were to act as a reserve and replacements for battle losses. Most of them were from Montreal's east end. They didn't like the Westmount boys, since they had to work for a living.

"Enright! Ryan!" a voice bellowed. "Get your fucking arses in line."

"Yes, Sergeant," replied Enright and Paul in unison as they picked up their kit bags and hurried to get into line. Finding their positions in the column was relatively easy, since the two sections disembarked from the train in the same order as they had embarked. Paul turned his head to the right to ensure that he was aligned with the marker, the first soldier at the end. Behind him the second section of ten men shuffled into their positions. None of them carried the Ross rifles that they had spent the last two weeks drilling with. They had been informed that new ones would be issued when they arrived at Valcartier.

That was one of the things that surprised Paul. He had enlisted in the artillery because he thought he would not be doing a lot of marching. However, on his first day the sergeant-major dispelled that notion by taking all of the volunteers on a six-mile route march, with full packs, and then they spent an hour of square bashing, where they were taught the basics of marching in a somewhat coordinated fashion. Who knew that so many men didn't know their left foot from their right?

He chafed in places he didn't know could be rubbed that raw. What was worse was that he had to march in brand new ankle boots. It had been an extremely painful week until the stiff leather was finally somewhat broken in. He was still wearing extra thick wool socks to protect the blisters on his feet. Every morning he wanted to report for sick parade, but he didn't want to give the rest of the men the satisfaction, especially when they found out that his uniform was custom tailored.

After Sergeant-Major Long completed his muster call, he ordered the section at ease. Paul mimicked the rest of the men by putting his sack at his feet. It contained a spare set of uniforms, a greatcoat, blanket, and other personal belongings. He then craned his neck to get his first view of the Valcartier camp.

To his right he could see an immense grass plain that ended at the foot of the Laurentian Mountains in the distance. Echoes of the musketry practice drifted across it. He assumed they were coming from the rifle range. He had caught a glimpse of a number of targets when his train rolled into the station.

A second train, with the same Canadian Northern Railway markings as those of the passenger car Paul had stumbled off, slowly stopped at the third platform. The loading dock was nearly the same length of the other two, which he estimated to be about 300 yards long. Men swarmed the cars to unload the horses and the wagons that comprised the brigade's ammunition supply. The boxcars contained nearly 18,000 artillery rounds. Uniformed men exited the passenger cars onto the gravel, since the raised platforms were reserved for unloading equipment.

Slightly to his centre left, he could see a white-painted water tower rising above the stand of trees behind the corrugated steel building. When he turned his head to the left, rows of white bell tents seemed to shimmer brightly in the early August sun. Like railway tracks, they converged into a single point in the distance.

Already he could feel that it was going to be a hot, humid day. He removed his flat-brimmed hat and wiped his brow with a handkerchief from his right breast pocket. He then used it to wipe moisture from his hat's inner band. He fingered the brass badge with the artillery gun motif on his cap for a moment.

He quickly put on his hat when he saw Captain Masterley, the brigade's adjutant, heading his way. The adjutant was being tailed by Lieutenant Gillespie, who was in charge of his section. Paul didn't have an opinion on the middle-aged lieutenant, but then Sergeant-Major Long was often quoted, "You don't know enough to have an opinion."

As they approached, Northern Railway employees and soldiers were starting to disembark the brigade's 18-pounders that were chained to the flatcars. Men were removing tarpaulins that protected the guns and limber wagons. They were intermingled with the passenger and the palace horse cars. Paul could smell the horses since the wind pushed the aroma toward him in an easterly direction. He had already endured their perfume during their four-hour trip from Montreal since his section rode in the last car.

The palace horse cars could carry sixteen horses at a time. They were designed so that the grooms could water and feed the horses while in transit. The 300 heavy draught horses were necessary as they were the only means of moving the brigade's eighteen field guns, plus the limber wagons that carried the ammunition, to, around, and from the battlefield.

Captain Masterley stopped in front of the sergeant, but the slamming of a ramp distracted him for a moment. He frowned when he saw a couple of men wrestling with a horse that was reluctant to leave the confines of the palace car. When he returned his attention back to the sergeant-major, it was Long who spoke first. "All the men are present and accounted for."

"Yes, yes," he muttered. He appeared somewhat distracted. He glanced at Lieutenant Gillespie then he remembered why he came. "They need to get everything off in an hour. Another train is scheduled to arrive."

Paul winced when he overheard. It had taken nearly four hours to load the trains in Montreal. The 18-pounders weighted slightly over a ton apiece. It took six horses to move them. Whether they could be unloaded in an hour, Paul didn't have a clue.

"Yes, Captain. Where do you need us?" asked Sergeant-Major Long with a veteran's lack of eagerness.

A brief smile flirted on the captain's face. "It seems that they were not quite ready for us. We need to build some temporary corrals for our horses."

"Of course, sir," replied Long. It was now his turn to frown.

"Lieutenant Gillespie will direct you to the location that has been selected."

As the captain moved away, he bellowed, "If you hurt that animal, I'll have you on report!"

Long turned to his section. "You heard the captain. Pick up your kit bags."

Paul picked up his canvas sack and set it on his right shoulder. He turned on the left turn order then started marching at the sergeant's left right cadence. Everyone in the squad gawked at the sight of the camp as the bell tents grew larger. A large gravel road ran down the middle of the camp. Six-foot drainage ditches were dug on both sides of the road. Wooden planks and footpaths were set at intervals to allow the men to cross over the trenches.

They had marched for half-hour when Lieutenant Gillespie led them over one of the bridges on the left. They marched between the tents to a small stand of shrubs and trees. In the middle of the grass meadow there was a Bains wagon with two brown horses hitched to it, waiting for them. Set in the ground there was a giant oval, marked by fresh-cut wooden stakes, which outlined the corral to be built.

Gillespie turned to the men then ordered, "Pile your bags here. Axes are in the wagon. Take them and go into that copse of trees and cut branches and scrub for the corral."

Sergeant-Major Long reinforced the lieutenant's command. "You heard him. Get to it."

Paul tossed his bag on top of the rest, and when he started to go to the wagon to get his axe, he was pulled up short when he heard Sergeant-Major Long say, "Not you, Ryan."

"Sergeant?"

"Stay here and guard the kit bags."

"Sergeant! I know how to use an axe," Paul protested. He could see Enright grinning from the corner of his eye.

"It was an order, not a suggestion!"

Paul felt his face flush. He knew that Enright was thinking. McGill always got the easy jobs.

CHAPTER 8

SEPTEMBER 1, 1914
MESS TENT, VALCARTIER CAMP

When Lieutenant Llewellyn pulled out his tobacco pouch from his tan haversack, he noticed that he was getting low. It was another item to add to the list for the quartermaster. He took pinches of loose tobacco and filled his pipe that was darkened with age. He dampened the tobacco so that it was relatively firm in the bowl and then lit it with a wooden match.

He didn't smoke very often. He was one of those who only smoked when he drank. He needed a drink. The news from Europe was not good. The British Expeditionary Force was suffering heavy casualties, nearly 5,000 so far, as they retreated from Mons. However, since he was in the middle of Valcartier and the camp was supposed to be dry, it would not a good example if he was seen to be shit-faced.

He suspected that the tents were not quite as dry as everyone claimed. He didn't find anything during his inspections. He did read the regulations and the punishments, if alcohol was found. He followed the orders with a lecture on the various techniques to be used for camouflage and concealment to avoid detection by the enemy. He had hoped that the subtle message was that if you were stupid enough to be caught, you would pay the consequences.

That was why the camp was relatively quiet that evening. At least for the next few hours, until the men returned from Quebec City. Then he suspected that it would be loud and noisy as most them would be drunk.

Quebec was not dry, and the men were paid today.

That morning he had been assigned to escort the paymaster from Valcartier's HQ to the battalion's mess tent that had been designated as the pay tent for the exercise. The major was easy to find, since he was the only one standing in front of the two-storey wooden building that was the camp's headquarters, with a CAPC badge on his cap. The initials stood for Canadian Army Pay Corps. Major Hayward was a portly man in his mid-forties. Based on Hayward's rank, Llewellyn suspected he was a twenty-year veteran. To get promoted to major in the pay corps, you needed to spend ten years as a captain first. Llewellyn soured slightly at the thought, since he had, like a lot of other officers, taken a reduction in rank in order to join the CEF.

"I'll take you to the pay tent," said the lieutenant after introductions were made. The major glanced at the two privates in the back of the horse-drawn wagon. They were armed with Ross rifles with fixed bayonets. The bare metal gleamed in the morning sun. Being a paymaster was a dangerous job.

"Lead the way, Lieutenant," said the major as he picked up the large tan canvas valise at his feet. He climbed into the back of the wagon and took his seat between the two privates. He held the valise on his knees. Llewellyn climbed up and sat beside the driver, who snapped the reins.

When they arrived at the pay tent forty minutes later, they could see a long line stretching from the entrance down the end of one of the bell tent's side streets. The mess tent was large and had the seating capacity of a hundred men per feeding. When the men heard the rumbling of the wagon, they turned their heads in eagerness.

"Hmm," murmured the major as he jumped out of the wagon, very lightly for a man of his bulk, onto the gravel road. "I need a few minutes with the pay sergeant," he informed Llewellyn.

The lieutenant nodded. "He's waiting for you inside the tent."

The major surveyed the men in the queue and followed the two privates across the small wooden bridge erected over the six-foot ditch to the mess tent's entrance. The men parted when the guards approach them. The major ducked his head under the canvas flap when he entered while the two privates took their guard positions at the opening.

"Major Hayward. Sergeant Marsh is our pay sergeant," indicated Llewellyn. Sergeant Marsh, a thin, sour-faced man, rose from his chair at a long mess table and saluted the major. On the table there were a number of memo books with the battalion's crest imprinted on some of the covers.

"Good morning, Sergeant. I just want to take a quick look at your nominal rolls before I start paying the men."

The sergeant's face became even sourer.

"Problem?" Hayward asked.

"As you are aware, the non-commissioned officers and the privates are paid by the commanding officers. To do that, we have to maintain a simple pay list of the men in the battalion."

"I'm well aware of the regulations," the major replied.

"Well, Major, I've been doing my upmost to maintain an accurate list, but I've encountered a number of difficulties," replied Marsh as he handed the pay officer an olive coloured ledger.

"What kind of difficulties?" Hayward asked sharply as he opened the book.

"As you can see, the rolls are not on the approved forms. I've requested them, but I have not received them from the quartermaster as of yet. I don't know when we will receive them. So I've been attempting to keep track using the materials at hand such as these books." He indicated by tapping the notebook in the major's hands.

Major Hayward glanced at the memo book, which was constructed with unlined paper. "I understand."

"Also, with the new recruits, transfers, and desertions, I have not been able to maintain as fulsome a record as I would like. Half the men have not fully completed their attestation papers yet."

Hayward examined the men through the openings that allowed a gentle breeze to cool the tent with a frown. He was well aware that it was not a very good idea to irritate men with guns. Technically, they were not currently armed, but they did have access to weapons.

"How many men in the battalion?" he asked.

"Approximately 850, give or take," replied the sergeant.

Llewellyn and Hayward made some mental calculations. As a lieutenant, he was entitled to $2.00 a day. The sergeant's pay was $0.75 a day. The major's take was $4.00. Privates were paid at the daily rate of $0.50.

"Okay. Do you have a blank memo pad?" asked the major.

"Yes, Major."

"What I would like to do is bring in the men in one at a time. We'll make a note of the man's name, service number, if he has one, rank, and days of service. At the end of the day we'll collate the papers, and we'll reconcile the amounts on next month's settlement day."

"Of course, sir."

"Good," said the major as he put the valise on the table. The first thing he took out of the satchel was a 1911 Colt automatic. The .45 calibre was not seen very often, but it was an authorized piece of equipment. It was an expensive piece of kit. Then he took out wads of one-, five-, and ten-dollar bills with the original bank wrappers and organized them neatly on the table. The money was the only explanation needed for the .45.

"Pen?"

After the sergeant handed him a pen, the major ordered, "Call the first man in."

A private marched up to the table and saluted.

"Name?" demanded Hayward.

"Peter Mack."

"Rank, private," the major wrote in his book after verifying the markings on the private's uniform. He also noted the private's unit as well.

"Date of enlistment?"

"August 20, 1914."

"Hmm. Today's the first, so that makes it twenty-one days' pay."

"Yes, sir!"

"So that is $10.50."

The private nodded. He couldn't keep his eyes off the money bundles. He watched in fascination as the officer broke the wrappers on the $1 and $5 wads and counted out five ones and one five.

"Here is $10.00. The $0.50 will be kept in your account. If you choose, you can designate a sum to be sent to your family."

"Oh, I didn't know that," blurted the private.

"You don't have to decide now."

"I guess that's fine. Thank you, Major," replied Mack as he clutched the money. It was probably the most that he ever held in his hands.

"Next!" shouted the major.

So it went for the next couple of hours as men filed in to get their pay. Llewellyn was getting bored as he watched the line. Some of the faces seemed to be familiar to him, but then again, men in uniform tend to look alike.

When a private in his mid-twenties entered the tent and marched up to the major, Llewellyn recognized the face. He was trying to place the man. He wasn't one of the men directly under his command. He gave his name as Peter Kent to the paymaster and took his money, but the private paused at the entrance. As he furtively put the money in a billfold, the lieutenant caught a glimpse of several bills already in the wallet.

The lieutenant sat up with a frown. He examined the remaining men in the line. He didn't particularly like the thought that entered his mind. He rose from his chair, informing the sergeant that he needed to stretch his legs, and sauntered out of the tent. He decided to circle around to the back of the line. Sure enough, Peter Kent reappeared and re-joined the line. He seemed to be buddies with several of the men. They gave each other conspiratorial grins.

He made his way quietly toward them. He overheard Kent say, "Well, I'm taking the train into Quebec. There's a bar there that I know where you can get two beers for a nickel ..." He stopped when his sandy-haired companion, who had spotted the lieutenant, nudged Kent in the chest. An annoyed look flashed across his face when Kent put his eyes on him.

"Private Kent, is it?" asked Lieutenant Llewellyn.

"Yes, Lieutenant," he replied with a poker face. It could mean anything. Privates always gave that look when questioned by an officer.

"In line for your pay, I see," he stated casually. Kent, putting a protective hand into the pocket that contained his wallet, confirmed the lieutenant's suspicions.

When Kent saw the lieutenant eye his hand, he knew that the jig was up. He casually took his hand out. "No, Lieutenant. I've already got my pay."

"Have you now?"

"I'm just keeping my buddy Eric here company while he gets his. We're going to Quebec to get a beer after."

"Hmm," said lieutenant, giving him a thin smile. "Well then, why don't you wait for him at the station rather than here."

Kent glanced at his companions as his shoulders slumped slightly. "Yes, Lieutenant. Of course," he replied as he and his two buddies left the line.

Lieutenant Llewellyn looked at the rest of the soldiers in the line watching the drama, then ordered, "If you already been paid, I would suggest you find someplace else to be."

As the lieutenant smoked his pipe, he smiled. He wasn't amused about the events this morning. He did admit took some imagination and nerve to run the scam. It also kept him on his toes. There was some hope for the CEF yet. As he puffed on his pipe, he pulled out his copy of the king's regulation. He was going to need it in the morning when he had to discipline some of his men for drunkenness. The question was how creative and legal was his punishment going to be?

SEPTEMBER 3, 1914
BAYONET TRAINING FIELD, VALCARTIER CAMP

"All right men, but try it again, and let's see if you can get it right," bellowed Sergeant Rawlings at the platoon of men who were standing in two rows facing each other. Behind the right row there were a couple of canvas bags hanging from wood frames. The heavy bags swayed slightly in the wind.

"What is the purpose of bayonet training?" he demanded, looking at a man who was still dressed in civilian clothes. They still hadn't received their allotment of uniforms, even though they had been bugging the regiment's quartermaster sergeant daily. There were sweat stains on the man's formerly white shirt, and the sleeves were rolled up, revealing tanned arms.

"Kill the enemy," he said brightly. Everyone chuckled.

"What the fuck is funny?" demanded the sergeant. Private Smithers was eighteen years old and had the false self-confidence of a youth with impressive physical talents. Rawlings needed to keep on top of him.

"Nothing, Sergeant," replied Smithers. The smile disappeared from his face under Rawlings' withering glare. From the corner of his eye he spotted Lieutenant Llewellyn scribble in the notepad that he constantly carried. He was supervising today, letting Rawlings conduct the lessons. The lieutenant was a great believer in letting his men develop knowledge and experience so they could move up the ranks, if they so desired.

"The purpose of bayonet training is to inoculate the fighting spirit. To close with the enemy and to deliver cold steel into this guts," Sergeant Rawlings informed them as he marched up the line. The new recruits looked at him at with a look of rapt awe, while the few veterans in the platoon had the look of men who had heard this lecture before. It was boring then, and it was boring now.

This was the second lesson in the schedule. Yesterday's was more of an evaluation of the men. They needed to know what level of knowledge they possessed so that they could develop a more effective training plan. It simply confirmed that he had his work cut out for him.

"Lance Corporal Booth will now demonstrate the guard position." Rawlings nodded to Booth. Booth, standing between the two rows, moved into the guard position.

Rawlings, using his swagger stick, pointed at key elements of Booth's stance. "Point of the bayonet is directed at the Hun's throat. The rifle held both hands with the barrel inclined slightly to the left about thirty degrees." When he touched the mock rifle with his rod, the twittering from some of his men brought another withering glare from Rawlings. They hadn't received their rifles yet, so the men were practicing with pieces of wood carved into a rifle shape. The bayonet was a long branch tied to the front end. "The right hand is belt high. The left arm is slightly bent with your left hand held under the barrel. Legs are in a boxer's stance, with your left leg comfortably forward and the knee slightly bent.

"Thank you, Corporal," he said. Booth brought the mock rifle to the order arms position. Then he relaxed in an at ease position. "Now face each other and take the guard position," Rawlings ordered.

The men lined up with their partner and took up what they thought was the guard position. Rawlings had made sure that they were at least five feet apart to avoid the men accidentally stabbing each other. He went down the lines to make corrections.

"Relax your arms, Matthews," Rawlings said as he tugged on the man's mock rifle. "You're too stiff. You need to be loose. The looser you are, the faster you can strike. That's better."

To the tall man beside him in khaki, he pointed at his left elbow and said, "Liam, your left elbow is too high. Bend down more. That's it. Your rifle needs to be set at thirty degrees. Don't lean too far back; you'll need your weight evenly balanced so you can move left or right to block a thrust. Better!"

As Rawlings moved to the next man, Liam asked, "Sergeant, when are we going to get real rifles?"

"When can you walk and chew gum at the same time," retorted Rawlings. Then he repeated it again. They needed the repetition. "When you can walk and chew gum at the same time. Is that clear, Private?"

Liam gulped. "Yes, Sergeant." He studiously avoided Rawlings' gaze.

"Okay, men, by the numbers," bellowed Rawlings. "So you want real guns then. Well, you won't get them until you can do this in your fucking sleep! Guard positions! Right eye! Thrust! Withdraw! Left eye! Thrust! Withdraw!"

He was so engrossed in shouting his orders that he didn't hear the noises of horses directly behind him until a voice said, "What the devil are you doing, man?"

He turned, ready to give the voice a piece of his mind until he saw the red tabs of a colonel who was sitting easily on his horse. He snapped to attention and saluted when he recognized Sam Hughes. Behind him was his usual entourage staff officers and reporters.

"Well, man?"

Rawlings was about to respond when Lieutenant Llewellyn interjected, "Sergeant Rawlings is instructing the recruits in the use of the bayonet." Rawlings could tell that the lieutenant was not happy. He had put out sentries with specific instructions that he was to be notified if the brass were in the vicinity. You couldn't let the red caps wander around by themselves. You never knew what trouble they could get into.

"You call that bayonet training?" Hughes said sarcastically as he hoisted himself down from his horse. "I'll show you bayonet training."

Rawlings couldn't help his eyes from widening in surprise when he saw Hughes remove his Ross from the sling he had on the left side of his horse's saddle. "Bayonet!" he demanded. One of the men from his entourage pulled a bayonet from his scabbard and handed it to him. The minister locked the blade into place.

With the rifle held in the port position, Hughes marched past Llewellyn and Rawlings and headed toward the hanging sacks. Rawlings gawked at the minister. He had heard that Hughes had a penchant for getting involved. However, it was never a good practice to publicly undermine someone's authority in front of his men. But the minister was doing it. When the lieutenant gave him a look that said to let it go, Rawlings understood, but he was pissed. The worst was yet to come.

"Nothing inspires fear in the enemy like cold steel," Hughes said to the men that had gathered around him at the wood frame. He waited for the reporters to take down his remarks before he continued. He even posed when one of the photographers snapped pictures. "This is how you do it!"

When he took the guard position, Rawlings nearly groaned. Llewellyn kept his face impassive. The positions that the colonel was demonstrating were the bayonet techniques that were in vogue during the Boer War. It depended on the "reach" concept. The prevailing thought was that a soldier needed an extremely long rifle and bayonet in order to stab his opponent without them being able to touch him. In South Africa, Hughes had fought with a Lee-Metford that came equipped with a fifteen-inch bayonet. It weighed nearly a pound. The method that was being used at the time was a fencing style. It was more suited where troops were standing shoulder to shoulder rather than the dispersed formations now being used. Also, it was designed to defend against cavalry charges where the opponent was sitting on a horse. With the introduction of machine guns, cavalry was essentially being used as scouts and flanking guards. What he and Rawlings had been instructing the new recruits in was a more naturalistic boxer bayonet style, which was easier to teach and learn.

When Hughes was finished cutting up the dummy, he handed the Ross to Llewellyn and said, "Well, Captain. Give it a go."

"I'm a lieutenant," Rawlings heard Llewellyn say as he took the Ross. He followed the colonel's example as he thrust the bayonet a couple of times into the dummy. When he was done, Colonel Hughes slapped him on the back and said, "When I tell you that you're a captain, a captain you will be. Well done, son."

He turned to Rawlings and said in a booming voice, "This is the proper way to teach the bayonet. Do it right from now on, Sergeant."

All Rawlings could do was to reply, "Yes, sir. Thank you, sir." He was barely able to get that out. What he was really thinking was *You're damn lucky I didn't give you the bayonet, you fucking bastard.*

SEPTEMBER 5, 1914
DRY CANTEEN, VALCARTIER CAMP

Rawlings knew why Captain Llewellyn had asked him to get a drink at the canteen. He wanted to talk to him privately away from the prying ears along the tent line.

The bottles of Allen's soda he held in his hands were sweating slightly in the September heat. When Llewellyn handed one of them to him, he was pleasantly surprised that it was cold.

"Cheers," said Llewellyn as he clinked bottles with Rawlings.

"Cheers."

They sat on the grass away from the other men who were crowding around the wooden shack that served as a canteen. From his angle, Rawlings could see the necks of soda bottles sticking out of buckets of melting ice, a coffee and teapot steaming on a small propane stove, and on the counter there were open boxes of chewing gum, candy bars, and cigarettes. The cigarettes were sold as packets or individually. Newspapers and magazines were pinned to the interior door panels.

"So I can't change your mind then?" asked Llewellyn.

"Nope," said Rawlings as he pulled a long draught from the bottle, emptying nearly half. He would have preferred a beer, but he would have to go to Quebec City for that.

Llewellyn pulled off his cap and dropped it into his lap. His face was showing some tired lines. Rawlings didn't like putting him on the spot.

"How many have volunteered?" Rawlings asked.

"At last count I heard nearly 2,000."

"Ouch, that many?"

"Yep."

"That's nearly ten percent of the men here."

"I know."

"That's not good."

"I could still take your name off the list."

Rawlings paused as he considered Llewellyn's request. He reluctantly said, "I've made my decision, and I'm sticking with it. Right or wrong."

While he would never admit it to Llewellyn, he wasn't really thinking when he stepped forward as Llewellyn read the request for volunteers for the Royal Canadian Regiment to the assembled company. He could still see the look of shock and disappointment on Llewellyn's face.

"How many from the Fusiliers?" he asked.

"Not that many. About a dozen or so."

"Anyone I know?" he asked.

Llewellyn gave him an enigmatic smile that told him that the regiment was trying to weed out some of the undesirables and misfits. At times he felt like he was one. They sat there for a moment as they heard buzzing of men gripe and laugh at someone's joke. Rawlings finally asked, "Anyone know why the RCR are going to Bermuda rather than being activated?"

"What do you think?"

"Hughes?"

"Yep. You know what he feels about the permanent force. This way he gets them out of the way, and he might even score points with the Imperials. But they still need men to bring them up to their authorized strength before they ship out."

"God. I can't stand that son of a bitch."

A smile appeared on Llewellyn's face. "That's why you volunteered?"

"Damn right." Rawlings finally admitted it, not only to Llewellyn but to himself. "Mark my words that he's going to end up as the GOC."

Llewellyn shook his head. "That's not going to happen."

"Yeah, right," Rawlings said in derision. "Why do you think he hasn't appointed a GOC yet? I read the papers. Every time someone asked him if he's going to command, he gives wishy-washy answers. He just looking for an excuse."

"I don't think that they are that stupid."

"Ya, right." Rawlings' voice lowered so he couldn't be overheard. "This is a mess. It's going to take awhile for this to be all sorted out. I really don't want to be in the same outfit with that blowhard."

Rawlings could tell that Llewellyn agreed with him and that he was right. "Why don't you put your name in?" he suggested.

Llewellyn took a sip of his soda and then he looked away. "I don't think so."

Rawlings sighed and nodded in understanding. He knew very well why his friend wouldn't leave. A sense of duty and honour was a part of it. The other was that even if he put his name in, it was unlikely that they would let him go because he was such a good officer. The likely result, if he volunteered, would that they would deny his request and then make his life a living hell because the senior officers would be resentful that he wanted to leave. But the real reason was that he was a man who would step up and take responsibility when no one else wanted to or could. He just hoped that it wouldn't get him killed.

CHAPTER 9

The blisters on Paul's hand were raw. He had them pierced with a needle to remove the fluid the previous night. He was hoping that the overlying skin would stay in place and would provide some protection, but it didn't take long for the wood shovel's handle to tear it away to reveal the red skin below.

Gloves would have helped, but even if he had them, he wouldn't wear them. That was all that he needed was to add to his woes as a pampered mother's boy. He tried to keep the tingling pain off his face as he tossed the shovel's contents into the wagon beside him.

He leaned on his spade as he swatted at the flies that circled his head. He didn't know why he bothered, since manure and flies went together.

"How can a horse create so much crap?" Paul asked his companion, who was wielding a similar weapon.

Reggie Ramus laughed as he used his thin but wiry body to toss a heavy load into the manure spreader beside them. It was painted a faded red with flaking black lettering, *Ferme Gauthier*, on the side. Sitting in the seat was a young boy, barely twelve, who was holding the reins to the three Canadian bay-coloured draughts that were hitched to it.

"Well, McGill," he said with a wide smile. Paul wasn't certain, but he suspected that the smile worked wonders with the ladies. "Ya never worked with them, have ya?"

Paul acknowledged by showing him his hands.

"Better put some salve on them. They'll callous in a day or two. Them beasts shit four to ten times a day. Depends on how much you feed them."

"Ten times? A day?"

"Yeah. Up to fifty pounds of the sweet stuff." Reggie, one of his tent mates, was known to be a practical joker. Reggie gave him a bigger grin. He pointed to the manure spreader. "This holds nearly two and a half tons. How many have we filled this morning?"

"Nearly four."

Reggie then pointed to the horses behind him with his thumb. There were only twenty or so, mainly draft horses, in the corral this morning.

A few were pacing lazily. Some were still chewing on their breakfast from the open hay bundles. A pair of chestnuts stood guard. One was keeping an eye on them while the other was standing in the opposite direction watching the makeshift barriers of branches and bush. "How many horses were here last night?"

"Don't know … a 150 to 200?"

"There you go. If they stayed in the corral all day, it would double our workload."

"The last I heard, we have nearly 6,000 horses. At fifty pounds …"

"I always wanted a government job," quipped Reggie.

"Why did you call this the sweet stuff?" Paul asked as he wrinkled his nose. He didn't know if he would ever get used to the smell.

The boy sitting on the backseat answered in a heavy English accent. "Good fertilizer for the fields."

"That's right. Good fertilizer, and its free." Reggie grunted as he tossed the last shovelful into the wagon."

"*Allez. Tout finished,*" Reggie said in bad French.

The boy rolled his eyes. He gave the horses a slight flick of the reins. The wagon hesitated, and then it started rolling toward the corral's gate.

"What the fuck are you doing, McGill?" demanded a voice behind him. Paul knew to whom the abrasive voice belonged. His hands tightened on the shovel as he turned to face the newly promoted Lance Corporal Hank Enright. Paul was mystified how and why the man had been promoted.

"We've just finished, Lance Corporal," said Paul as he stood at attention. He sensed that Reggie did the same thing.

"Yeah, right," Enright said with derision.

"We did, Corporal," Reggie added.

Enright turned his head and glared at him. "Was I talking to you?"

"No, Lance Corporal."

"Then shut the fuck up!" Ryan noted the gleam of satisfaction in Enright's eyes when Reggie did. He was going to have to talk to Reggie to be careful. He didn't want Enright's enmity be transferred to Reggie simply because he was Paul's friend. "Now you layabouts need to clean and dry out the nose bags before the brigade comes back. You also have to report for harness training at nine o'clock. You better not be late, or I'll put you on report."

Paul nearly groaned. Not about the threat of being put on report. He knew that even if he arrived a half-hour early, Enright would find something to put him on report for. No, it was the harness training. The first thing the instructor would ask him would be to identify each and every part and in a specific order. He couldn't help pulling the order from his memory: padded collar, breast collar, hames, breeching, traces, harness saddle, girth, belly-band, back-band, sliding back-band, fixed back-band, surcingle, false martingale, crupper, back strap, shaft tugs, turrets and reigns, and bridles and bits. He also had to explain the purpose of each part and when it should be used and how it should be maintained.

Movement behind the corporal drew his eyes. He saw two middle-aged officers approach the corral gate, which was two sets of poles with a heavy cord between them. They seemed to be lieutenants, but he wasn't sure. They were watching with considerable interest the horses in the corral.

"What the fuck are you looking at, McGill?" The corporal turned his head to see what Paul was gazing at. When one of the officers saw that they had been noticed, he waved the corporal over.

"He's got it in for ya, doesn't he?" remarked Reggie.

"I know," replied Paul. He winced in pain when he retightened his grip on his shovel. His blisters were getting worse.

After a brief conversation, the corporal waved them over. "These gentlemen need to take a look at the horses. You're to do what they tell you to," ordered the corporal. "I'll be back shortly to check on you."

"Thank you, Corporal," said Lieutenant Haile. Paul liked Lieutenant Haile, the husky Saskatooner who was in charge of the brigade's horses. He was curious about the other lieutenant, who wore steel-framed glasses. He was still learning the bewildering array of unit insignia in the Canadian army. He was trying to decipher the bronze letters CVAC on the officer's collar when Haile introduced him.

"This is Lieutenant Fuller from the veterinary corps. He's here for an inspection."

Haile's lips pursed when he saw Paul wince in pain as he saluted the officers. Fuller gave him an absentminded glance because his focus appeared to be directed at the horses. "Are these the only animals you have?"

"The brigade is on manoeuvres today." Haile's statement was accentuated by the sound of rifle fire that drifted in from the range. "Most of these are remounts that have been trickling in. We're been working them up to make sure that they are in good shape and they have proper training before we allow them into service."

"Quality's been good?" asked Fuller.

"On the whole, not bad. There have been a few that have been questionable. Mainly because of age. Some had bad temperaments and were not suitable."

"They couldn't be retrained?"

"Maybe," Haile said. The slight shaking of his head indicated he was doubtful. "But it takes time and patience that we don't have."

"And their health?"

"Pretty good, considering. I've got a couple of horses that I have concerns about. If you have a few minutes, can you take a look at them?"

"Not a problem," answered Fuller.

"Ramus, can you bridle that mare that has been listless for the lieutenant?" ordered Haile.

"Yes, sir," said Reggie as he placed his shovel in its usual place beside the corral gate. From the crooked railings he took a bridle and went to get the mare.

"What have you been doing for water and feed?" asked Fuller. He followed Haile as he led him to a water trough that Paul had helped build using waterproof canvas and two by fours. "We have to haul the water in using carts from taps down the road. We need to let the water stand for several hours to get rid of the chlorine smell, otherwise the horses won't drink it."

"You water them from the same trough?"

"No. We have a number of different troughs, and each horse is led to an assigned one. That way if one trough somehow gets infected, we don't lose the entire herd."

"What about the feed?"

"It's been sporadic, but the supply has been improving." Haile pointed to the open hay bales that were scattered around the corral. "I don't like them feeding off the ground, but until we build proper feeders I don't have much of a choice. Regulations state that they need at least twelve pounds of hay and ten pounds of oats per day. Quality of the forage we have been getting is good. We've been trying not to work them to hard until it becomes more stable."

"Sounds good," Fuller stated as he pushed his glasses back up. "Let's take a look at those questionable horses of yours. If they are not in good shape, we'll have to leave them behind. I really don't want to deal with a sick animal on a two-week sea voyage."

"Understood," replied Haile. "Go ahead. I need to speak with the Private Ryan a moment."

"Mr. Ryan?"

"Yes, sir," said Paul.

"May I see your hands?"

"My hands, sir?" replied Paul in surprise.

"Yes."

Paul placed his implement beside Reggie's then held up his hands. The lieutenant motioned him to turn them over. When he saw the blisters and the red skin, he frowned. "Have you seen the medic yet?"

"No, sir. They're just blisters."

"Sometimes men don't have the sense ..." Haile shook his head. "See the medic about getting a salve for them. I don't want them to get infected because you've been mucking all day."

"Thank you, sir."

"Don't thank me, Mr. Ryan. You're government property now. Like the horses." He waved at the animals in the corral with a grin. "I need to keep you in good shape so I can get a good day's work out of you."

Paul watched as Haile headed toward Reggie, who was holding the reins on the mare as Fuller examined the steed. Paul wondered, as he left the corral to find a medic, *Would they shoot me if I broke a leg?*

SEPTEMBER 7, 1914
DOMINION ARSENAL, QUEBEC CITY

"Good morning, Minister," said Lieutenant-Colonel Lafferty, greeting Colonel Hughes as he stepped out of the car.

"I'm pleased to see you again, Colonel," Hughes replied warmly after he returned the man's salute.

Hughes eyed the Dominion Arsenal complex located at Artillery Park. The lilac bushes that decorated the well-maintained grounds had lost their purple blossoms months ago. The complex was comprised of seven main buildings that sprawled from the top of Palace Hill and ran to Angele Street. The arsenal was a complete production facility where they smelted metal ingots and transformed them into finished munitions. It even had a small workshop to build the wooden containers for their transport.

When the plant was first built in 1881 to meet the needs of the British and Canadian militaries, it had been on the outskirts of Quebec City. As the city grew, businesses and homes started to surround the site. He had major concerns that it was too close to the sea, making it vulnerable to attack. He hadn't gotten anywhere with his proposal to move it.

"Things seem busy," Hughes said approvingly.

"Yes, Minister. We've hired additional workers to increase production."

"Good to hear," replied Hughes with a wide smile. He was pleased that the colonel was doing an outstanding job of reorganizing the arsenal since he had appointed him as superintendent.

For a number of years, Hughes had been getting reports about the quality of the .303 rounds being produced at the factory. When he became minister in 1911, he decided to look into the matter, especially since he had plans to double the ammunition training allotment.

What also factored into his decision was the introduction of the new Mk VII .303 round in 1910, which was to be manufactured at the plant. The Mk VII round was a more modern design that took advantage of the developments in smokeless gunpowder and the spitzer-style rounds that various militaries were experimenting with. The new round resembled the spitzer. It was a full metal-jacketed bullet. Where it differed was that the front third of the projectile was lighter, since the interior had an aluminum, wood pulp, or compressed paper core. This meant that the tail of the bullet was heavier so that when it struck its target at high velocity, it would tumble, creating a more severe wound.

While he was loathe to do so, Hughes didn't have much choice but to ask that two British munitions experts review the Quebec arsenal and its production procedures. When he read their report, he hit the roof.

He was pissed at the British officers for being blunt in their private report, but he was more upset at the superintendent. One of the findings was that the plant had run out of cordite, the propellant used in the shells. It took nearly six months before they replenished their supply. During this time, they continued to manufacture empty rifle and artillery casings and stockpiled them. The other finding was that the quality control inspections were cursory at best. This meant that nearly $300,000 worth of .303 ammunition, mainly Mk VI, had to be destroyed. This was nearly the country's entire ammunition reserve.

86

What really got his blood pressure to rise were the problems they found with the 18-pounder shells the facility was producing for the rapid-fire artillery guns. None of the rounds had ever been test fired. Not a single one! When a seventy-five round sample was taken for proofing they discovered that fifteen of the rounds would not fit any of the guns. The remainder were highly inaccurate. Some overshot their targets by a thousand yards. It was totally unacceptable!

He forced the former superintendent to resign. Retire, actually, since he was talked out of firing the man. He replaced him with the thirty-eight-year-old Ontario-born Colonel Lafferty.

Like him, the colonel had served in the Southern African War; however, Lafferty had been a lieutenant with the Royal Canadian Artillery. When he returned he became DSA of Military District 4, headquartered in Montreal. In 1905, he became adjutant to the RMC in Kingston. In 1912 he graduated from the Ordnance College at the Woolworth Arsenal in England.

"Have they arrived yet?" he asked as Lafferty escorted him into the main administration building.

"Yes, Minister. They are waiting for you in my meeting room."

"Excellent," replied Hughes. "I would like to thank you for the presentation you did last Wednesday in Ottawa. Even I learned a thing or two about the manufacturing process. I didn't quite realize that it required seventy different steps to produce a single round."

"Thank you, Minister," replied a pleased Lafferty. "I thought it was essential that all the executives there be informed in what they are being asked to do."

"Quite, quite," replied Hughes. He had ordered the colonel to report to a meeting he had arranged with Canadian manufacturers to discuss the viability of producing artillery shells in Canada. The War Office had sent telegrams asking about the feasibility of obtaining empty shrapnel shell cases from American companies. He had met with the senior executives of Bethlehem Steel. They didn't see any problems with supplying the empty shrapnel shells. When he asked whether Canada could produce them, they had informed him that it was not practical since Canada didn't have the facilities or the steel. Their attitude annoyed him greatly.

He had been extremely pleased that, after the presentations by Colonel Lafferty as well as by Colonel Benson, his Master-General of Ordnance, and Lieutenant-Colonel Harston, his Chief Inspector of

Arms and Ammunition, that the assembled chief executive officers had indicated they could fulfill the contracts.

He had been gleeful when he heard that piece of news. He really wanted to prove the Americans wrong and show that his countrymen could produce the goods.

"Please remain seated," he said when the seven invited gentlemen began to rise to their feet as he stepped into the room. He naturally took the empty chair at the head of the table. He barely glanced at the paintings and mechanical drawings of various cartridges and shells that covered the walls. He ignored the items that were on display in the glass cases. Lafferty sat at the opposite end of the table.

"I would like to thank you for attending today, especially Colonel Bertram, Mr. Cantley, and Mr. Watts. I know that you are very busy men."

Colonel Bertram, who headed the John Bertram & Sons firm based in Dundas, Ontario, acknowledged this with a nod. His firm manufactured machine tools for working iron, steel, and brass. He had commanded the 13th Regiment of Hamilton. He had volunteered, but he was deemed too old — he was fifty-one — for the contingent. Thomas Cantley, who headed the Nova Scotia Steel Company, gave the sitting men a brief smile. James Watts rose from the table and made a slight bow. He was the general manager of the Canadian General Electric Company, which held interests in various steel and irons manufacturers, as well as electrical and power plant firms. It was one of the largest conglomerates in the country.

"As you know, last week we discussed the feasibility of manufacturing shells in Canada. Ideally, I would have liked have Canadian firms produce them, since the Dominion Arsenal does not have the capacity to construct them in the numbers that the War Office requires." He looked at the Lafferty for confirmation.

"I'm afraid that is correct," he stated.

"Since the September 2nd meeting, I've received word from the War Office that they were desirous of having shrapnel shells made in Canada. I've informed them that we would entrust the work to a committee of manufacturers. I also took the liberty of providing them with your names, which they have approved."

"Excellent," replied Colonel Bertram.

"Good. I would like you to be chairman of the committee," Hughes said.

"I would be honoured," said the colonel.

"As well, I've decided to add Colonel Lafferty and Colonel Benson." Hughes indicated to the colonel sitting on his left. Colonel Benson was the Master-General of Ordnance based in Ottawa. The master-general was mainly responsible for artillery pieces, fortification, and military supplies.

"Thank you, Minister. I would suggest adding a technical expert to advise the committee."

"Do you have someone in mind?" asked Hughes.

Benson bobbed his head. "I do. A Mr. Carnegie. I'll contact him to see if he's available."

"Very well. What are the next steps?"

Colonel Betram glanced at his fellow manufacturers and then said, "It will take some time to plan for production. Gauges are needed to be designed and made, inspection and test laboratories built, and distribution channels developed."

"Don't forget we need to gunproof the shells before we ship them," added Colonel Lafferty.

Watts interjected, "I feel we first need to decide whether the contracts will be given to a single firm or split among various companies. If split, small shops can make components then ship them to a plant for final assembly and testing."

"I'm glad that everyone seems to know what needs to have done. I'll leave it in your capable hands," said Hughes as he rose from the table, calling the meeting at an end. "One thing. I like to be kept abreast of your process."

"Of course, Minister," Lafferty assured him.

When he left the building and entered the waiting car, he realized he needed to confirm the creation of the Shell Committee and its legal authority. *I'll just write a note when I get to Valcartier*, he thought.

SEPTEMBER 10, 1914
RIFLE RANGE, VALCARTIER CAMP

"Not a bad pattern," remarked Major Cooke, the range officer, as he lowered his binoculars.

Llewellyn was somewhat pleased as he peered above his sights at the paper targets that were on a raised mount above the beaten-down grass.

"I'm still hitting the upper left, aren't I?" said Llewellyn as he turned his head to the major, who was down on one knee on his left, where he could avoid the ejection of hot brass.

"Yes, but all five were hits." The man's tone suggested that hitting the target with all five shots at 300 yards was good shooting.

"It's taking me too long to get used to the new sights," muttered the captain. This elicited a smile from the officer.

Llewellyn reached up with his right hand and made a slight change to the sight using the thumbscrew. He was more used to the Mk IIs' sights. On the Mk IIs the Sutherland sight sat just in front of the breech. On the Mk IIIs they had been moved back so it sat just above the bolt carrier, a few inches away from his right eye. The new position meant that he didn't have to reach as far to make adjustments.

He shifted his weight to his left side so he could gain access to the right ammo pouch. The Oliver gear made lying prone uncomfortable, as it always seemed to dig into his chest. He removed a charger strip loaded with five shells, aligned it with the carrier, and forcibly pressed down into the magazine. That was another thing that he liked with the Mk IIIs. He never liked the Mk II's Harris-type magazine, which meant the rounds needed to be carried loose. When he needed to reload, he had to grab a handful, press the magazine's release spring, and then shove them in. No matter how careful he was, he always dropped one or two. He could never find them later. With the box magazine just in front of the trigger guard, it meant that he could use a charger. The metal strips were designed to hold five cartridges in place by the bullet's extractor grooves. His standard load was ninety rounds neatly arranged in five-round charger strips. All the soldier needed to do, if the factory loads were not available, was fill them in his spare time. This meant that reloading was a lot faster and simpler.

When he pushed the bolt forward, it didn't lock. Thinking maybe the shell had got misaligned, he pulled the bolt back, and the shell ejected to his right. He pushed forward, and it still didn't lock.

"Problem?" asked Major Cooke.

"Don't know," replied Llewellyn as he worked the action to remove the second shell. When he looked into the breech, he saw some grains of sand lying in the chamber. He puffed his cheeks and blew to clear the debris. From one of his pouches, he took out another round. He had ten loose in case he needed them to top off. As he went to drop it into place, it slipped and it tumbled off the sandbag that the rifle was resting

90

on. He clenched his jaw in irritation. He pulled another clean one out and inserted it in. This time it locked when he pushed the bolt forward.

He rode the recoil five times. Each time he paused. He was shooting for accuracy rather than for speed. He had already passed the proficiency tests at 100 and 200 yards for prone, kneeling, and standing, as well as snap shooting and rapid fire. Every man had to fire fifty rounds before he could graduate. Those who didn't meet the standards would have to redo the exam. He didn't want to be one of them. It set a bad example. At 300 yards, it was more learning the effect the wind conditions had on the rounds as they hit the target, rather than speed.

"That should do it," said the range officer as he rose to his feet. "You have a nice pattern around the centre. You want to take a look?" Cooke offered him his binoculars.

"Sure," Llewellyn replied as he made his rifle safe by pulling back on the bolt ensuring the breech was open. He then stood up. He arched his back to remove the kink that was developing in his right shoulder. When he peered through the lens at the paper targets, he was happy to see the five shots arranged around the centre. At this range, he didn't expect them to be tight, but at least they had landed in the chest area. The rifle was fresh from the factory, and it fired true.

When he turned his head, he saw the eagerness on Private Cummings' face as he stood behind him, waiting impatiently to take his place. Not enough rifles had yet arrived to equip everyone, so they had to share. When the major indicated that it was safe to take his position, Cummings extracted a charger from his ammo pouch and then dropped to the prone position on the ground. He lifted the rifle and pushed the rounds into the magazine.

"Don't put your goddamn finger on the trigger, Private, until I order you to shoot!" Cooke demanded.

"Yes, sir," replied Cummings. He looked over the rifle at the targets and then peered at them over the sights. His index finger vibrated slightly on the trigger guard as he waited for the order to fire.

Llewellyn took a couple steps back to observe his company. Today, the Fusiliers were in the middle of the nearly three-mile rifle range. Three brigades were assigned to rifle practice today, while the fourth was on manoeuvres. The range had been built on the grass plain and could accommodate nearly 1,500 targets. In front of him, where the grass was beaten down, there were markings for the 200 and 100 shooting positions. In the distance, he could see slight smudges of red and orange among the green forest. Autumn was coming.

He smiled when he heard Sergeant Bassets say to Acting Sergeant Booth, "That's better. You kept your eyes open this time."

"Fuck you," was his friendly reply. The instructor chuckled. Booth was having some trouble adjusting to the Ross, as he was more used to the Lee-Enfield. He had been trying to figure out why his shots were slightly off. One of the major differences between the two rifles was the bolt action. The Canadian rifle was a straight pull, while the British required a quarter turn to extract and load the shell into the breech. This meant that theoretically the Ross had a greater rate of fire because the motion was simpler and faster. However, if you had spent countless hours practising the motion of lifting the bolt, pulling it back, pushing it forward, and dropping the bolt to lock it place, it was a difficult habit to unlearn. It took time to be comfortable with the new motion.

Llewellyn was glad they had a couple of the instructors today. The company was progressing well because of them. There were only thirteen of them available to run everyone on the base through the course, and they were running out of time.

At the far end, he saw a troop of horsemen wearing red band caps observing the battalion next to them practice.

"Is Hughes giving them a lesson?" he asked as he pointed at the horsemen.

The major turned his gaze at Hughes' entourage and snorted. "He gave one this morning. He was pissed when a couple of new volunteers kept missing the target. He grabbed their rifles and showed them how to do it."

Why doesn't that surprise me, thought Llewellyn. "How did he do?" he asked.

"All five in the bull's-eye. He wants to make sure that we can 'plink' the enemy."

The captain grunted in amusement. "Well, our men are beginning to sound good, don't you think?"

"They sure do," the instructor acknowledged. "But some of the former Imperials are griping about the Ross. They don't like it."

"What else is new ..."

He was interrupted by a rifle crack that was followed by a scream of pain. When he snapped his head around, he saw Private Cummings was on his knees, clutching his face. At first the nearby men turned their heads to find out what the fuss was about. Private Duval, on Cummings' right, had a shocked look on his face. He pulled back sharply when blood spurted toward his eyes.

By the time Llewellyn reached Cummings, blood was streaming between the private's tanned fingers. He didn't know how serious the wound was but wasn't taking any chances. When Duval rose to his feet, Llewellyn ordered, "Private, get a medic and an ambulance. Report back to me once you have done so."

"Yes, Captain," Duval replied as he rushed off. He recognized an order when he heard one.

"Let me take a look," said Llewellyn. When he lifted Cummings' hand to view the wound, blood spurted out. It didn't look good to him. There was a gash on his cheek, and nearly half his ear was torn off. It was difficult to tell how serious it was because head and face wounds tended to bleed a lot. From his pouch, he pulled out the bandage that every solder was supposed to carry. He ripped the external wrapping and pulled out the cotton gauze. He pressed it against the wound.

"Use your hand to put some pressure on it," he demanded of the private. The bandage didn't cover the wound completely. He motioned for one of the soldiers to hand him his. He used the second one to cover the rest. "Lie down on your side," he said. Cummings groaned as he complied.

When Llewellyn looked up, he noticed a crowd of curious onlookers had gathered around him. "Give us some air," the captain demanded. Then he ordered, "Get back to your positions."

"You heard the captain," said Sergeant Booth as he took charge. "Get back to your spots."

At that moment Private Duval arrived with a two-horse drawn wagon with red crosses painted on its sides. A couple of body snatchers jumped out, went to the back, hauled a stretcher out, and then hurried over.

"We'll take care of him," they said. They took a quick glance at the bandage. Deciding it would do, they carefully placed Cummings on the stretcher then loaded him into the wagon.

"Can I go with him? He's my buddy!" asked Duval anxiously.

Llewellyn shook his head. "No, they'll look after him. You better go back and pick up his things. You can bring them to him when you visit the hospital."

"Yes, sir." Duval's eyes followed the wagon for a moment as it disappeared, heading for the camp hospital. He then turned to comply with the captain's orders.

Llewellyn went over where Cummings had been lying prone. Sergeant Bassets had picked the blood-splattered rifle. He and Major Cooke were examining it.

"What happened?" he asked them.

Cooke pointed to the mangled breechblock. "The bolt blew out of the carrier."

"How the hell did that happen?" demanded Llewellyn. He didn't have any problems when he was firing it.

"I have no idea," the major replied gloomily.

SEPTEMBER 10, 1914
NO. 3 CLEARING HOSPITAL, VALCARTIER CAMP

"Here you go," said Emily as she handed Samantha a pile of white sheets.

When Samantha saw the letters V and I marked on them, she made a face. "Are these the only ones you could get?"

"I know," said Emily with a similar face. The sheets marked with the V were intended for patients with venereal diseases, while the I marked linens were to be given to those who were infectious. "That's what the nice man at the quartermaster said. We're short on supplies, and we're lucky to have these."

"Oh, well," Samantha said as she arranged the linen in the storage area of the field hospital. True, there were quite a number of female visitors at the camp. However, based on her experience, she doubted there was much spreading going on. The hospital's CO had made it perfectly clear that the nursing sisters would not be allowed to sleep in the camp. This meant that every morning and evening they had to take the train back to Quebec City, which was irritating to say the least. As well, the colonel had issued orders that they couldn't wander around the camp without an escort. This was for their own safety, since they didn't have the training to recognize some of the dangers that a military camp posed. She noticed that the order did not apply to the male orderlies, who had even less training than she had. She gave the linen a couple of whacks, which gave her some satisfaction. Giving a whack at the CO was against some kind of army rule.

"Better mark the linen in the log book," she suggested to Emily. They were required to keep a daily log of the linen usage.

"We have one?" she teased as she headed toward the haversack hanging near the tent's main entrance.

"Nurse! Nurse!" yelled a voice.

Samantha needed to look around the centre post that was supporting the canvas roof that was nearly twenty feet above the planked floor. In her section there were twelve black-framed cots that lined the oval tent's walls. Canvas mesh, where the roof and wall met, allowed sunlight to stream in and air to circulate. Most of the patients suffered the same injuries and ailments that she had dealt with at the Toronto General, like colds, fevers, cuts, bruises, sprains, and broken bones.

The patient that was trying to catch her attention was Leroy Longhurst, a member of the Canadian engineers who broke his arm when he was helping to put a pontoon bridge across the Jacques Cartier River. "Water, please?" he asked as he waved an empty glass with his good arm.

"Of course," she replied as she retrieved the water jug from the supply cart near the centre post.

When she was refilling the glass, she heard Emily say, "Good afternoon, Major."

When she looked toward the tent entrance, she saw it was Major Creighton performing his usual rounds. She also noted how Emily's face had lit up. She had her sights set on the thirty-five-year-old doctor from Windsor. She had initially been keen on some of the better-looking privates. She had to change her mind when she was informed that because she was a lieutenant the military didn't allow fraternization with the enlisted men. Samantha had to admit that Emily did look good in the light blue uniform with a white frock apron on top.

"So, how are our patients today?" the major asked Emily as he nervously shifted the stethoscope hanging around his neck.

"They are doing fine," said Emily with her best smile.

"Nurse Emily, can you check to see if we received more sheets from the laundry?" Emily's smile became icy.

"Yes, Doctor," Emily replied. She gave Samantha a glare before she left.

Dear God! Samantha thought. *She thinks I'm after the doctor. That's all I need. I'm going to have to talk with her and work it out.*

"Let's take a look," he remarked. He had stopped fiddling with his stethoscope when Emily left the tent. The first patients that he went to examine were the Lyne twins, Ian and Errol. They had caused some excitement when they came in and had become minor celebrities.

"Hmm, it looks like there's minimal blood. That's good. Very good," Creighton said after he examined the men's wounds.

"Thanks, Doc," said Ian — or was it Errol? Samantha didn't know them well enough to tell them apart.

"Don't thank me," the major admonished with his finger. "What the hell were you thinking?"

"It seemed like a good idea at the time," replied the other brother.

"Really! Bayonet practice with bare blades. With no supervision! You are both damn fools."

"It wasn't my fault," said the brother on the right in a petulant tone. "He didn't zig."

"Well, you didn't zag," retorted the other.

"I don't really care," the doctor shouted. His patience was beginning to wear a bit. "You could be brought up on charges for this." This finally silenced the two. "I've talked with your CO, and he indicated that if he charged everyone for stupidity, he wouldn't have anyone left."

The two men looked relieved until the doctor said with a wicked smile, "He did, however, leave your punishment to me. It's obvious that you both will not be healed in time for embarkation. So you will remain here until I sign your medical clearance."

"How long will that take?" Errol demanded.

"When you two stop being idiots."

"Faint hope of that," said the engineer. The twins winced in pain when they snapped their heads toward him as the other patients started laughing.

Samantha thought it was wise not to join in. The opening of the tent flap caught her attention when she saw a captain and a private enter. The private had a kit bag slung over his shoulder. They both took off their caps. The captain put his under his arm while the private kept a stiff grip on his.

"May I help you, Captain?" Samantha asked.

"I'm Captain Llewellyn, and this is Private Duval," he stated. She was impressed that he looked at her eyes rather than her breasts, as most men tended to do. He had deep blue eyes. "I wanted to check on Private Cummings, who was brought in this morning, and to bring him his things."

"Of course," Samantha said with a sympathetic tone. Although she was on shift when the casualty arrived, she did not take part in the actual surgery. Major Creighton had been called in since he was the doctor on duty. The tent wasn't fully equipped yet. From what she had heard, he used what equipment was available from the medical panniers. Most of the medical equipment was still in the quartermaster sheds here on base or at the Quebec City docks, waiting to be put on a ship.

"The doctor is here making his rounds, if you want to speak with him."

"I would," replied the captain.

"Doctor," she said as she turned toward Creighton.

"I heard," said the doctor, waving him over to Cummings' cot, several over from the twins.

"So, Major, how is he?" asked the captain as he glanced at the heavily bandaged soldier.

Samantha saw Cummings' free left eye move from the captain and then to Duval. He tried to smile, but it came out very weak.

"He's been stabilized. We cleaned out the wound and stitched him up. We gave him some morphine to dull the pain. The only concern that I have is whether or not he's suffering from concussion. We're going to watch him overnight. In the morning he'll be transported to Quebec."

"That's a relief. I was worried." Both Fusiliers relaxed when they heard the news.

"An inch to the left, and he would have lost an eye. Or worse, he wouldn't have made it. What the heck happened at the range?"

"Your guess is as good as mine. The rifle breech exploded. It's been sent back to the factory for them to determine if there was a defect," the captain informed the doctor. "It could have been me, as I was firing the same weapon minutes before it exploded." Samantha caught the tone of guilt in his voice. "You'll send me a report for my files."

A flicker passed behind the major's eyes that Samantha didn't understand. She would find out later what the captain was hinting at.

"I brought his things," stated Duval as he unslung his kit bag.

The major grinned. "Give them to Nurse Lonsdale. She'll write you a receipt."

When he gave Samantha the bag, he asked, "Can I stay with him for a while?"

"If the captain doesn't object," said the doctor.

"As long as you are back for dinner parade, I don't have a problem," answered Llewellyn.

SEPTEMBER 11, 1914
ROSS RIFLE FACTORY, COVE FIELDS, QUEBEC CITY

Marc waited impatiently as the steam excavator made its slow way toward the construction site that was facing the green expanse of the Royal Quebec Golf Course. He had beeped his horn a couple of times because he had a schedule to keep. But all that he got for his effort was a get lost gesture from the massive vehicle's driver. In a contest between the two vehicles, he would lose. Besides, he didn't want to scratch up the new truck. It would come out of his pay.

Once the road was clear, he drove up to the platform and parked it below the painted sign, *Ross Rifle Factory Receiving*. By the time he had the truck's back gate opened, the receiving clerk was waiting for him. This was a familiar routine. They had been doing the same thing every day since the factory opened in 1902.

"*Salut!*" said André as he rolled his cart into position. "What do you have for me today Marc?"

"*Comme d'hab,*" Marc replied as he tossed him packages of various sizes. "So they have started construction?"

A long rifle box was the last item he handed over. When André read the box's label, he frowned.

"The construction?" repeated Marc.

"Huh?" said André, who hadn't heard the question. "*Oui,*" he replied as he looked over at the construction zone. "They want to have it finished by the end of October, early November."

"It looks big?"

"It's 240 by 200 feet. We need the extra space for all the orders that we are expecting. Those soldiers up at Valcartier need them."

"You're hiring?" asked Marc.

"*Pourquoi?*"

"My cousin needs a job. My wife has been bugging me to find him something." Until the war started, the city had been suffering a mild depression. A lot of people were out of work.

"Send him around to see my manager," suggested André. "Can't promise anything, but you never know."

"Thanks. I'll tell my wife. She wants him out of the house. *A demain,*" Marc said as he slammed the truck's gate shut and jumped into the cab.

As the messenger sped away, André sorted the packages for his mail run. The factory's three floors housed the production lines of the Ross rifles. The bulk of the space was being used to produce the .303 military pattern, while a second line was producing the civilian versions. The most popular was the .280 magnum high velocity rifle used for target shooting and for big game hunting.

The ground floor was mainly devoted to the small parts department, which manufactured and inspected the seventy parts that went into the finished weapons. It also contained the marketing department, which sent out catalogues to prospective buyers. On the second floor lathes turned steel bars into metal rods and walnut into the appropriate shapes to receive the breeches and barrels. On the third floor, the drill presses turned the rods into rifle barrels, after which they went to the bluing room. On the same floor the wood stocks were sanded, stained, and then oiled. All the components were then sent down to the main floor for final assembly and inspection.

After he had delivered the mail to the various departments, he carried the last parcel to the general manager's office. It was at the back of the building with a splendid view of the St. Lawrence River. Through the door's large window he could see that General Manager Denton was talking with Superintendent James Fleurbaix, the head of final inspection.

"Good, it has arrived. *Merci*, André," Denton Edgars said as André entered and placed the rifle case on his desk and then left. Denton had been expecting the parcel since he had been informed, via telephone, of the accident at Valcartier. They have been asked to prepare a report on what may have caused it. He opened the box and peered at the gouged steel and wood.

James reached in and pulled the rifle out of the case. There were dried bloodstains on the stock and on the blue steel.

"What do you think?" Denton asked as he leaned forward in his chair.

James examined the weapon with a critical eye. "To make this kind of damage, either there was debris in the chamber, or they put the bolt in improperly. I'll need to take it apart to make sure."

"Give me a report once you've completed your examination. If they put the bolt in incorrectly, is there anything we can do to prevent it happening again?"

"I'll take a look at our instructions to make sure that they are clear. We can send out a notice to the armourers to check that the bolts are installed correctly. The only other thing we can do is to look at some redesign work."

"No redesign work!" Denton stated firmly. "We're going to get an order from the Imperial government for a 100,000 rifles. I do not want to delay completing it." He knew that James and his design team loved nothing more than make modifications to the Ross. Since its introduction in 1902, it had been under constant development. It had seen modifications to the ejectors, mainsprings, firing pins, extractors, trigger-guards, swivels, butt plates, bayonet mounts, sights, and magazines. The rifle also had grown in length to thirty inches and weight to slightly over nine pounds. Most of these changes were based on input from the militia department. There were so many of them that officially and on paper there were three standard marks. In reality there were so many variations that essentially there was no standard pattern. What was worse was the parts were not interchangeable between marks. For example, the bolts from the Mk II's could not be used in the Mk III's because they used a different tread design. This was an administrative nightmare for the firm trying to keep track of the various models to ensure that there were sufficient parts to make repairs.

"See if we can get away with revised instructions. If it is absolutely necessary, we'll make improvements for the next pattern."

"Alright! Alright!" replied James grumpily. "At least it's good news about the contracts. What price?" James asked as he placed the rifle in the box.

"Twenty dollars apiece."

"That will keep us busy. With the new addition, we can add an extra 200 staff and increase production to 500 a day," he said. "The problem is finding qualified machinists. They don't grow on trees, you know. I'm going to take people off the other lines."

Denton grimaced at the news. The civilian versions of the rifle kept the firm profitable, since the United States was its biggest market. "Damn it! Go ahead. But don't strip those lines completely bare. We may get away with being slow in fulfilling the civilian orders. I mean, we may."

"Okay, okay," replied James as he picked up the rifle box. "I'll disassemble it and give you a report in the morning."

"Sounds good," replied Denton as James left his office. When he turned his chair toward the St. Lawrence, he observed khaki-dressed officers test firing newly assembled rifles on the plant's thousand-yard range. They hadn't reported any problems yet similar to what occurred at Valcartier.

When he turned his head toward the construction site visible from his office, he watched as workers shovelled concrete into the foundation forms. The expansion seemed to be going well. They needed the additional space. Especially if they were going to get further orders from the War Office.

He sighed when he viewed the some golfers course next door. The members of the Royal Quebec were not happy that they had to reduce their golf course from fourteen to nine holes. They were not very happy at all.

CHAPTER 10

SEPTEMBER 14, 1914
FUSILIERS' LATRINES, VALCARTIER CAMP

The latrine stank! It was bad enough that even Major Creighton, Samantha's escort, was wrinkling his nose as they approached the wooden structure covered by a corrugated metal roof. This particular one had been designated for the privates and was the longest of the three they were inspecting. The NCO and officers' outhouses were located farther down the line.

When a private exited it, she could see that he was concentrating on buttoning his fly underneath his white apron. When he lifted his head, his eyes widened in surprise when he spotted her. Embarrassed, he quickly turned around to complete his task before facing them.

"I hope that you are going to wash your hands before you touch food," said the major as he indicated to the cook tent that was twenty yards to their left. Samantha could see smoke rise gently from the stovepipe. The smell of eggs and bacon drifted toward them, a much more pleasant aroma. There was a long dining tent beside it that was partially blocked by a line of tethered horses and service wagons. The tent walls were pulled up to allow the air to circulate. The drone from several squads of men could be heard as they ate breakfast under the canvas that was protecting them from the early morning sun. A squad that had finished eating were dipping their mess tins in a hot water vat to clean them. Farther right, in front of the shower tent, bare-chested men were shaving with straight razors as they stood at a waist-height wooden bench. Flanking them were several men seated at a picnic table getting haircuts.

"Of course, Major," the cook replied quickly. He knew that it was an order, not a suggestion, especially when he saw the CMAC on the officer's collar. One did not mess with the Canadian Medical Army Corps officers. They took sanitation very seriously.

"Who's responsible for these latrines?" demanded Creighton.

"I don't rightly know."

"Find the officer of the day. I want to see him."

"Yes, Major!" The cook hurried away to find him.

"Wait here a moment. I want to take a look inside," he told Samantha as he opened the thin pine door. Inside she could see a long white porcelain trough before the door closed behind the doctor. The major had suggested that she accompany him on his inspection tour as part of her training with the army way of sanitation. In the field or in an encampment, arrangements had to be made to ensure that there was sufficient space to accommodate the men's needs. Also, the primary rule was always cleanliness.

The cook, she saw, was pointing out her and the major to an officer. She got distracted when the latrine door banged behind her. "That was the most disgusting thing that I have seen in a long while," he stated.

When she saw Major Creighton's frown deepening as he examined the cook tent, she asked, "Problem?"

"The cook tent is closer than I would like," he remarked. "The regulations required one latrine for every seven men, and they need to be at a minimum twenty yards away from the food preparation. Also, they are required to empty them and clean them on a daily basis." He then gave her a wry smile. "I'm rambling again, aren't I?"

"Somewhat," replied Samantha with a grin. The major was quite enthusiastic about sanitation, to the point that some of the staff took great pains not to broach the subject. His attitude was not that unusual in the medical profession. She remembered the instructor she had for the sanitation course that she needed to pass before she could get her nurse's credentials. After the war, maybe she should introduce the two, if Emily hadn't married him by then. The one thing that was different between the military's and the civilian's fight against communicable diseases, as the major was fond of saying, was that they needed to ensure that the men were healthy enough to fight.

"Can I help you, Major, Lieutenant?" asked a deep voice behind her.

When she turned her head, she recognized the face of the officer who had come to see Private Cummings several days earlier. She was rather embarrassed that his name escaped her at the moment. When the captain saluted the major, his blue eyes seemed amused as he posed for a moment. She finally realized that he was waiting for her. She returned the salute that Matron Rita had drilled into all of the nurses. She hoped it was better than her first salute.

"You're the officer of the day?" demanded Creighton.

"Yes, Major. I'm Captain Llewellyn."

"Well, Captain, the latrines are quite disgusting. The pails haven't been emptied for several days."

The captain's face turned grave as he examined the three latrine buildings. "I see. I noticed that with the officers myself this morning. I was going to broach the subject with the adjutant. We've had a lot of units being transferred in and out. It seems that the responsibility fell through the cracks." When he saw the look on the major's face, he added, "It is not an excuse. Simply an explanation."

The shouting of men near the showers drew the captain's and Samantha's attention. Samantha noticed that he moved a bit closer and took a step to the right to block her view when he saw that some of the men were naked.

The major, oblivious, continued, "There are contractors who have been hired to clean them on a daily basis."

"I was not aware of that," replied Llewellyn. "Until it gets sorted out, I'll assign some men to clean them." He smiled with private amusement. "For some of them it would be a rather appropriate punishment." Samantha wondered what infraction would result in latrine duty.

"Good," said the major as he took out a notebook and made a note.

"How is Private Cummings, Lieutenant Lonsdale?" he asked Samantha. "If I recall, you were his nurse when I visited him in the hospital."

Samantha cocked her head. She was pleased that he remembered her name. "He's improving. I saw him last night. He's at the immigration hospital in Quebec City where we are staying. It'll be several months before he'll be fully recovered."

The captain appeared relieved at the news. "That's good to hear. I'll let Duval know. He was asking me about him. If you can inform Private Cummings that we inquired, I would appreciate it."

"I will," said Samantha.

"Well, Captain. That will be all for today," the major said, dismissing the man. "We'll be re-inspecting the facilities tomorrow to ensure that everything is satisfactory."

"Of course, Major. I will be expecting you and the lieutenant," he replied after he saluted the major. Creighton glanced at Samantha and then back to the captain. He didn't like what he saw in the captain's eyes. "I'm afraid it will be just the MO of the day."

"I see," replied the captain. There was hint of disappointment in his voice.

After she gave the captain a goodbye salute, she couldn't resist saying to him, "Thank you for being so gallant, Captain Llewellyn. But I am a nurse!"

She liked the way the captain blushed when he caught her meaning. As she marched away with the major, she wondered if he was still watching her. She resisted the temptation to peek over her shoulder to find out.

SEPTEMBER 14, 1914
65TH HORSE ARTILLERY BELL TENTS,
VALCARTIER CAMP

"Watch were the fuck you put your feet, McGill," groused Reggie when he entered his assigned bell tent.

"Yeah, close the fucking flap," yelled Sandy Cranston, a twenty-four-year-old former schoolteacher, as he tried to protect his newspaper. "You're letting the rain in."

"Go fuck yourselves," Paul retorted. The sound of the rain drumming on the canvas roof seemed to increase when he closed the flap. The wool cap he was wearing provided limited protection against the elements, but it wasn't enough against the torrential rain. He could feel the dampness seep through the fabric and the lining.

When he turned, he saw seven men with whom he shared a tent grinning at him. The hanging oil lamp that was swaying gently as the winds buffeted the walls lighted their faces.

"McGill is learning to talk like a soldier," remarked Shawn Pelletier, the twenty-two-year-old store clerk from Shawville. He was holding playing cards in his hands, as were four of the others. Paul suspected that he was a card shark, since he had the uncanny ability to take nearly everyone's money.

"Now all we have to do is find you a woman," remarked Brandon Meran, a twenty-seven-year-old bank teller from the Eastern Townships, as he reorganized the cards in his hand. He peered over them and asked, "You have had a woman, haven't you?"

Their grins became wider when Paul felt himself blushing. "Fuck you," he muttered as he took off his cap and tossed it onto his cot. On the whole, he liked the men with whom he shared his accommodations. He still hadn't gotten used to such crowded quarters, since he'd grown up sleeping in his own room. The tent was even more cramped since they brought their rifles and other equipment in to protect them.

He sat on his blanket and sighed with relief when he removed his muddy boots. The blisters on his hands were finally callusing over. But now his boots, that he had paid a considerable sum for, were still blistering his feet. He didn't know what was worse.

"Good god, man!" Shawn said as he held his nose. "When was the last time you washed your socks?"

Paul looked at him innocently. "I was supposed to wash my own socks?"

Shawn stared at him and then chuckled as he shook a finger at him. "You nearly had me there."

"Are you in or out?" demanded Tim O'Malley, a mechanic from the east side of Montreal.

"Yeah, yeah. Hold your horses," replied Shawn as he stared at his cards.

"So did you get all of the work done?" asked Reggie. In his lap, he had his housewife open. He was trying to extract a needle and thread to sew a loose button on his tunic. "I'm surprised he didn't put you on guard duty tonight."

"Don't give him any ideas," Paul replied sourly. He was physically exhausted, because he had spent most of the day mucking the corrals, cleaning tack, and any other dirty job that Corporal Enright could find. He was really beginning to hate the man.

"So how's the war going?" he asked Sandy. The camp was hungry for news. Especially on how the British Expeditionary Force was doing in France.

Sandy looked over the paper and was about to respond when a loud thunderclap rattled the tent. A few muted ones followed it. Everyone looked up as the drumbeat on the roof increased and got louder. "That was close," remarked Sandy. He shrugged and then continued his reading from the paper. "Things seem to be looking up. We don't seem to make much headway against the centre and west German armies, but we're driving the east wing back."

Paul suddenly felt the earth beneath him tremble. He sat up and was about ask Reggie if he was feeling the same thing when he saw a puzzled look appear on his friend's face.

"Shit!" exclaimed Reggie when he heard faint sounds of a frightened whinny.

Reggie was scrambling for the tent's opening as the thunder of hooves grew louder. Suddenly, the tent collapsed and they were all plunged into darkness. Everyone swore vehemently as they struggled to get out from under the heavy, water-laden fabric. Paul finally managed to slide under one of the edges. He was greeted by a gust of wind and rain that slapped him in the face. In the dim light from the street lamps he saw that a cavalry horse had become entangled in the tent's support lines. The stallion's eyes were bulging, and it was screaming in fear and pain. Every time it kicked, the ropes tightened. A hoof skimmed Sandy's emerging head. He scrambled to get away from the horse.

"Did everyone get out?" asked Paul. He did a quick head count. All the men were accounted for and, miraculously, none were injured. Through the slanted rain he saw several other tents had collapsed. One was on fire, probably from a broken oil lamp. Men were slapping at the flaming tent with what they had at hand in an attempt to put it out.

Reggie went over to check on the horse. When he came back, his face was grim. "Paul, see if you can find a rifle."

"Why?" asked Paul.

"He broke his leg. There's nothing that can be done. I have to put him down."

"Are you sure?"

"Of course I'm fucking sure," he snapped. He gave a tired sigh. "Sorry, McGill. I don't like it. But I need to put him out of his misery."

Paul wiped water from his brow as he lifted the canvas to search for a weapon. He finally spotted a protruding rifle butt a few feet away. He retrieved it, and when he checked, it wasn't loaded. He also found a pair of boots, which he hoped were his, since he was still in his bare feet.

He gave the rifle to Reggie. As he hopped on one foot and then the other as he put on his boots, he said, "It's not loaded."

"Fat lot of good."

"Need a bullet?" said Sandy.

"You got one?"

"Yeah. The fucker nearly took my head off," Sandy stated as he handed him a cartridge.

Paul looked away as Reggie loaded the rifle and pointed at the horse's head. The shot seemed to be louder than the thunderclap that followed. When Paul looked back, the animal had stopped thrashing, and Reggie was slinging the gun over his right shoulder.

"What the hell happened?" demanded Paul.

"The lighting and the thunder must have spooked the horses, and they broke out of the corrals," Reggie said as they watched a small herd of five draught horses gallop past them down the centre of the road.

"What are we going to do?" asked Sandy.

"We'll have to round them up and put them back," replied Reggie.

Paul couldn't keep his eyes from returning back to the horse lying motionless near the tent. "Okay. How do we do that?"

Reggie paused to think and then looked at the tangle of cords that were lying on the ground. He pulled out a pocketknife and cut them from the tent. Then he started to wind the rope around his left arm. At the end, he made a slipknot.

"We'll use this as a lead rope. If you spot a loose horse, gently talk to them as I've been showing you. Get close enough to rub their foreheads. They like that. Then slip the rope around their neck and lead them back to the corral. If they spook again or decide to run, let them go. If you don't, they'll run you over. We'll find them later when they calm down."

"Okay. I think," replied Paul. He rummaged around the tent to find a cap. The rain falling on his bare head was starting to irritate him. When he put it on, it was obvious it wasn't his because it fell below his ears. It was better than nothing.

"Let's get to work. I don't think we're going to get any sleep tonight," Reggie ordered as he led the squad down the road after the horses.

SEPTEMBER 15, 1914
JACQUES CARTIER RIVER, VALCARTIER CAMP

Captain Llewellyn was kneeling on a small hill overlooking the Jacques Cartier River. Through his binoculars he was watching logs from the timber cutting operations farther upstream that were gently bobbing and bumping against a wooden pontoon bridge that the military engineers had built. The bridge swayed and dipped slightly as the heavy draught horses of the Royal Canadian Artillery were attempting to cross it.

The horses were skittish as they placed their hooves down. The rider sitting on the front left lead horse was urging his reluctant team forward using his whip and boot spurs. The wind blew off his cap into the water. They were pulling a heavy 18-pounder and its limber to this side of the river. Two of the heavy guns had already traversed and were parked a hundred yards in front. Once the gun had crossed over, the wagons of the ammunition train would follow.

When he lowered his glasses, he turned his attention to his men. They were down on one knee with their rifles in the ready position.

The company still looked motley, with only about half wearing khaki and Oliver gear. A scattering were wearing white pith helmets. When he spotted several privates just watching the river, he stared at them, hoping they would get the message.

When Sergeant Booth, twenty paces away, felt his eyes, he turned to toward him. He followed the captain's stare. "What the fuck are you looking at? Eyes front, you bastards! The enemy is that fucking way," Booth declared as he pointed to the tree line.

The captain continued to observe the men. They were all tired, since they spent most of the night chasing horses. The lightning storm had created a mess. When the herd had broken out, it attempted to use his section of the camp as their escape route. Half the men's tents, including his, got knocked down. He had to spend a couple hours putting it and his scattered contents back together.

The lack of sleep made him more irritable than usual. It didn't help that he didn't know where in the hell his CO was. He hadn't heard from him since this morning's briefing.

Oscar Henricks, who led the 1st platoon, a twenty-six-year-old lanky insurance salesman from Toronto, scurried over and asked, "Have you received word yet?"

Llewellyn shook his head. "I sent out a runner a half hour ago. He isn't back yet."

Henricks glanced back at the pontoon bridge. "They'll all be across soon, then we'll have to move."

"I know," replied Llewellyn. His company of Fusiliers was positioned to provide a protective screen for the RCA so they could cross the river into Redland. The field artillery was needed to provide support for the 4th Brigade's attack on the Red forces' supply depot.

At the morning meeting, the tactical scheme had been laid out. The Jacques Cartier would act as the border that separated the two warring countries: the Redland and the Blueland. Reconnaissance had discovered the location of a critical Red army supply depot. The capture and destruction of the base would be a critical blow to the Red forces' operations. There were nearly 2,000 men involved in today's exercise. The 1st Brigade would act as the Reds, while the Fusiliers would be the Blues.

The one thing he could say was that his men were eager. It would be a pleasant change from the nearly continual reviews that they had to endure. The men were still grousing about last Sunday's parade. Hughes had forced everyone to march in a torrential storm. At least he had the decency to apologize to the men for the discomfort he had put them through.

So where the hell was Colonel Topham? When he saw a rider on a bay appear and canter up to his position, he was hopeful he would finally have an answer. "Captain Llewellyn," the rider said when he stopped his panting horse in front of him. "Message for you." He leaned down from his saddle and handed him a folded piece of paper.

Llewellyn took the note and read the handwritten orders. One thing he could say about the colonel, he wrote in a fine hand. He had to read the orders twice before he was able to figure out what message his CO was actually trying to convey. He looked up at the messenger and asked, "The colonel instructs that we are to meet at the rendezvous point two miles north of this road with dispatch. It doesn't mention the field artillery?"

The messenger shrugged. "I was informed that you are to bring your company as soon as possible. Do you have a reply?"

Llewellyn paused to think. He hated vague orders. The colonel knew that he was to protect the RCA, so why didn't he mention them? On the bridge, he could see that the last of the ammunition train wagons were coming across. The draught horses could do about eight miles an hour at a walking canter. At a gallop, they could do up to thirty miles per hour, but that was only sustainable for a max of a quarter-mile at best. His company could do the three and half miles, if they stayed on the road, in about an hour.

The hell with it, he thought. "Tell the colonel that we'll be at the rendezvous point in an hour and half with the field artillery."

"Yes, Captain," replied the messenger. He turned his horse around and spurred it into a gallop in the direction he had just come from.

With a finger, Llewellyn beckoned Sergeant Booth. "Tell the lieutenants I want to see them."

Henricks, who was still in earshot, came over. "News?"

"Yes," replied Llewellyn as he knelt on one knee. He picked up a broken branch from the ground and began to draw a crude map in the dirt. They were short on paper maps for the surrounding area.

"Gentlemen." He greeted the other leaders of the three platoons under his command. He was familiar with Henricks and John Troope, a thirty-year-old broker on Bay Street, since they'd been with the Fusiliers for a number of years. Rather, the 18th Provisional Battalion, as they were now to be called. One of Hughes's announcements from on high.
110

It was not that far from the truth, actually, since Hughes read orders and speeches from a small dirt hill in the middle of the camp. All of the CEF units were to be assigned official numerical designations, which they were to use from then on. But, dammit, they were the Richmond Fusiliers and always would be.

He was just getting to know the new lieutenant, who had transferred in from the Strathcona Horse to replace him after he got promoted. Jeremy Vernon was a twenty-five-year-old grocery store manager from Edmonton. He had requested a change to the infantry because he was not a very good rider. Llewellyn's first impression of him was positive, and he seemed to be efficient. Time would tell.

"Since the artillery has nearly crossed the river, I want Vernon as the advance guard." Llewellyn indicated in the dirt with the branch. He looked up at Vernon. "Put the scouts outs. I really don't want any surprises." Vernon acknowledged with a nod. "Second will be on the left flank and third on the right. For the rear guard, I would like a section from both of your platoons." The platoons were made up of thirty men organized into three sections of ten men each. The sections were normally led by a sergeant or a lance-corporal.

"I'll give you Sergeant Bryan's section," stated Henricks.

Troope said, "I'll give you Sergeant Stone. He gets along with Bryan, so there shouldn't be a problem."

"Where will you be?" asked Vernon as he lit a cigarette.

"I'll be between you and the RCA," replied Llewellyn. "I don't want them to feel lonesome." Vernon's lips lifted into a smile, and then he grunted in acknowledgement. If Vernon thought that Llewellyn had placed himself were he could keep an eye on him, he was correct. However, he was far enough away that he could not be an undue influence on his former platoon. Vernon led the 3rd platoon, Llewellyn didn't.

"Is everyone clear on their jobs?" Llewellyn took the silence as acknowledgement. "Let's get to it."

* * *

"May I ask a question?" Llewellyn requested.

"No, you may not!" replied Colonel Topham testily. "You are to comply with my orders. Do I make myself clear?"

"Yes, Colonel," Llewellyn replied. He tried very hard not to grit his teeth. There was a glint of satisfaction in Colonel Topham's eyes as he used the reins to turn his horse in the direction of his command post about 300 yards away. The four officers that formed his entourage followed suit.

When his company had arrived at the starting point, he knew by the way the colonel was handling his horse he was extremely displeased. His first demand was, "Where the devil have you been?"

After Llewellyn gave his report, Topham still was not impressed. What really put the CO over the edge, besides lack of sleep, was the royal standard that was flying near the Fusiliers Headquarters. The governor general was observing today's mock battle. The colonel really wanted to impress the duke.

He needed Llewellyn's company to launch his attack, and he had been embarrassed that it was missing. It was a classic case of miscommunication. While it hadn't been his fault, it didn't matter; he still was being blamed for the fiasco. As punishment, the colonel had changed the battle order. He had put the captain's company in reserve so they would not take part as the Fusiliers made their initial assault on the Red forces' supply depot, which was located on the knoll in front of them.

When he turned to face his three lieutenants, he saw they had looks of disappointment and resentment. They had done a good job protecting the RCA. The platoons held their formation well, with good separation between the men. It was a shame they would not take part in the attack.

"You heard the colonel," said Llewellyn. "Get the men into columns of fours."

As the junior officers went to organize the men, he examined the battlefield through his binoculars. The 1st Brigade pennant was fluttering above the knoll at about a thousand yards distance. They had selected a very good spot. The Jacques Cartier River was at the defenders' backs, so the only way to dislodge them was a frontal assault. Also, they had the advantage of firing downhill, while the Fusiliers had to fight on the upslope.

"The men are ready," reported Vernon. The captain turned his head to verify that the company were in columns of fours. They were in a hollow, which provided them some cover from the 1st Brigade's watchful eyes.

"What do you make of this?" asked Llewellyn as he waved at the battlefield.

112

"I don't rightly know," admitted the lieutenant. Which didn't surprise the captain. To the untrained eye, the attack looked somewhat confusing and impressive at the same time.

"The two companies will be moving into extended order shortly," the captain said. "The artillery," he stated as he indicated the three 18-pounders strategically placed near the tree line, "will open up with a barrage to disrupt the Red forces' trench line. The first platoon will provide covering fire when they get to the 500-yard marker. When the second company reaches its position, it will then provide covering fire for the first platoon. They'll leapfrog each other until they can get into the appropriate range to use their bayonets."

Since the Boer War, the British Army had changed its infantry tactics when attacking a defensive position. The hard lessons it had learned from the Boer's high-powered, accurate, and magazine-fed rifles meant that they could no longer attack in solid mass formations disciplined in firing in volleys. The new tactics required that the units attack in a four-line extended formation. This made it more difficult for a machine gun or for enemy rapid fire to annihilate a company.

"Damn!" exclaimed Llewellyn.

"What?" asked Vernon.

"Look at that platoon on the left there," Llewellyn said as he pointed to the line that was marching toward the hill. "See how they are clumping up? They should be further extended. You notice some of the men are also going around the small bushes rather than stepping over them."

"I see it," said Vernon.

"The men have a tendency to do that. When that happens the line starts to bend and get off step. Which means that the second line will slow down because they are getting too close to the first line."

"Ouch! Did you see that?" interjected Vernon.

"What?"

"The horse on the right there. He just threw his rider."

When Llewellyn turned his head he saw a horse cantering across the field with an empty saddle. Several men were standing around trying to help the fallen officer. One of them began to signal that they needed an ambulance wagon. Based on the armbands they were wearing, they were the judges and instructors for the exercise.

"That does not look good."

"No, it doesn't," said Llewellyn. He then saw a messenger running toward him. He was pretty certain that the colonel was going to order them into the mess in front of him. Llewellyn raised his glasses to scan the field, trying to figure out how he could take advantage of the confusion in front of him. He smiled when he spotted the opening.

"Vernon, this is what I want to do," he said as he outlined his scheme to his subordinate.

CHAPTER 11

"They are not going to like it," stated Lieutenant Vernon emphatically.

"I know," replied Captain Llewellyn. They were sitting at a picnic table where the movie tent used to be. It had been burned down when some of the men took exception to the proprietor's business practice of repeat showings of the same movies and charging the soldiers exorbitant prices. The rumour was that the cash box was never found. A dry canteen had taken its place. Vernon was sitting across from him with a mug of coffee with Henricks. Parker was sitting beside him stirring his tea. The setting sun was hitting the left side of his face. He glanced at the orange glow. He estimated he had another hour of daylight before it got dark. It had been a pleasant September day of route marches and training. His feet ached a bit, but his day was not over yet.

"At least we will be able to get rid of the undesirables," remarked Henricks.

"True. There's that," answered Llewellyn. He tapped the pad of manila paper, with a wooden pencil on top. "I need to prepare and submit a return of the men we feel we can leave behind by tomorrow at nine o'clock sharp."

"Do you think that they will still send everyone?" asked Parker in a hopeful tone.

"I don't know," replied Llewellyn as he rubbed his chin. "I hope so. But the government authorized 25,000 thousand, and we have over 33,000 here already. Every day we are getting a new influx of recruits. Hell, we've got men walking up to the front gate begging to volunteer. Most of the sentries spend their time signing them up."

"Will those left behind be sent later as reinforcements?" asked Parker.

"Probably."

"If the war lasts that long," stated Vernon.

"I certainly hope so," replied Henricks. He was keen on seeing action.

"If we have to, it means it's nearly 8,000 men who are going to stay here."

"That's twenty-five percent. Nearly eight battalions," whistled Henricks. "Why don't they simply designate eight battalions and be done with it?" Llewellyn gave him an incredulous look. "Oh, right, what was I thinking?"

Llewellyn agreed that the simple solution was to simply pick eight battalions to continue their training in Valcartier and then ship them out at a later date. The problem was politics. Rather, military politics. None of the senior commanders wanted to be left behind. It was their chance for glory. Any attempt to cut them, and Hughes would probably have a revolt on his hands. Especially since he was the one who picked them in the first place. It was much easier for the commanders to weed out individual men, since all that the men could do was grouse and complain.

"We can always cut the quartermasters," joked Parker.

"You can try. See how far that gets you next time you need supplies," remarked Vernon. He turned to the captain. "What criteria are we going to use to select the men for the list?"

"I'm open to suggestions," replied Llewellyn with open palms.

"Last in, first out?" suggested Parker. "I think it's only fair. All the recent recruits and transfers can be put on the list."

"Wait a minute," protested Vernon, as he was the only recent transfer at the table.

"Not you, of course. You're such a nice fellow," Henricks said, patting him on the back as he winked at the other two men.

"Thanks. I think."

"Let's get back to the task at hand. I'll need at least twenty-five men for HQ. I could always arrange a parade and walk down the line and point and say 'you and you,'" Llewellyn mimicked, pointing with his hand.

"Good as any," stated Henricks. He shut up when Llewellyn gave him a glare. To mollify him, he said, "You can put Hutchison and Cramer on the list. I just got word from the medical officer before I came. They have VD."

"Damn!" replied Llewellyn. "They were good soldiers."

"I hate losing them, but there's nothing we can do about it."

Llewellyn picked up his pencil and wrote their names and indicated the reason: *Discharge. Venereal Disease.*

116

"We have a couple of men who have refused to have their vaccinations. I was hoping to convince to take their shots. If they don't, we'll have to discharge them, so we can put them on the list. We also have Cummings on sick parade," added Parker. Llewellyn grimaced, but he wrote down the injured man's name. "Put McCormick also as an undesirable. I can't get him to do any work. Every morning he reports for sick parade, and I'm getting sick of it."

"That's a good point. We'll add anyone that is not getting along well with the men and have been on report." The three lieutenants provided nearly a dozen names that met that criterion.

Llewellyn paused when Henricks said, "Add Rosenberg."

"Why?"

"He's a Jew."

"No, he stays," stated Llewellyn. "He's a good soldier." He glanced at each of the men. "Let me make myself clear. I don't care what religion the man is. I'm only interested is whether or not he has the potential to be a good soldier."

Llewellyn knew that it was easier said than done. If his company was any indication, most of the men were Church of England. About a quarter were Baptist and Methodists, and a similar number were Roman Catholics. Rosenberg was the sole Jew. On the whole, the men got along well. The men who indicated they were Anglican were required to report for church parade, while it was optional for the other denominations. Still, nearly everyone attended a religious service in one form or another. Since Rosenberg was from Montreal, the captain was well aware that the Jewish press had a special interest in those of their faith who had joined the CEF.

"So, if someone can't get along with the one other men or if he's a drunk, we'll put him on the list. Am I understood?"

"Yes, Captain," they replied, nearly in unison.

SEPTEMBER 19, 1914
TRAIN STATION, VALCARTIER CAMP

Borden stared out of the train car's dusty window as it slowly rolled to a lurching stop at the platform.

"Oh dear," said Laura, who was sitting beside him. "Is that a band?"

"I believe it is," replied Borden with a sigh. Waiting on the platform was an honour guard and a small marching band wearing kilts. "I wouldn't be surprised if he has a twenty-one-gun salute planned as well." Laura *tsked* in agreement as he eyed the two men dressed in colonel's uniforms standing in front of the squad of soldiers.

When he felt the train's final shudder, he helped his wife gather her things. A conductor jumped out to put down a footstool so they could step out onto the loading dock comfortably. Laura adjusted her white ostrich feather cap and then brushed some lint off his brown suit jacket before she allowed him to step out of the car.

"Please watch your step, dear," he said as he helped her down. When he took his first footsteps, the band struck up "The Maple Leaf Forever." Hughes and his aide-de-camp, William McBain, saluted him as he approached. Both men wore colonel insignia on their shoulders. A red band circled their caps. However, McBain's commission was an honorary one. Hughes had rewarded the land agent with militia officer's post, with pay, for acquiring the 5,000-acre site. The original plan was to use the land as summer camp to train Quebec-based soldiers.

"Thank you, Sam. It is a pleasure to be here again. I'm looking forward to seeing what you have accomplished since I was last here," he said. The main purpose of his visit was to review the soldiers before they embarked for England in a week's time. However, he was also there to have a chat with his minister of Militia and Defence about his language and behaviour. The reports that he had been receiving were not flattering. The officers from the Nova Scotia regiments, his native province, were upset at Hughes. What also bothered him was how he had treated the visiting US army officers. He wanted to maintain good relations with the US government. Verbally abusing the senior American generals who had come to observe the Canadian mobilization was not good diplomacy.

"It would be my pleasure, Prime Minister. Once you have inspected the honour guard, we'll be taking a motorcar tour of the camp to see how far we have progressed. The camp's commandant will not be joining us for lunch, as he has other matters to attend to."

"My wife and I are looking forward to it," Borden replied as he followed Hughes for the inspection of the honour guard on the platform.

* * *

The motorcar was parked on a hill overlooking the Jacques Cartier River. Borden and Hughes were sitting in the middle row of the three-row seat motorcar while Laura and Lieutenant-Colonel McBain were sitting on the rear bench. The view was magnificent. Across the river, he could see the gleaming straight lines of the camp's bell tents as they reflected the sun. In the far distance, where the rifle ranges were located, very faint rifle reports were heard when the wind shifted.

"The camp has progressed extremely well," Borden remarked to Hughes. The camp had indeed advanced greatly since he last visited on September 6th. At the time, he only stayed for a day, and he had half his cabinet with him. They had been hearing rumours that the conditions at the camp were very poor and that the soldiers were suffering. They had discovered that there were indeed problems at Valcartier, but they were what one would expect when a brand-new facility was being constructed. From what he had seen, great effort had been made since then to ensure that the men were well cared-for.

"Yes. We have made great strides. As you know, as soon as I announced that Valcartier would be our assembly point, the land was cleared for the tents and the parade ground. I had the men that were working on the Connaught rifle range in Ottawa come down here by train. They did spectacular work. In less than ten days they constructed three and half miles of rifle pits and put up 1,500 targets for the men to practise on.

"But not only that, we ensured that there was adequate water, sewage, lights, and telephone and telegraph lines. And we continue to make improvements for the men's health and safety. We have lain in twelve miles of clean water pipes and fifteen miles of sewage drains to remove the effluent from 7,000 horses and 31,000 men. We built the Service Corps and Ordnance buildings. I would like to have permanent barracks for the men, but we don't have the time. I want to get the contingent to England as soon as we can.

"I'm very pleased with how the men's training has progressed. We can see them coming in from an exercise right now." Hughes pointed to the column of 2,000 men that were marching toward the pontoon bridge to return back to the camp for lunch. It was an impressive sight as they marched in nearly perfect synchronization. The left arms swung to shoulder height, while they carried their rifles in their right hands.

"Have you heard from London who they have under consideration to command the CEF?" Borden was almost afraid to ask. He saw the look of disappointment on Hughes' face. Borden knew he wanted to command the force himself. In August, George Perley, the acting high commissioner in London, had replied to his trail balloon to appointing Hughes as the contingent's commander. Perley stated that he had spoken with Lord Kitchener, and his opinion was that it wasn't wise to change ministers at this time. Also, it would have meant that he would have to promote Hughes to major-general. Hughes had asked for the promotion in the past. Last Sunday, Fiset, the surgeon-general, and Macdonald, the quartermaster-general, suggested the same thing. He told them that he would consider it. However, he didn't want Hughes to be in command of the force. What was needed was an officer with combat experience and tact. It was obvious that his minister did not have those qualities.

"We requested the names of the top three Canadian-born officers that are currently serving in the British Army. Sadly, none are currently above the rank of brigadier-general. If we select one, he'll have to be promoted. It looks like a British officer will be chosen," Hughes grunted in disgust.

"Did they provide any names?"

"Yes they have. I've been considering Lieutenant-General the Earl of Dundonald. As you recall, he served with the Canadian Militia as the COC in 1907 for two years. Major-General Sir Reginald Carew and Lieutenant-General E.H. Alderson are also candidates. They both served in the Boer War."

"Which one do you like?"

"I like Alderson the best. During the Boer War he commanded two regiments of Canadian soldiers."

"If you feel that he is suitable, I don't have any objections," Borden replied. He was somewhat relieved that this was relatively painless. He doubted that his afternoon meeting with the Nova Scotia officers would be.

"Thank you, Prime Minister. Once I've made up my mind, I'll inform you and then London. Have you decided how many men we are going to embark next week?" Hughes asked as he glanced at Borden.

Borden frowned. He and his cabinet had numerous discussions as to whether or not to send everyone at the camp or only the authorized number of troops. Gwatkin had pointed out that the CEF would need reinforcements. Current estimates were that there was going to be a ten percent casualty rate. White, his finance minister, was getting alarmed at the expenditures being incurred. Also, the current plans were to contract sufficient ships to transport 25,000 men and their equipment to England. If he decided to send the additional 6,000 to 7,000 men, they would have to find more vessels. He only had a few days to decide.

"Not at the moment. That is one of things I'm here to discuss with you and the brigade commanders."

"I can assure you, Prime Minister, that all of the men are raring to go and are the best-trained soldiers in the world. I would really hate to leave good men behind."

"I understand," replied Borden as he watched the last of the soldiers cross the bridge.

"Dear, I hate to intrude," said Laura behind him. "I believe that you have a lunch meeting scheduled."

Borden turned to his wife and grinned. "Thank you, Laura."

"Driver, please proceed to the railway station," ordered Hughes. He turned toward Borden and said, "I have arranged lunch at the CPR dining car. The brigade commanders will be present. In the afternoon, we will have a tour of the camp hospital and meet some of the men."

CHAPTER 12

Llewellyn waved away a black fly, which was buzzing his ear. He stood in a freshly washed khaki uniform. He was using a small metal mirror to verify that he was properly dressed, from the khaki puttees that were wrapped from the top of his brightly polished black boots to just above his knee. A dark Sam Brown belt was cinched at his waist, while a thin leather strap crossed his shoulder. He gave one of the brass buttons on his uniform a quick rub with his thumb to remove a speck of dirt. His Colt .45 felt heavy in a covered holster as he adjusted it on his belt to a more comfortable position. He picked up his cap, with the brass badge of the Richmond Fusiliers on the front, and his swagger stick from his cot just before he exited his tent.

For late September, the weather was nearly perfect. Llewellyn looked up at the blue sky with a few wisps of white clouds drifting lazily westward. When he looked at the hills in the distance, the trees were beginning to turn beautiful shades of yellow, orange, and red.

Booth was waiting for him with new sergeant stripes on his uniform and a drill cane in his right hand. He was pleased that the man he and Rawlings had recruited turned out to be a solid NCO. He sighed when he thought of Rawlings. He was probably on a beach by now with a bottle of rum and a girl on his arm. The last he heard was that the Royal Canadian Regiment had set sail on the 10th for Bermuda.

"Are all the men back yet?" he asked Sergeant Booth.

"Yes, sir. They better be. Told them to be back by one after this morning's church parade," he replied.

Llewellyn nodded. While the men were not compelled to attend, almost everyone in the unit mustered for the morning Mass that was held on the parade ground. Nearly 20,000 men were present. The front section, reserved for the dignitaries, had been full, with Sam Hughes, the governor general, and his wife and daughter, as well as the prime minister and his wife.

What amused Llewellyn was that the Signalling Corps had been drafted to use their flags to announce the hymn numbers. An officer was stationed near one of the chaplains, and as the Mass progressed, he would raise a flag sequence, which would relay to the other signallers on the field the next hymn number. It was quite a sight as he listened to the entire contingent singing in unison, or at least trying to as they fumbled through their hymnbooks.

After the morning Mass, the men had been given fatigue duty to prepare for this afternoon's review. Llewellyn pulled out his steel pocket watch and checked the time. It was nearly one thirty. The parade was scheduled to start at three. "Call the men."

"Yes, Captain," Booth said as he turned and started bellowing down the length of the bell tents for the men to assemble.

The men grumbled as they assumed formation. At least they dressed the lines relatively quickly. Booth didn't need to use his cane to straighten the lines more than once or twice. When the ranks were finally ready, he marched to the first of the four rows of men and began to inspect their uniforms and their rifles. From a distance the men appeared impressive; however, at closer inspection one could tell that the men suffered from the army's notion of appropriate sizing. Some of the tunics were a size too large, while for others the sleeves were a inch or two too short for the man's arm length. Thank goodness for the puttees, as they masked the various pant lengths. The tunics hid that some of the men's pants were a couple of sizes too wide. A couple of men had to be sent back to their tents to get the wire frames for their caps. They liked to remove them to give themselves a jaunty look. When he completed his inspection, he returned to the front of the column. They were not really soldiers yet, but they were presentable. He gave the left turn marching order and then led his company toward the parade ground.

Llewellyn knew that it was a big day for the contingent, since it was their final parade before they boarded their ships for transport to Britain. In fact, it was really no secret. The GTR railroad was advertising special $10 weekend excursion rates to Valcartier so tourists could view the festivities. Guards had to be posted around the camp to prevent visitors walking off with souvenirs.

As he marched toward the review field, the murmuring of voices from the large crowd began to increase. What he had been told during the morning briefing was that they expected 10,000 civilians in attendance. Llewellyn recognized the political necessity, but for some reason he couldn't get out of his head the American civil war's first battle of Manassas, where the spectators from Washington had come to be entertained. They fully expected the Northern Army to trounce Robert E. Lee's southerners. When Lee broke through, the crowds fled in horror.

Llewellyn could now see the crowds that were held back by a makeshift fence. Some people were standing in motorcars to get a better view of the festivities. Others had climbed the trees just outside the perimeter. In the distance, the royal standard fluttered gently in the wind in front of the headquarters building.

When he moved his eyes to the saluting post, he could see empty seats where the Duke of Connaught, his wife and daughter, his military staff, the prime minister, and other invited guests were to be seated.

"Fix bayonets," he ordered. Behind him he could hear them being removed from their scabbards and being locked in place on their Ross's.

"Forward march," he commanded as he led his men to their assigned location on the field. It was anticipated that they would be inspecting some of the troops before the actual review would begin at three. Once it started, it would take slightly over an hour for the entire force to pass the saluting post. Above the heads of the troops in front of him, he could see Colonel Hughes, the Duke of Connaught, and Colonel Williams riding their horses as they examined the men in the lines.

When the Royal Canadian Artillery and the Royal Canadian Garrison bands struck up the "Royal Artillery Slow March," he knew that it was starting. The music from the brass and reed instruments battled with the sounds of the horse artillery rumbling past the post. They were followed by the Lord Strathcona Horse. The troops were wearing their distinctive Stetsons.

As the cavalry passed, a squad of men with spades and buckets would scoot out and clean up any droppings that the horses might have left behind. It would not do if a man's foot slipped. A fall could take out an entire company, marring the occasion — something that Hughes would be livid about.

Llewellyn's jaw clenched when he thought of Hughes. The latest rumours indicated that three British generals were being considered to command the force. He knew that his men were placing bets Hughes would resign being the minister and appoint himself as the force's CO.

Just before each unit arrived at the saluting post, the bands would change the music to reflect the units' designated march, if they had one. Behind them, waiting patiently, were the field ambulances, which were to be the last units to past the post. It took nearly half-hour of waiting patiently until the bands played the Richmond Fusiliers' theme.

124

As he crossed the white post, he ordered eyes left. He could feel the 200 men behind, with their left arms swinging to shoulder height, snap their heads to face the stand. He snapped a smart salute as he crossed the line. Colonel Hughes, beaming from ear to ear, returned the salute.

CHAPTER 13

SEPTEMBER 22, 1914
HEADQUARTERS, VALCARTIER CAMP

As a low-level captain, Llewellyn had been surprised when Colonel Topham ordered him to attend such a high-level meeting. Normally the adjutant or the senior captain would accompany the colonel to meetings that included the four brigade commanders, Mercer, Currie, Cohoe, and Turner and Williams, the camp commandant. He suspected that his name was on the list of men to be left behind. If that was true, it made sense since his absence would have little impact on the Fusiliers' efficiency.

But there he was, seated in an uncomfortable rattan chair set against the wall. No one paid any attention to him as Lieutenant-Colonel Price said, "I just want to clarify my orders, sir."

Llewellyn had been watching the honorary colonel's left profile when he was informed why he had been required to report to today's meeting with the minister of Militia and Defence and the prime minister.

Price did a pretty good job of not allowing his jaw to drop when he heard Hughes say, "After a lengthy discussion with the cabinet and the brigade commanders." Hughes pointed to the officers sitting at the three tables arranged in a U shape. "And taking in consideration that the imperial government has recently issued orders to raise a third new army of six divisions, the government has decided to send all of the men and the horses in this camp to England."

Llewellyn heard someone shout, "Yes!"

At least it wasn't him. The mood in the room had lightened considerably. With the exception of Price, the officers were all smiles. Hughes, he noticed, was wiping tears from his eyes. Llewellyn glanced at the only three men in the room that were in civilian dress sitting at Hughes' table: George Foster, Robert Rogers, and Prime Minister Borden. He wondered how much of a beating did Hughes have to do before he got his way? Everyone knew that Hughes wanted to get into the fight.

The more he considered it, the more he thought it was a smart move, since it solved a lot of political problems. He had heard that the Nova Scotia officers had met with Borden to air their grievances. It was painful for the minister to decide who was or wasn't going, since he was the one who had chosen them.

Llewellyn glanced over at the table where the senior officers sat. He was well aware of the infighting among the brigade commanders over this issue. Just because three of the four brigade commanders had conservative connections didn't make them incompetent.

The first brigade commander, Malcolm-Smith Mercer, a fifty-four-year-old with a bushy moustache, was an experienced militia commander. From what Llewellyn had seen and heard, he had an aptitude for training and organization. He commanded the three Ontario battalions.

Beside him was the forty-three-year-old Lieutenant-Colonel John Edward Cohoe, the acting commander of the 3rd Brigade. The brigade was composed of the three prairie battalions. Of medium height, he carried weight around his waist, and he wore a walrus-style moustache. In civilian life, he was the local register to the high court.

When Llewellyn turned his gaze to Lieutenant-Colonel Richard Ernest William Turner. He was cleaning his wire-frame glasses with a white handkerchief. The forty-three-year-old with a neatly trimmed moustache had been a wholesale merchant in Quebec City. Llewellyn's eyes fell on the ribbons on Turner's thin chest. The first one, on a red field, was a miniature Victoria Cross that was awarded for his actions saving an artillery battery during the South African War.

The odd man out, moustache-wise, was Lieutenant-Colonel Arthur Currie. He was, along with Hughes, the only ones in the room without facial hair. In civilian life he was a real estate agent and insurance broker in Victoria, B.C. He was tall, and his uniform didn't seem to fit properly on his pear-shaped body. His brigade was mostly comprised of the Western battalions. The other reason was that he was odd man out was that he was a Liberal, which should have automatically disqualified him for command. However, his second-in-command of the 50th Regiment, Gordon Highlander of Canada, was Garnet Hughes, the minister's son.

Llewellyn wondered what other fine officers had been excluded. The one that came immediately to mind was the well respected and experienced Major-General François-Louis Lessard of Quebec. Besides being a Roman Catholic, Lessard and Hughes had several run-ins, which explained why the major-general hadn't been given a command in the contingent.

Llewellyn returned his attention back to William Price, a business-man involved in the pulp and paper industry in Quebec. He had raised two companies for service during the Boer War. He had been elected twice as a Conservative member of parliament, until he suffered a defeat in the 1911 election. It was Price that Hughes had tasked to build the camp's electrical and water supply. And Hughes was now asking him to be the embarkation-general.

He suppressed a chuckle when he wondered if Carl von Clausewitz had the Canadian army in mind when he wrote that war was the continuation of politics by other means.

He refocused on the meeting when Hughes said, "In August, I met in Ottawa with the representatives from the largest British, American, and Canadian shipping companies. I had informed them that we needed suitable ships to transport 25,000 men across the Atlantic by what I hoped would be mid-September. I've been extremely pleased with the progress of the men's training. What yesterday's review has shown is that we have one of the finest bodies of men in the world.

"By the 15th we had contracts for twenty ships. Nine are dedicated to transporting the horses. The imperial government requested additional communications units, so we had to add four more passenger liners." In military parlance, communications were quartermaster and supply personnel. "The ships will be paid based on current admiralty rates. The men will be provided nourishment on board at $1.10 for officers and $0.65 for the men. The vessels will be allowed to carry private cargo, if space permits."

"Will the ships be coming directly to the Quebec City harbour?" Price asked.

Hughes shook his head. "It is my understanding that the ships will first dock at Montreal. There, a Fisheries and Marine officer will inspect them after they have been refitted to make them suitable for military transport. Once they have been passed, they will sail for Quebec City."

Hughes ruffled through several sheets of papers in front of him until he found the one he wanted. He handed it to the colonel. "This is the original plan that was finalized last Thursday."

Several officers in front of Llewellyn shifted papers. Curious, he leaned forward. He couldn't read the small print, but the header columns indicated: Unit, Ship, Number. Number, he assumed, meant the number of men and horses per ship.

"Once they are inspected, each vessel's cargo capacity will be noted, and they will be transmitted to you before they sail. Also, each unit will prepare returns indicating the number of men, horses, and equipment tonnage."

"I see," said Price as he looked up from the list. "Do we have a date for embarkation?"

"Yes," replied Hughes. He stabbed at the table with his finger as he said, "It is absolutely essential that the force sail on September 27th, the 28th at the latest."

Price's Adam's apple bobbed as few times before he replied, "Understood."

"Since we are sending every man and beast here, you will need to use the current capacity as much as possible. If the men have to sleep in hammocks, it will be allowed as long as the men's safety is not endangered. If you need additional ships, you have the authority to obtain them at the current admiralty rates without consulting Ottawa."

Borden gave Hughes a sharp look after that statement.

Price reluctantly nodded. He said, "With this many troops it will be difficult to keep it quiet."

Borden finally spoke. "The governor general and I will be making announcements that we will be sending the entire contingent. I will also state that there will be a delay in sending troops due to the difficulty in obtaining the appropriate ships. It is our hope that this will deceive the Germans."

"Thank you, Prime Minister," said Hughes. He then spoke to Price. "That is why the ships must sail on the 27th. I don't want a reoccurrence of what happened to the PPCLIs," said Hughes.

Llewellyn grunted. The Princess Patricia Canadian Light Infantry was to have sailed on August 28th. The unit created by the wealthy industrialist Gault was composed of ex-British servicemen, and it had been formed in Ottawa. They were ready to board the *Megantic* when orders came down from the admiralty that they were not to sail without an escort. The Patricias had been training for the last month at Levis, Quebec.

He had encountered several of the Patricia's officers in Quebec City when he had taken a day's leave. They blamed Hughes for the delay, believing that he was jealous of them. He didn't want them to get there before the CEF did.

"Understood," replied Price. "Has staff been assigned?"

Hughes glanced at Williams, who frowned and then said, "Visit me tomorrow and I'll see what I can do."

Hughes slapped the table with his hand. "We have a busy schedule today. Lady Borden will present the camp's flag and the Union Jack at ten. Then the prime minister will visit the troops to say a few words before he takes the train to Quebec City at three thirty."

Hughes didn't repeat naming the PPCLI. The prime minister was to meet them later today, as published in the morning orders. As far as he was aware, Hughes had never visited them at Levis.

Actually, Llewellyn had some concern about the Princess Pats. As far as he was concerned, either they were part of the Canadian army or they were not. They shouldn't have been allowed to circumvent the chain of command because their senior officers wanted to.

Llewellyn tossed his concerns in the waste bin as he walked out of the room. He had enough problems getting his men ready for embarkation. His boots seemed to be lighter. He was looking forward to England.

* * *

"So what is your name?" Sir Borden asked.

In his nervousness he nearly blurted out, "McGill!" It would not have gone over well with the entourage that was accompanying the prime minister. It included the prime minister's wife, along with Captain Masterley and Lieutenant-Colonel Marshfield, the regiment's commander. It took a couple of seconds before his blank mind finally engaged. "Paul Ryan, sir!"

"And where are you from?"

"Montreal, sir."

"Montreal!" Borden replied with a politician's smile. "I'm very proud that you have responded to our call. I wish you Godspeed. I'm confident that when you are asked to perform your duty in the face of the foe, you will bring pride to the hearts of your family, Montrealers, and your fellow countrymen."

"Thank you, sir!" replied Paul. Borden shook his hand before he moved on to the next soldier in the line that had been drawn for his and Lady Borden's inspection after the flag presentation. Lady Borden gave him a brief warm smile as she shook his hand, and then she followed her husband.

When Paul considered the prime minister's statement, he would have snorted if it wouldn't have brought down the sergeant-major's wrath upon his head. He didn't think that the duty he had been performing would have brought pride to the hearts of his family or Montrealers.

His family had come up yesterday for the military review. After the parade, he met them at the rendezvous point at the dry canteen near the train station. His fourteen-year-old brother, Cameron, and his eleven-year-old sister, Eloise, were dressed in their Sunday best. They looked upon his uniform with undisguised glee and pride. His father, however, had a resigned look. The first thing that he said was, "You look fit. Army life appears to agree with you."

"It's all right." He looked around for his mother then asked, "Where's Mom and Marie?"

A look of dismay and distress appeared on his father's face. "She didn't come. And I have a letter from Marie for you," he said as he handed him a letter from his vest pocket.

He couldn't disguise his feelings of hurt and disappointment. "I wanted to see her before we embarked," he said flatly.

"Are you embarking?" replied his father in surprise. "I heard that not all of you may go."

Paul acknowledged with a shoulder twitch. "I'm hoping that I get picked." He fingered the letter. He didn't think that it was good news.

Changing the subject, his father said, "Were you in today's drill? I didn't see you."

Paul smoothed his face as he lied, "Everyone looks the same in uniform."

His little brother and sister's knowing smiles told him that they knew what he was actually doing on the parade ground. He was embarrassed to inform his father that his pride and joy was cleaning up after the horses.

Initially, he was not happy standing at the far end of the review stand with a shovel and pail. It didn't take long for him to appreciate the view of the contingent marching past. He watched as Hughes rode his horse at the front of the first units. From time to time, he would have to dart out and clean up a mess. Surprisingly, Hughes' horse was well behaved.

"I see," replied his father. "Do you know when they will be embarking?"

"I don't know, Dad. Rumours are in a week or two."

His father's eyes appeared to be slightly dim when he offered his hand. "Godspeed, son." After Paul took his hand, he continued, "Write to us and your mother. Let us know how you are doing."

"Yes, Dad, I will," he replied. He hugged his teary-eyed sister and shook his brother's hand before he watched them walk away to the waiting train. He cried that night when he finally read Marie's letter, informing him that she found someone else.

The news that everyone was going had spread like wildfire throughout the camp. Everyone in his unit whooped when it finally reached them. Paul dreaded the letter that he would have to write to his parents, telling them he was being shipped to England.

SEPTEMBER 22, 1914
CHÂTEAU FRONTENAC, QUEBEC CITY

"The falls were lovely," said Claire as she sipped her tea. A scone covered with powdered sugar rested on the plate beside her saucer.

"Yes, it was," replied Samantha. She liked her tea black with a thin slice of lemon.

"It's too bad that we have to report back," replied Emily as she sliced a piece of lemon cake with a fork. Her lips rose in delight as she slowly enjoyed the flavour.

"True. Matron Rita did say the hundred nurses would be arriving soon," Samantha stated as she leaned back in her chair. From the letters she was getting from Irene, nurses from the Toronto General Hospital would be included in the group.

She glanced through the window at the Château Frontenac's courtyard. The shadows were beginning to lengthen on the Dufferin Terrace as the sun was starting to set. They were sitting in the coffee room, and they were lucky to find a table since the hotel was booked solid. Scattered around the room were well-heeled American tourists for whom the CPR had built the plush hostelry. The rest were Canadians who had come up to view yesterday's review at Valcartier. Also, at several tables sat officers from the Princess Patricia's, who, from snatches of overheard conversations, were here to attend some kind of meeting.

The matron had given them a day's leave to enjoy the sights of Quebec City. With a sad smile, Samantha thought. Since they didn't know when or if they would be back, they did the typical tourist things. They visited Montmorency Falls, the Plains of Abraham, the Citadel, and finally the Governor's Gardens. As she strolled with Claire and Emily along the Dufferin Terrace toward the seven-storey red brick hotel, passersby gawked at the formal nurses' uniforms they were wearing. Some of the gentlemen even tipped their hats at them.

They had entered the hotel from the ladies' entrance. They were impressed by the large, open vestibule with black and white mosaic tile floor, antique oak furnishings, and rich tapestries that covered the walls when they exited the staircase. They had gone up to the ladies' room on the second floor and were disappointed when the maître d' directed them to the coffee room. The restaurant reserved for the women was booked solid with the out-of-towners. He gave them assurances that they would be accommodated. Samantha would have preferred the ladies' room. From what she had seen, the white-painted room had a light, airy feel rather than the coffee room's more sombre brown walls above the dark oak wainscoting. The view from the second floor of the terrace and the St. Lawrence would have been spectacular, rather than the courtyard and the limited view of the Dufferin Terrace from the angle she was sitting.

"Yes, the hospital will be crowded," remarked Emily. She had enjoyed sharing her room only with one person.

Claire shrugged. "It'll be only a few days until we embark."

Emily grinned. "I think we'll be kept busy on the ship. They ordered 20,000 boxes of sea sickness medicine."

Samantha laughed. "My God, imagine ministering to all those men with heads hanging over the side."

Claire started to cackle. She then put a hand over her mouth to muffle it. She blushed in embarrassment. Emily simply giggled girlishly at the image.

"It must have been quite a sight watching all the men at the review," Claire asked. Her eyes lit up when she bit into her scone.

The corner of Samantha's mouth turned down slightly. "I unfortunately didn't see very much. I spent most of it staring at the person in front of me. When you march past the review stand, you turn your head to the left for a minute or two. After that I concentrated on not tripping over my skirt."

Claire pursed her lips. "Beats cleaning bedpans." Claire and Emily had shift duty at the Immigration Hospital yesterday — one of the reasons the matron had given them a day's leave.

"My Lord!" Emily exclaimed.

Claire turned her head toward her, as did Samantha. "What?"

demanded Claire.

"Isn't that Borden?" Emily raised her hand off the table enough to point to the window. When they turned their heads, they saw an open touring motorcar drive in from Carrière Street and stop in front of the Château Frontenac's main entrance. A man who they presumed to be the hotel manager made a hurried but dignified approach to the vehicle. When the uniformed doorman opened the car's door, he helped the prime minister and Lady Borden out.

Emily squealed, "The prime minister looked at us."

Claire was excited as well. "So did Lady Borden."

"What luck," said Emily as they watched them disappear into the hotel. "Did you see Lady Borden's dress? It was very pretty."

Samantha nodded in agreement, and then her eyes widened when she saw both Sir Robert and Lady Borden walk down the coffee room's corridor. The officers rose to their feet and stood at attention when they saw the prime minister. Seeing what the officers did, Samantha, Claire, and Emily did the same. When the prime minister acknowledged the officers' salute, they returned to their seats. Samantha suddenly got the distinct impression that the couple wanted to meet them.

A smile appeared on Borden's face when he acknowledged their crisp salutes. "Please sit, ladies," he said, waving them down. "When Lady Borden and I saw you three ladies through the window, we just had to meet you."

Stunned looks appeared on all three faces. "T—thank you, Prime Minister," stammered Samantha. Claire and Emily simply nodded.

"I just wanted to thank you for volunteering. I really do hope that your services will be required for a very short period."

"Yes, Prime Minister."

"Are you the only nurses here at the moment?"

"Yes, Prime Minister. But we are expecting another hundred nurses in a few days."

Lady Borden spoke. "The prime minister has a special interest, you see. Our dear cousin Jessie Jaggard is quite keen on volunteering."

"She is a nurse?" asked Samantha.

"Oh yes," she replied. "She was a superintendent of nurses at a hospital in Philadelphia until she married. Her husband is a president of an American railway."

"We would be quite honoured for her to join," replied Samantha.

"Quite," replied Borden. "I'm sure that you will bring great pride to the hearts of your family, city, and the country."

The khaki-clad officer standing behind the prime minister whispered in his ear. Samantha watched as Borden put on his politician's face. "I'm afraid that duty calls. It was a pleasure meeting you," he said as he and his wife were led away.

Samantha, Claire, and Emily watched in stunned awe as the couple disappeared down the oak-panelled corridor.

CHAPTER 14

"Oh my God!" exclaimed Emily when she saw the second-class stateroom they had been assigned.

"This is beautiful," marvelled Claire as she examined the luscious space. The cabin that normally accommodated two passengers had been reconfigured with four bunk beds. A dark wooden mirror and a white porcelain washbasin were set between them.

Samantha, who was right behind her, and Emily were impressed by the Cunard passenger liner *Franconia*. And this was second class! She was really eager to see first class.

From the moment the nursing sisters had marched in, they were nearly struck dumb by the vessel's opulence: the oval glass-domed main entrance with its white-painted panels, intricate moulding, fluted Grecian columns, and the mahogany staircase with its wrought iron railings.

Samantha had been nervous in the morning when she was getting ready to leave the Immigration Hospital. One of the reasons was meeting Matron Macdonald again, the senior commanding officer of the Canadian nursing sisters. Samantha nearly died when she had stopped in front of her. She was worried that she somehow messed up her uniform, but the matron's blue eyes were smiling as she gave her an approving nod. From the corner of her eye, she had followed her as she inspected the rest of the nurses in her line.

Matron Macdonald was a legend among the nursing sisters and the community at large. Samantha knew that the matron was born in Baily Brook, Nova Scotia. She had graduated from the New York City General Hospital. She seemed to like military nursing. She did eighteen months in Panama when the US army was completing the canal, served at Camp Wikoff in New York State during the Spanish-American War, and ministered to the wounded in the South African War.

Samantha had been so deep in thought that she only caught the tail end of the command to board the buses. When she had clambered aboard and found her seat, she asked Emily, "I didn't get all of her speech. Did I miss something important?"

Emily gave her a quizzical look and replied, "Nothing important. Just pride and all that."

From the way Emily had said it, Samantha suspected that she hadn't heard it either in her nervous excitement.

It didn't take long for them to arrive at the dock where the ship was being loaded. The bus carrying the nurses stopped at the gangplank while the other vehicles continued to the nearby warehouse and cargo areas for unloading. When she got off the bus, she had taken her place in the column. Matron Macdonald asked for a head count to make sure that they didn't lose anyone along the way.

When Samantha gazed upon the ship, it looked rather new to her. It was. The 18,000 gross ton ship had been launched four years earlier. It was the pride of the Cunard line and it had been designed for the Liverpool to New York run. It had two black funnels in the centre, and there were two masts, one in the bow and one in the stern. She had a rather elegant look, even with the fresh grey paint.

A couple of longshoremen, with their backs toward the women, were cursing as they tried to manhandle an ambulance wagon. The frame that held the canvas roof refused to budge. When the foreman spotted the nurses, he shouted in French, "Watch your language. There's ladies present."

When the men turned their heads toward the ladies, they simply shrugged then returned to cursing at the wagon.

Matron Macdonald glared at them and then gave the order for the nurses to march toward the entrance in formation. On the railings, soldiers appeared and then started cheering. The cheering energized the nurses. Their arms seemed to swing a touch sharper. So did the echoes of their black boots as they hit the gangplank.

The feeling dissipated once they entered the ship, broke formation, and made their way to their rooms.

Emily giggled as she tested the bed. "This is quite comfy."

Samantha replied sternly waving her forefinger at her. "Don't get any ideas!"

"What ideas?" Emily said with a wicked grin. The *Franconia* could carry 2,850 passengers: 300 in first class, 350 fifty in second, and 2,200 in third. That meant that there were nearly 270 men for each woman aboard the ship.

"Did you see the guards at the ends of the corridor?" said Claire.

"Tisk tosk," replied Emily humorously. "They are not going to be a problem."

Samantha sighed. It was going to be a long voyage.

SEPTEMBER 25, 1914
DOCKS, QUEBEC CITY

"Isn't she a fucking beautiful sight?" Reggie said with a tired excitement as the ship came into view. The last few days had drained much of his enthusiasm.

Paul lifted his head from watching his feet and tried to focus on the gangplank that thrust from the hull of the large grey vessel with the name *Lapland* painted in white on her bow. The Red Star Liner, based out of Antwerp, was nearly 600 feet long and was nearly seventy feet at the widest point. In the centre there were two black funnels that in the dark blended easily with the night sky. She had a gross tonnage of nearly 18,000 tons and a 1,500-passenger capacity: 350 in first class, 450 in second, and the rest in third class. Paul so tired that he really didn't care which class he was assigned to as long as he got a bed.

The four masts were being used as king posts for the loading of cargo. It took a few moments for him to understand how an 18-pounder gun could be flying through the air until he realized it was wrapped in a black net that only became visible when it passed through the glare of Shed 19's electric lights.

When his eyes traced the path back to the dock, he saw the rest of his unit's guns waiting patiently for their turn. Beside the guns there were a mountain of various crates, boxes, sacks, and trucks waiting to be hoisted into one of the ship's four cargo holds. Farther down, he saw the heavy draught horses waiting to be loaded.

"They should have taken the wheels off the guns," remarked Paul.

Reggie glanced at the gun. "You're right. It would make it easier to store more supplies." He turned his attention back to the guns that were waiting on the platform.

"It looks like the rollover didn't do any damage."

"Tell that to the guy with the broken arm and legs," replied Paul. He was there when the horses and guns took the corner a bit too quick, and it had rolled over onto its side. The horses screaming in fear and panic was something he really didn't want to hear again. But his training kicked in and he was able to cut the animals free. However, the lead rider got thrown and had his right arm broken. Another man got crushed when the 1.2-ton steel wagon rolled over him. It took a combination of a couple of horses and his squad to push the gun back on its wheels. By then the body snatchers had arrived. They took the wounded and the dead artilleryman away.

Paul didn't even have the energy to shake his head. He was tired, hungry, and thirsty. What should have been a simple march from Valcartier to the Port of Quebec City was rather farcical, if it wasn't so sad.

The litany of things that went wrong was astonishing. It started with leaving Valcartier Camp at noon rather than 6:00 a.m., as they were scheduled. So they arrived at the city in the dark. They had difficulty finding the industrial park where they were assigned to stay before embarking. Because they arrived late, they weren't fed. In the morning, they were directed to the *Bermudian*. However, the ship didn't have the capacity to accommodate them, so they had to get off it and wait for a new one to dock. They didn't have breakfast or lunch, since they expected to be fed onboard ship. Since Paul's section was among the last to enter, he hoped that they had some food left for him.

Finally, the gangplank trembled under his section's boots. When Paul entered the ship, he could tell that it was relatively new. It had been launched in 1909. One of the *Lapland*'s claims to fame was that she had carried some of the stricken passengers of the ill-fated *Titanic* back to London.

They were led into the vessel's bowels to the third-class dining room. The plain white enamelled room with a dark-tiled floor was so large that it needed pillars strategically placed to support the deck above. It had the capacity of feeding 1,100 passengers in two seatings. The tables and chairs were bolted to the ship's deck to prevent them from moving when she rolled in stormy seas.

Paul frowned when he saw the sign that stated that evening meals were served at six and at seven. He hoped that they would make an exception in their case. His frown turned into a grimace when he saw how filthy the floor was.

"What's that smell?" he asked Reggie. He had been expecting food cooking. It smelled rather like the camp he had just left. He would learn later that due to the haste with she was contracted, the third-class quarters were never fumigated after they had shipped nearly a thousand immigrants to New York.

"I really don't want to know," replied Reggie with a frown that matched Paul's.

They heard a dull thud behind them. When they turned toward the sound, they saw Lance Corporal Hastings with a couple of buckets of soapy water and two mops. Paul really hated the grin on the man's face when he handed him one of them.

SEPTEMBER 27, 1914
DOCKS, QUEBEC CITY

Captain Llewellyn ordered the 4th Battalion to a halt when he saw the unit in front of him stop. All four battalions, a thousand men in uniform, carrying their kit but no rifles, had marched from Valcartier to Quebec City. From his vantage point he could see a part of the harbour and a ship that was tied to the dock. He hoped that it was the vessel on which they were to embark for their voyage to England. He called up Private Duval, who was his runner today. "Run on up and get a report on why we have stopped."

He turned to Lieutenant Vernon. "Order the men to fall out. But they are not to take their gear off. We could be marching and embarking in a few minutes." When he saw the crowd of civilians looking on, he ordered, "Tell the men no smoking. We still want to look sharp."

"Yes, Captain," said the lieutenant, giving Llewellyn a snappy salute. Llewellyn was pleased with Vernon. He was shaping up nicely.

When a puffing Duval returned, he said, "The colonel requested your presence."

"Acknowledged," said the captain as he dismissed him.

When Llewellyn arrived at the front of the column he found the other three battalion captains, Joseph Percival of the 1st, Fred Lamb of the 2nd, and Gavin Lime of the 3rd, already there. This was no surprise, since the colonel had specifically ordered the 4th Battalion to be in the rear to eat the dust of the first three. As a general rule, the battalions would rotate in sequence during a route march. It allowed all of the men to get relief from the sand that was kicked up by the men in front. In wet and soggy conditions, the lead battalion would have it tough as they sloughed through the mud. It gave them a bit of rest by moving them to the back.

He arrived just in time to overhear the colonel say, "We have orders to embark on the *Lapland*."

The major with a clipboard shook his head. "I'm sorry, Colonel, but according to my schedule you and your men were to arrive and embark at nine o'clock this evening. You're ten hours ahead of schedule."

"Why can't we board the ship? It's right there," the colonel argued with a pointed finger. Llewellyn knew that the colonel was not about to tell the major that he had arranged for reporters from his hometown to take photos of him leading his men on horseback to the harbour. Nine at night wouldn't do.

"Colonel," said the major with a slight aggravated tone, "we have a very delicate situation. That is not your ship." He used his thumb to point to the boat behind him. "The *Lapland* is designated for the 2nd Battalion's HQ. They are boarding as we speak. Also, we are loading cargo and supplies. Your unit arriving ten hours early has thrown a spanner in the works. We are still waiting for the 7th Battalion to arrive to complete the loading. We can't because your men are in the bloody way," snapped the major.

Captain Llewellyn admired the major's gall to address the colonel in that fashion. As the designated embarkation and control officer, he was in charge. Also, since he was in a different chain of command, there was very little that the colonel could do.

The colonel, his face turning red, gestured at the ship again. "So what do you want me to do! We are here now!"

So engrossed was everyone in the conversation they didn't realize a second officer had arrived. The lieutenant-colonel, with medical service insignia on his cap badge, was tapping his swagger stick impatiently against his right leg. "The 2nd General Hospital reporting for embarkation."

"Ah yes, Colonel. I'm glad that you're on time. If you will take your unit to Shed 19, the officer will see that your people are taken care of."

"Thank you," said the medical officer as he returned the major's salute. He gave the Fusiliers a half-gloating smile before he turned on his heels and headed toward his people.

"Major! What about my men?" demanded Topham.

The major's face hardened. "There is a holding area a few blocks away. You can park your men there until they are ready to embark. It's about half-hour or so march from here."

Captain Lamb from the 2nd Battalion spoke up. "Will there be food and water for the men?"

The major raised the tip of his cap as to stare at Lamb. "Instructions were issued that all men should have been fed before they were marched today. They were to be issued a day's rations."

Colonel Topham turned and glared at Lamb and then eyed Captain Percial, "Your men don't have food and water either?"

He shook his head. "We never received any orders or instructions, sir. We were only informed that we were to get the men ready for embarkation."

"Do any of your men have food and water?" Topham demanded. All three captains shook their heads.

Llewellyn sighed. "My men do."

The colonel glared at Llewellyn. Another blot that the colonel would place in his copybook. "Why do your men have food and water?"

Llewellyn shrugged. "Crap happens."

* * *

"Crap," said Lieutenant-Colonel Price as he stared in disgust at the corkboard on the wall. Pinned to it, with brass tacks, were six sheets of eight by fourteen accounting paper that had been glued together; two sheets down and three across. On the far left, near the window that overlooked the docks, was the "units" column that listed in black ink all the units to be embarked. The next column, labelled "strengths," provided the number of men and horses for each unit. The rest of the columns, in red, displayed the names of the thirty-three ships of the embarkation fleet. Printed in blue crayon above some of them was the word "complete," indicating that the vessel had been fully loaded with its cargo, fuelled, watered, and provisioned. They were ready to sail once they received their sealed orders.

With a finger, he found the square that intersected the SS *Lapland* column and the 2nd Brigade HQ row. His pencil ticked it to indicate that the unit had been boarded.

Price watched through the window as a steam crane loaded the ship moored at the quay. A phone ringing caused him to turn toward to his staff sitting in the office that he had requisitioned at the Quebec City docks to manage the embarkation. On the table in front of him were neatly stacked telegrams; the green ones were CPR's, while the yellow ones belonged to the Great North Western Company. A couple of black telephones were arranged at the far wall, where Staff Sergeant Middleton just replaced a receiver on a hook. He didn't look happy.

He glanced at the four Boy Scouts that were sitting on a wooden bench. One of the boys yawned while the two others were trying hard to keep their eyes open. He had been using the local scout troop as runners and messengers. He was glad to have them, since the moment he took over the docks he had all telephone and telegram lines, except those in this office, cut. As well, the 12th Battalion, who had been placed in charge of the docks, ensured that only authorized personnel were allowed in or out until the embarkation was completed.

"Has the loading of the *Lapland* been completed?" he asked the officers sitting at a long table. They looked just as tired and haggard as the Boy Scouts. Which was not surprising, since they'd been working around the clock, snatching a few hours sleep whenever they could. They were running out of time, since all of the ships needed to sail by tomorrow.

Mr. Gorrie, who was assigned to look after the loading of the Red Star liner SS *Lapland*, said, "She arrived in port on September 17th. We didn't start loading her until the 23rd, the day after you took command. We managed to put on her two 60-pounders, forty-one 18s, nine 13-pounders, twenty-three horses, sixty-one rifles cases, 600 boxes of S.A.A. ammunition, and 450 Red Cross packages. She already had 13,000 sacks of flour when she sailed from Montreal."

"And the number of men she can carry?" Price asked.

"She has a 2,000-passenger capacity. Headquarters staff was originally assigned to her, but when they decided that they wanted be the last to leave we had to find another unit to fill her cabins. The 65th Artillery boarded her late Friday night. I think she still has room. She has 450 in first, 400 in second, and 1,500 in third."

Price turned to Colonel Layton, who was sitting to his left and was responsible for arranging troop movements from Valcartier. "What do you have to fill the *Lapland*? I want to clear space for the next ship."

Layton frowned and then sighed. "I think I can get most of the 2nd Infantry Brigade aboard. I might even get their headquarters and the 5th and 6th Battalions on her. I won't know for sure until they give me an accurate head count. I could have spare cabins, or I might have to crowd some men in. Also, it means I have to shift the hospital and the machine gun units, since they were assigned to the *Lapland* as well."

"More crap."

"I know," replied Layton. "I have to find slots for the 2nd Brigade's 7th and 8th Battalions and the transport units."

All that Price could do was nod. "See what you can do."

"It would have been helpful if the commanders of the 1st and 2nd Artillery hadn't handled the embarkation in such an incompetent manner," stated Gorrie in exasperation.

"I agree," replied Layton with same irritation. It was his job to coordinate with Valcartier. The plan had been that Colonel Gordon-Hall was to send a telegram to the embarkation office informing them of the unit, the numbers of men and horses, the quantity of equipment that was accompanying them, their mode of transport, their departure time, and their estimated arrival time.

"I still can't believe that some of them proceeded without direct orders," groused Gorrie. "They were not the only ones. I just received word from the embarkation officer that the Richmond Fusiliers have arrived at the docks ten hours early," said Layton.

"It wouldn't have been that bad if the artillery and the damn Fusiliers had gone to the rendezvous point," continued Gorrie as he began to work himself up again. The exhibition grounds had been designated as the rendezvous point for the arriving troops. Contracts had been arranged to supply provisions so that the men and horses could be fed and watered. "That's why we fell behind schedule. They created traffic congestion at the docks. Not only did we have to figure out how to get them out of the way, we then had to try get the scheduled units aboard onto their transports before the ship was supposed to sail. And," he stabbed at the table with his finger, "the way the artillery loaded their guns was an absolute disgrace. If the wheels had been removed, we could have packed more ammunition onto her. Now I have to find another ship that can handle the excess cargo."

Staff Sergeant Middleton interjected, "I hate to add more water to the torrent."

"Now what?" demanded Price. He was immediately sorry he had snapped at the sergeant. He was glad to have the man, since he was the only staff clerk he could get his hands on. He had to get him from Toronto, since he couldn't pry any people from Valcartier. Seven additional officers were to report later today, but he wondered how useful they would be.

"I just got a call that some of the motorized trucks of the supply column and the ammunition park are too large for the hatches."

"All of them?" asked Captain Murray, the harbour master, as he rubbed his chin. Middleton nodded. Murray's job was to regulate the arrival, departure, and inspections of the transports. "Maybe the *Manhattan*'s hatches are big enough," the captain said. The ship was a small one, with only an 8,000-ton capacity. It was a freighter, so her holds were designed to carry a wide variety of cargo.

"If she isn't already filled," stated Gorrie. Many of the ships already had cargo in the hulls. In some cases, they had to be removed to make space for the assigned military supplies.

"Right!" said Colonel Price. He ran a hand through his sparse hair. "Is there any good news?"

"Actually, there is some," stated Major Dixon, who was sitting beside Lieutenant-Colonel Layton. The major was in charge of collecting the statistics as to the number of men, guns, and wagons that were loaded onto the ships. "The *Leonard* has been a godsend. That mechanical deck of hers has allowed us to load most of the herd onto the horse boats without any problems." Price finally cracked a smile. The *Leonard* was an icebreaker that was intended for service on the Quebec City–Levis run. Designed to carry passenger and freight trains, her tidal deck could be raised and lowered by twenty feet to compensate for the local tides. This allowed the horses to be walked onto the transport vessels. Otherwise, he would have had to train them to Montreal for loading.

"As well, the *Alaunia* completed her loading with 1,500 tons of drinking water. Nearly 2,000 tons of coal are in her bunkers, which should give her nearly fifteen days of steam at full power. We provisioned for twenty-one days. We loaded her with 40,000 rounds ammunition, 2,000 tons of cheese and grain, fifty tons of wood, nineteen horses, forty cars, and forty tons of regimental baggage." With a grin, he added, "We even managed to find room for fourteen bicycles."

"Ah, so the bikes might explain why she was listing to the port side then," quipped Layton, which caused the men at the table to chuckle.

"When will she be ready to sail?" asked Price with a sigh of relief.

"Actually, she should be leaving the dock as we speak."

"That is good news!" replied Price. He found a blue crayon on the table, rose, and went to the corkboard. Above the *Alaunia* he printed "complete."

CHAPTER 15

OCTOBER 03, 1914
GASPÉ HARBOUR, QUEBEC

As Llewellyn was watching the *Canada* steam for her anchorage in the Gaspé Basin, he wondered how Rawlings was enjoying Bermuda. The White Star-Dominion passenger liner was the vessel that had transported the RCR, the Halifax based unit, to the Caribbean island. On board her now were the men of the 2nd Battalion of the Lincolnshire Regiment that the RCR had replaced. He smiled when he first viewed the boat's familiar profile, a single funnel amidships and the two masts fore and aft. He had sailed on her to South Africa during the Boer War. Whether the Lincolnshires were anxious to get into the fight or pissed that they had to leave the sun and the beach, he couldn't say. It was probably a mixture of both.

The Basin was teeming with vessels of various types. There were motorized launches, tugboats, and single-, two- and triple-masted sailing fishing boats that manoeuvred among the thirty-one ships of the embarkation fleet. There were also four cruisers the Royal Navy had sent as an escort. They had positioned themselves to keep a protective eye on the convoy.

The *Canada* dropped her anchor in the second column of the three-column flotilla, between the *Monmouth* and the *Franconia*, which was directly across from the *Alaunia*'s deck that he was standing on. All of the ships were arranged about two cables apart. According to what a steward explained to him, a cable was the naval measure for 600 feet. This gave the vessels ample room without putting their neighbours in danger. It also allowed the small supply boats to easily manoeuvre as they delivered mail, and reading material as well as fresh provisions for those who left Quebec City without an adequate food supply for the voyage.

It had taken the *Alaunia* nearly a day and half to sail the 377 miles to the historic Gaspé Harbour, where Jacque Cartier had landed when he explored Canada. The port used to be an important destination for international cod fishery ships. A number of consulates used to have their offices here until Halifax and Montreal grew in importance. Fishing and lumbering were now the main local industries.

"Captain Llewellyn," said a voice behind him. When he turned his head, he saw Lieutenant Vernon approaching with one of the ship's officers in tow. The officer was dressed in a dark blue uniform with gold braid on the sleeves. Llewellyn turned away when he heard and felt the vibrations of boots pounding on the wooden deck. A platoon was in the midst of their morning exercise. One of the first things he had insisted on was that the daily camp routine be maintained. Nothing destroyed a unit more than idleness. It was a good thing that he had. From reasons that were never explained, the *Alaunia* had remained parked in the St. Lawrence directly across from the Château Frontenac for two days. They could see the evening strollers on the terraces. What made it worse was the colonel's decision to leave the ship on a daily basis to have supper at the hotel. If he hadn't kept the men busy, he would have had a mutiny on his hands.

The daily routine started with reveille at six, followed by breakfast, then sick parade, morning parade, a couple of hours of drill and exercise, a break for lunch, then in the afternoon more drill, exercise, lectures, supper, fatigue duty, and more lectures. Lights out was at 10:15.

"Yes, Lieutenant," he said as he followed the platoon jogging toward the bow. A five-mile run was eighteen circuits of the deck.

"We have to do a recount," said the lieutenant. There was a hint of frustration in the young officer's voice.

"Why?"

"We have a discrepancy in the number of men on the nominal rolls, as compared with the actual number of men that we have on board."

Shit, thought Llewellyn. *Not again.* Llewellyn kept it out of his voice when he said, "Really?"

"I'm afraid so, Captain," said the ship's officer. Llewellyn had been introduced to him, but the man's name just wouldn't come to his tongue. He looked like he was in his late thirties or early forties, with a greying beard and hair. "I need an accurate count for the lifeboat assignments. I want to make sure that each man has a life belt and the appropriate number of men are assigned to each boat."

Llewellyn understood the reason for the officer's demand. The frustration was the Fusiliers' counts were never correct. They always seemed to be off by a hundred men. The problem was Llewellyn was frequently given the task to correlate the figures. No matter how much he tried, he could never seem to get the other captains to give him an accurate count. "When do you need the information by?" he asked.

"I would like it by this afternoon so we can begin making the arrangements. I would like to start on the fire and muster drills as soon as possible."

"I'm meeting with the colonel shortly, and I'll get you some numbers by one o'clock," he replied. He hoped that they would be right this time.

"Thank you, sir," replied the officer.

Cheering from the bow caught their attention. When they looked to identify the cause, they saw the men were looking at a launch that was making its way toward the white clapboard houses that lined the wharf. The fleet was using the white church's steeple as an alignment marker. In the boat, a man standing upright near the tiller pointed at his ship and then started waving with his cap when it turned directly toward them.

"Oh dear God! It's Hughes!" exclaimed Vernon.

"Yes, it is," said Llewellyn. There he was, Sam Hughes, indeed larger than life.

"I was hoping that we had left him behind," stated the lieutenant. He examined Hughes then said, "He doesn't look happy."

"What irritated him this time?" asked Llewellyn.

The ship's officer spoke. "He's not pleased with the escort that the Royal Navy provided."

"I saw that we only have four warships. I wondered if that was enough to protect a fleet this large," said the lieutenant.

"Actually, it is. Problem is explaining it to a landlubber." He indicated Hughes with a thrust of his beard. "Essentially, what the navy is doing is ensuring that the German fleet does not get out of the North Sea. So the home fleet has been deployed to find and discourage German vessels from sailing into the North Atlantic. There are some German ships in the American harbours that can act as raiders. That is why we have four protected cruisers."

"What's a protected cruiser?" interrupted Vernon.

"When these ships were built fifteen years ago, armoured plating on the hull was impractical. The ship would be too heavy for the engines to drive her at a reasonable speed. They compromised by building a protective deck to guard the ship's essential machinery. They are second-class ships mainly used for trade protection. The *Eclipse*, the *Diana*, and the *Talbot* are *Eclipse* class while the flagship the *Charybdis* is an *Astraea* class cruiser. The *Diana* and the *Talbot*'s armaments were upgraded a few years ago. They currently carry eleven 6-inch guns, seven 3-inch and nine 12-pounders, and three 18-inch torpedo tubes. The *Eclipse* for some reason was not upgraded, so it still has its original five 6-inch and six 4.7-inch guns, six 3-pounders, and the same number of tubes. The *Charybdis* is a bit smaller, so it has two 6-inch and six 4.7-inch guns, ten 6-pounders, and four tubes for her torpedoes."

"How fast can they go?" asked the Llewellyn as he watched the crew of Hughes' launch hand bundles of mail and newspapers to one of the *Alaunia*'s crewman. He spotted Sergeant Booth eagerly grabbing one of the bundles. The men would need something to read during the next two weeks as they crossed the Atlantic. The ship had a library, but the men would probably go through it in a couple of days.

"They can do about eighteen to nineteen knots at full power. However, the convoy will be probably travel at about nine to ten knots. We can only go only as fast as the slowest ship.

"So when we go, we'll be sailing in three columns. The X column will be led by the *Charybdis*," he stated, indicating the column two over. "*The Scotian, Arcadian, Zeeland, Corinthian, Virginian, Andania, Saxonia, Grampian, Lakonia, Montreal,* and the *Royal George* have been assigned to her. The Y column with the *Caribbean, Athenia, Royal Edward, Franconia, Canada, Monmouth, Manitou, Tyrolia, Tunisian,* and the *Laurentic* will be guarded by the *Eclipse*. Our column, Z, will have the *Megantic, Ruthenia, Bermudian, Alaunia, Ivernia, Scandinavian, Sicilian, Montezuma, Lapland,* and the *Cassandra*. The *Eclipse* has been assigned to take care of us. The *Talbot* is assigned as a rear guard and to take care of stragglers."

"So when we do actually set sail?" asked Llewellyn. He was watching Sergeant Booth walking toward them with a bundle of papers in his hands.

The sailor shrugged. "We're still waiting for the *Manhattan*. If she doesn't arrive soon, I think that we'll sail without her. Or we could be waiting for more warships to arrive. You'll know as soon as we raise our anchor and the *Alaunia*'s engines start humming. Blackout regulations will then be in effect, and we will not be allowed to use our wireless."

When he saw the look of disgust appear on Booth's face, he felt compelled to ask, "Bad news?"

Booth raised his eyes from the broadsheet he was reading and shook his head in despair as he handed each of them a copy. The naval officer widen in surprise when he read the title. He gave Booth a glance of understanding. When Llewellyn scanned the newsprint he was given, he finally understood. The minister of Militia and Defence had felt compelled to share with the men his latest speech.

OCTOBER 04, 1914
READING ROOM, HOTEL CECIL'S, LONDON

Lieutenant-Colonel Carson was sitting with Lieutenant Spittal in the Hotel Cecil's reading room at one of the card tables in the corner. He scanned the ornately decorated room to ensure that no one was near enough to hear his conversation with his subordinate.

There were about ten or so other people in the room. Several were seated on the plush chairs reading newspapers for the latest war news, a couple of others were writing letters using the hotel's stationary, one person was struggling with a telegram since he kept erasing the message he was writing with the eraser on his pencil, and a middle-aged, well-dressed woman was playing solitaire at the table across the room.

He doubted that there would be German spies at the luxury hotel located in the Strand. The 800 rooms were booked solid with stranded Canadian and American tourists who were trying to book passage back home. Cecil's was a comfortable place to be left high and dry, since the restaurant was well known for its exquisite cuisine. From the large windows, one could look on the Victoria Gardens, and the view of Westminster was spectacular. If the restaurant wasn't your taste, there was the Grill Room below. In the evenings, dancing was available in the Palm Court. Not that the fifty-year-old, slightly over six-foot-tall, iron-grey-haired Carson was doing very much of that these days.

"I've read your report on Salisbury Plain," said the former commander of the 1st Regiment of the Canadian Grenadier Guards. When he had been offered the command of the Guards in 1911, he had insisted that he be given a free hand in selecting its officers, that it become a regiment of the Foot Guards, and a new armoury be built. He had wanted to lead his unit he had rebuilt into battle. At least he had the satisfaction that he had accomplished that before he sailed to England with a small advance party. They were to liaison with the War Office and to prepare the ground, so to speak, for the arrival of the contingent.

"The turf at Salisbury Plain looks good," Lieutenant Spittal said. "I think that our boys will like it better than the sandy plains they are currently accustomed to."

Carson examined the officer that the Militia Department had assigned to him. At age forty, he still looked very fit, which was not surprising since Charles Douglas "Baldy" Spittal had been a professional ice hockey player in his younger years. Spittal had played in the 1903 Ottawa Silver Seven Stanley Cup game and professionally for the Pittsburgh Victorias and the Canadian Soo of the International Hockey League. He had been well known as an aggressive player and had been arrested twice for on-ice incidents. The lieutenant was also was a competitive cyclist, lacrosse player, and shooter. Spittal had been on several Canadian teams to the annual Bigsby shooting competition in England. He missed winning one year by a few points.

"After your visit to the camps, do you think that they'll be ready for our arrival?"

Spittal shook his head. "Not after I met with Colonel Johnston, the QMC for General Althuac. He had made arrangements for 25,000 men. He doesn't know how he'll provide for the additional men that the government has decided to send."

"That explains their request that we send waterproof tents with the contingent."

"Equipment here is in short supply. Especially since they are recruiting for Kitchener's new army." Kitchener's call for volunteers had resulted in 750,000 volunteers. "Waterproof tents would be useful. Currently, the plans are for the contingent to land at Southampton. Trains will bring them to the Lavington, Patney, and Amesbury train stations. From there the unit will be assigned to four different camps; the Bustard, the West Down North and South, and the Pond Farm."

Spittal noticed Carson's frown under his moustache when he mentioned Southampton. "Problem?"

"I'm afraid so," replied Carson. "It may not be Southampton."

"Why not?"

"There've been reports of German submarines in the approaches to England. It also didn't help that Ottawa telegrammed the details of the contingent to the War Office in the clear," Carson replied sourly. "Winston Churchill is the one who's going to make the final decision on which port we will disembark at. I have a meeting with him at the admiralty."

"What's the alternate port?" asked Spittal.

"It looks like Plymouth. I suspect they won't announce it until the last minute, for security reasons."

Spittal looked up at the pastoral scenes that were painted on the panels above their heads. "From the Salisbury Plain end, it shouldn't have much of an impact. Getting the men to the train stations will be the logistical problem the War Office will need to solve.

"Once the men get there, they have to march to their assigned camps. The Bustard is nearly seven miles from Amesbury stations, while Lavington is six miles from West Down. The Pond Farm camp is five. Colonel Johnston has informed me that he was assigning 5,500 to Bustard, 10,000 to the West Down North and South, and 7,500 to Pond Farm. In my report, I indicated the units that will be assigned to each one."

"I saw the sketches you included in the report," remarked Carson. "What about the accommodations and the messes?"

"Unfortunately, the men will be under canvas, but all of them will have floors. They are considering huts in the future. Currently, the only ones they are building are for the canteens. They will be dry, by the way."

Carson grunted in agreement. "I'm going to come down and take a look for myself."

Spittal informed him, "If you go, I would recommend a car. A horse would not be much use."

Carson nodded. One of the amenities that Cecil's offered was car rentals. "Okay, let's get a bite to eat before we call it a day," said Carson as he rose to his feet. Spittal followed Carson as they exited the room.

OCTOBER 10, 1914
SS *LAPLAND*, MID-NORTH ATLANTIC OCEAN

Paul grunted as he pushed the bale of hay off the cart onto the ship's deck. It landed with a dull thud. He pulled out a pocketknife, flicked it open, and sliced the twine that was holding it together. The nearby horses neighed and stamped their feet in anticipation. As he picked up a pitchfork, he said to Reggie, who was pushing the cart, "I thought I was done with this when we left camp."

Reggie chuckled as he picked up a pitchfork as well. "What, and miss all this fun?" he replied as he tossed some hay into a galvanized steel feeding trough that was hanging on the front of the stall. The 600 horses onboard were located onto two decks just below the main one. The metal-framed stalls had been installed for the steeds, half on the port side and half on the starboard side to ensure that the vessel remained balanced. Most of the men were bunked on the decks below.

"Yeah right! Hay, water, lunch, hay, water, supper," Paul muttered.

"We can always mix it up with water, hay, water, hay," teased Reggie.

The routine was very simple. After they had breakfast in the morning, they came up to the cargo hold and got the forage for the beasts. The regulations required that each mount at sea be fed five pounds of oats, three pounds of bran, two pounds of corn, and twelve pounds of hay. Normally, watering and feeding was started at 5:30 a.m. It was the usual practice to give the horses the hay about two hours later. This allowed the horses to fully digest their breakfast. If the hay were given too soon, their small stomachs would force out the corn undigested. At noon and six they were given water and fed, while hay was given at two and at eight.

After Paul tossed the hay into the feeding trough, he pushed down two metal rods to keep the animal from throwing the hay out. The amused laugher of Corporal Hastings caught his attention. The corporal had a carrot in his hand and was teasing one of the horses with it. They gave them carrots as a treat. Paul frowned in annoyance. He didn't know much about horses, but he knew that the animals liked to be approached from behind. The steel eight by six feet stalls were built so that they were facing toward the middle of the ship. Paul and the rest of the grooms were trying to be careful so that the steeds didn't get into the bad habit of biting and nipping.

"Corporal! What the hell are you doing?" said a voice behind Paul.

Lieutenant Fuller was standing in the corridor with an open hatch behind him. All the hatches were kept open during the day to aid in air circulation and temperature control. With 600 horses in a confined steel hull, it was quite easy for the temperature to rise and for the animals to overheat.

"Just feeding the horses, Lieutenant," said the corporal as he allowed the horse to snatch the carrot from his hand.

The lieutenant's eyes narrowed. "Go get a sling. We'll need to have a horse moved to the promenade deck," he ordered brusquely.

"I'll get one of the men …"

The lieutenant interjected, "I prefer you to do it, since I want it be done right."

"Of course, Lieutenant," said the corporal. He gave Paul a smirk as he rushed past him.

The officer gave Paul a warm smile. "Private, can you help me move the horse?"

"Of course, Lieutenant," replied Paul. "Right now, sir? I was about to muck out the stalls."

"I'll take care of it," said Reggie as he lifted the board attached by bolts to the front of the stall and led the horse to the empty one beside it. Empty stalls had been strategically placed on the deck to allow them to temporarily move the animals out while the men cleaned them. The dung was tossed in a wheel barrel, which was then dumped over the side.

"I owe you," said Paul.

"I know," replied Reggie. Paul turned to follow the veterinarian as he strolled down the coconut mats that had been set on the deck. All the stalls and horse decks were covered with them to prevent the horses from slipping and falling. If their feet slipped, they would struggle trying to stand, which could lead to serious injuries.

The lieutenant led him to a heavy brown-black draught. Her head was drooping and her breathing was laboured.

"We need to move her to the promenade deck," said Fuller. "Get a halter. I want to lead her to the hatch so we can lift her out."

"We can always set up a double stall," suggested Paul. The stalls were built so that one of the walls could be removed, which would allow the horse to rest on her side.

"I'm afraid not. I believe that she has a pulmonary decease. I don't want it to spread to the others. They are prone to communicable diseases in a confined space. That's why we have designated the promenade deck as the sick ward for them."

"Yes, sir," Paul said as he retrieved a halter from a hook a few stalls over. When he picked it up, he noticed that the horse in the stall was bleeding from a cut on her shoulder. "Sir. This horse is bleeding."

The lieutenant came over and gave it a glance. "Nothing serious. I've got a number of them with cuts from rubbing against a sharp edge. We have to watch their tails, since they get damaged as well. After we take care of our patient, I'll come back and clean it up," he said with a tired sigh. He was the only vet on board, and his services were in constant demand. He gave Paul a speculative look. "Do you want to learn horse first-aid?"

Paul shrugged. "Sure." Anything to get out of mucking.

"Good," the vet replied as he took the horse to the cargo hatch that opened to the deck above. "Where the hell is the corporal?"

A moment later, a huffing Corporal Hastings arrived with a heavy canvas sheet with ropes that met at two metal rings on either side. "Sorry, Lieutenant, I had to go to the D-deck to find it," he stated.

Cupping his hands, the vet yelled up the hatch, "Lower the hoist." A moment later a steel cable with a hook appeared.

"Did you feed her?" asked the lieutenant. Generally, when hoisting one of the animals it was best if the horse had an empty stomach.

"No, sir. I don't think so," replied Paul as Hastings slid the sling under the animal's belly and hooked the metal rings onto the hook.

"Okay. Take it up slowly," the officer shouted up at the hoist operator. The sling gradually tightened, and the horse gave a faint neigh of fright when its hooves left the deck.

"Let's get up there," ordered the lieutenant. They took the flight of stairs to the deck above. When they arrived, they saw the horse clear the hatch.

"Easy! Easy!" Fuller yelled, indicating to the boom operator to swing the animal toward the wooden box stalls set on the deck. With his hand, he gave the signal to lower the draught down.

The horse was tentative when her feet touched the cork covered deck. "Get her into the stall." Paul gently pulled on the halter and led the animal into the stall that was covered with a dull white awning that provided the six patients with shade from the sun. He stroked the horse's neck gently to calm her.

"Corporal Hastings, if you please, gather the sling again. I think I'll need it in a moment," demanded Fuller.

Paul turned his head toward the lieutenant because of the man's unhappy tone. He was examining a bay riding horse. Paul could tell that the bay was not doing well. Her head was down, and her breathing was raspy.

"Shit," muttered the vet when he finished his exam. "Paul, can you get me my bag? You'll find it on the shelf a couple of stalls over."

"Yes, sir," replied Paul. It took Paul a couple moments to find the bag. It felt heavy when he carried it over to the doctor. By this time, Fuller had the animal out of the stall and had led her to the nearby railing. He and Hastings had the sling set up and were indicating the operator to lower the hook again. The sling this time was set with a quick-release mechanism. When the sling was tightened, he turned to Paul for the bag.

"Thanks," the lieutenant said as he set the bag on a nearby ledge. From it he took out a .45 Colt revolver. He broke the cylinder open. His hand dipped into one of the satchel's side pockets and removed a single shell. He slid the cartridge into the cylinder and closed it. He turned it carefully so the bullet would be next in line when he cocked the gun.

"You're not going to shoot it, are you?" demanded Paul.

A tired look reappeared on the doctor's face. "I'm afraid that I have to, son. She's not going to make it. It's best this way. To alleviate her suffering."

"What, McGill? You squeamish about a bit of blood?" said Corporal Hastings sarcastically.

Paul glared at the corporal. He didn't care if he would be put on report.

Fuller took careful aim at the horse's head, ensuring that if the lead passed through it would go out to sea. He fired. Several of the men nearby turned their heads toward the sound. A couple of the horses neighed in fright. The horse slumped into the sling. The doctor waved at the boom operator, who started the lift.

As it rose, it swirled slightly, causing the horse to turn. Paul saw the hooves coming toward his head, so he ducked. Corporal Hastings was not so lucky, and a hoof gave him a glancing blow that knocked him sideways. To Paul's horror, he saw the corporal frantically trying to grab the railing.

He tried to get a hold of the corporal. He did try. Not very hard, mind you, but he did try. When they heard the splash, Paul and the lieutenant looked over the railing. Fuller turned to Paul then said, "It's the Christian thing to do."

"I suppose," replied Paul. He turned, cupped his hands, and yelled, "Man overboard!"

OCTOBER 12, 1914
SS FRANCONIA, MID-NORTH ATLANTIC OCEAN

"Now, army regulations require that upon admission the name and other necessary particulars regarding the patient be entered in the Admissions and Discharge Book. The A and D book is the official record of patients staying in a military hospital. It is the basis upon which we calculate statistics. It documents the official length of stay of the soldier, his diagnosis, and his disposal. Namely, whether the patient has been returned to his unit, transferred to another hospital for further care and convalescence, or if he becomes deceased. All admissions for the day should be entered in sequence in the A and D book," Major Creighton said in an earnest tone as he turned the page of the manual he was reading. "It is also especially important that the patient's particulars be entered in a fine, legible hand."

Some of the nurses in the second-class dining room tittered. He gave the nearly one hundred feminine eyes a flustered look, not realizing that what many in the audience heard was "fine eligible man." He shot a glance at Emily, who was sitting beside Samantha. He then dropped his head quickly to his notes.

Samantha turned her head slightly and asked, "What is that on his upper lip?"

"It's a moustache," Emily whispered in reply.

"Really?"

"Oh yes," replied Emily. "The officers have been ordered to grow one."

"It doesn't look like much." The growth was very thin and spotty.

"That's what I told him. Besides, who wants to kiss a man with a moustache?"

Oh dear, Samantha thought, *the poor fellow doesn't have a clue what's going to hit him.* Feeling that someone was staring at them, Samantha became slightly concerned when she saw that it was Matron Macdonald. She was sitting at the table that the doctor was using as his lectern. Samantha didn't think she was frowning at them concerning Emily's infatuation. She didn't have an issue with the nurses becoming romantically attached, if proprieties were followed. Her look was more along the lines of "Pay attention, you are going to learn something."

The white linen-covered tables in the dining room had been arranged lecture style with the nurses sitting ramrod-straight in their seats. In front of them near the glasses of water and cups of tea were sheets of paper and pencils for note taking during the lectures, which the matron had arranged to instruct them in the finer points of military nursing. The twittering hadn't pleased her, and she stopped it with a stern glance.

Today's lecture was on hospital administration and the paperwork that it would entail. Samantha tried to stop a yawn by clenching her jaw, but it failed so she had to cover her mouth with her hand. She glanced at the head table to see if the matron had seen it. She didn't want to receive a warning from her superior. Samantha viewed paperwork as a necessary evil. However, in the last few weeks she discovered that the military carried it to new heights, or depths, depending on your point of view.

Macdonald was keeping them busy. Besides, the daily lecture there was training with the field ambulance staff. They were learning the appropriate techniques for treating the battlefield wounded, placing them in stretchers and then transporting them for medical attention.

Also, the nurses had to endure the first-aid courses that the medical officers taught the privates. It took a while, but they were able to convince them that they were quite capable of training the enlisted men.

As well, the nurses were also required to work shifts in the vessel's infirmary. Most of the work was giving physicals and inoculations for smallpox and typhoid. Some of the men had such bad reactions to the vaccines that they needed to be hospitalized for observation. With nearly 3,000 people aboard, there were the usual occurrences of run-of-the-mill ailments. They did have one case of meningitis, recovery from which was looking doubtful. Thankfully, they hadn't needed the 20,000 boxes of seasickness medication on board. The seas were remarkably quiet for this time of year, according to the ship's crew.

On the whole, she was so pleasantly tired that she fell asleep when her head touched the pillow. She slept so dead to the world that Emily and Claire complained about her snoring. What added to her tiredness were the daily parade drills and the hour's exercise in the *Franconia's* gymnasium. Naturally, guards were posted to keep the men out when they were in the room.

What the nurses really enjoyed were the evening recitals and dances that allowed them to socialize with the other officers in a more informal manner. This resulted in a number of shipboard romances blooming. On a vessel this large, there were plenty of hidden spaces where couples could smooch. Even Claire, who was sitting across from her, seemed to have caught love fever. When she glanced down at Claire's blouse, she saw that all her buttons were done up correctly, thank God. When she had come into their cabin last night, the shirt had obviously been redone in haste and was slightly askew.

Samantha wondered how long these attachments would last once the voyage ended. She had to admit some of the officers had taken an interest in her. Most of them were nice, but none really appealed to her. Still, the nightly entertainment was a pleasant way to end the evening before lights out.

At that moment a long blast from the ship's steam whistle overwhelmed the doctor's voice. Everyone automatically looked up at the ceiling. When it was repeated, a look of relief appeared on the doctor's face. His current ordeal was over.

Matron Macdonald rose to her feet and ordered, "Ladies, please go to your cabins and get your life belts and report to your designated stations. No dilly-dallying now!"

Samantha grinned at Emily and Claire as they rose. The lifeboat muster and fire drills had added some excitement to their daily routines at first. However, after the tenth one they were getting rather tiresome. The ship's crew was rather insistent on them. It was to be expected since the sinking of the *Titanic* several years earlier. The other major concern was running into a German warship or submarine, since they were slowly approaching the English coast.

"Well, at least it got us out of the lecture," Samantha teased Emily as they hurried to their cabin. Emily replied by sticking out her tongue at her.

When they got to their cabin, they helped each other put on their life vests then ran to their designated lifeboat on the upper deck. The drill was being timed, and thankfully they weren't the last ones. Since the lifeboat had a sixty-one-passenger capacity, the space around Samantha filled in quickly. When she felt a hand caress her bottom, she gave a sharp elbow to the offender. She was quite satisfied with the whoosh he expelled when she hit his solar plexus. Emily, attracted by the noise, gave the man a glance then gave Samantha a disapproving shake of her head.

Then everyone stared at each other. The last thing that they were expecting was the faint strains of "O Canada." As the sound came closer, it changed to the "Maple Leaf Forever."

"Look," shouted one of the officers standing at the rail. When Samantha followed the arm, she saw a very large warship, pennants streaming on her masts and the ship's band on her bow, steaming toward them.

"That's the *Princess Royal*," said one of the men standing beside her.

"She's beautiful," someone said an admiring tone as they watched the ship steam at full speed between the convoy's columns. Samantha recalled the discussion the officers had at her dining table concerning the arrival of the *Princess Royal* and the *Majestic*. They had been concerned when the HMS *Glory* and the armoured cruiser HMS *Lancaster* had left them on the 8th. Due to wireless blackouts, the commander of their naval escort wasn't expecting them. As well, the two battleships

160

had not been informed of the exact date that the convoy had left Gaspé Harbour. They had been waiting two days for them.

The men interpreted the arrival of the two largest ships in the British Navy as an indication of how much the imperial government valued the contingent. The men bored Samantha, describing the *Princess Royal* and the *Majestic*. That *Princess Royal* was the largest warship in the world at 700 feet in length. She was armed with eight 13.5-inch guns mounted on four turrets, one on the bow, one midship, and two on the stern. She also carried sixteen 4-inch guns. She had the top speed of twenty-two knots. The *Majestic* was slower, at sixteen knots. While a pre-dreadnought design, she was still formidable, with four 12-inch guns, twelve 6-inch, sixteen 12-pounders, twelve 3-pounder guns. She also carried five 18-inch torpedo tubes.

"Isn't a glorious sight?" asked Emily as she took off her cap and started waving it at the warship.

"I wouldn't have missed this for the world," agreed Samantha as she watched the *Princess Royal* gracefully slide past them as if they were standing still. She took off her cap as well and joined the soldiers in cheering as the ship steamed forward to take its place at the front of the convoy.

CHAPTER 16

OCTOBER 16, 1914
BAR, PLYMOUTH, ENGLAND

"Where the hell do you think you're going?" demanded the constable who had stopped Paul Ryan.

It was two in the morning, and the light, misty drizzle made Buckland Street rather slick. Paul had just staggered out of the local tavern and was trying to use Reggie as a crutch. His first thought was that they were in trouble. The second thought was *There goes my chance at a promotion.* He glanced at Reggie and the rest of the men of his unit who just spilled out of the Harley & Bros Public House.

"Royal Marine Barracks," he slurred politely. He then remembered to add, "Sir." He had lost count of the number of drinks that he had during the evening. Normally, Paul didn't partake very much. He had an occasional cold beer when the weather was unbearably hot or a dram of whiskey to remove the chill after a hockey game. Reggie and the rest of the men wanted to blow off steam since they'd been cooped up in a ship for nearly two weeks, and they had spent a better part of the last two days disembarking the horses.

To get the horses off the ship, they had to load them into stalls, which would then be hoisted from the cargo holds to the dock. Paul would lead the horse into one that was open at both ends. Once inside, Reggie would lock the rear panel. Then they would put a collar on it and attach it by rope to rings found on the walls. The rope would help prevent, as much as possible, the animal from moving around. Paul would then placed a blinder on the horse to prevent it from panicking when it lost sight of the horizon as the stall was raised. If it became agitated, it would be a danger to itself and the men working around the draught. It was then a simple matter of hooking a metal hook onto the ring on the top of the cage to hoist it up and then down.

On the dock, one of the men would lead the animals to the stables, where a vet from the British Army would inspect them to see if they were fit for service. Most of the horses were unsteady on their feet when they landed on terra firma. After nearly two weeks of inactivity, it would take some time for them to get their land legs back. Horses needed daily exercise to keep in top form. That was next to impossible while on a ship.

After the vet's inspection, he had ordered that several of the horses be put down. When Paul had spoken to Lieutenant Fuller about the losses, he had sighed and replied, "Sadly, it happens. However, they have been minimal. You should have seen it during the Boer War. It wasn't unusual that half would die during transit."

"Why?" Paul had asked.

"We have learned much since then. Why do you think I was so insistent on feeding, grooming, and sanitation? And why I taught you to look for signs that a horse was doing poorly? Mind you, we didn't have to cross the equator, and thank goodness the seas were calm. If we ran into storms, we would have lost more. A ship rolling through rough seas would have caused us no end of trouble."

"Well, they are finally here, all safe," Paul had said.

Fuller chuckled as he shook his head. "We need to give the horses a couple of days to recover before we can put them on the train."

"If we don't?"

"We could lose more of them. We need to work them up slowly. In South Africa we shipped them directly to the field, and we lost nearly half them in a month's time. This is a more efficient way of doing things."

"So you want us to exercise them for a day or two. Then, once we get to Salisbury, light work until they're back in shape."

"That's correct. You're learning," replied Fuller. "By the way, you're doing such a good job, I decided to recommend you for promotion to corporal."

Paul was surprised. He hadn't realized that he was being considered to replace Corporal Hasting. It would take another month or two for the corporal to recover from his mishap.

When he had gotten back to the barracks, Reggie and the rest of the squad were heading out to find a bar. When he protested, saying that they had been ordered to remain in the dockyard, they asked him where his sense of adventure was. Against his better judgement, he had decided to go with them. Since he was almost a corporal, he thought he should do his best to keep them out of mischief.

They had found the tavern that one of the marines had suggested on Buckland. There they discovered that they were not the only ones with the same idea. The bar was packed with Canadians. Also, they had been pleasantly surprised when the first round of drinks was on the house. After that, everyone bought a round. Paul had lost count after five beers.

"Canadians, eh?" said the Metropolitan Police sergeant as he eyed his partner. The Devonport branch of the London Metropolitan Police was responsible for policing the Royal Navy facilities at Plymouth. They also had the authority to police military personnel up to twelve miles outside the dock's legal boundaries. Ever since the Canadians had arrived and started disembarking, they had their hands full. For some strange reason, the first thing they asked when they got off their ships was, "Where's the beer?"

The sergeant looked at the bunch and then made a decision. "Look, lads. You haven't given me and my partner any trouble. We'll take you back to the barracks and call it a night."

"Thank you," Paul hiccupped. "It is much appreciated."

As the officers ushered them back to the base, the constable muttered to the sergeant, "I want to know how they are getting out of the docks. The place is supposed to be locked up tight as a drum."

"Damned if I know," replied the sergeant.

OCTOBER 18, 1914
DOCKS, PLYMOUTH

"It's about bloody time." Llewellyn overheard Colonel Topham mutter as they watched the tugboats at the *Alaunia's* stern push her toward the docks.

The colonel had been impatient to get ashore as soon as the liner had sailed around Mount Edgcumbe and then anchored in the Hamoaze. Many of the men, anxious to get a view, had crowded the ship's decks and masts. They had cheered when the massive HMNB Devonport dockyard appeared. Their arrival had not been expected, so it took a while for the local residents to react. When the word spread, large crowds appeared on the shoreline waving their colourful hats and Union Jacks. Steamboats and launches of various sizes had zigzagged among the convoy's vessels as they parked in pairs. From their megaphones the welcoming captains had sung, "It's a Long Way to Tipperary."

A launch soon appeared and they had requested permission to come aboard to meet with the senior military officer on board. Colonel Topham met the officer in his cabin, and he had invited his senior captains to attend. Llewellyn, standing in the corner, had eyed the lieutenant-commander. The man was in his early thirties, with a pear-shaped body, a neatly turned beard, and hazel eyes. He looked rather haggard, as if he had just been roused out of bed.

"Colonel Topham, I'm Lieutenant-Commander Belvedere. I've been assigned to the Disembarkation Office," he said as he shook the colonel's hand. The colonel indicated that the commander should take a seat.

"Commander, how can I be of service? We are quite anxious to disembark," stated the colonel.

"Quite. If you can provide me with returns of the men and equipment aboard the *Alaunia*, it would be extremely helpful in ensuring that the disembarkation will proceed smoothly and with a minimal of friction."

"Of course," replied Topham. He nodded to his orderly officer, who handed the commander a thick folder. "You should find everything in order."

"Is all of your equipment aboard this vessel?" the commander asked as he glanced at the folder's content.

The colonel grimaced as he gave Llewellyn a glance then answered sourly, "I'm afraid not. They were scattered among several other vessels when we embarked in Quebec."

"I see," said the commander with a frown. "And your sick nominal roll is included in here as well?"

Captain Moore, the Fusiliers' chief medical officer, asked the colonel, "If I may?"

The colonel indicated to proceed with a nod.

"We have about a 120 men on the nominal rolls. We have a case of meningitis, which we would like to disembark as soon as possible. There are about twenty patients that may need some hospitalization for a short period before they can be returned to their units. The others I expect will fully recover. My report is included in there," the doctor said as he pointed the papers in the lieutenant-commander's hands.

"Very well." Belvedere rose to his feet.

"When can we expect that we will be able to disembark?" asked the colonel.

"Patience, Colonel, patience," he replied. "It will take a bit of time to organize the disembarkation of this many troops and to coordinate train transport. Also, the chief of the disembarkation has issued orders that no one is to disembark without his specific instructions."

The last statement had not pleased Colonel Topham. He was rather

FRANK ROCKLAND

terse when he said, "Thank you, Commander. If you require any further assistance, it would be our honour."

It had been nearly four days since their arrival, and each day the colonel became more and more impatient. So did the men. He had to put half a dozen on report this morning. What really set the CO off today was what Captain Moore had said when he returned from the dockyard. He had been ordered to the hospital to confer on the meningitis case. Moore made the mistake of informing him he had seen a number of Canadian officers and men on leave at the port. What the doctor didn't know was that Topham had just been denied permission to attend a parade that Canadian troops were putting on for the mayor of Plymouth. The mayor had been away on business when the contingent arrived in port. The colonel fired off a blistering message of complaint to the chief embarkation officer.

Llewellyn didn't think that it had been a wise thing to do. You never knew how the officials would react. Either they would be accommodating or decide you were such a pain in the rear that they put you at the end of the queue.

From the port side railing he could see the well-maintained grounds of Mount Edgcumbe. Three crew members on the conning tower of a British submarine, running on the surface, waved to him as they sailed out to sea. Steam and grey-black smoke rose in the blue sky from the construction dock where they were working on building the next warship. On his side of the deck, Stonehouse, an enormous white stone classical style building, dominated his view. From there, the mast of the wooden training vessel HMS *Impregnable* was visible. It was at this dock that the HMS *Dreadnought*, which revolutionized warship design, rendering destroyers built before her obsolete, had been launched eight years ago.

The dock was so vast he didn't have a clue what the count was for the number of wharfs, slips, and basins there were in one of the most important naval bases in England.

When the tugboat released the ship, she gently settled against the bumpers on the wharf as the longshoremen secured the vessel. As they were doing so, he noticed a group of red-capped officers in olive drab were being escorted by a man he assumed was the base's admiral.

He didn't recognize the major-general, but he did recognize the man beside him. He had seen that walk many times before at Valcartier.

166

Colonel Topham recognized him as well. "How the hell did he get here? Did God give him wings?"

Strutting on the dock was the minister of Militia and Defence, Sam Hughes. He had an ear-to-ear grin.

Llewellyn blurted out something without thinking and that he would regret in the coming months. He said, "I wonder what the weather's like in Bermuda."

CHAPTER 17

Since Borden had a few spare minutes after lunch, he decided to practise his chipping with his niblick in his backyard while he waited for John Hazen and Colonel Gwatkin to arrive for the afternoon meeting that he had called. He was careful to hit away from his large, two-storey stone home. He couldn't damage the house when he pitched his ball about a distance of ten to fifteen yards. His wife didn't approve of him practising his swing in the house — something about the furniture.

Laura had fallen in love with the two-and-a-half acre property that ran from Wurtenburg to the Rideau River when she first saw it. The house was set back from the street with a large lawn and plenty of trees for shade. The architect who had designed many of the CPR hotels had been involved in its construction.

He hummed the remnants of Hymn 665 from the Anglican songbook that he had enjoyed singing at this morning's All Saints Church Mass. It didn't seem to help with his swing tempo very much. When he sculled the ball, he swore and then said a prayer in repentance.

What had caused the poor shot was the intrusion of politics. Most of the week he had been consulting with his ministers about whether or not to call an election. Foster, Doherty, and Meighen were opposed, but everyone else was in favour. His party was reorganizing the Quebec wing in preparation for a quick election campaign. They had one more year, or maybe a year and half in their mandate before he was required to call an election. Most of the ministers were in favour. The thought was a fresh mandate would go a long way to hamper any future opposition by the Liberal-dominated Senate, which kept opposing every bill his government brought forward. Naturally, the Liberals would view this as breaking the truce both parties had agreed to for the duration of the war. When he had informed Rogers and Cochran that he had decided not to call an election at this time, their strong disagreement forced him to reconsider.

After determining how much support they had in the cabinet, he had informed the governor general that there wouldn't be an election. His meeting with his cabinet didn't go well. He had lost his temper. What didn't help was Hazen's statement concerning Hughes' poor administration of the Militia and Defence department.

Also, he had an interview later this evening with Louis-Philippe Pelletier, his postmaster general, where he would try to persuade him not to resign. Louis-Philippe had been suffering from ill health for some time now, and the additional strain from his current heavy workload was making him consider quitting the cabinet.

Borden sighed as he went to his ball and gave it another whack.

"Robert!" shouted his wife from the porch.

"Yes, dear?" he replied.

"John Hazen and Colonel Gwatkin are in your study."

"I'll be in in a moment," he replied as he slid the iron into his golf bag and the ball in the side pocket. Golfing season was coming to an end here in Ottawa. He and Laura were planning a trip to the healing spring baths in Hot Springs, Virginia. While there, they would play some rounds before they put the clubs away permanently for the winter.

John Hazen and Colonel Gwatkin rose to their feet when he entered his study. Actually, it was soon to be Major-General Gwatkin, although he hadn't informed him yet about the promotion. Both men had the tired look of long hours and little sleep. He felt the same exhaustion.

"Gentlemen, thank you for coming," he said as he motioned them to sit in the dark brown leather couch along the wall. The other wall had a bookcase filled with his law books, which he was loath to get rid of. "I know that you are both quite busy."

"I'm here to serve, Prime Minister," replied Gwatkin. Hazen simply acknowledged with a twitch of his bushy black moustache. Borden had asked his minister of the Canadian Navy to bring Gwatkin to this afternoon's meeting. Since Hughes was in England, Hazen was the acting minister of Militia and Defence. From the leather folio the colonel had placed on the coffee table he pulled out several sheets of paper and handed them to the prime minister. "This is the latest draft that you requested."

"Thank you," Borden said as he put on his reading glasses. He took out the black fountain pen that he had clipped to his shirt pocket so he could make edits and notes.

For the last week, he had been discussing with the GOC the raising of a second contingent. He, Gwatkin, and Colonel Denison, the adjutant-general, had spent all day Saturday hammering out the details.

"I know that we've been over this, but will we have adequate manpower to defend our borders and coasts?" Hazen asked. He was concerned about possible attacks on the key naval installations at Halifax, Quebec City, and Esquimalt. "I'm just asking because we need to reassure the public that we are doing everything we can."

Borden raised an eyebrow at the colonel, suggesting he respond. "We still have the permanent force of approximately 3,000 men available. They have been augmented by the activation of nearly 5,000 more from the militia for the duration of the war. The ports are being garrisoned, and we are mounting patrols to ensure the security of the Welland Canal and the St. Lawrence River.

"What we are proposing is to have 33,000 in continual training. If we need additional forces, we'll draw on the trainees. When we are able to fully equip 10,000 men, we will then dispatch them to England."

Hazen looked thoughtful. "So we're not going to send them all at once, like we did with the first contingent?"

Gwatkin shook his head. "We've stripped the cupboard bare. Nearly all of our 18-pounders are in England. Most of the clothes, boots, and other accoutrements can be produced quickly. But it's not much use if we can't arm the men. The cavalry units need a certain amount of time to acquire horses and work their men and mounts up appropriately.

"Also, this produces less strain on our administrative capacity. Nearly everyone in the Woods Building is near exhaustion just getting the first contingent to England."

"I was relieved when we got the message that they reached Plymouth safely," said Borden. Both men nodded. Many had spent sleepless nights worrying.

"I spoke with Admiral Kingsmill," said Hazen. "He had heard that Admiral Wemyss had complained to Winston Churchill about the voyage. It was the admiral's opinion that the passenger liners should have sailed individually, not in a convoy. If a German cruiser or submarine had found them, we could have lost them all. Sending them over in small batches would have minimized the risk.

"I do have a major concern about the German reservists in the States," Hazen continued. "There have been rumours that they were mobilizing."

"I've spoken with Commissioner Sherwood and Inspector MacNutt. They've increased their intelligence operations in the northern states for any unusual activity along the border," said Sir Robert. Commissioner Sherwood ran the Dominion Police, and Inspector MacNutt ran its

170

Secret Service, which kept an eye on possible threats to Canada's security.

"There are other ways that the Germans can do mischief," Hazen pointed out.

"They have been trying," stated Gwatkin. "Our censorship unit discovered a message that was transmitted to the United States from Berlin that stated they were making a sweep of the Allied forces. It was only a matter of weeks before they would be in Paris, dictating terms. Supposedly, it had been sent by an American military attaché. When we investigated, we discovered that it was fake and the officer in question didn't write it."

Both men's eyes widened at Gwatkin's story.

"Returning to the second contingent," Gwatkin said. "Basically we should only recruit infantry, mounted rifles, and service units until we get word back from London. Once they provide instructions on what they need, we can make the necessary adjustments."

"The scheme seems workable to me," remarked Borden. Some of his ministers had suggested that they wait for word from the War Office before they committed themselves to a second contingent.

Borden returned to the press announcement and stroked through a paragraph and made some notes in the margins. He handed them back to Gwatkin. "If you can make these changes and have it back to me by seven for my final review, I would be pleased. I want to provide it to the press this evening."

"Of course, Prime Minister," Gwatkin said. He glanced at the changes that the prime minister requested before returning them to his portfolio.

It was then that Borden decided to inform Gwatkin of the good news. "Colonel Gwatkin, it is not official yet, but I have decided to promote you to major-general."

A look of surprise crossed Gwatkin's face. His demeanour became sombre when he realized the implications. Borden knew exactly what he was thinking. "I'm also promoting Minister Hughes to major-general as well."

Relieved, Gwatkin said, "Thank you, Prime Minister. This is most unexpected."

One thing he didn't mention, but Gwatkin would find out soon enough, was that he made Hughes' promotion retroactive to May 1912. This made Hughes, except for the governor general, the most senior military officer in Canada. He hoped that on this particular matter he could get some peace. At least until Hughes created another crisis. He dearly hoped that it wasn't soon.

CHAPTER 18

OCTOBER 19, 1914
TRAIN STATION, AMESBURY

It was late at night when the train pulled into the station. From the windows, Llewellyn could see the forlorn lights of the red brick building. The light accented the drizzling rain that fell at a slight angle. Through the other windows, he could see darkened passenger cars on the track beside him. He wondered what unit of the contingent that particular train had carried.

"End of the line! Amesbury station!" shouted the train conductor as he marched down the corridor crowded with soldiers. "End of the line! Amesbury station!"

"Sergeant!"

Booth's head appeared from the cabin next door. "I believe that we have been asked to leave the train," the captain informed him.

"Yes, sir. We're ready," he said as he held up two rucksacks, Llewellyn's and his own. When the captain made a motion with his hand for his bag, the sergeant pulled it back with a look of consternation. "Sir, it simply isn't done!"

The captain was about to argue then decided that it wasn't worth the effort. If the sergeant wanted to be his batman, so be it, for now. He glanced down the corridor and spotted his four platoon commanders. He waved them over for an impromptu meeting.

"I'm going to find out what the situation is. Start getting your men ready, and I want them disembarking in an orderly fashion starting with the first platoon." He glanced at the drizzling rain and then said, "Have the men get their waterproof gear on in case we don't have transportation and we have to march."

"Yes, Captain," replied the lieutenants.

Llewellyn nearly fell when he misjudged the last step to the platform. The conductor had neglected to put down a stool. He settled on his feet as he watched several officers stepping down from the other cars. When he spotted Major Edwards, the adjutant, he greeted him with, "Lousy evening."

"I know. I did hear that England was damp," said the major as he adjusted his collar on his greatcoat. Llewellyn got along well with the major, even though he was a close confidant of the colonel.

"Was someone supposed to meet us?" asked Llewellyn.

"So I was informed," replied Edwards.

"Let's go into the station and find out," suggested Llewellyn.

As they were turning, a major stepped out from the train station and approached them. "Richmond Fusiliers?" he inquired.

"At your service," replied Major Edwards as he saluted the other officer.

"I'm Major Withers. I've been assigned to direct you to the Lark Hill camp."

"Has transport been arranged?" asked Captain Llewellyn.

"I'm afraid that none are currently available," Withers replied.

"My men have been on the train for the last two days, and they're exhausted," protested Llewellyn.

Major Withers replied tersely, "It's only a two-hour march to the camp."

"I see," Major Edwards said with a frown. "Can you provide directions on how we can get there?"

"Of course. The directions are marked on this map," said the major as he handed them a folded tourist map with "Wiltshire" printed on top. "If you exit the station then march down Albert Street to St. Annes, it will lead you out of the city. Then simply follow the road signs. You can't miss it."

"I'll inform my colonel," replied Major Edwards. "You wouldn't by chance know if our tents have arrived and been set up?" The Fusiliers' equipment had been loaded onto a cargo train two days prior. The unit's tents were in that shipment.

"I'm afraid I do not. If you need anything further, I will be at your convenience in the station," Withers replied as he returned Major Edwards' salute. He turned on his heel and returned to the warmth of the station.

The major shook his head. "Well, Captain Llewellyn, sort out your men and get them ready."

"Yes, Major."

"It looks like we won't be fed until we get to the camp." There was a hint of disbelief in the major's tone, which the captain shared.

"Right, Major."

174

"Let's get going then. The quicker we get started ..." he said as he began to shout orders to the other companies.

It didn't take long before the men were assembled, and they were on the move with their rucksacks slung on their shoulders. As they marched through the city, some of the townsfolk stuck their heads out of their doors and windows and gave them friendly waves. When they had marched for two hours, the column came to a sudden halt. A runner appeared in front of Llewellyn. "Captain, the major wants to see you."

When Llewellyn arrived at the front of the column, he found the three other company captains and Major Edwards gathered around a map. It was lit by a torch in Captain Lime's hand. The major's jaw was clenched. Llewellyn was afraid to ask what the problem was.

"According to the map and the instructions we were given, we should be at the camp by now," replied the major tersely. "Unfortunately, we can't locate it."

"Have runners been sent back the way we came?" asked Llewellyn. "We may have missed the landmark in the dark."

"We have, Captain. We are waiting for their return," replied Edwards curtly.

"We should fall out the men," suggested Captain Percial.

"If I may," said Llewellyn, "I would suggest that we don't. I don't want to lose any men in this bush, especially if we don't know where we are."

The major glanced at the other captains, who didn't appear to have any objections. "The men can rest, but as long as they stay in the line."

"Thank you, Major."

"Return to your units. As soon as the runners get back, we'll decide what we need to do," ordered Edwards.

In about half an hour, a runner found Captain Llewellyn at the head of his company. "Major. The orders are to get the men ready. We will be marching shortly."

"So we found the camp?"

"Yeah! We found the signpost five minutes back. We missed it," replied the runner.

When they finally staggered into the camp, Colonel Topham was waiting for them. He had been given a ride to the base. "Where the hell have you been?" he demanded, as usual.

He was not pleased to see that the men had arrived late. When Major Edwards attempted to provide an explanation, the colonel cut him off. Then he looked at the gather captains.

"The men will have to put up our tents," said the colonel.

"The tents aren't ready for us?" asked the major.

"No, they're not. I have also been informed that we're missing thirty of them," said the irritated colonel. The captains glanced at each other, wondering who would ask the question.

It was Edwards who finally broke down. "What happened to the tents, sir? Where will our men sleep?" The missing equipment meant that 240 men would be sleeping without cover in the rain.

"The unit who arrived before us took them," answered Topham. "I'm going to have a word with them in the morning to get them back." He then addressed the captains. "Now get going. We need to get the men under canvas as soon as we can. We have a parade tomorrow."

"Yes, Colonel," they replied.

As Llewellyn turned away to go to his unit, he nearly started to laugh. *What a dismal end to a perfect day*, he thought.

OCTOBER 20, 1914
YE OLD BUSTARD INN, BUSTARD, SALISBURY PLAIN

Lieutenant-General Alderson's horse skirted around the two-ton Gramms truck as it rumbled past them on the Great Bustard Road toward the line of bell tents behind him. A captain at the head of a column of men loaded down with packs and rifles saluted as he led his men on an early-morning march. He was pleased to see smiles and grins on the men, an indicator that their morale was good.

He twisted in the saddle to look at the camp behind him. Smoke rose in the dawn sky as the cook tents were making breakfast. Squads of men were preparing for their morning ablutions. On one side of the tents, Bains wagons were unloading boxes and equipment.

When he returned his gaze back to his steed's head, he stroked the animal's neck as he examined the square tents that had been set up in the field next to his headquarters. They housed his staff, since there was insufficient room in the Ye Old Bustard Inn. Alderson chuckled at the name. He had dealt with the Canadians before, and he knew they would soon be calling it the Bastard. The bustard was a species of ground bird that used to make its home on Salisbury Plain until it became extinct nearly fifty years ago. Originally, the inn was a way station for travellers to London, which was 200 miles away, and for those who had come to hunt game. The inn itself was a two-storey stone building with a reddish brown clay tile roof. The main floor housed the public room, kitchen, manager's office, and the servant's quarters. On the upper floor were the bedrooms for the guests, one of which was his. Beside the main building was the sixty-six-foot-long stable. Part of the stable had been converted into a garage and housed several staff cars.

When he swung out of the saddle with practiced ease, one of the grooms had already appeared after being notified by the sentries that were stationed around the HQ's perimeter. When he entered the Bustard, most of the men in the rooms that had been converted to offices were occupied answering ringing telephones, and some of the clerks were stabbing at black Oliver typewriters. He gave them warm smiles as he made his way to his office in the back. On his desk, waiting for him, was a cup of steaming tea. He barely sat down when his adjutant, Lieutenant-Colonel Sweeney, entered his office with a sheaf of papers in his hands.

"Good morning, General. How was your morning ride?" he asked. The colonel had been seconded to Lieutenant-General Edwin Alderson's staff from Southern Command. Southern Command was responsible for ensuring the defence of southern England. Headquartered in the city of Salisbury, ten miles south of the Bustard Inn, General Alderson reported to its commander, Lieutenant-General W. Pitcairn Campbell. Initially, the War Office had acquired ninety square miles of the plains for cavalry and artillery training. Since then it had expanded its holdings.

"It was pleasant. I'm happy to see that the camps are starting to fill," he remarked as he took a satisfying sip from his cup.

"Yes, but it is taking longer than we anticipated. We had planned for six days, but it's being stretched to nine," Sweeney replied.

"I was expecting that there were going to be some issues," Alderson replied. The announcement that he had been selected to become the GOC of the Canadian contingent was made on October 15. However, the actual transfer of the command between him and Colonel Williams took place on October 14 at ten p.m. aboard the *Franconia*.

Lieutenant-General Alderson stroked his greying bushy moustache. Now fifty-five, he had been in the army since he was seventeen. He had joined his father's regiment the Royal West Kent, which was then based in Halifax, Nova Scotia. The regiment was subsequently transferred to Gibraltar and then finally to South Africa. He was attached to the Mounted Infantry Depot. During the Boer War, he developed a well-founded reputation for commanding irregular troops and developing innovative tactics.

It was there that he met and became lifelong friends with General Edward Hutton. Hutton had once been the GOC of the Canadian Militia before he was recalled because he had published mobilization plans without getting the Canadian government's approval.

Governor General Minto had approached him about becoming the Canadian GOC, but after listening to Hutton's stories about Canadian politicians, he was happy that it didn't take place. After meeting Hughes, he was glad that Gwatkin had taken the job, not him. Nearly everyone who had served in the Boer War was familiar with Sam Hughes. He did get along with Hughes, who he thought was prickly.

Contrary to what Hughes believed, the contingent was simply not ready for combat. It was a given that the current Canadians officers did not yet have the training or the experience to operate effectively in the field. That was what he and his staff were planning on correcting during the next several weeks as they ran the contingent through the training syllabus.

"So how are the dispositions coming?" he asked.

"There is going to be some crowding with the men until we get additional shelters. From what I have gathered, they didn't heed our request for waterproof canvas and tents. I've got the list of the units and the camps we assigned them to." Sweeney pulled out a report from the stack of papers he was carrying.

"Read them to me, please," asked Alderson. It would help him memorize the names of the units under his command.

"The Bustard Camp will be home to the 1st Infantry Brigade, commanded by Lieutenant-Colonel Mercer and its four battalions. In addition, so will the No. 2 Company Divisional Train, No. 1 and 4 units of supply, the Ordnance depot, No. 1 Field Ambulance, and a depot company.

"At the West Down South Camp, they will have the Divisional Ammunition Park, the No. 2 Field Ambulance, and the base depot. At the West Down North Camp we have assigned the Divisional Artillery Headquarters, A & B Batteries, the 1st, 2nd, and 3rd Field Artillery, and the 1st Heavy Battery with their ammunition columns. Also, room was found for a headquarters divisional train company.

"Lieutenant-Colonel Turner's 2nd Brigade and Colonel Currie's 3rd Infantry Brigade, and their four battalions, have been assigned to

Lark Hill South. Located there will be the Divisional Engineers plus two companies of divisional trains and two supply units.

"The 4th Brigade and her battalions will be at the Sling Plantation Camp. The reserve park will be there, as well as a supply and field ambulance." He then turned the sheet to the second page. "Pond Farm Camp will have the Royal Dragoons and the Lord Strathcona's Horse."

He looked up and said, "I would suggest that returns be prepared to get an accurate picture of where everyone is once things settle down."

"Agreed," said Alderson. "Have we set up communications yet?"

"The telephone and telegram lines are being set up as we speak. We'll be using gallopers, cyclists, and motorcyclists as messengers. Channels with the Southern Command are being arranged. Last I spoke with them, they'll be forwarding the intelligence summaries and field observation reports, which we can use for the training syllabus."

"Good, put the syllabus on the next meeting agenda. I want to get the men started on it as soon as possible. I need an assessment done to determine where they will require improvements. Also, I've been made aware that a number of surplus officers were included in the contingent. I would like them identified."

"You want to transfer them to other imperial units?"

"No! It's been my experience that we'll be short on officers, so I would prefer to keep them, if I can," said Alderson.

"Yes, General. It will be difficult to conduct training until all of the unit's supplies and equipment have arrived. It may take a week or two to sort out the mess."

"I'll inform the senior commanders," Alderson acknowledged.

Sweeney frowned when he read the next page. He looked up at the general. "They finally discovered how the Canadians managed to get out of the dockyards," he stated.

"Oh?"

"It seems that as each unit marched through the gates, some of the men acted as if they belonged with them. Once they were out of sight, they would drop out of the line and find the closest public house."

When Lieutenant-General Alderson chuckled, the Adjutant looked at him in surprise. "You approve?"

"Not exactly. But it shows their resourcefulness. It will be an extremely useful quality once they learn discipline."

"If you say so, but I've been getting report that they been finding the bars in the local villages and causing problems. The mayors have lodged several complaints already."

"I was expecting that with the dry canteens," replied Alderson. "When I went out on my morning ride, I saw two or three empty whisky bottles outside nearly every tent."

"Dear God!"

Alderson nodded in agreement. "I was expecting this. When I learned that there would be no beer, I knew that this would lead to trouble. That's why I've been lobbying Southern Command to cancel the order. If they don't, the problem will continue. With wet canteens, they would be in the camps where we can control them, and it will improve our relations with our civilian neighbours."

"I certainly hope so. Otherwise, we will be authorizing a lot of Field Punishment No. 1s," Sweeney replied. Field Punishment No. 1 was where an offender was tied to a wagon wheel or fence for up to two hours a day for the length of their sentence.

"That I would like to avoid, if I can," Alderson replied.

OCTOBER 20, 1914
LARK HILL, SALISBURY PLAIN

"It is rather muddy, isn't it?" Captain Llewellyn said as he pointed to the plank floor to Lieutenant Henricks. One of Llewellyn's regular duties was to inspect the kit of his soldiers to ensure that they were properly equipped and determine what he needed to order as replacements from the quartermaster. Today, he was inspecting Henricks' platoon.

When he entered the first bell tent, the slight smell of rot hit his nostrils. The plank floor was rather muddy from the heavy rains that had fallen for the last several days.

"Yes, Captain," said Private Duval. He pointed to the back of the bell tent, where a small swell of water and mud was creeping under the canvas. "We have to keep all of our kit on our cots, otherwise they would be all wet."

"I can see that," replied Llewellyn.

"We have to sleep with our rifles in our cots and our boots on." It was obvious that Duval would rather be sleeping with something softer and warmer than cold steel. "We can't leave the rifles out, because they'll rust."

"I certainly hope not!" stated Llewellyn. "Just make sure that they are kept well oiled."

"Of course, Captain. Whenever we can get a supply from the quartermasters."

Llewellyn grunted an acknowledgement then ordered, "Lay out your kit for inspection as best you can."

Private Duval quickly laid out his kit on the cot in the prescribed form. The Canadian kit was comprised of one metal identity disk, normally worn around the neck on a cord; a Ross rifle, with an oil bottle and letter sling, bayonet with a scabbard, Oliver pattern belt, straps, ammunition pouches, and pack; ration bag; mess kit with plate, spoon, fork, and knife; a folding clasp knife; shaving kit with a razor, brush, and soap; a first aid field dressing; haversack; a khaki greatcoat; a soft cap with a brass badge; a field jacket and trousers; a pair of socks; a pair of underwear; puttees; and black boots.

"Everything appears to be here," replied Llewellyn, somewhat surprised. He never been able to do an inspection without finding that a piece was lost, stolen, or traded for some doodad that had caught one of his men's eyes. He cocked his head to the side when he noticed that the private was wearing a pair of British pattern boots.

"Where did you get the boots?" asked Llewellyn.

Duval looked down at his feet and then stared Llewellyn directly in the eye. "I bought them at the general store," replied Duval. The general store at Salisbury Plain sold everyday necessities to the British and Canadian soldiers.

"Really?" said Llewellyn in disbelief.

Duval's eyes dropped slightly and gave a sheepish grin. "One of the Imperials was kind enough to give me one of his spares." From the looks on the faces of the other five men in the tent, that wasn't the true story either. "He did put up a rather difficult fight when he woke up, but he did volunteer them in the end."

"Private Duval, I don't know quite what to do with you," said Llewellyn with laugh. "Are they comfortable?"

"They hurt like hell, but me feet are dry. They aren't falling apart like the junk they gave us at Valcartier," he replied.

Everyone was complaining about the boots they were given. Even Llewellyn needed to get an extra pair. He had been dabbing his with water proofing to keep the torrential rains out. This, combined with his feet's perspiration, meant that his boots were always damp at the end of the day. It wouldn't be a problem if he could take them off so they would dry overnight. With the amount of water they were getting this was not happening. Since they only had been issued one pair of boots, it just compounded the problem. With a second pair they could rotate them on a daily basis, having a dry pair always available.

"I'll talk with the quartermaster again about getting more boots. I need a second pair too," said Llewellyn. The captain glanced down at Duval's feet then asked, "What size are they?"

"Nine."

"Hmm," Captain Llewellyn said as he stared at the boots to the point that Duval was beginning to think that he was going to ask for them. "Pity," he said with a regretful sigh, "I take a size ten."

CHAPTER 19

OCTOBER 20, 1914
PRIME MINISTER'S OFFICE, EAST BLOCK,
PARLIAMENT HILL, OTTAWA

Borden was looking forward to his yearly vacation to Hot Springs, Virginia. He couldn't wait to soak in the Jefferson Pools. Fed by natural springs, the hot mineral water seemed to always penetrate deep into his bones. He enjoyed taking a morning and an evening bath, especially after playing a round at the nearby golf courses. What he also liked was the interesting people that he met at the spa. Last year he and Laura were greeted by former President Taft when they stepped off the train.

He needed a restorative after this hard week. On Tuesday he swore in two new ministers to his cabinet: Thomas Cosgrain as his new postmaster general and Pierre Blondin as his new inland revenue minister. Also, he officially announced Gwatkin's and Hughes' promotions.

His mouth soured slightly when he thought of Hughes. White was complaining that too many of the ministers were trying to interfere in the Militia Department's contracts. And the telegram he received from the War Office concerning his government's proposal disturbed him. London had suggested that he wait until the imperial staff fully assessed the first contingent. It had ominous implications. Hughes had assured him that his boys were first-rate and ready for battle.

In his desk journal, he made a note to send a telegram to Perley in London. He knew that Perley and Hughes didn't get along, but he needed someone to find out more of Kitchener's intentions concerning the CEF.

Borden had just completed the note when a knock on his office door distracted him. It opened, and Blount, his principal secretary, entered. "These have been signed," Borden said, indicating the stack of folders beside the journal. Blount replaced the stack with a stack of new ones he was carrying.

"Commissioner Sherwood and Inspector MacNutt have arrived for your appointment," Blount informed him. Borden blinked. *Where did the time go*, he thought.

"Show them in," said Borden.

The two men who entered wore civilian clothes. The older man, in his sixties, was Sir Percy Sherwood, the head of the Dominion Police.

The police's offices were just below him on the ground floor of the East Block. The second man, in his mid-thirties, was Inspector Andrew MacNutt, who ran the Secret Service for the commissioner.

The Dominion Police and the Royal Northwest Mounted Police handled federal policing in Canada. The Ontario-Manitoba border delineated their duties. The Dominion police handled all crime in the east, while the Mounties dealt with the crime in the west. Also, Sherwood was responsible for Parliament Hill security and, like the London Metropolitan Police, was responsible for policing the Halifax, Quebec City, and Esquimalt naval bases.

The force's Secret Service ran a network of covert agents along the US–Canadian border to prevent a repeat of the Fenian raids and against other threats against the Empire. Considering the current situation, there was a distinct possibility, with the large number of German reservists living in the States, that a similar attack could be planned.

"I understand your son James has volunteered," remarked Borden to Inspector MacNutt as he and the Commissioner sat in the two wooden chairs in front of him.

"Yes, he did. He's with the Princess Patricia's," the inspector said proudly. Borden knew that the Princess Patricia's Light Infantry tended to prefer men with military experience, so MacNutt's son must have shown exceptional skills or character to be allowed in. Having dealt with the Dominion Police officer for a number of years, he wasn't at all surprised.

"Excellent," replied Borden. "Also, I heard from my wife that Katherine is helping with Belgian Relief." Katherine was the Inspector's wife.

"Katherine and the Women's Canadian Club are doing excellent work for Belgian Relief," said Inspector MacNutt.

Sherwood nodded. He was a past president of the men's Canadian Club of Ottawa. Changing the subject, he said, "Since you requested this meeting, I took the liberty of asking Andrew to prepare an oral report on our current activities. If you wish, we can submit a written one as well."

"An oral report will be fine. Please proceed," said Borden as he leaned back in his chair. He was willing to procrastinate with his unpleasant task that he was going to assign.

"As you are aware, on August 15th we were given the authority to arrest and detain German and Austrian reservists who attempted to leave Canada. Also, anyone we feel will assist the enemy and those who engage in espionage and sabotage were to be confined. At last count, nearly 10,000 are currently under detention."

"Ten thousand?" blurted Borden in surprise. The issue of German reservists had emerged at the cabinet meetings, but he hadn't realized the numbers involved.

"Yes. Most of them have been arrested by the militia, and they are being held at various armouries. My understanding is that the army is planning to take steps to centralize the detainees. We have initiated fingerprinting procedures, and they are being sent to my colleague, Inspector Foster's Fingerprint Bureau in the Langevin Building.

"We've increased our surveillance along the Ontario and Quebec borders. So far the borders have been pretty quiet, no reports on any activities by German reservists. Also, we've contracted the Pinkerton Detective and the Thiel Detective agencies for their services during the duration of the war. They'll help us keep tabs on possible efforts to resupply German navy vessels with fuel and provisions.

"We do have concerns about the military attachés, Captains von Papen and Boy-Ed at the German embassy in Washington. We're implementing plans to keep a close watch on them."

"Hazen mentioned to me an incident at the Cornwall Canal last night. One of the sentries fired on three men who were attempting to lay a charge?" Borden probed.

Inspector MacNutt sighed. "We've investigated a number of such incidents. In nearly all them they claim that the suspects escaped across the border. A fair number of them involve young men who are shooting at shadows."

"Basically, this is what we have accomplished to date. Would you like to add anything, Commissioner?" the inspector asked as he looked over at his boss.

"No, you did a fine job," Sherwood said. The inspector looked pleased by his superior's words.

Borden cleared his throat. "I appreciate the report, Commissioner." He paused as he considered his words carefully. "On Wednesday I received some distressing news," he said with a hint of anger in his voice. "There is a possibility of graft in the militia department."

He saw the men's faces pale. "Are you certain?" asked Sherwood.

The prime minister pointed at the chair that the commissioner was sitting in and replied, "I interviewed the man myself on Wednesday. He claimed that he overheard a Mr. Allison boast that he was making profits on Canadian and British government contracts."

MacNutt retrieved a police notepad that he always carried in his inside left breast pocket of his blue suit. "May I have the particulars concerning this Mr. Allison?"

"Actually, he goes by Colonel Allison, and he is from Morrisburg. He's been a friend of Minister Hughes for some twenty-five to thirty years. I don't know exactly when the minister made him an honorary colonel. Supposedly, General Hughes asked him for assistance with some gun contracts. He was to ensure that he got the best possible price. I've requested General Gwatkin to find copies of the contracts in question. As you are aware, the people at the Woods Building are a bit overwhelmed, and it might take a while."

The process of issuing and approving contracts was a sore point with Borden. When he formed the government in 1911, one of the first things he did was commission a study on how to improve the organization of the civil service. The study confirmed what he already knew. A considerable amount of time at cabinet meetings was spent on what could be considered minor or trivial matters. The cabinet issued 3,000 to 4,000 orders-in-council on a yearly basis. Some dealt with serious issues such as a ratifying a treaty or appointing a court judge. Others dealt with a small pump contract, promoting a clerk up a grade level, or the hiring of a lightkeeper. The report recommended that ministers should set out the policy and leave the administration of the policy to the civil service.

That did not sit well with many of his ministers, like Hughes, who wanted to have a more direct say in the contracts. Because of the sheer volume, only contracts above $5,000 were to be sent to the cabinet for approval. He hoped that it was an isolated incident, not a systematic one.

"Mr. Allison," Borden refused to use the military honorific. "Has a number of interests and contacts in the metal business in Canada and the United States. He is a former director of the Cramp Steel Company then was a promoter of the Tin Plate and Sheet Steel Company. Supposedly, his company made the first tin plate in Canada. Also, a number of years ago he and Hughes were involved in a St. Lawrence River dam project."

"This is very helpful," stated MacNutt as he closed his notebook. "I may need to contact Pinkertons and have one of their operatives make inquiries in his current activities in the States and conduct a thorough background check."

"I would ask that you exercise discretion in this matter. It is highly sensitive."

"Of course, Prime Minister," the inspector assured Borden.

"In the meantime, I have informed Mr. Perley in London to inform the British authorities that contracts are not to be granted to him. Also, I will have a frank discussion with the militia minister on this matter when he returns from England."

Sherwood said, "Yes, Prime Minister. Is there anything else you want us to take care of?"

"That's it for now. On Saturday afternoon I'll be taking the train to Hot Springs. I can be reached by cypher telegram," Borden informed them.

Sherwood and Inspector MacNutt glanced at each other. "We think that it might be prudent that one of our officers accompany you," suggested Sherwood.

"I really don't think that's necessary," said Borden. "I will be quite safe."

"Prime Minister…!"

"No!" stated Borden firmly.

"Yes, Prime Minister," replied Sherwood unhappily.

"I hope that you have a pleasant and safe vacation," Inspector Mac-Nutt said as he and the commissioner rose to their feet.

They are two good men, thought Borden as he watched them leave his office. *I wish that I had more like them.*

CHAPTER 20

Colonel Topham had called a muster parade to prepare for an inspection of the troops by the new contingent's commander, Lieutenant-General Alderson. He wanted to impress the new GOC with the Fusiliers' sharpness. He was not happy when he saw that over half of Llewellyn's company was missing.

"Captain! Where in the Sam blazes are your men?" he demanded.

"Tactical exercise," replied Llewellyn as he stood at attention in front of what was left of his company.

"What tactical exercise?"

He was considering informing the colonel that he had sent his men to retrieve their missing tents. His lieutenants were all for going over to give the sons of bitches a good trashing when they found out that their tents were stolen. When he asked if that was their plan, they gave him blank looks.

"Plan, Captain? It's simple enough. We march over and demand our tents back," said Lieutenant Troope.

"If they don't give them back?"

"We'll make them," he replied as he cracked his knuckles.

"I suppose. If that is your objective," the captain said casually.

Lieutenant Troope looked annoyed, but Llewellyn was pleased when Lieutenant Vernon picked up his hint.

Vernon interrupted Troope to say, "I think what the captain is suggesting that we consider it as a military operation against an enemy position. They have it, and we want it."

"Possibly. If it was against an enemy, a friendly enemy so to speak, how would you plan it?" asked Llewellyn.

The lieutenant stopped to think as he considered the problem. When Henricks spoke, Vernon, Troope, and Parker looked at him. "We'll need to do a reconnaissance to determine our enemy's ... our opponent's, disposition, strength, and weakness. Identify when the appropriate time to strike is with the least resistance. Then call in the reserves to exploit the opening."

"Why don't you four go out and discuss it among yourselves," Llewellyn suggested.

When they left the tent, he called for Sergeant Booth. "Yes, Captain?"

"Can you pass the word to the other sergeants that while it was a grievous error on our comrades' part, when it is said and done we will still have to get along."

The sergeant smiled. "Understood."

"Colonel, we did forward to your command last evening that my men were conducting a tactical exercise to recover supplies that were captured by enemy forces."

The colonel squinted at Llewellyn as he tried interpret what Llewellyn was saying. "I've received no such message," he replied.

"Colonel," interrupted the Sergeant Booth. "I delivered it this morning, sir."

"I see," the colonel glared at the sergeant.

"I will see you, Captain, after parade to discuss this so-called tactical exercise." It was an order, not a request.

When the colonel was out of earshot, the captain said with a bit of concern, "That was not a good idea, Sergeant."

Booth snorted. A moment later, a runner came up to Llewellyn and saluted.

"Lieutenant Vernon has requested your presence, sir."

Captain Llewellyn raised an eyebrow. "You lead. I'll follow."

"Yes, Captain," said the private as he led the captain to the far side of the camp, to where the offending regiment, the 10th Kanata Rifles, was located. As they got closer to the line of canvas, Llewellyn noticed that stacked neatly on tarpaulins were various rucksacks, laundry, cots, and other personal effects. Standing in front of each of the tents were two of the men from the Richmond Fusiliers. When Lieutenant Vernon spotted the captain, he marched over and snapped a smart salute, which the captain returned.

"Captain, I'm pleased to report that our tactical exercise has been a success."

"So it seems," said Llewellyn. From what he could tell, the lieutenants had arranged their attack when the unit was on their inspection parade, leaving the tents relatively unguarded except for a couple of sentries to protect against petty theft.

Those sentries were sullen, but they had been facing two- or even three-to-one odds. The men had carried groundsheets around their necks and had spread them on the ground to protect the unit's clothes, blankets, and other equipment from the damp ground.

"What is the meaning of this?" demanded the husky Kanata Rifles' captain who came to a screeching halt in front of Llewellyn.

"I would like to thank you for taking care of our tents. But we decided that we have need of them," Llewellyn said cheerily.

The captain sputtered, "That's ridiculous! You can't do that!"

Captain Llewellyn cocked his head. "Be thankful that the weather forecast is for sun for the next few days." It shut the man up.

OCTOBER 22, 1914
SALISBURY PLAIN

It was just before noon when the entire battalion halted in a sloped hallow just off the gravel road they were using for their morning's route march. Greyish smoke curled from the black steel stovepipes of the four mobile kitchens that were already parked. Eight horses, two per wagon, were picketed twenty feet away, still wearing their harnesses. They would soon be hitched once the men were fed.

The men stacked their rifles, pyramid style, to keep the metal off the damp ground. There had been some gentle rain showers a few hours earlier. Once they dropped their packs, they pulled out their mess tins and started to line up for their chow.

As a couple of men walked past him, one said in a voice that carried, "Wonder what the weather is like in Bermuda?"

A small smile appeared at the corner of Llewellyn's lips. He didn't react otherwise, because he knew that his men were watching his reactions. His remark aboard ship had spread quickly. Most of the teasing was of the good-natured variety, so he let it go. However, he still had to keep an eye on it, because if it got out of hand, it could impact discipline. He already had some problems with his men. Several of them had gone, without his permission, into the nearby town and had gotten drunk. He had no choice but to impose punishment on them as an object lesson.

When the line began to thin out a bit, he approached the field kitchen with his plate. He liked to eat after his junior officers and men were taken care of. He was pleased to see that his lieutenants were following his example.

At one of the wagons on the far right a cook opened a small door at the bottom of the stove. He used a metal rod to rake the glowing red coals before he threw in several more scoops of charcoal. The chefs had prepared their lunch several hours earlier. As the men marched, the wagons followed, and the hot steamers would slowly cook the meat, the potatoes, and the vegetables over several hours. Each of the wagons weighed nearly two and a half tons. The heaviest load they carried was the nearly 400 pounds of water and 300 pounds of meat. The water was also used for making soups, coffee, and tea. In addition, the kitchens carried an assortment of dried goods and condiments to liven up the meal.

Llewellyn watched as the young man cleaned his coal-covered hands on his apron and then lifted a lid from one of the wagon's bins. When a cloud of steamed swirled up, he decided to move to the next wagon, where the food appeared to be more appetizing. He also turned his face away since he didn't want to watch that particular cook plunk stew into someone's plate.

He had just got his food when he noticed a small party of horses approaching from his left at a trot. When he saw the flash of red on the men's caps, he sent a runner to Colonel Topham. A few moments later he appeared riding a deep brown, almost black horse — he had wisely left his white charger at Valcartier — and headed for the officers.

When he saluted the leading rider, Llewellyn realized who the man was. He motioned to Sergeant Booth. "Tell the men that the general is here."

The sergeant didn't bat an eye. He shrugged and then went to warn the lieutenants and the other NCOs. It wasn't his first general, and it wouldn't be his last.

There was rustling among the men as the news quickly filtered through. As the general approached, Llewellyn had suspicions that Alderson had timed his arrival quite carefully. Talking with the men after a belly full of hot food made them more receptive to what he had to say. His escort stopped near the wagons, but Alderson continued to ride another ten feet or so. All of the men had a good view of him.

"Can I ask all the officers form a semi-circle in front of me?" Alderson said. His voice carried even to the men near the back of the slope. Llewellyn joined the semi-circle that formed around the steed. "Now, all of you men, break ranks and form a semi-circle around the officers. I want it done quietly."

As the men rose to their feet, a slight buzz of voices were heard as the men muttered to each other. His men behind him had risen but had not joined in when Alderson lifted his right hand. "Stop!" his voice boomed out. "I said I wanted it done quietly, and I meant it." He turned his head so that every man could see that he was serious.

He seemed to note that the men behind Llewellyn had done what he commanded. "Now go on!" When the men were crowded around the semi-circle of officers, he ordered, "Close up, just as if you were listening to a speech."

When Llewellyn threw a glance behind him, he saw that the slope allowed all of the men to have a clear view of their new commanding officer.

"I want you all to have a good look at me so that you will know me in the street, or if you see me in camp. I am your general, and I hope that before long I will take you out to fight the Germans."

When cheers broke out, Alderson's horse started slightly. The general didn't seem at all disturbed by the movement. He kept his seat well. He waited until the cheering stopped before he continued. "Talking about fighting the Germans reminds me that I have been fighting for the past week or more. It was only last night that I finally heard. Some of you can guess what I have been fighting for and won?" he asked with a grin.

Several of the men shouted out, "Canteens! Canteens!" The cheer quickly spread.

When it died down he continued, "Yes, it is the canteens, and you are going to have one in the camp. I have fought for you about this, because I always try to treat men like men, not like schoolboys. If you behave as such, I will treat you as such. I have fought for you because I do not believe that trying to make men teetotallers by order is the right way to go about it. I don't see why a man, at certain times and in moderation, cannot have his glass of beer. However, if there are any problems at the canteens, I will order them shut.

"I have placed myself in your hands. I'm quite happy to do so based on my experience with your countrymen who fought for me in South Africa. Now, I know that some you have been causing trouble in the neighbouring towns. Some of you have been going absent without leave and annoying the inhabitants. This has got to stop! If I have to put half the contingent on guard around the camp in order to keep the other half in, I will do so. I will have discipline! You are soldiers, not a mob!"

When Alderson stared at the battalion, many of the men bowed their heads in shame. Others stood taller with pride.

"I had the honour to have the 1st and 2nd Canadian Mounted Rifles under my command during the Boer War. Some of the young ones were hotheads, but it has been my experience that the hotheads were some of my best fighters." Grins and chuckling broke out around Llewellyn.

"Now it is in your hands. I will have no more on this topic. I want every man to know that if your commanding officer deems it fit to bring you to me, I am quite ready to see him at any time and help in any way," Alderson said, looking directly at the Fusiliers' officers.

"On my command, I want you to form in your units." He paused then ordered, "Go!"

Llewellyn quickly made his way to his men. He was pleased that all four of his lieutenants were in position and that the men of their squads had quickly assembled into their standard platoon formations. Alderson nodded in approval when he saw how quickly and efficiently they had completed his order.

With a slight kick of his boots, he directed his horse toward him. "You have good-looking men," he stated.

"Thank you, General," the captain replied. He wasn't quite sure how to take the compliment.

"And your name, sir?" he asked.

"Captain Llewellyn," he answered. He was surprised by Alderson's look of recognition when he heard his name. He didn't know if it was a good thing or not.

"Keep up the good work," he said as he rode his horse to inspect the next unit.

After Alderson rode away, Llewellyn ordered the men to gather their packs for the march back to camp. As the men were getting their gear together, Lieutenant Vernon sauntered up to him and asked, "What do you think of our new general?"

"He seems to be all right," he replied.

"Well, one thing we can definitely say about the man. He has guts," Vernon said with a grin.

"How so?"

"I wouldn't want to be the one to tell Hughes about the wet canteens."

Llewellyn was pleased when his frown communicated Vernon might have overstepped his bounds. Truthfully, he agreed with the young lieutenant. The man did have some gall going up against Hughes.

OCTOBER 26, 1914
ST. THOMAS HOSPITAL, LONDON

"If one more person says 'My, what a pretty hat' I'm going to scream!" declared Samantha as she and Claire exited the nurses' home.

"Well, it is cute," said Claire as she tilted her head to view the blue cap with the CMAC badge sparkling in the early morning sunlight. It was set at a rakish angle, not quite regulation. Samantha's blond hair was perfectly set in a bun.

"Not you too!" she snapped.

Claire chuckled. "Someone got up on the wrong side of the bed this morning."

"Sorry, Claire," Samantha said. "I didn't mean to take it out on you. It's just that all of this sitting around waiting is so ... so frustrating!"

It had been nearly a week since they had disembarked from the *Franconia*. Their march, parade, actually, through Plymouth with the headquarters staff seemed to take forever as they had to stop several times because they were being overwhelmed with small gifts from the cheering local residents that lined the streets. When they finally got to the train station, they were required to remain in columns of fours as they endured speeches from visiting dignitaries as well as a presentation of pans of Devonshire cream, a gift from Mrs. Waldorf Astor, the wife of the MP for Plymouth.

It was there that Colonel Jones had informed them he had accepted a kind invitation for the nurses to stay at the St. Thomas Hospital in London. He seemed to be relieved, as if one worry had been lifted from his shoulders.

Nearly all of the nurses, including Samantha, were thrilled at the news. It was at St. Thomas that Florence Nightingale started the first nurse's training school. It was on her foundation that all of the other schools were built.

They were all wide-eyed for the first couple of days as they walked the hallowed grounds. The hospital was a complex of six buildings separated by lush quarter-angles of green grass. They were connected by covered open-air corridors that allowed plenty of sunlight and air. The nurses had been informed that the wards held 581 beds, and they treated nearly 7,000 in-patients and 22,000 out-patients per year. There were two additional buildings, the 185-bed nurses' home behind them, and at the south end of the complex there was the medical school.

She had to admit that she had written gloating letters to Irene at Toronto General, describing waking in the morning and looking out of the window at the House of Parliament directly across the Thames. When she looked down she could watch the barge traffic moving on the river. She could hear the traffic on the Westminster Bridge, and if she stuck her head out she could see a part of Buckingham Palace. She failed to mention, due to the recent aerial bombing of Paris by the Germans, that London at night was dark. They were starting to enforce blackouts to reduce the threat of German Zeppelin raids.

"Matron Macdonald is meeting with the War Office again today, trying to get it sorted out," Claire pointed out tersely.

It was true that they hadn't seen much of the matron since she was tied up in meetings with Colonel Carson, Sir George Perley, and Dame Ethel Becher, the matron-in-chief of the Queen Alexandria's Imperial Military Nursing Service.

She acknowledged with a nod and then asked Claire, "So what is on our social calendar today?"

Claire coughed softly as she extracted a small black notebook from her blue overcoat pocket.

"Are you okay?" asked Samantha. "You seem to be coughing a lot lately."

"I'm fine. I just not used to this dampness," Claire replied as she turned the pages. "After the lecture at the teaching hospital this morning, we are required to attend lunch at Hotel Cecil's, where we are to be introduced officially to Colonel Carson. He's going to speak to us about what a wonderful place Salisbury Plain is."

Claire looked up at Samantha. "From what I heard, the entire contingent has finally arrived and are starting their training."

"Let's hope that it is a small lunch. With all the lunches, teas, and dinner parties, I might have to let my dress out a bit."

"I'm told that men like women with a bit of roundness to them," Claire said with a straight face. Samantha was surprised. It seems that Claire was developing a sense of humour.

"After that we're to report to the Queen Alexander Military Hospital for duty," she continued. The hospital was fifteen minutes down river, on the other side of the Thames. Samantha was looking forward to it, since she would feel as if she was contributing to the war effort. The matron had ordered that the nurses work two-hour shifts there to familiarize themselves in the care of wounded soldiers.

Samantha had already done two shifts, and she found it interesting the differences between the Queen Alexandra's Imperial Military Nursing Service and her own service. When the war started, the QAIMNS had 300 permanent nurses with nearly 2,200 in the reserve.

At the Millbank, as the military hospital was known, its 280 beds were full of casualties from the recent fighting near the port city of Ostend in Belgium. There was a nurse and an assistant staff nurse for eighty beds. For each ward of ten beds, there was a male nurse and a general duty orderly private who reported to an NCO. Both the nurse and the NCO accompanied the medical officers when they made their rounds. She had assumed that the nurses were officers, like she was, but she discovered that while they were attached to the British Army they were not military personnel. In the Canadian hospitals, the NCOs and orderlies reported to her because she outranked them.

"Then we have tea with Lady Deville." Claire looked up at Samantha. "She's a great supporter of the VADs."

The VADs were the Volunteer Aide Detachments that have been called into service for additional nursing support. From Matron Macdonald's attitude, she had gathered that she wasn't impressed by them. Many were upper-class women with great enthusiasm but little medical training.

"I wonder if anyone wants to trade shifts?" she asked.

"Oh, no you don't!" Claire said sternly. "You know the matron's orders about never travelling in London alone."

"It was just a thought," Samantha replied contritely.

"Right!" Claire said in disbelief. "After that we've been given tickets by some Viscount for *Pygmalion*."

"Really!" Samantha said in surprise. "That might be fun, actually."

"You! Having fun! A moment ago all you wanted to do was work."

"Well, a lady can change her mind, can't she," Samantha said as they headed toward the corridor that led along the river to the medical hospital.

As she walked, she started humming some of the tunes from the play that she had heard on the voyage. The sheet music was very popular. She actually did want to see it. At least for tonight, she was glad they had not received their orders to move to Salisbury Plain.

CHAPTER 21

Colonel Carson watched as his friend paused at the entrance of the Hotel Cecil's Grill Room. The restaurant was decorated with the oriental blue and yellow tiles that were in fashion. Normally there was fine view of the Thames River, especially at night with the illumination from the nearby buildings and the streetlights. With the imposed blackout, the view was rather dim, except for the occasional running lights from barges and launches. The eatery was nearly overflowing with hotel guests. Most were wearing evening dress, but a significant number were garbed in olive drab with red officer patches.

He rose to his feet when Hughes, escorted by a waiter, reached his table. Carson's eyes naturally fell on the minister's new shoulder boards. The colonel's crown and two stars had been replaced by a major-general's crossed baton and sword below a single star. It was, in Carson's opinion, a long time coming.

"I apologize for being late. A Canadian Press reporter waylaid me wanting a story," Hughes said as he took the chair opposite. He waved away the wine list the waiter offered and ordered a glass of water.

"What kind of story?" asked Carson.

"About the fighting near Ypres. Is the contingent going to join the BEF there?" Hughes said. Carson's lips tightened. The Germans had assaulted the Belgium army near the Yser River on their drive to take the port cities of Boulogne-sur-Mer and Calais. In desperation, the Belgians had two days ago opened the dykes and flooded a twenty-mile area. From the reports, it looked like the Germans were planning an attack on Ypres.

"Are they?" he asked. He had not been invited to the high-level meetings the minister had held with Lord Kitchener and the War Cabinet.

"Damned if I know," retorted Hughes as he slapped the table with his hand. "Lord Kitchener feels that my boys need more training before he allows them to embark to France."

"He and Lord Roberts seemed to be impressed by them when they reviewed them last Saturday at Salisbury," Carson pointed out.

"That's true. When I had dinner with Lord Roberts at his estate, he told me personally that they were a fine body of men. It's Kitchener. He is not a bold man. He wants to train the spirit out of the men before he sends them to the front," Hughes said in frustration.

"So what are you going to do?"

"There isn't much that I can do at the moment," Hughes said sourly. "When I met with him, he told me that George Perley had informed him that our government would have no involvement with our boys here in England or at the front."

Carson blinked at Hughes's statement. "Perley told him that?"

"He did. When I spoke to our so-called acting high commissioner, he told me to my face 'You do not pretend, surely, to have anything to do with Canadian soldiers in Britain.'"

"What did you tell him?" he asked. Carson was well aware that Hughes resented the man. He had been surprised when he introduced himself to Sir Perley that he had not been informed by Ottawa of his arrival. The commissioner had been perplexed as to what Carson's role was in preparing for the contingent's arrival, since he was in constant communication with the War Office. He suspected that Hughes' enmity with Perley was due mainly to the fact that Perley was one of Borden's most trusted advisors and part of Borden's inner circle — something Hughes had not been able to achieve.

"I told him what I told Kitchener," he sneered. "They needed to study Canadian Military Law and the British Army Act. They needed to appreciate the spirit of the constitution. As far as I'm concerned, since we are paying for the contingent, I should have absolute control of them in Canada or in Britain. I'll grant you that the War Office will have a say concerning them while they are at Salisbury or at the front. But I'm going to be the one who will select its officers and commanders."

Carson sat back in his chair as he considered his friend's position. He understood Hughes' point of view, but it was going to be a difficult sell.

Hughes turned his steel-blue eyes on Carson. "That's one of the reasons that I wanted to talk with you before I sailed for New York on Saturday. I need someone that I can trust to keep an eye on things for me. I don't trust Perley, and I certainly don't trust the War Office. They haven't said anything yet, but I'm certain that they want to break up the contingent. As far as Kitchener is concerned, they are imperial soldiers and he'll try to use them as reinforcements. They tried that in South Africa, and they didn't get away with it. I sure as hell don't want them to try to get away with it now."

198

"So what do you want me to do?" asked Carson.

"I'm going to appoint you as my personal representative and give you the authority to look after financial issues and any other questions in regard with the contingent. I also want you to send me regular reports on my boys," he stated.

"Of course, Sam," Carson replied happily. He immediately recognized the implications of what the minister was offering him. "I would be glad to."

OCTOBER 31, 1914
LARK HILL, SALISBURY PLAIN

When reveille dragged him out of bed that morning, Llewellyn knew that he was going to have a hard day. It didn't help that he hadn't slept much last night. It had been rather nippy, and he had woken several times shivering. He winced as the headache in his frontal lobe throbbed when he looked down at the list of charges that had been lodged against four of his men.

Through a watery left eye, he noticed that there were only two men standing in front of him just outside his command tent. He turned toward Sergeant Booth and asked, "Where are the other two?"

The sergeant's face was a blank mask when he replied, "Privates Eric McBain and Kelly Storer broke guard last night, Captain."

The throbbing got worse. "Why wasn't I informed?"

"I just found out, sir. The guards thought they were sleeping off their drunk. They didn't check on them until they were ordered to bring the men to you." Booth then added, "Sir."

"Well, they just got docked three days' pay and four days of punishment drills," he ordered. "And a week's C.B."

"Yes, Captain."

From the faces of the two men, he saw they were worried. Their colleagues' escape had certainly splashed on them. What punishment the captain had in store for them could be doubled as an object lesson for the rest of the company. Especially since the two men standing in front of him in the wispy rain were two of his better soldiers. He sighed when he saw Private Toby Duval. He was a pain in the butt but was proving to be quite good at scouting and reconnaissance. Almost as good was Private Tyrrell Dack, an American from Albany, New York.

"Have you heard anything from Private Cummings?" he asked Duval. Llewellyn was pleased to see his surprise that he remembered. It was difficult to forget nearly losing a man when the breech of his rifle exploded.

"Thank you, sir. He was doing fine. The last I heard," he replied.

He then turned to the American and asked, "Are you having fun?"

There were a fair number of Americans in the contingent. At one point, creating an American battalion was considered, but it was decided it was too political. Instead they scattered them among the various units. Most of them had joined for the excitement and the adventure.

Dack, a tall, burly man in his early twenties, assumed that the captain was asking a rhetorical question, so he didn't reply.

Being in a foul mood, Llewellyn decided to twist the knife a bit. He flipped a page in his black notepad and then asked Booth, "The men who broke guard. Do you have descriptions?"

"Yes," replied the sergeant as he removed a similar notebook from his breast pocket. "Private Eric McBain, age twenty-nine, height five foot seven, complexion fair, eyes brown, hair fair, distinctive marks, tattoo, right arm, serpent. Private Kelly Storer, age twenty-five, five foot five, complexion dark, eyes blue, hair light brown, distinctive marks, vaccine, upper left arm, tattoo, anchor, right forearm."

When Llewellyn finished making his note, he returned the book back to his breast pocket and said, "I'll send a report to the military police to arrest them and bring them back in chains."

He was about to pronounce his sentence when he saw the Fusiliers' chaplain arrive. "Sergeant," he said, "take over for me for a moment. I need to have a word with the chaplain."

The chaplain was in his mid-thirties and on the slightly plump side. "Please come into my tent for a moment."

The minister glanced at the two men standing at attention with a certain degree of sympathy. He removed his khaki cap with the Canadian Service Chaplain badge and entered the tent. Llewellyn sat on his cot and offered his guest the canvas stool.

"You called for me, Captain?" the chaplain enquired when he had settled uncomfortably in the stool.

"I wanted to speak to you because we have a bit of a problem, Father Stoat."

A hopeful look appeared on the priest's face. "I was hoping that you would find the word of God."

200

The good father had been the minister of the St. James Presbyterian Church in Flin Flon, Manitoba, before he volunteered. He was cheerful and likeable. The man's only failing, if you wanted to call it that, was that he was a strong supporter of the men's temperance league. He wasn't too happy with General Alderson's decision concerning the canteens.

"Thank you, Father. I believe you misunderstood. We have a bit of a problem in that based on the wartime establishment, we don't have a position for a chaplain."

"There isn't?"

"I'm afraid not," Llewellyn replied. One of the administrative tasks that he had to do was to prepare a return on the reorganization of the Fusiliers. At Valcartier, the battalions had been organized in eight company formations. Each company had a captain and four lieutenants. However, the British war establishment organized battalions in four company formations. If implemented, it would mean four captains and eight lieutenants would be looking for new jobs. He was well aware that his name was at the top of the list for being declared surplus. In the meantime, what he was trying to do, and hoping that Colonel Topham didn't catch on, or at least not until it was too late to stop it, was to staff as many competent officers in positions where they could do the most good.

"What you may not be aware of, Father, is that since there isn't an official slot for a chaplain, technically you do not belong to the battalion. Which means we cannot pay you, nor can you draw rations."

Stoat gave him a startled look. "Where do I belong then?"

"We're not exactly sure," replied the captain. When he saw the man's concern, he hurriedly said, "We have a proposal as a stopgap measure until the situation is resolved."

"I'm listening."

"What we would like to do is make you an intelligence officer, on an acting basis."

"But I don't know anything about intelligence work," protested the father.

"We really don't expect you to. I can lend you my intelligence handbook for you to read to get a general gist of the work. You can continue to minister to the spiritual needs of the men. The only difference is that you will receive pay and rations. Also, we'll be assigning several men to you who will do the actual work. However, I must warn you that you may, on occasion, need to associate with some unsavoury men."

"I see," replied the chaplain thoughtfully. "Sinners, I take it."

"Oh, the worst, Father," the captain assured him with a hint of a smile. "They have been known to take a drink or two, swear, and even take God's name in vain."

The father nodded as he regarded Llewellyn, who became a touch worried that he had figured out what he was doing and would turn down the offer. In his experience, he found clergymen rather difficult to fool.

"I'll take it."

"Excellent," beamed Llewellyn. The intelligence slot had been a concern. The person that had been occupying the position was, to be blunt, an idiot. Llewellyn managed to have one of the captains in another battalion entice him with a job offer, which he had accepted. By filling it with the chaplain, it gave him time to find someone competent. He suspected the Fusiliers needed a good one.

He gave Father Stoat a congratulatory handshake as he escorted him out of the tent. He was then faced with the punishment of the two soldiers.

He thought they had suffered enough, at least for today. "Privates Toby Duval and Tyrrell Dack. For being drunk and causing a disturbance, I'm docking you three days pay, four days of punishment drills, and you are being transferred to the intelligence section."

Llewellyn saw their relief that the punishment was not going to be as severe as they expected. He would have loved to see their faces when they discovered who their new commanding officer was. You never knew, the good minister might be able to moderate their drinking.

CHAPTER 22

Samantha and Emily were riding in the front seat of a Bains wagon. It was rather crowded, but the driver didn't seem to mind that she was pressed against him. At least he was keeping his hands to himself. She glanced down at the gold band on Emily's left hand. When she looked at her friend's face, she had the sleepy look of a newlywed.

When the sisters finally received their orders to report to Salisbury Plain, Major Creighton was waiting for her on the platform at Amesbury. Emily had squealed with delight when she saw him. She was even louder when he went down on one knee and proposed. Rita, who was the matron-in-charge, had put on a displeased face at the disruption, but Samantha could tell that she was secretly pleased. There was no regulation against the nursing sisters marrying. The wedding ceremony took place the next day and was officiated by Father Stoats, the Fusiliers' chaplain, who was a good friend of the doctor. Samantha and Claire acted as the bride's maids of honour.

After the ceremony, the happy couple had been escorted to their matrimonial bell tent. A guard was posted to protect the couple's privacy. When Samantha checked on them in the morning, the young private was blushing as he glanced at the tent behind him.

Samantha looked at the dark grey clouds that were rolling in as they entered the village of Amesbury. "It was rather cold last night," she remarked. The tent she was sharing with seven other nurses didn't have a stove. All the stoves and heating elements that the doctors and orderlies could get their hands on were requisitioned to provide heat for the No. 1 General Hospital's main marquee.

"I didn't really notice," Emily replied with a wistful sigh. Samantha raised an eyebrow. She had expected Emily to face the marital bed like a wide-eyed doe.

"We're near the train station, ma'am," said the orderly sergeant who was driving the horses. Sergeant MacCullen was a burly, clean-shaven man a couple years older than her. They were in the lead wagon of the four wagons that had been tasked to retrieve and sort the medical equipment that was stored at the train station's warehouses and storage facilities.

They had been informed that their unit had been declared a clearing hospital, and they were expecting nearly one hundred patients in the next day or so.

The senior officers were busy organizing the staff into the appropriate surgical and treatment divisions. However, the medical facilities at West Down North were woefully inadequate. The medical tents didn't have wooden floors, no electricity to run their equipment, and water was being pumped from local wells. Even the requisitioned heaters weren't enough to keep their current patients at a comfortable temperature. They had borrowed what they could from the No. 2 Hospital, but it still wasn't enough. And they needed to put up additional tents to accommodate the expected influx.

What was worse was the kitchen. Samantha had nearly gagged at how bad her breakfast was. Emily merely laughed with an expression that said it was she who had wanted to leave St. Thomas Hospital.

Major Creighton had indicated they could only provide limited treatment. Serious cases would be transported by motorized ambulance to Tilsworth, to the military hospital there. Emily's husband admonished them, saying, "Yes, the CO has complained to General Alderson that the facilities were not up to snuff to treat patients properly."

Before they left he had informed Emily and Samantha that they didn't have all the medical forms they needed, especially the diet and the medical history sheets. They had put in an emergency request for them and asked them to check if they had arrived.

Traffic on the narrow road between the two-storey buildings was rather heavy. Amesbury was relatively small. Until August, it had only a thousand souls or so. They mostly lived on sheep and wheat farming. The local stores supplied the soldiers with the luxuries that the British Army couldn't supply. Business was booming with the influx of Canadian, Newfoundland, Australian, New Zealander, and imperial troops.

The closer they got to the train station, the more Canadian accents they could hear. There was a traffic jam of beeping car and truck horns and horses neighing at the entrance. It took nearly half hour before they managed to get to the front. When they did, the skies opened up and poured on them.

At the guard gate, a military police officer armed with a Lee-Enfield rifle slung over his shoulder greeted them. Other guards patrolled the exterior to protect against pilfering. Some of the boxes that had arrived at the hospital had been opened, and the contents were damaged.

The guard directed them where they thought their equipment might be. When they drove up to it, they stared at the huge mountain of boxes of various sizes.

"Oh my God!" said Emily in dismay. A fair number of the boxes had lettering for other units of the CEF. It meant that they had to pick through hundreds of them to find the equipment that they needed.

Samantha saw how the sergeant and the other orderlies reacted to Emily's reaction. Samantha looked at the mountain and then at the NCO and his men. "Sergeant MacCullen, what is at the top of our list?"

"Tents, ma'am."

"Tents it is. Let's jump to it," she ordered. She was very pleased with the firmness in her tone. More importantly, the look of respect that appeared on the sergeant's face gave her much satisfaction.

NOVEMBER 2, 1914
WEST DOWN NORTH CAMP, SALISBURY PLAIN

Acting Corporal Paul Ryan rode up to the small farmhouse on the outskirts of the War Office lands, or at least he assumed that was the case. He still felt uncomfortable riding a draught horse. The steed he was sitting on was nearly eighteen hands high and had a gentle disposition. However, the animal's girth was putting a strain on how far he could stretch his legs.

It had been nearly a week since his artillery unit disembarked from the trains at Lavington and had marched the six miles to the West Down North Camp. Paul had not been impressed with the base or with the tent that he and his squad had been assigned. It had seen a lot of years of hard use. There were a variety of stains, running from ugly yellow to dark brown, and that was on the inside. Patches had been sewn over top of the bad spots, and they leaked when it rained. When they complained, the British quartermaster clerk got sharky, saying they should have brought their own tents when they had been ordered to do so.

They had been given a black iron stove, placed in the middle to provide heat for the other seven men who bunked with him. The problem was they hadn't received their supply of firewood or coal to actually use the stove. The same quartermaster clerk simply shrugged and pointed out that since they were Canadians, they should be able to handle a bit of cold weather. They were tempted to go to a small copse of trees in the distance to gather some firewood. It wouldn't have been a problem at Valcartier, but it seemed that it was a court-martial offence on the Plain to gather branches or trees without authorization.

Paul was grateful that Sergeant Lawrence had ordered him to find this farm and retrieve property that belonged to the CEF. He consulted the handwritten address on the orders he had been given. He was having a difficult time figuring out where the farm was. He hoped that this was the correct one, since this was the fourth that he had visited. The others had given him directions, but their accents made them difficult to understand.

As he passed a pasture, he stood up in the stirrups to get a better view. He saw a black stallion munching contently on the short grass. As he rode up to a two-storey white plaster farmhouse with a thatched roof, several dogs barked out warnings to their masters. A woman in her early forties with steel-wool hair came out with a broom to see what had attracted their attention. When she glared at him with green eyes, he straightened his cap and his back.

"Your beastie is in the south pasture," she yelled out at him as she pointed in the general direction of the white barn twenty yards away. The riding steed he saw earlier was watching him curiously over a white post fence. He was somewhat perplexed as to how the horse managed to wander off. They were normally housed in open-air corrals, since there weren't sufficient stables to handle all of the contingent's horses. Also, they were supposed to be tied to piquet lines and hobbled to prevent them from leaving the camp. This was the fifth one that he had been ordered to retrieve.

"I be giving ye fair warning. If he comes back and eats my flower garden again, I'll be selling him to a glue factory," she threatened.

It was then that Paul noticed that half the plants in the neatly harrowed bed beside the house were gone. "Sorry, ma'am. It won't happen again," he apologized.

"Mum! Who is it?" asked a voice from the cottage.

"Never ye mind!" she snapped, without turning around.

A moment later a pretty girl in her late teens or early twenties peered over her mother's shoulder. His heart stopped for a moment because she looked like Marie, except for the hair, which was wiry like her mother's.

"Paul Ryan," he said as he tipped his cap. "Canadian Expeditionary Force."

"A Canadian!" she exclaimed. Her cheeks dimpled with her smile. "Mum, invite him for breakfast."

"I will not," her mother declared quite emphatically. She waved her broom at her daughter and ordered, "Get back in the house." She then turned on Paul. "Don't ye be getting any ideas. Get your horse and be on ye way."

"Yes, ma'am," he replied as he turned his draught horse toward the south. He caught another glimpse of the girl's dimples before the door was slammed shut. He wasn't too sure whether or not it had been an invitation.

NOVEMBER 2, 1914
65TH HORSE ARTILLERY, WEST DOWN NORTH CAMP

It was late afternoon when Paul rode into the West Down North Camp with the riding horse trailing behind him. The recent rains had softened the ground, and he could see the ruts leading to the maintenance tents that the heavy 18-pounders had made. As he passed them he saw men scraping mud off the wheels using bayonets and wire brushes. Buckets had been placed outside the tents to catch rainwater to help with the cleaning.

He eyed the corrals and the horse lines, and on the other side of the tents he could see that the heavy horses were chewing up the soft ground with their hooves. They had sunk enough that they were no longer visible. He waved a hello at Reggie, who was leading a squad of men that were tossing hay from a wagon as it slowly crawled down the line. Other men were using brushes to clean as much mud as they could off the draught animals.

When he arrived at the veterinarian tent, the recently promoted Captain Fuller emerged from it. "Well, Corporal Ryan. Another patient for me?" he stated as he went to examine the black stallion. When he saw the identification brand on the horse's haunches, he said, "He's not one of ours. Where did you get him?"

Paul replied, "A women sent word and said there was a horse eating her pansies, and would we come get him before she turned him into glue."

Fuller chuckled and then looked thoughtfully at the saddle. "He was saddled when you found him?" Paul nodded. "We could have someone out there who got thrown. I haven't seen any alerts that this horse was missing. I'll send a message to Bustard HQ to see if someone hasn't reported in or they simply lost him."

"Sure," replied Paul. "By the way, are we having another review?" He was getting sick and tired of them.

The captain gave him a cherry smile. "The orders came in today. The king and queen are dropping by for a visit on Wednesday."

"They're coming for tea, are they sir?" replied Paul with a sigh. It meant that he would be spending that next couple of days cleaning tack.

Fuller read his face then said, "The men call you McGill?"

"Yes, sir," Paul responded warily, wondering why the officer was asking.

"Can you type?"

"Type, sir?" Paul was wondering what typing had to do with his nickname.

"Yes, type." Fuller pantomimed typing with his hands.

"Yes, sir. I can do thirty-five words a minute," he replied when he realized the captain was trying to determine, since he had intended to go to McGill, if he had such skills.

"Good. Good. I'll put your name in for the Remount Depot we are trying to establish. We need someone who can type to keep records for us. Are you interested?"

"Yes, sir. I would like that," replied Paul. He'd do almost anything to get out of cleaning tack.

NOVEMBER 4, 1914
LARK HILL, SALISBURY PLAIN

Llewellyn watched as Private Duval, wearing a greatcoat to protect against the rain, waved the oncoming car to a stop. As he approached the driver-side window, it rolled halfway down. In a thick Scottish accent, the driver asked, "Road closed?"

"Yes, sir," said Duval indicating the barricade that the Fusiliers had placed on the intersection of Stonehenge and Bustard.

"You with the Canadians?" the driver asked.

"Yes, sir," replied Duval.

The woman sitting in the passenger seat leaned over her husband's chest then said, "We're the MacClouds. Here to visit our nephew. You may know him. Adrian MacCloud."

"No, ma'am."

"Why not?" she demanded.

"There are 30,000 men here," he pointed out.

"We came all the way from Glasgow," she whined. Then she demanded, "How long will the road be closed?"

"For another hour or so, ma'am," the private said. "You can park your vehicle over there if you wish to wait until we open the road." He pointed to the field next to the barrier that the Fusiliers had erected to block traffic.

When Captain Llewellyn had received orders that the road to the Bustard camp be closed while the king and queen were reviewing the contingent, he hadn't anticipated the number of visitors who had come to meet relatives in the CEF. They came from all over England, Wales, and Scotland. A few even from Ireland. Many turned back to Amesbury or Salisbury to try later. Some, like the thirty or so cars, trucks, and horse-drawn wagons, waited in the field next the gate until the roads were opened. He had a squad keeping a watchful eye on them.

At the morning operational briefing, Colonel Topham had read the special order issued by Lieutenant-General Pitcairn Campbell, the commander-in-chief of the Southern Command. Based on the schedule provided, the royal couple would arrive at 11:15 at the Amesbury station. Via motorcade, they were to proceed to Stonehenge then to the Bustard. At 11:40 they would inspect the troops there and then proceed to the West Down and Pond Farm camps. They were to be back to Amesbury by 1:45 to catch their train back to London. Llewellyn highly doubted that the train would leave without them if they were a few minutes late.

When the phone beside him rang, the signal sergeant raised the black receiver to his ear. When he hung up, he informed Llewellyn, "They're on their way."

"How was the signal?" the captain asked.

As a training exercise, the engineers had run miles of telephone wire to the various outposts for the Canadian Signal Corps to provide communications between them and the Bustard HQ. It supplemented the semaphore, runners, and gallopers being used to keep him informed on the progress of the visiting dignitaries. Due to the rainy conditions, the heliograph system was not of much use. One thing he did notice was the fact that his men were in good spirits, despite the rain. It was mostly due to the fact that they didn't have to suffer another review.

A few minutes later he received a semaphore message by one of the patrols he had sent out to protect the road. He was glad that he did, as a number of the visiting family folk wouldn't take no for an answer and had tried to sneak around the main barricade. They weren't too pleased at being caught.

"Sergeant Booth, get the men ready," he ordered. The sergeant was standing on his right-hand side near the white pole gate. He acknowledged with a grin. "Okay, you bloody sods. Form up! Form up!" he ordered as the ten men lined up. The men guarding the vehicles straightened their uniforms but still kept a wary eye on the small crowd waiting in the field. When the line was formed, Captain Llewellyn took his place in it.

When the lead car appeared, it slowed to a crawl, not only to give time for the gate to lift, but also so the wheels wouldn't splash the men as it rolled through the puddles of water. When he saw the royal pennant on the third car, he yelled, "Present arms!" He then raised his hand in salute. There were four people sitting in the three-bench seat car. In the seat behind the driver sat a couple of civilians who were facing King Edward V and his consort, Queen Mary, sitting in the back seat. The royal couple waved as they passed him. Even the people in the crowd behind him straightened and stood at attention when they recognized the royal standard. It wasn't until the last car, with the security detail, had passed that he lowered his hand.

* * *

"They are a fine body of men," King George remarked as the limousine rolled past the checkpoint. "They seem to be in good spirits considering the weather conditions."

"Thank you, Your Majesty," George Halsey Perley replied as he watched the guards recede through the rain-spattered window. He returned his gaze back to the King of England. As the acting Canadian High Commissioner, he knew that he and his wife, Millie, were being granted a singular honour riding with the head of the British Empire and his consort, Queen Mary.

King George was wearing a greatcoat over his field marshal uniform. The coat hid the medals and honours that he wore on his left breast. Queen Mary was dressed in a blue coat and a matching hat. Like Perley, the king had a neatly trimmed beard. He was in his late forties and was in the fourth year of his reign. As the second son, he had not expected to become king. He had been quite happy serving in the navy until the death of his older brother, due to pneumonia, had forced him to give up his career.

"So what do you think of Salisbury Plain?" he asked Perley.

"It would make a great golf course," Perley replied. It elicited chuckles from the king and queen. Millie, sitting beside him in a black dress and matching hat, smiled with a raised eyebrow. She was the more social of the two. Like the king, Perley preferred a quiet life. If the king had been briefed on him, he would know that golfing was one of his favourite pastimes. He was the past president of the Royal Ottawa Golf Club and the Royal Canadian Golfers Association. He knew that the king did play some golf, but it was not his favourite sporting activity. He preferred stamp collecting and shooting. It seemed that every time his majesty played golf, it made him angry. It was not an uncommon sentiment.

"It's unfortunate that Lord Strathcona was not here to see his regiment. He would have been quite proud of them," stated the king.

"I'm sure that he would have been," acknowledged Perley. Baron Strathcona and Mount Royal had been, until his death in January, the Canadian High Commission to Great Britain.

Perley had been impressed when he accompanied the royals as they reviewed the Strathcona's Horse and the rest of the Canadian contingent. He had to grudgingly acknowledge Hughes' feat of getting the contingent to English soil. He did have concerns when Borden sent him a telegram informing him that Hughes was coming to London for a vacation. That he didn't believe for one minute. Perley knew that Hughes really wanted to command his boys. In his discussions with Lord Kitchener, Winston Churchill, and the War Office, it was clear that they were not keen on Hughes being in command. Also, whenever Hughes' name came up, so did the Boer War. It was obvious they had not forgotten his behaviour there.

When Perley met Hughes after his arrival to London, he was somewhat startled that Hughes took it for granted that he would still be involved in the decisions about the force. Perley had assumed, as in the

Boer War, once the soldiers landed in England the Canadian government would have little involvement. He had suggested that to Lord Kitchener. He wasn't happy that Hughes had contradicted him and Borden.

Perley had fairly good idea why they didn't get along. The first was that Hughes held his American birth against him. He had been born in Lebanon, New Hampshire. The second was he had made his fortune in the Ottawa Valley's lumber trade before he decided to enter politics. Since 1902 he had represented the riding of Argenteuil, Quebec. The final reason was Hughes was envious of how he and Borden had cemented their relationship by playing golf regularly at the Royal Ottawa.

For his part, he disliked the disorganized manner in which Hughes ran his office. One of the reasons that Borden had asked him to become the acting high commissioner was his management and organizational skills. The role of the high commission was to look after the Canadian government's interests and to promote immigration and Canadian business. Borden hadn't been happy with the state of the high commission. One of the problems was that there was no coordination, in London, among the various Canadian departments and agencies. In some cases, departments either ignored or bypassed the high commission. One of his tasks was to bring them to heel. Also, the prime minister had mandated he finalize the move of the offices from the cramped and gloomy facilities at 9 Victoria Chambers that had been on going for two years.

Borden had added to his agenda discussions with Winston Churchill, the First Lord of the Admiralty, about the naval question and his government's contribution to the Royal Navy. The prime minister had requested that Perley be invited to sit in the Imperial Defence Committee meetings, where external affairs and defence matters were discussed. It wasn't until the crisis hit in August that he, the first dominion ministerial representative, had been finally invited to attend this key committee.

Prior to July, he was getting a handle on reorganizing the offices and was bringing order to the chaos among the Canadians working for the government in England and Europe. In some cases, he discovered that they were working at cross-purposes. He had a major concern when he found out that Colonel Carson was still in England after his work preparing for the contingent's arrival was done. Now, it seemed that Hughes had appointed Carson as his personal representative. According to what he had gathered from Lieutenant-General Alderson's staff, Carson was responsible for certain financial and other questions concerning the contingent. The problem was that it overlapped with Perley's purview. It was going to create no end of complications.

Perley refrained from sighing as he continued small talk with the king and queen as they made their way to Amesbury. His problems would have to wait until he got back to London.

CHAPTER 23

Major-General Gwatkin walked from his bachelor apartment in the Victoria Chambers building located on the corner of Wellington and O'Connor Streets to his office in the Woods Building on Slater Street, since it was only ten minutes away.

He usually enjoyed the morning walks, since the streets were relatively empty at this hour. There was a chill in the air, so he was wearing his greatcoat. The days were getting shorter and the sky was turning a grey steel colour. Soon he would be arriving and leaving work in the dark. This morning, however, he couldn't help thinking about the four Royal Canadian Navy sailors who recently died at the naval battle at Coronel just off the coast of Chile. They were the first official Canadian battle casualties in this war. He was sure that there were more to come.

As he approached the entrance to his office building that was flanked by two small black cannons, Lieutenant-Colonel Septimus Denison stepped out of his car. "Good morning, General," he greeted him with a salute. The colonel was his acting adjutant-general, replacing Colonel Williams, who had been assigned as the commandant of Valcartier and was now with the contingent at Salisbury Plain. Denison was another Boer War veteran who had served with the quartermasters and on Lord Robert's staff during that conflict.

"Good morning, Colonel," he replied as he returned the salute. Gwatkin paused as Denison opened the entrance door for him. "So what is on the agenda for today?" he asked as he took the stairs.

The colonel would had preferred to take the elevators, since he knew that he was going to be breathing hard once they reached the sixth floor where the general's office was located.

"There are several items we need to discuss," he answered. "The first is that we received a telegram from the War Office concerning the second contingent."

"What are their requirements?"

"They suggested that the second contingent be arranged to balance with the first to create a Canadian Division with a line of communication units. What they would like to see are two infantry brigades, three brigades of field artillery, a heavy battery, a divisional ammunition column, two field company of engineers, a cyclist company of 200 men, a signal company, and three field ambulance units.

"For the line of communications units they indicated a divisional ammunition park, a supply column, reserve park, and field bakery and butchery units."

"How many men all together?" asked Gwatkin when they hit the third floor. Through the wall he could hear the rattling of typewriters from the steno pool. He didn't think that all forty were in at this hour. The bulk of the women were involved in typing up the militia contracts.

Once the adjutant caught his breath after pausing on the landing, he continued. "Altogether they're asking for nearly 16,000 men, 5,000 horses, sixty guns, and sixteen machine guns."

"We should be able to use the twelve infantry battalions we are currently recruiting," the major-general remarked.

"We have to equip them first," the colonel pointed out.

Gwatkin snorted. "The Château and the Russell are full of manufacturers. They are looking to cash in on our lucrative militia contracts."

"We have also to keep in mind the request we received from the Quebec politicians concerning recruiting and fielding a French-speaking battalion," stated Denison. In late September both the Liberals and Conservatives had petitioned Borden to form one to serve with the CEF.

"What has the recruiting been like?"

"Not very good," admitted the Denison. "We had to transfer men from the 23rd and the 24th Battalions to bring the 22nd up to full strength."

"Hmm. We'll include the 22nd in the second contingent for now," Gwatkin stated as they reached the six floor. "The sixty guns concerns me, as we've already shipped all we can spare. I don't want to strip what little defence we have. We'll have to inform the War Office we can supply the artillerymen, but they will need to supply the 18-pounders for the units. We don't have the capacity to manufacture artillery pieces. And I just read the report from Colonel Bertram of the Shell Committee. They are not going to be able to meet the production schedule for 4,000 artillery shells a week they had promised."

"Did he state why?"

"The main problem is the specifications demands acid steel. Canada only produces basic steel. Their expert, Carnegie, is looking into seeing

215

if the War Office will accept basic steel shells. As well they have only ten sets of gauges they need for the process. They have to make copies of them for the fifty or so companies they have lined up. They are parceling out the work to various firms across the country."

"The minister will not be happy about that?"

"It can't be helped."

"Yes, sir," replied the colonel.

"As for the machine guns, I suppose we can contract them from the Americans," he said as he passed his empty outer office. The orderlies had not yet reported for duty.

When he saw the colonel's frown, he asked, "Is there problem?"

"I don't know if it's a problem or not, but Rideau Hall sent us a message from Spring-Rice," he stated. Cecil Spring-Rice was the British ambassador to Washington. "He's concerned about reports of gentlemen making themselves out to be agents of the British government making extravagant offers for contracts."

"Do we have any authorized agents in the United States?"

"Not as far as I'm aware of. The minister may have. But I haven't found any records to that effect."

"Did the ambassador supply the names?"

"Yes, he did. He was concerned because the Americans are currently favouring us."

"I agree." There was a difference between earning a profit and profiteering. "Let's bring it up with the minister when he returns next week and see if we can clear up the matter."

The adjutant pulled a pencil and a notebook out of his breast pocket and made a note.

When Gwatkin sat in his chair, he asked, "Has General Otter settled into his new position?"

"That is my understanding."

General Otter was the first Canadian-born chief of the Canadian General Staff and had a long, distinguished career with service in the North-West Rebellion and the Boer War. He had retired in 1910, but Justice Minister Doherty had asked him to take charge of the internment operations.

"I'm pleased. Just let him know that he'll have to coordinate his activities with the Dominion Police."

"Done."

"Is there anything else?" he asked as he glanced at the stack of folders on his desk.

"We got a gram from Salisbury concerning Captain Janey and Lieutenant Sharpe." Gwatkin frowned when the officers' names were mentioned.

"Why?"

"They were asking if they had the authority to accompany the CEF. It seems that their airplane was damaged in transit and they are looking to repair it."

Gwatkin frowned as he recalled that in September Hughes had authorized Captain Janey to buy an aircraft for reconnaissance and artillery spotting. That fact that the captain was not a certified pilot didn't seem to bother the minister much. Janey had spent $5,000 buying a used Burgess-Dunne float aircraft from the US Navy. The craft was a tailless swept wing design with a wingspan of forty-six feet and the fuselage of twenty-six feet in length. The two-seater, powered by a Curtis engine, had a top speed of fifty-five miles per hour.

"Inform them that they had been authorized by the minister. They should be paid the standard aviator rates for their rank. Also, let them know that we don't have the intention of creating an aviation unit."

"I'll take care of it," Colonel Denison said as he made another quick note in his book.

"Anything else?" Denison shook his head no.

When the colonel left, Gwatkin paused for a moment before he buried himself in the latest war intelligence summaries. He wrote a reminder in his datebook to start the process for replacing Denison as his adjutant-general. He was being considered as a commander of one of the battalions in the second contingent. Whoever he would get, he had to look seriously at making him permanent. The position was starting to become a revolving door, and it was too important for that.

NOVEMBER 6, 1914
YE OLD BUSTARD INN, BUSTARD, SALISBURY PLAIN

The tent just outside the Old Bustard was packed with senior officers. *If an artillery shell landed, there goes the contingent's entire command structure*, Captain Llewellyn thought. The captain was sitting on his greatcoat on one of the wooden benches that were set up to face the table at the front of the tent. Sitting at the table were the four brigade commanders, Mercer, Turner, Williams, and Currie, chatting amiably. From time to time one of them would glance at the empty chairs beside them. To the right of them was a covered easel.

Llewellyn was sitting near the end of the bench. Colonel Topham was sitting near the aisle, and the three Fusiliers' captains were seated in order of precedence, with the captain brushing against the tent wall. The other benches were similarly arranged by units. Those officers who had arrived late stood at the back.

"Attention!" a voice commanded when Lieutenant-General Alderson entered with his headquarters staff. All the officers rose to their feet.

"Please be seated, gentlemen," said the general as he took his seat, "we have a lot to cover today."

Once everyone had taken their seats, he continued. "I've called all of the senior officers to outline my plans for the contingent for the next couple of weeks. I'm well aware that you are all anxious to get to the front. However, my staff and I have noted some deficiencies in your training that need to be rectified.

"Before we start, my adjutant would like to address some housekeeping items," added Alderson.

Lieutenant-Colonel Sweeney rose to his feet. "First, we are pleased that the incidence of drunkenness has decreased significantly since the wet canteens opened. However, there are still too many. Lieutenant-General Alderson would like you to restate to your men his concern about the consumption of alcohol. If a man is found drunk on duty, punishment up to and including No. 1 will be imposed. He is endangering himself and his fellow soldiers. That will not be tolerated."

The adjutant took the officers' lack of response as acquiescence. He continued, "The recent storm that caused a stampede of 700 horses also caused the collapse of the administration tent. I'm afraid that most of the attestation papers has suffered severe water damage and need to be redone." There was a collective groan from the sitting officers. Captain Llewellyn was one of the men groaning. A small smile flashed briefly on Alderson's face.

"If you have copies, please send them to HQ. We'll forward them to the pay office that has been established in London. For those who don't, you'll have to redo the paperwork."

When the muttering continued, Sweeney said flatly, "I'm well aware of the inconvenience, but it needs to be done."

After the officers were silenced, the Lieutenant-Colonel said, "We requested returns for the men to attend the Lord Mayor's Show next week in London. We would like to send 300 men to represent the contingent." Llewellyn had read the orders, and they were quite emphatic that reliable men were to be selected. As if they were going to send the unreliable. He and the other captains had selected men who had worked hard and deserved a chance for a two-day leave in London after the parade.

Llewellyn had never heard of the Lord Mayor's Show. As it had been explained to him, the mayor of London was appointed every year. On the day after the mayor was sworn in, he led a parade from the Guildhall to the Royal Courts of Justice, where he swore allegiance to the crown. It was held every year on November 9.

"It is of great importance," stated the adjutant with a touch of heat in his tone, "that returns requested for eleven o'clock be received on time. It is of great inconvenience when they are not received when due. Those who submit them late will be severely dealt with." From the corner of his eye, he saw Colonel Topham's face turn pale when the adjutant fixed his gaze on him. Llewellyn was somewhat pleased by that. The colonel was lackadaisical concerning paperwork.

"Next. All firearms, especially sidearms, must be discharged on the rifle ranges. Pistol practice in the camps is forbidden and must cease immediately.

"The First Field Hospital is moving from the West Down North Camp to the Bulford Manor House that General Vaughan was so gracious to provide. Until the move is completed, continue to send patients to the West Down.

"We are developing a schedule for the collection and delivery of official correspondence between the camps and headquarters. Riders from the Royal Canadian Dragoons and Lord Strathcona's Horse will be detailed daily under the command of the Signal Corps. It is expected that the riders will depart at 9:30 a.m. and 12:15 p.m. for the Bulford and Sling Plantation. This will be separate and apart from the contingent's regular postal service. This is all I have for the moment, General."

"Very good," Alderson acknowledged. "As you are aware, it's been rather wet for the past week."

"It sure ain't Bermuda weather!" someone from the back of the room remarked, which caused the gathered officers to chuckle. Llewellyn grimaced. From the corner of his eye he saw Colonel Topham give him a glare.

Alderson chuckled as well and then sighed. "Unfortunately, the forecast for the coming week is not favourable. I'm aware that there have been issues with footwear. We are working on getting additional supplies from Canada. Failing that, we'll have to look at obtaining them from local sources."

The general paused then nodded to the orderly standing beside the easel. He lifted the covering sheet to unveil a coloured map of France and the surrounding countries. A thick black line ran downward, indicating the current battle line that separated the combatants. At the top of the map, near the English Channel, arrows indicated a void between France and Belgium.

"This," Alderson indicated with a finger, "is the current positions of the Allied and German forces. As you are aware there, is currently heavy fighting in Belgium. Based on the latest intelligence summaries, there have been heavy assaults on the French left wing between Dixmude and the Lys. It appears that the Germans' objectives are the port cities of Calais and Boulogne-sur-Mer. Recently, there has been fierce fighting near Ypres. We cannot afford to lose the ports, since they are critical to our line of communications. The Germans have been thrown back with heavy losses."

He returned his gaze back to the contingent's officers. "I know that you are all eager to enter the front lines and do your bit." With a finger he indicated to the orderly to pass out the stack of papers that were set in front of him. The orderly started handing them out to the officers sitting along the aisles. When a pile was passed to Captain Llewellyn, he took the one of the sheets and passed the rest to the officer behind him.

He scanned the typed text, and the infantry section caught his attention. It was the only section that provided specific hours needed for the next seven days: physical training six hours, musketry instructions nine, squad drill six, extended order nine, route marching two, and four hours of night work. The total at the bottom was thirty-six hours. He wondered about the musketry, since space at the ranges was limited.

The rest of the syllabus had sections for the cavalry and cyclists, categorized as mounted troops, the artillery, and the engineers. All of the units had squad and section drills, physical training, route marches, map reading, night operations, patrolling, reconnaissance instruction, and basic field engineering.

The largest section was devoted to the artillery. Added to their learning plan was battery tactics, ranging, distribution of fire, ammunition supply, entrenching and concealing guns, and communications and orders. The artillery commanders were to give daily lectures on discipline, organization, and causes and history of the war. Llewellyn put a question mark beside that one. Also, they were to give lectures on sanitation and health, gunnery, ammunition, and internal economy.

"As you can see, you have a lot to learn," stated General Alderson grimly. "Based on General Campbell's reports that he has prepared from interviews of injured officers and men who have returned from the front, we will be placing emphasis on the following:

"Attacks by cavalry, especially small mounted units on small infantry units. I want the Strathconas and the Dragoons to practice the handling of weapons while mounted. This means the use of the sword while charging in a melee, and in pursuit of retreating enemy troops. Also pistol shooting while mounted. I want the infantry to practice defending against such attacks.

"As for the infantry, the spade has been found to be quite effective. Trenches best suited are nearly four feet deep and three feet wide, with a berm nine to ten inches in front. This has been found to be adequate for protection.

"The bayonet has proven to be a great factor to date. Inform your men to keep them sharp, as they will be getting plenty of practice.

"Deficiencies have been noted in night operations. Manoeuvring, taking up positions, and retiring at night with minimal sound will be practiced. Also, when taking up positions, care must be taken in setting up field of fire and obtaining accurate ranges for rifle and artillery.

"All units, mounted and dismounted, will practice rapid rifle fire on a daily basis. It has been proven to be quite effective.

"As for the artillery, the fullest use of cover afforded by gun shields and wagons should be used. Enemy fire has caused considerable casualties among the gun crews. Section commanders and detachments should stay as close to the shields as possible. Attention should be taken as to where the horses are picketed. It seems that guns have been captured because of casualties among the horses.

"I also want to emphasize the importance of keeping in touch and cooperating with neighbouring troops. This is especially important during a retirement to avoid gaps in the lines.

"This is all for the moment. As we receive and gather further reports, we'll be refining the training. Are there any questions?" asked Alderson.

Llewellyn had plenty of questions, but he wasn't about to raise his hand, especially when the more senior of the officers didn't.

"Good," said Alderson. "Please take a few minutes to study the map before you return to your units."

As the meeting was breaking up, Llewellyn rose and made his way to the easel. Already, there was a crowd examining the battlefields that they would be soon fighting on.

CHAPTER 24

Samantha walked briskly down the hallway to the ward that she and Emily had been assigned. It had taken several days to transfer patients from West Down North camp to Bulford Manor, in the small village of Bulford, that General Vaughan and his staff had vacated.

The manor had been built in the seventeenth century out of stone and flint. It had changed hands over the years, and the last owner had added service wings in the southeast and northeast corners. The newer sections had a red brick exterior. When Samantha arrived she found, the edifice quite pretty with its covered walls, white painted windows, and the four dormer attics. A three-foot-high black iron fence was its only protection against intruders.

The hospital had quickly moved sixty patients into the building. In the rear courtyard they had erected tents to accommodate those with minor injuries or those that were in the final stages of recovery. They also designated two rooms on the ground floor as operating theatres and one room for a lab for blood work. The manor had electricity, so they could run lights, sterilizers, and X-ray equipment. The motorized and horse-drawn ambulances were parked in the stables. Several cottages on the property had been assigned as the nurses' residence.

When she heard shouting and swearing outside, she glanced out one of the windows and saw the stretcher-bearers going through their daily drill. With the imminent departure of the No. 2 Field Ambulance, the training tempo had increased.

"So they finally arrived," said Emily when she saw the forms that Samantha was carrying. She took them from her and put them into an eighteenth-century armoire that they were using as a pantry. The ward Emily had been assigned had six beds that were all occupied. One of the patients, a Royal Dragoon, had broken his pelvis when his horse kicked him. Beside him was a Queen's Own Rifle soldier who had his feet wrapped because the poor man's boots had rubbed his feet raw and they had become infected. The other two were from one of the kilted regiments. They were recovering from deep slashes on the backs of their legs from their mud-encrusted kilts after a ten-mile route march. The two at the far wall had ailments the doctors had not yet diagnosed.

"Are we ready?" Emily asked, her forehead creased with worry.

"As well as we can be," replied Samantha. They hadn't received much warning for the inspection.

"Do you think that they'll be sending us to France?" Emily asked. Rumours were flying that the nurses could soon be deployed. They also heard that the PPCLI would be next, since they were the most ready at the moment.

"If they are, they are more likely to send the nurses from West Down. I don't think that they're going to pull nurses from here."

Emily frowned in dismay. She said, "What I've been hearing is that the London hospitals are full, and they could be sending patients here."

Samantha snorted and was about to reply when she heard voices that carried from the ground floor. "Oh my God. They're here," she exclaimed.

She and Emily hurried to their assigned posts in the ward. The six men looked on with wry amusement, as they were not the ones required to pass inspections. Both of them stood at nervous attention. It took awhile for Matron-in-Chief Macdonald to arrive with Lieutenant-Colonel Murray MacLaren, the commander of the No. 1 General Hospital, and Matron Rita Newman, the hospital's matron.

Macdonald gave the nurses a brief smile. "Miss Lonsdale and Miss Richard … I mean, Mrs. Creighton. It is good to see you both again."

"Thank you," the two nurses replied, pleased that the matron knew their names. Samantha's eyes fixed on Matron Macdonald's shoulder boards. She was finally learning to recognize the military insignia system. She nearly gasped when she saw that a major's crown had replaced the captain's stars. What Samantha didn't realize, until she was informed later, was that the promotion made the matron the highest-ranking woman officer in the Empire.

"Do you have everything you need to perform your duties?" she asked after she had greeted and chatted with the patients. "I noticed that the history charts are missing."

Both Samantha and Emily blushed in embarrassment. "We just received them, ma'am. We didn't have time to complete them prior to your arrival," Samantha explained.

Major Macdonald cocked her head toward Colonel MacLaren, who confirmed. "We've had some shortages in our supplies. It took a devil of time to get proper boots and socks for our men. Their feet are constantly wet. I'm hoping that this building will ameliorate the situation."

"Understood," replied Major Macdonald. She turned to Emily and asked, "How is married life?"

Emily blushed. "It's been fine, ma'am." She paused. Samantha could see that she was struggling with asking the matron a question.

The major saw it as well. "Out with it."

"When will we be sent to France? I mean …" she blurted. "No disrespect, but the No. 2 Ambulance are in Boulogne. When will be we sent out there?"

"Anxious to leave your husband so soon?" the matron replied in amusement.

Emily shook her head. "I just want to do my bit."

"You are," Macdonald said with a sweep of her hand. "Don't you think?"

Emily dropped her eyes as she replied, "Yes, ma'am."

"Matron, we need to move along. We have a meeting in half an hour," said MacLaren.

"Of course, Colonel," she replied as he pointed her down the hallway. Before they disappeared down the staircase, Matron Newman gave Samantha and Emily a displeased smile.

* * *

"Are you certain you want to include Miss Lonsdale?" asked Matron Macdonald. Her and Matron Newman were meeting in the Bulford Manor's reading room. It had been stripped bare of its books, and the cases were now being used as storage for the hospital's records. The major flipped through the pages of the list of names on the nursing return.

"Yes, I believe that she has leadership potential. She gets along well with the other nurses and the orderlies. She still has a lot to learn, but I think that she is capable," replied Matron Newman.

"Hmm," murmured Macdonald, gently tapping her teeth with her pen as she considered the suggestion. At the urgent request of Sir Alfred Keogh, the director of the British Army's Medical Services, the CEF's No. 2 Stationary Hospital was being deployed to France. Colonel Jones had ordered that fifty of the one hundred nurses accompany the unit. "Frying pan to the fire?"

Newman shrugged. "Sink or swim."

Macdonald sighed. She knew the feeling. She recalled she had been rather apprehensive when she had knocked on the door of the director-general of Medical Services office in the Woods Building in Ottawa. She had generally tried to avoid militia headquarters, since she had to spend most of her time between the Kingston and Montreal military hospitals. She had been on a camping trip when the urgent telegram ordering her to report to Ottawa had been sent, so she was a couple of days late.

"Where the hell have you been?" he had demanded when she had entered his office. She had known the fifty-year-old colonel for nearly fifteen years. He and Surgeon-General Fiset had worked hard in modernizing and training the Canadian Medical Services Corps. It took them years to convince the militia that they were not only healing but preventative doctors. Now they were going to see if all of their efforts were worthwhile.

"I'm sorry, Colonel. It won't happen again," she had replied.

"I certainly hope not," he said tersely. "I'm going to get directly to the point. I want you to be the matron of the nursing sisters we are sending to Britain."

She was surprised by the offer and felt that she was not ready for the post. She told him so. "Thank you, Guy. I don't think that it would be wise. I'm most unsuitable to be a matron."

"May I ask why?"

"There are a number of reasons," she told him. "The first is that I don't have any administrative experience."

Jones waved that away. "I believe that you have the aptitude. You will learn the rest on the job."

"Georgina has seniority." She was referring to Georgina Page, who was nearly ten years older than her and had more time in the militia than she did.

Jones snorted. "Just because she has seniority, it does not mean that she is suitable."

"Also, I'm too old. The regulations state that you need to be between the ages of eighteen and thirty-eight to qualify."

Jones gave her a wry smile. "It's been my experience that some women tend to be non-committal about their age."

When he saw she was still not convinced, he leaned forward.

"Sister Macdonald! Whether or not you feel that you are not suitable is immaterial in this particular case. You are a military officer, and you will comply with my orders."

"Yes, Colonel."

Jones leaned back in his chair with an air of satisfaction. "Good. I'm glad that I've made myself clear. The first task you will perform is to review the applications. Nearly 2,000 have come in so far. Regulations state that we need a nurse for every eight wounded soldiers. For the initial intake, we are looking to staff No. 1 and No. 2 General Hospitals. We will need a hundred nurses."

"Yes, sir."

"If you have any problems or you need assistance, come and see me. My door is always open."

"Thank you, sir."

"Well, Margaret. You might as well get started."

And that was exactly what she did. She had ploughed through nearly all of the applications. The criteria she used to select the final candidates were relatively simple. The women needed to have military nursing experience or training. Three of five nurses in the permanent nurses made the cut. Geraldine, due to her age, was not included. Nearly forty-two nurses in the pile had militia reserve training or had attended an annual militia training camp. The remainder had to be graduates from a nursing school to be considered. Any application from women who didn't have nursing experience or training received a polite "we regret to inform you" letter. Once she weeded down the pile, she interviewed all of the candidates to ensure that they had suitable characters and disposition.

Samantha Lonsdale had impressed her from the beginning and seemed to have the qualities that she was looking for.

"If the war is going to be a long one, we'll need experienced supervisors and administrators. What do you think of Miss Richardson?"

"Emily? She's a good nurse, but she hasn't shown administrative skills to date. If she was at West Down, I would send her along, but I wouldn't put her on the list."

"That's fine. Let's cut orders for Miss Lonsdale," the matron-in-chief decided. She then looked pointedly at her subordinate. "I've been reading your reports. I've been finding them rather thin. In future, I like more detail in them in order to base my decisions."

Newman's face blanched slightly. "Yes, ma'am."

"Good," Matron Macdonald said briskly. "Let's take a closer look at the rest of these names."

NOVEMBER 12, 1914
LARK HILL, SALISBURY PLAIN

Samantha had been dancing for nearly an hour before Captain Llewellyn approached her with a gold ticket. She and the other nursing sisters that were not on duty had agreed to attend a YMCA fundraiser at Lark Hill. They were the star attraction, since an attractive woman could entertain the men for a dime a dance. When they arrived, a long line of men was waiting impatiently to buy a ticket. Samantha could hear music from a piano and brass instruments emanating from inside the large tent.

When the guard at the entrance spotted them — the nurses were easy to spot in a sea of olive drab uniforms — he escorted them past the lineup into the marquee. Inside, Samantha saw that the front third of the space was filled with tables of various sizes, colour, and types ranging from card to picnic. Many of the men looked up at them from the postcards and letters they were writing to their folks back home. The buzz dimmed slightly as their procession made its way through the centre aisle to a set of tables near the dance floor at the far end.

On the stage, an upright piano was being hammered by a madman, Samantha thought, from the way he was playing. There was no style and grace but frenetic energy as he pounded the keys and jumped about on his stool. The military brass band seated beside him tried gamely to keep pace with him. What surprised her was that her toes were tapping to the music. It was that good.

Running along one of the walls were the refreshment tables. The YMCA was a strong temperance proponent, so the drinks were dry. The glass bowls were filled with fruit juices, there were urns for the coffee, hot water for tea, and soda pop bottles were in vats of crushed ice.

Samantha spotted Claire, who was waving to get their attention. She had saved a couple of chairs for her and Emily.

"Look at all the men," Emily said cheerfully.

Samantha laughed as she took off her jacket and hung it on the back of her chair. "I think that we are outnumbered."

"Maybe I should surrender," Emily replied.

"I thought you already did," answered Claire with a teasing smile.

"I wouldn't raise the white flag just yet. Wait until later this evening?" Samantha stated as she adjusted her blond hair. "How is this going to work?"

"The soldier will present you with a ticket," replied Claire. She was interrupted by a coughing fit.

"Are you okay?" Samantha asked. She noticed that Claire seemed tired of late.

"I'm fine. I'm just not getting as much sleep as I would like," Claire replied with a rather thin smile. Before Samantha could question her, Claire continued, "Like I was saying, they set different prices for the tickets. The ten-cent white tickets are for the privates. The NCOs are given red tickets for fifteen cents. The officers get the gold tickets for a quarter. Now, if you don't like the man who presents you with a ticket, you can turn them down. If a man gets fresh, tell the sergeant." Claire pointed to a muscular military police sergeant standing guard near their table.

"Miss Lonsdale, may I have the pleasure of a dance?" the officer asked as he offered her his hand. She was about to refuse, because it had been announced that the next dance was a waltz. She disliked the intimacy that it implied. She smiled and said, "It would be my pleasure, Captain Llewellyn." She somehow trusted that the captain would behave properly.

When they stepped out on the dance floor, she asked, "So how is Private Cummings?"

"Last I heard, he was doing fine," replied the captain, cocking his head. He seemed somewhat pleased that she remembered. When he raised his arm, she slid comfortably into them. For a big man, he moved very well. He gently steered her through the crowded dance floor with soft pressure from his left hand that rested gently on the small of her back, just above her waist.

"I also heard that some of the nurses are going to France tomorrow." She looked up at him and said proudly, "Yes. I'm one of them."

Samantha had been shocked when she received orders that she was to report to Boulogne. She was puzzled why she had been given the assignment, since she had not asked for it. She had mixed feelings about her deployment. She was excited, but at the same time nervous. She didn't know what to expect or whether she was up to the task.

She had wanted her last evening at Salisbury Plain to be a quiet one. Emily had looked into having dinner at the Rose and Crown, the pub that was just a few minutes away from Bulford Manor on High Street. However, orders had been issued that the eatery was off limits to military personnel. The rumours were that a number of her countrymen had gotten into a drunken brawl once too often, and the owners had had enough with the Canadians.

"Nervous?" he asked.

"Yes," she replied honestly.

"Good. I would be worried if you weren't."

"Oh?" was her startled reply.

He gave her a wry smile. "It's been my experience that the more competent and reliable ones tend to be the most nervous."

Samantha blushed at the compliment. "Thank you," she replied. "Aren't you anxious to get to the front?"

"Time spent training is never wasted," he replied with the same wry smile. She found his reply curious. It was unlike the responses other men had given her. They had been quite eager to get to the front. Some nearly gushed telling how they would make quick work of the Boche.

When the song ended, she asked, "Do you have another ticket?"

"I'm afraid that I only had the one," he replied as he walked her back to her table. "I enjoyed the dance, Miss Lonsdale. It was a pleasure seeing you again." He acknowledged the other ladies sitting at the table with bow. Samantha tracked the man as he strolled away toward a table on the other side of the tent.

"Here's your fruit punch," Emily said as she handed her a tin cup. She had finally found her husband, and he was keeping a protective eye on her. She tilted her head and followed Samantha's gaze. "You like him, don't you?"

"He's all right," said Samantha thoughtfully. Since she was leaving in the morning, it was unlikely she would ever see him again. Pity.

CHAPTER 25

NOVEMBER 16, 1914
ADVANCED REMOUNT DEPOT,
SALISBURY PLAINS

"Where did you get it?" Paul Ryan asked as he stared at the green Oliver typewriter sitting on a plank table in the Advanced Remount Depot's administrative tent.

"Found it in a second-hand shop when I was in London for the Lord Mayor's Show," replied Captain Fuller.

"So the quartermaster still didn't want to order one?" Paul said as he struck a key. A hammer flew out from one of the twin towers that rose a couple of inches above the keyboard to strike the paper in the paten. He was more familiar with the Remington, where the hammers were set in a U-shaped well, which gave him an unobstructed view.

"The idiots," groused Fuller. Paul had been with the captain when the clerk had refused to order a machine for them. He had instructions from the War Office not to issue typewriters to anyone. There was a concern that the machines resulted in excessive paperwork and that some of the men were using them for personal correspondence.

"What are we going to do when the ribbon wears out?"

"If you can believe it, those we can requisition." Fuller grumbled at the foibles of the line of communication system.

"How was the Lord Mayor's Show?" Paul asked, changing the subject. The captain had been in command of the thirty men from the battalion that were sent to London.

"I must admit it was quite a spectacle. There were nearly 3,000 troops that marched. There was us, the Newfoundlanders, New Zealanders, and the territorials. We had to stand around for a while for the speeches by Lord Kitchener, Winston Churchill, and Prime Minister Asquith. Our nursing sisters drew quite a bit of attention," he said with a proud grin.

"I just heard that half of them left for France yesterday," said Paul.

"They did," he acknowledged. "We may be going soon."

When he heard a whinny, he glanced toward the tent wall. "How many do we have today?"

Paul knew that he was asking how many horses were in the sick paddock. "About thirty, sir. We also got requests from the Strathconas for replacement chargers, and one of the brigade commanders needs a rider."

"Anything serious among the sick?"

"Not as far as I'm aware."

"I'll take a look before I turn in. By the way, I had a word with General Alderson's adjutant concerning whether or not we need to establish a base remount depot."

"What did he say?"

"He indicated that it was a good idea, but he will bring it up with the War Office and Ottawa."

"That sounds promising," Paul said. The captain had explained to him that their unit were considered part of the line of communications. When the Canadian Division moved, they would move with it and supply the various units with replacements from the 300 or so animals available at the depot. It meant that they needed to be fit and nearly fully worked up, ready for work.

Captain Fuller said that the expected attrition rate was about fifteen percent. That meant based on the nearly 8,000 horses currently on the nominal rolls, they would need to purchase, train, and supply nearly 1,000 new horses on a regular basis. There were a number of reasons why the horses were cast from service, other than death or capture during combat operations. The main one was medical, such as disease or chronic disability. Remount cases were where the steed in question was prematurely worn out, had bad vices, or was simply too dangerous or unsafe to ride. Age was another factor. Any animal that was over fifteen years old and didn't meet the standard that was expected of them was considered worn out.

"Any news on stables for the horses?" Only the sick horses were under canvas to protect them from the elements.

"Nothing yet," replied Fuller. "They'll looking into either building some, or if there are some suitable barns nearby that could be converted. Have you completed the paperwork for the sick animals?"

"Yes, Captain," said Paul, indicating to the ledger on the table beside him. He was actually surprised at the amount of paperwork that was needed for the depot. Every horse in the division had a file. It contained a form that listed the breed, age, where and when it was acquired, and how much was paid for the horse. The horse's serial number, which was branded on the near forefoot, was recorded. On the off shoulder, "CA" was branded to indicate it was a Canadian horse. Included were the horse's medical history and the unit it was assigned to.

The captain flipped through the pages, and Paul waited anxiously as Fuller inspected his work. "It looks fine," he said. "You can go and get some rest. We're going to have a busy day tomorrow."

NOVEMBER 16, 1914
65TH HORSE ARTILLERY, BELL TENTS,
WEST DOWN NORTH CAMP

It was nearly nine before Paul entered his quarters. He missed Reggie, but when he got reassigned, he had to transfer to a new tent. He used the wooden board, set beside the entrance, to scrape the mud off his boots. Once inside, he unlaced them and padded across the plank floor to the oil stove in the centre. Sixteen cots were arranged in a circle around it. The wood under his feet was damp, and as he put his weight down, water would seep through. His wool socks were already wet, so he didn't notice the additional dampness. As he got near it, he could feel the heat from it as it had been topped with firewood. However, it was still not strong enough to heat the extremities.

"So how is it going, Corporal?" asked Ned Kennedy, who was sitting on his cot playing chess with Edwin Mackay. Both men were from Regina and were grooms at the depot.

"The usual," Paul replied, "Mud, mud, and more mud."

"And that's just what they serve in the mess," quipped Edwin as he moved a pawn.

"Ha-ha," replied Paul sarcastically. It was an old joke, and it was getting older.

He stared at the stove, trying to find room for his boots. There were about half-a-dozen on the floor beside it, another four or five pairs on stakes around the stove as if it was a bonfire, and others above hanged from the guide wires. Everyone knew that heat damaged the leather, but they were all tired of wearing wet boots.

"Take it easy with my boots. They're the only pair I have," growled Ned when Paul moved a pair in order to fit his in. They all only had one pair. The drubbing they used to waterproof didn't help much when mud and water reached above the top of their boots.

"Yeah, yeah," Paul replied as he made his way to his neatly folded cot. One thing he was grateful for was they hadn't learned about his nickname, which would have made the teasing worse.

When he sat down on his cot to take his socks off, he saw his neighbour, Jerry Neilson, a Yukoner and a stable hand, bare his stomach and carefully set his socks on his belly. "What the hell are you doing?"

Jerry gave him a toothy grin. "Someone told me that if you put your wet socks on your belly, your body heat will dry the socks out."

"That's the most ridiculous thing I ever heard," declared Ned, looking up after he had moved his knight.

"We'll see who will be laughing the morning," Jerry said defensively.

When Paul reached down to remove his left sock, he thought, *What the hell, it doesn't hurt to try.*

NOVEMBER 18, 1914
SALISBURY PLAIN

"Well, Privates Harrison and Grayson, I must say that I'm extremely disappointed." Captain Llewellyn shook his head at the two men who were kneeling before him on the wet grass with their hands behind their heads. "To be captured so quickly and easily. A real shame."

"Yes, Captain," they replied as they stared at the ground, crestfallen.

Llewellyn had selected the sneakiest and most cunning men in his company to try to infiltrate the outposts that had been set up as part of the day's training scheme.

"Take them away for interrogation," he ordered Sergeant Booth, who led the guard detail.

"Get up," the sergeant said brusquely. When they got to their feet, he gave them a shove with his rifle butt. "Get going."

"Hey! Take it easy, for Christ's sake," retorted Grayson. "We're only playing."

"You're just a dirty Hun to me, Private Grayson," chuckled Booth as he gave him another shove. "I'm going to love interrogating you," he added as they headed toward the detention area where the other six men were being detained.

The captain wasn't concerned with the sergeant getting too rough. Part of the training scheme was to practice prisoner of war procedures. The captured men were to be stripped of their equipment and any military documents they had confiscated. They there were to be interrogated to determine their unit designation, formation, commanding officers, where the men had slept the previous evening, how far they had marched, and their unit's morale. This all had to be done while respecting the 1907 Hague Regulations, which stated that captives were required to provide their real name and rank and were to be treated humanely.

"So we got them all," said Lieutenant Vernon with a satisfied grin. It was his outposts that the two men had tried to sneak past.

"Looks like," lied Llewellyn. The eight men would not be happy with him when they found out that he had informed the outposts where and when to expect them. But then again, he hadn't told his three lieutenants that there were actually sixteen men involved in this evening's exercise. Eight men who had reported for sick parade in the morning were conveniently missing.

"So should we pull the men in?" asked the lieutenant.

"No, leave them out there 'till morning," he replied. He wanted to assess how well they managed when things went wrong.

For the night operations, the scheme was that the brigade had stopped for the night, and his company had been selected to provide security for the temporary camp. The Red Force, of brigade strength, was in the vicinity, but they had lost contact. They were to bivouac for the evening and see if they could find them at first light. He had been ordered to protect the flank and the road they would be taking in the morning.

Llewellyn had been given the frontage that his unit was to cover, and he had provided it to his three section commanders to come up with a plan. The three had agreed to have two platoons out in front, with three-man teams about a half-mile away from the main camp. The men would have two-hour rotating shifts. If they sighted or encountered the enemy, they were to send a man back with a report. The first platoon would act as a reserve, ready to move to delay the enemy and protect the camp if there was an attack in force, until the CO decided on the appropriate response.

The captain knew quite well that there was a great bit of difference between what the book said and what actually happened in the field. A lot of small things could trip soldiers up. No could appreciate how spooky observing at night could be. Especially since the men had been up since five thirty, had extended order drill in the morning, and then a ten-mile march in the afternoon to get to the assembly point. The men were tired, hungry, and wet.

In the dark, even with a full moon, the movement of grass by the wind and the amplification of sound made men jumpy. Standing guard for any length of time at two in the morning without falling asleep was difficult. That was why there were severe punishments for the offence. In actual combat, falling asleep could result in the death penalty.

"I want to do an inspection to see if everything is to my satisfaction," Llewellyn stated. One of the things that he was doing was evaluating his lieutenants. There was a mark against Vernon because he had left his post instead of sending one of his NCOs back with the captured prisoners like the other two had.

"When is your examination?" asked Vernon.

The captain grunted sourly. "I'm writing it in two weeks." He was still an acting captain until he obtained the appropriate certificates for his rank. He was struggling to make the time to prepare for the written test.

"Good luck," the lieutenant said. He then changed the subject. "I heard that the PPCLI is being sent to the front."

"So did I," replied the captain. On the 16th, the PPCLI joined the 27th Division in Winchester. He was of two minds on the Princess Patricia's. Since they were supposed to be Canadian, they should continue to remain part of the contingent. However, Colonel Farquhar, the commander, felt that his battalion was ready for combat, and he had been lobbying strongly to be split from the other units. This did not sit very well with many of the other senior officers, but it seemed that the colonel finally got his way. He had also learned from the armour that the PPCLIs were replacing their Ross's with Lee-Enfields. Llewellyn grudgingly acknowledged that it made sense, since it would be the only Canadian unit in a British division.

"What is on tomorrow's menu?"

"Entrenching at Lark Hill."

"Joy."

The men tolerated digging trenches at best, even though they knew that it would save their lives. With the constant rain they had been enduring, no matter where they dug, the trenches quickly filled with brown murky water.

Suddenly Llewellyn's nose was hit by the pungent smell of body odour. By then he knew it was too late. He was knocked down to the ground and his hands were roughly tied behind his back. Vernon sputtered as he tried to raise the alarm, but he was quickly gagged. Something was stuffed in his mouth, a sock from the woolly taste, and then he was

236

lifted to his feet. He and the lieutenant were force marched for about a half-hour to a small hallow between two high mounds.

There they faced the grinning faces of Privates Duval and Dack as they removed their gags.

"You're been a good prisoner, Captain," Duval said with a satisfied tone. "Didn't mean to rough you up."

"I see that your time with the good father hasn't been wasted," he replied.

The two privates glanced at each other and then back to Llewellyn. Actually, Father Stoat had been proving to be an excellent intelligence officer. It must be due to all that religious training. Llewellyn could see the wheels turning. They weren't going to say it to his face, but he knew that they were going to call him a right bastard when his back was turned.

"I thought the exercise was over!" exclaimed Vernon.

"Whatever gave you that idea, Lieutenant?"

"You told us eight men, and we captured them all."

Llewellyn gave Vernon a puzzled frown. "I'm fairly certain that I said sixteen."

CHAPTER 26

Captain Llewellyn had stopped noting the weather in the Fusiliers' war diary, in which he was required to record the regiment's daily activities. He had already filled the "Remarks and References to Appendix" column of the three-column page with adjectives like gentle, misty, soft, drizzling, spitting, hard, sideways, flooding, torrential, drenching, and in buckets.

Today was no different as he and his twenty men stood at ease in the London rain waiting for the order to march. Nearby was a section of New Zealanders. A squad of Newfoundlanders were a couple of rows back. The men from the rock were a bit standoffish, since they disliked being mistaken for Canadians. In a way, Llewellyn didn't blame them, since his countrymen were developing a bad reputation.

From his position, he could barely see Charing Cross train station, where the body of Lord Roberts was to arrive at 10:30 by special train from Ascot. Britain had been stunned by the sudden death of one of her greatest and popular soldiers. The eighty-two-year-old field marshal had died last Saturday when a chill he had contracted while inspecting British and Indian troops in France turned into pneumonia.

When news had arrived at the Bustard Camp, the senior staff was surprised, since the field marshal had visited and inspected the contingent just a few weeks before. Orders were transmitted that 300 men, under the command of Lieutenant-Colonel Turner, would be sent to the ceremony at London's St. Paul's Cathedral, while an equal number would attend the memorial service that was to be held at the nearby Salisbury Cathedral.

The body of Lord Roberts had been transported back to his home in Ascot, where a private ceremony had been held. From what Llewellyn had been told, the same gun carriage that had carried Lord Robert's son, who had been killed during the Boer War, was used to take the casket from his home to the Ascot train station for this morning's trip to London.

Llewellyn had taken the train with his men the previous evening, and they had been briefed on their role. Due to his rank, he had not been granted a seating in St. Paul's Cathedral for the service. Llewellyn had not been put out by this, since being assigned to take part had been honour enough. He did feel it was somewhat unseemly that Colonel Topham tried to jockey for a seat among the Canadian senior officers who were fortunate enough to be granted a spot in one of the back pews.

When he heard the cannons of the Hampshire Artillery at St. James Park start the nineteen-gun salute, he knew that the procession was about to start. The London Scottish, Royal Sussex, Grenadier Guards, Irish Guards, and Indian Mountain Artillery Battalions began their sombre march. The Indian Battalion intrigued Llewellyn as he could see red turban handlers lead mules, with disassembled 10-pounder cannons tied to their packs. Lord Roberts had been their commander during the Afghan wars.

The casket, draped with a Union Jack, followed behind on the Royal Horse Artillery's 'P' battery's gun carriage. There were twelve pallbearers; Lord Kitchener was at the head, followed by four field marshals, four generals, two admirals, and one colonel. Cavalry squadrons of the Life Guards, Royal Horse, and King Edwards followed them.

When the order was finally given, Captain Llewellyn and his men, with the thousands of Dominion and Imperial soldiers that had been assembled, began their slow march through the quiet and respectful crowds that lined the route from Northumberland Avenue, along the Embankment, New Bridge Street, and Ludgate Hill, to St. Paul's Cathedral, where the king and queen and other dignitaries were waiting.

NOVEMBER 19, 1914
SALISBURY CATHEDRAL

Paul Ryan was impressed by the Salisbury Cathedral. He and Reggie had visited the building a few weeks earlier when they had an afternoon's leave. He had felt somewhat uncomfortable entering the Anglican church, since he was a Roman Catholic. God didn't seem to mind, since he was still alive. They had taken the "Tower Tour," during which they climbed the tallest spire in England. He didn't believe that the church was over 700 years old until he saw the ancient wood scaffolding during the tour.

They had lucked out, because the weather had been, like today, quite pleasant. The sunlight streaming through the stained glass windows had illuminated the long nave, with its grey stone and dark marble columns. It was awe-inspiring. The guide informed them that the church had one of the four remaining copies of the *Magna Carta*. Paul had wanted to take a look, but they weren't allowed.

The opening salvo of artillery fire caught his attention, and he looked over to the single battery of the Royal Canada Artillery that had the honour of giving the nineteen-gun salute for Lord Roberts. Smoke emanated from the barrels of four 18-pounders as the crews reloaded blank shells for the next salvo. The CEF's artillery had been recently ordered to reorganize into 4-gun batteries. Paul was used to seeing six guns, so it seemed rather odd to him.

He did wonder why it was only nineteen guns, since he thought it was supposed to be twenty-one. He made the mistake of asking Sergeant Mackenzie. "McGill, did you miss a class, or you weren't paying attention?" he had said derisively as if it was a silly question and that every artilleryman should know. "Only the royals are entitled to twenty-one guns. The prime minster gets nineteen. Hughes, bless his soul, gets seventeen. Since Lord Roberts was a field marshal, he gets nineteen guns."

Paul glanced back to the main entrance as he waited impatiently for the ceremony to end. He had been ordered to attend the Mass, but he managed to escape when he pointed out his religious affiliation. He didn't completely escape, since he was sitting in a Peerless two-ton truck that he had used to drive the squad from the remount depot. He was one of the few men there that had a driver's license. It was a civilian one, but he was in line for the class to get his military permit.

When the traffic co-ordinator sergeant signalled that the ceremony was nearly at an end, Paul started his engine, as did every other vehicle in the car park. The vehicles had been arranged so that the senior officers would be picked up first, followed by the lower ranks. The sergeant pointed at the Southern Command cars and motioned them forward. The Canadian units were next in line. Paul started up his truck, and it lurched when he engaged the clutch. In the side mirror he saw the New Zealand and the Newfoundland trucks were on his bumper as they followed him toward the church's main entrance.

CHAPTER 27

NOVEMBER 20, 1914
PRIME MINISTER'S OFFICE, EAST BLOCK,
PARLIAMENT HILL, OTTAWA

"They are screaming for his head again," said John Hazen.
"Who this time?" asked Sir Robert Borden as he looked up at Hazen, who was standing in the doorway of his office.

"*The Toronto World*," Hazen said as he waved a newspaper.

"Sit," ordered Borden, pointing to the chair in front of his desk. "What did he do this time?" Borden suddenly felt tired. He was hoping that he would have a few days to catch up with the correspondence that had accumulated during his three-week vacation in Virginia. The hot springs and the daily rounds of golf with Laura had rejuvenated him. Most of the letters had already been dealt with by his staff and his ministers. For some, only he could make the decision. There was the list of judicial candidates for the vacant seats on the Ontario and Western benches. He needed a replacement for Casgrain on the International Joint Commission. When to recall Parliament, as well as the vetting the candidates for the by-elections in Terrebonne, Jacque Cartier, and Westmoreland ridings were sitting on his desk. He had six vacancies in the Senate; two were the results of senators being booted out for lack of attendance.

"Major-General Lessard decided to test his revised mobilization plans. On the 16th he called out three militia regiments in Toronto. He gave the men only a four-hour warning before he ordered fifteen hundred to gather at their assigned assembly points."

Borden gave him a puzzled look, trying to determine what the issue was.

"Unfortunately, the test alarmed the good citizens of Toronto. They thought that they had been called out to repel an invasion by German-Americans."

Borden leaned back in his chair. "I would think so, with all this talk of German spies. I've been informed that the good women of Toronto have been keeping the target ranges busy," Borden said. "When I was in New York last week, the British Ambassador, Spring Rice, spoke to me at length on the topic. Even the duke has been informed that Germany has a perfect spy system. I'm certain that the ambassador bent the duke's ear on German espionage in the States when he was here this week."

His wife Laura was one of the dignitaries who had greeted the Ambassador Spring Rice when he arrived in Ottawa. He was required to visit the governor general twice a year.

"The story would have died if Sam hadn't publicly castigated General Lessard in a speech the next day." He lifted the paper and read, "'It was the worst military tactics possible and it needlessly encouraged speculation of a raid on Canada. Also, it would have a negative impact on recruitment.'"

"In public?"

"I'm afraid so. Toronto is up in arms, and the militia officers that I've spoken to are not very happy. You know how respected Lessard is. The *World* is running a campaign to have Hughes fired, and I've gotten some angry telegrams from our supporters saying Hughes has got to go."

"What are the other papers saying?"

"The *Toronto Telegram* is saying the same thing. The others are making fun of Toronto."

"Will it impact recruiting for the second contingent?" asked Borden.

"I doubt it. All the reports that I've read say that it's going well. There is some difficulty recruiting in Quebec. They are not making their targets," replied Hazen.

"I read in the *Citizen* that some of the volunteers are refusing their typhoid vaccination."

"I'm afraid so. Gwatkin is looking into the matter. They did sign their attestation papers, and it clearly indicates they are to pass their medicals. Some of the men don't want foreign germs in their systems. If they don't submit, we'll have to discharge them." Hazen paused. "I might as well tell you about Eliot's Horse."

"What the hell is Eliot's Horse!" demanded the prime minister.

"The Eliot's Horse is a regiment raised by a Winnipeg lawyer as mounted troops. However, the militia department said they didn't need them. Their officers were eager to go to England, so they convinced eighty men that they would be accepted once in they arrived in Great Britain. Now they are stranded there without money."

"Why doesn't General Alderson take them?"

"General Alderson doesn't want them. He suggested that they either join a British regiment or sail back to Canada and join the second contingent."

"That's ridiculous! They are there already. There must be some room in the contingent," demanded Borden. "Especially since we have been discussing increasing the number of men in Canada under arms to 50,000."

Hazen nodded in agreement, recognizing an order when he heard one. "Yes, prime minister. I'll pass your request on."

"Where is Hughes at the moment?" asked Borden.

"I don't rightly know," replied Hazen. It wasn't his job to keep track of the minister of Militia and Defence. "By the way, were you informed that Lady Otter passed away?"

"Yes. Heart trouble, wasn't it?"

"So I have been informed. Also, Lord Roberts' funeral was yesterday. He passed away suddenly in France earlier in the week as well."

"I know. I've sent my condolences to General Otter and to Lady Robert as well," Borden said with a touch of sadness.

Borden glanced at the paperwork on his desk and sighed. "I have to get back to it. Have you read the latest suggestions from Jackman?"

"Yes, I have," replied Hazen. Edward Jackman was sent by the Newfoundland government to negotiate possible terms for Newfoundland joining Confederation. In public, Jackman espoused anti-Canada sentiments, but in private he was pro-union.

"If you have time, I want to go over his proposals before I meet with him again."

"Of course," replied Hazen. He took a fountain pen from his breast pocket so he would be able to make notes in the margins.

NOVEMBER 20, 1914
ORDNANCE, SALISBURY PLAIN

The ordnance officer put up his hand when Captain Llewellyn entered his busy office. "I know. You want 30,000 rounds of .303s."

Llewellyn chuckled amiably. "You saw the orders."

"Of course," replied the ordnance officer. Major Hampstead, a Cape Bretoner, was a portly man in his mid-thirties with thinning hair. "They had to talk to me before they were issued. I wonder what that's all about," he said as the captain handed him a requisition form. Bustard HQ had issued an urgent order, effective immediately, that all battalions were to ensure that 300 rounds were available for each rifle in the unit. Each man was to carry one hundred while the remaining 200 would be carried in the S.A.A. carts. Since each battalion was supposed to have the authorized strength of a thousand rifles, it meant that they had to draw the 30,000 from the reserve.

"A German naval squadron was spotted twelve miles off the channel," replied Llewellyn.

Hampstead looked up at him, startled. "That's rather close, isn't it?"

"They're worried that the Huns may shell or land a raiding party along the coast to disrupt our lines of communication. Southern Command is responsible for the channel's coastal defence. Since we are under their command, we can be called up in an emergency. A battalion is being kept on alert, ready to move."

"Really? You mean we may actually get to fight?" the major said in wonderment. He glanced at the form and said, "You didn't indicate the quantities your battalion currently have on hand."

"Our supply is rather low," replied Llewellyn. "Somehow it got misplaced during transit. We were hoping that it would show up eventually."

"You haven't been using ammo for rapid fire training?"

"We've been doing dry firing so far." Llewellyn's shoulder twitched when they remembered the daily half-hour instructions he had endured with his company. The muscles in his shoulders and forearms burned after holding a nine-and-a-half pound rifle steady and on target for thirty minutes.

The imperial sergeant-major who had been assigned as their instructor was relentless. He didn't say anything when he first laid eyes on the Ross, but there was a hint of derision in his gaze. Be that as it may, the sergeant insisted, "The key to rapid fire is practice, practice, and more practice." When one of the men in the company groaned, he made them all run ten circuits around the muddy field near their tents with their rifles at the port position above their heads.

"Gentlemen! I use the term loosely. I have never seen such a sorry sight of soldiers in my twenty years in the Yorkshire Yeomanry." He then held up a bullet for the men to see. "This is a Mk. VII .303 dummy round. It has two small holes drilled in the casing. The bullet, the pointy thing at the front, is painted red. That is the only colour that I want to see. If I see a live round, I will put my foot so far up your arse, you will be able to lick it with your tongue! Do I make myself clear?"

"Yes, Sergeant-Major!" the company yelled back.

"I haven't lost a man during training, and I sure as hell ain't going to now," he said as he stared at the company. "You have been issued six chargers. Thirty rounds. At the end of the exercise, I fully expect all the rounds to be turned in. If they are not, my foot goes up your arse.

"You will be given the command *Rapid fire!* I will then give you following commands. *Charge magazine! Aim! Fire! Eject! Load! Lock!* Do you understand?"

"Yes, Sergeant-Major!"

The sergeant-major announced each command in a slow, steady cadence. When five rounds were fired he yelled, "Stop!"

He looked up at the grey sky and said, "God give me strength." He returned his gaze back to the company. "That was the worst display of musketry that I have seen in my fucking life. You!" he pointed a private in the front row. "Keep the damn rifle steady. Quit dancing about. Keep your cheek on the butt at all times.

"And you!" he shouted to the private beside him. "If you handled a women's teat like you did with that bolt, she would slap you silly. Gentle lad, gentle." When the private blushed a bright pink, the sergeant shook his head. "Mother of God, a virgin!" When some of the men tittered, he turned on them. "Port arms, ten circuits. Now! Move! Move! You lazy bastards!"

When they had finished their punishment, he said, "God give me patience. Let's do it again."

And they did, again and again for two weeks. The muscles still burned, but the motion of aiming, firing, and reloading was being done more smoothly. With the smoothness, the speed began to increase. Most of the men were now capable of firing fifteen rounds in a minute. A few even managed twenty rounds. In a few weeks' time they should all able to fire thirty in the allotted time. The true test was going to be when they got on the range, where they had to put fifteen rounds in a twelve-inch target at 300 yards.

Llewellyn informed the major, "The schedules at the rifle ranges are rather tight ..."

"What the hell!" he blurted when he saw something through the office window behind the captain. When Llewellyn turned he saw a truck being towed by two horses.

"What the fuck happened?" Hampstead demanded as he stomped out of the office.

"The engine got flooded. We didn't think the puddle in the middle of the road was that deep," replied the private sourly. He didn't seem to be bothered by the major's tantrum.

"Problem?" asked Llewellyn as he eyed the vehicle.

"You can say that. We got twenty-three of these three-ton Gramm Trucks. They've been giving us nothing but trouble. The Continent engines are crap, and there are cracks in the chassis. Maintenance is so backlogged that I've no idea when they can even take a look at it, let alone get it fixed. This screws up our delivery schedule."

"So what are we going to do for transport?"

Hampstead frowned and then said, "We're going to have use wagons or pack horses. The fucking roads have been pretty hard on the trucks."

Llewellyn glanced at the open warehouse, where crates were stacked to the ceiling. He was calculating how he would be able to transport thirty cases of ammo. Each box contained a thousand rounds and weighed nearly sixty pounds. The pack horses could handle nearly 200 to 240 pounds of dead weight under ideal conditions. With the rain and mud, they would have a heavy workout, so he would need to lighten the load. So on top of six or seven horses he would need an extra two or three. He would have preferred the truck, because he wouldn't have to make the extra trip to return the animals to the ammunition park. *Might as well turn it into a training exercise,* he thought.

"Okay. If you have sufficient packhorses, we'll do it that way. We'll return them in the morning."

"As you wish," the major said with relief.

The captain motioned to Sergeant Booth, who had accompanied him. "We'll be using pack animals. Get the men to help out with the loading."

"Yes, sir," replied Sergeant Booth.

"Will they all be in bandoliers?" asked Hampstead. The ammunition came in cartons of loose cartridges or prepackaged in web bandoliers of fifty rounds, which the men could wrap around their chests.

"Twenty-five in bandoliers and five in cartons," replied the captain.

"Sergeant, come with me. I'll show you where they are," said the major as he turned on his heels and went back into the office with Booth right behind him.

As Llewellyn turned away, he saw the armour riding up to the ordnance office. He and his horse were splattered with mud.

"Sergeant McCormick! Just the man I wanted to see."

The sergeant, even on top of the horse, barely met the height requirements for the CEF. However, he was a genius at keeping the Fusiliers' weapons in working form. He leaned forward as he rested his elbow on his saddle, a serpent tattoo on his left wrist clearly visible. "How can I help you, Captain?" he asked.

"When can you visit my company? We're having some problems with our rifles."

"Let me guess. The sights and the bayonets are falling off," he stated confidently.

"I'm afraid so," replied the captain. Llewellyn didn't like the implications that the issues with the Ross were that common.

"What is your company's schedule for tomorrow afternoon?" he asked.

"Outpost training, if it isn't raining," Llewellyn rhymed.

"If it is?"

"I'll think of something."

"Can you leave them where I can take a look at them?"

Llewellyn paused to think. "I'll leave them with Corporal Edwards."

"Good enough."

"Thank you, Sergeant," replied the captain, returning the sergeant's salute.

NOVEMBER 28, 1914
LARK HILL, SALISBURY PLAIN

The shouting, jeering, and cheering caught Captain Llewellyn's attention as he made an inspection tour to ensure that the tents were secure for the evening. He had to cancel the afternoon's extended order drill, and the forecast for the evening was dismal. His men needed the training, but there was really no point. Within ten minutes they would be exhausted as they tried to swim through the sea of mud. He was so intent on investigating the noise that he nearly tripped over a tent's guide wire as he made a turn.

What he saw displeased him greatly. It seemed that his men were not quite as tired as he had supposed. A small circle had gathered around two men who were doing a pretty good job of imitating drunken prize-fighters. They were having a difficult time maintaining their balance as they exchanged blows. He was really pissed when he recognized Duval blocking the other man's punch.

"Break it up!" he commanded. When the two men ignored him, he stepped in and shoved the two men apart. Both splattered into the mud.

"What the fuck?" declared Duval as he came up to a knee.

"Yeah," agreed the other man. Captain Llewellyn finally was able to place the man. Private Henderson was a burly miner from Timmins, Ontario.

When they both recognized him, they backed off. They knew what the penalty was for striking an officer. "What the hell is this about?" Llewellyn demanded.

Henderson raised an angry fist at Duval. "I'm going to punch his lights out."

"I didn't do nothing," replied Duval with an innocent face that immediately raised Llewellyn's suspicions.

"Didn't do nothing? Didn't do nothing?" shouted Henderson. "The fucker dug a trench around his tent to drain the water away."

When Llewellyn gave him a confused look, Henderson pointed to a muddy, water-filled trench aimed at a tent. "It's draining into my tent."

"Did not!" retorted Duval.

"I saw you, you fucker!"

Keep a straight face, Llewellyn told himself. *Keep a straight face!* "I don't really care. I don't condone fighting to resolve disputes. Both of you are under house arrest until I decide what your punishment is going to be."

"What about my tent?" demanded Henderson.

Llewellyn turned to Duval. "Move the trench. Now!"

"But Captain ..." Duval tried to protest, but Llewellyn overrode him. "Just do it."

"Yes, sir," replied Duval grumpily.

The captain turned to the spectators. "I believe that you have some place you need to be."

As they scattered, Sergeant Booth appeared, "What did I miss?" Llewellyn explained the situation while they sloughed their way back to his tent. "I'm going to be glad when we move into the new huts," Booth said.

Llewellyn glanced at the small rise a half-mile away. Through the drizzling rain he could see a team of carpenters starting to construct wood-framed huts covered with corrugated thin sheets as the outer skin. About a quarter of the contingent had been moved into the new quarters. They hoped to have sufficient huts built to house the rest of the men by the end of December.

"I saw today's orders. They need some 300 carpenters, so they're asking for volunteers," stated Llewellyn.

"We're going to have everyone in the unit volunteer," Booth pointed out.

"I know. Everyone who can swing a hammer thinks they're a carpenter."

"What do you want to do?"

Llewellyn removed his soft cap and squeezed it to remove some of the water and then replaced it on his head when he considered the problem. His first thought was to go through the attestation papers, which listed the men's civilian occupations. However, since half the papers had been lost in the storm a few weeks back, that was not a viable option. Then, he remembered, "Corporal Innis was a carpenter, wasn't he?"

"I believe so," replied Booth.

"Get him to vet the volunteers. He'll be able to tell the real ones from the slackers."

"Sounds good," the sergeant replied. "Also, the adjutant sent out a message that we are to return the ammo that we requisitioned."

"Why?" asked Llewellyn. It had been a painful hassle to get the ammo and to distribute it to the men.

"According to what he said, each battalion was supposed to have 1,000 rifles with 300 rounds per rifle, max. We weren't to draw 30,000 rounds, we were just to top up if we didn't have that amount."

"Great. So how much do we have to return?"

"About 25,000."

"Okay," said Llewellyn as water started to drip off his hat again.

"There is a bit of a problem."

"Oh."

"We don't have the ammo boxes."

Llewellyn turned his head sharply to the sergeant. The empty ammo boxes were kept so that spent brass could be returned to the ordnance officer for recycling. "What happened to them?"

Sergeant Booth gave a resigned shrug. "Well, you know that we've been short of fuel to heat the tents. So we smashed them up and used them instead. They burned quite nicely. We didn't think that they were going to ask for them back."

"What's done is done. I'll try to square it with the adjutant," the captain stated.

As he neared his bell tent, he saw two men waiting for him. He became grim when he saw the MP brassards on the left cuffs of their greatcoats. They were never bearers of good news. When he glanced at Sergeant Booth, his face was as grim as his was.

"How can I help you?" he asked after he returned the warrant officer's salute.

"Captain Llewellyn?"

"Yes."

"I have orders to detain ..." His hand entered the right pocket of his jacket, removed a tan notebook, and flipped open to a marked page. "Corporal Henke and Private Kramer."

"May I ask what they have done?"

The warrant officer didn't seem to be happy with his task. There was a hint of distaste when he said, "The War Office has ordered that all men with German-sounding names be detained and questioned. There is a possibility that they could be German agents."

"I know those two men. They are not German agents," protested Sergeant Booth.

"I'm sorry. I have my orders," replied the warrant officer.

Llewellyn glared at the two cops. He really didn't want to do it, but he had no choice. "Let's get it done," he said sourly. "Sergeant Booth, if you would please lead the way."

The small group marched down the muddy path between the tents. He stopped at a tent that was five columns over and eight rows down.

Captain Llewellyn called out, "Corporal Henke, please come out."

A weathered face with a premature greying moustache appeared at the tent opening. He gave them a questioning look. "Captain?" he queried.

"I'm afraid that you must accompany these two gentlemen," he said with distaste. The corporal was a Boer War veteran.

"Why?"

The man deserves an answer, Llewellyn thought. "They are questioning all soldiers with German-sounding names. I'm afraid that includes you."

"But I'm loyal!" he protested.

"I know." He was a very good soldier and diligent in his duties. Llewellyn couldn't recall any complains concerning the man from his men or his superiors. "I'm sure that it will be cleared up and you'll be back," he felt compelled to say when he saw the man's concern.

"If you say so, Captain," Henke replied as he put on a cap and greatcoat.

It would be the last that the captain would see of Corporal Henke. When he enquired about him he learned that all of the men who were detained were discharged and shipped back to Canada. He never would discover that when they arrived in Halifax they would all be sent to concentration camps.

DECEMBER 01, 1914
YE OLD BUSTARD INN, BUSTARD,
SALISBURY PLAIN

"He didn't seem pleased," said Sweeney as he watched Colonel Carson stomp out of the office. The stomping was rather muted, since he was wearing black, mud-streaked rubber over boots.

"I'm afraid not," remarked Lieutenant-General Alderson. He tugged at his uniform jacket as he rose to his feet.

"Let me guess," said the lieutenant-colonel. "He wanted you to revisit your decision to continue having our men housed in tents."

"He was rather emphatic about the poor conditions," the general admitted.

Hughes' special representative had somehow managed to get a personal appointment with the war secretary during the Lord Mayor's Show a few weeks prior. Kitchener had been surprised, never a good thing, when Carson informed him of the conditions that the contingent was labouring under. The adjutant was aware that Alderson was embarrassed when Lord Kitchener had offered to move some of his new territorials from the huts into tents to accommodate the Canadians. It had put the general in an awkward position, because either he would be upsetting Lord Kitchener or the officers and the men of the units that were going to be displaced. He declined with an explanation that a construction program had been initiated to replace the canvas.

"I did explain to him that we are building huts as fast as we can at Lark Hill and Sling Plantation. Units are being moved as we speak," said Alderson.

"He was not impressed?"

"I'm afraid not."

"Was it wise to antagonize him?" asked the adjutant.

Alderson stared after the departing colonel. "Maybe, maybe not. Well, he'll be out of our hair for a while. I've been informed that he will be sailing back to Canada next week."

"Yes, sir."

"What do you have for me? I'm to inspect the engineers."

"I got a preliminary report from Major Russell concerning our mechanical transportation before he returns to Canada," replied Sweeney as he gave him a report.

This caught Lieutenant-General Alderson's attention. He was most impressed by Major Tommy Russell. Prior to 1914, the Canadian militia really didn't have much mechanization. When the war began Russell, the general manager of the Russell Motor Car Company, had met with the minister to discuss selling trucks for the contingent. Hughes was so impressed with the man that on the spot he ordered eight trucks and made him a purchasing agent for the Militia Department, with the honorary rank of major, responsible for buying motorized vehicles for the force. He had accompanied the contingent to Salisbury and was instrumental in organizing and maintaining the various vehicles that had been acquired.

"I'm in agreement with his recommendation concerning the Port Arthur wagons. The front wheels need to be set for a small radius. It's the motorized vehicles that I have a concern with."

The adjutant agreed. "He submitted a detailed report concerning having a mechanized transport base be designated where replacement vehicles can be inspected, repairs made, and spare parts maintained. He also suggested that we standardize on the Peerless, as that is the most popular model we currently have."

"I saw that," replied Alderson. "He also mentions that fifteen percent be kept as a reserve. I prefer to have at least twenty. And what I would like to do is replace all our current vehicles. They've been put to heavy use. We'll keep the new ones in reserve until we are sent to the front. When the second contingent arrives, they will get the older models."

"We still have to maintain two separate transportation organizations: the horse and the mechanized. We might consider centralizing them," Sweeney pointed out.

The general paused. "I don't know. There could be considerable friction between the two." One of them was the wave of the future, while the other, he thought as a horseman, sadly was the remnant of his past.

"Speaking of which, did we receive a report on the remount depots cost?"

"Yes, I did. It's based on 5,000 horses. Estimates on buildings, including sanitation, are included, as well as the number of personnel needed to run the base."

"How many are we talking about?"

"About twelve hundred officers and men."

Alderson nodded in agreement. "That's about what I expected. I'll send the report to the War Office and Ottawa for authorization."

The lieutenant-colonel pulled out another report. "This is the latest personnel assessment of the senior officers." The report was a delicate one, and very few were privy to its contents. With good reason, the report was not very flattering concerning the quality of the senior Canadian officers.

"Thank you," remarked Alderson as he took the report. He unlocked his top desk drawer and relocked it once he dropped the report in. He would review it later.

"On the topic of senior officers, I noted that Colonel Topham has declared Captain Llewellyn surplus," Sweeney said.

It took a moment for Lieutenant-General Alderson to recall the captain. "Ah yes, the Fusiliers officer. He was put on the surplus officer list?" he queried with a frown. "What reason did Topham give?"

"The captain was a substantive lieutenant and the colonel wanted to replace him with a qualified captain."

"He did, did he! What do you think the real reason is?"

"The tactical exercise last week," said the adjutant firmly. The previous week, his staff had arranged a training scheme where a hostile force had landed on the Southern Coast of England. A cavalry force from the invading army was seen near Shaftesbury-Blandford. The defenders were to advance southwest from Marlborough, Newbury, and Basingstoke. During the exercise, the Fusiliers were to dislodge the enemy's defensive line on a small grassy knoll to allow the Strathcona's Horse to engage the enemy cavalry. Lieutenant-General Alderson had been observing the Fusiliers' attack. The plan was for Captain Llewellyn's two companies to attack the enemy's centre, and the third company would be the reserve to be thrown in when necessary. Unfortunately, things didn't go as planned, as only one company launched its attack. When the captain saw that one of his companies was missing, he ordered his reserve in.

"If I recall, there was a miscommunication. The company was lying in the grass, and they didn't hear the orders," said Lieutenant-General

Alderson. "I was impressed that the captain adjusted his sections and still managed to penetrate the lines to allow the Strathconas through."

"Yes, the judges gave him the victory but assessed sixty to seventy percent casualties," pointed out Sweeney.

Alderson winced at the casualty figures. "I know. You've been reading the intelligence summaries as well as I have." He had seen too many familiar names on the lists.

"Well, he's not likely to make that error again," stated the adjutant.

"If he had made one?" replied Alderson.

"True, but Colonel Topham does have it in for him. I pulled the captain's file. Topham put him on surplus on the morning that Llewellyn was supposed to write his exam for his captain's certificate."

"Did he pass?"

"With flying colours. What I've learned about him is all favourable, and he seems to be actually running the Fusiliers."

Lieutenant-General Alderson frowned. Technically, he could override Colonel Topham's decision, but he was worried about the discipline that he was imposing on his unruly command. He had to take another approach.

"I hate losing a good officer. Especially one who has that mental toughness. The one thing that impressed me was that he took the blame. He didn't pass it off to a subordinate, like Colonel Topham did."

He paused to ponder the problem, then he decided. "Why don't you have an unofficial word with Colonel Currie? He may find him useful."

"That's a good idea. I'm meeting with him concerning the boot issue this afternoon," Sweeney said with a tired sigh. The footwear for the contingent was a pressing issue, as evidenced by the several filing cabinets filled with correspondence from George Perley, Colonel Carson, the quartermasters, the War Office, and Ottawa.

"Let me know what the colonel says after your meeting."

"Of course, sir," the adjutant replied with a conspiratorial smile.

CHAPTER 28

"Smart aleck," muttered Captain Llewellyn when he arrived at the surplus officer's hut. Either someone had a sense of humour or had known that he was coming. Just above the black digits was a hand-painted sign that read *Bermuda*.

He shifted the kit bag so that the strap would stop digging into his right shoulder as he glanced at his orders and then the hut number. There was no mistake. The hut was approximately fifty feet long and twenty feet wide. The exterior was made of plywood, and a dull corrugated tin roof topped the building, with a black stovepipe poking through the centre. There were windows every ten feet to let in sunlight and air. It sat above the ground on red brick pillars.

When he entered, the interior was spartan, with a black iron coal stove in the centre. The air seemed stale and stuffy, even though the stove was unlit. There were twenty-two plank beds, eleven on both sides nailed to the floor. Half the planks had grey woollen blankets, and the bed sheets had a similar colour. The owners' kit bags were hanging from brass hooks that were nailed to the wall's visible studs. They didn't have enough material to hide some of the nails that had missed them when they nailed the exterior siding.

It was empty, since the officers were on parade at this hour of the morning. He picked one of the vacant planks and dropped his bag on it then took a seat with his elbows on his knees. He stared at the floor. He didn't notice the mud that he had tracked in.

He felt a bit lost and tired. He hadn't felt ennui for a long time. He knew why he was feeling this way. He had experienced it before, after the Boer War. It didn't make it any easier going from not having time to think one day to having as much as you wanted the next.

He was pissed at Topham, and he knew that there was very little he could do about it. He was also well aware that he hadn't been on the colonel's good side, and the mistake that happened under his watch was all that his CO needed to can him. Topham had tried very hard to bury him with a certain amount of glee.

At least passing the captain's exam was a finger in the man's eye, but it might be a pyrrhic victory. He had hoped that what he tried to impart to the men under his command would stick, but there was no guarantee. He had seen the devastating effect when a poor leader took over a well-run unit. It was not pretty.

The news had spread fast. By the time he got to his tent, lieutenants Vernon, Henricks, and Troope were waiting for him. He could tell they were upset, especially Lieutenant Vernon. It was his platoon's mistake that had triggered his firing. He pointed out they had a job to do and they better get on with it. He didn't have very much time to wallow, since he had an exam to write in an hour or so. After the exam, he was busy getting Lieutenant Troope up to speed on his new temporary command until the replacement captain arrived. He was to clear out the next day.

In the morning, he was touched when the entire company was lined up on parade. He did a final inspection and had a few final words with some of the men. When he finished, he gave them a final salute. He was tempted to say that they needed to watch their asses. Instead he wished them well and the best of luck.

He was rather astonished when Private Duval stopped him before he got into a truck. "It has been a pleasure to serve with you, Captain Llewellyn. If you need a good scout, keep me in mind."

"I sure will. And watch your ass," he replied as he shook the private's hand.

"Always do," Duval replied as he gave a respectful nod and then joined the company for their morning drill. Llewellyn had thought it was best not to look back as he was driven away.

Now he had to decide what he was going to do. He was well aware of the reputation the surplus officers had in the CEF. He needed to put out feelers as quickly as possible. He had to find a new job soon, or he would be shipped home. If that happened, and if he wanted to come back, he would have to join the second contingent currently being organized. But there was no guarantee. It did seem a waste going back and forth across the ocean, but that was the direction the force's policy was moving in.

When the door banged opened, he jumped to attention when he saw the red bands of two senior officials enter.

"I'll have that sign removed," stated one of the colonels, irritated. Captain Llewellyn was startled when he recognized Lieutenant-Colonel Currie standing beside the man who was speaking. He assumed that

Currie was being given a personal tour of the new huts being built that would eventually house the 2nd Brigade.

"As you can see, the huts can accommodate twenty-two men. It will be much more comfortable than being under canvas …" He stopped when he saw the captain. "Captain, why are you not on parade?"

"Sir, I've been just assigned to this hut. I was going to square my things before reporting in."

"What's your name?"

"Llewellyn, Henry James, sir."

Currie cocked his head. "Formerly of the Fusiliers?"

"Yes, Colonel." Llewellyn didn't know if it was a good thing that the Currie knew his name.

Lieutenant-Colonel Currie glanced at his fellow officer then asked, "Are you sure that you have been assigned to this hut?"

Llewellyn's lips parted in surprise. He pulled out his orders and handed them to Currie.

Currie read them then clucked his tongue. "Colonel Harrison, didn't you mention that you received new orders for a Captain Llewellyn?"

"Actually, yes," Harrison said upon consideration.

"New orders?" Llewellyn asked, perplexed.

"Yes. If I recall correctly, you are to report to Hayling Island for the machine gun course."

"I am?" He was trying to remember if he had put his name in.

"You have a problem taking the course?" demanded Lieutenant-Colonel Currie.

"No, sir," Llewellyn replied quickly. He was trying hard not to look like an idiot, especially in front of a potential boss. "I think it is important to familiarize oneself with such an important weapon."

The CEF had several machine gun units established. Some of the armoured cars were being equipped as platforms for the weapons.

"Good. I like my officers to learn their trade."

"Report tomorrow to the Amesbury train station at 7:00 a.m. sharp," said Harrison.

"Yes, sir." Llewellyn was so surprised, he hadn't picked up that Currie had said, "my officers."

DECEMBER 4, 1914
MESS TENT, LARK HILL, SALISBURY PLAIN

"I would suggest replacing your underpants if you set the fuse to zero," Captain Masterley said expectantly as he held aloof a brass metal cone for the men in the tent to see. The thirty men sitting in a semi-circle in front of him chuckled politely.

Paul Ryan, standing at the back of the cavernous marquee, noticed that some of the men looked bored. He assumed it was not the first time they had heard this particular lecture and joke. It was Paul's first, and he found it interesting.

Technically, he shouldn't be there, since he was on leave for the afternoon. He had come to find Reggie to see whether he had the afternoon off as well. He was going to suggest travelling to Bulford to get a hot bath. It had been a week, and he reeked. At Reggie's tent the sole occupant told him that he and the rest of the section were in the mess tent. He didn't feel any need to inform Paul, since he was with the quartermasters, that Battery C was holding a lecture and a drill there. Paul had been surprised to see that an 18-pounder had been wheeled into the hall. Raindrops beaded on the dull, grey-painted steel barrel. He would have backed out if the captain hadn't locked eyes on him, compelling him to stay.

He took a sharp breath when the captain set the fuse on the top of a shrapnel shell and then screwed it in until it was tight. He let out a sigh of relief when he spotted the four holes that were bored into its side, indicating that it was a dummy shell. They were marked that way to avoid confusion with live ammunition.

"Now use the fuse key to set the correct timing."

Paul watched as he put a circular steel clamp onto the British Army's standard type 80 fuse and then turned it. Originally designed by the German firm Krupp, the Imperial Government had been manufacturing it under licence for years. "You can set it from zero to twenty-two seconds."

Paul recognized the hand that rose from one of the seated men. "Yes, Private Ramus? You have a question?" asked the captain with a slight hint of impatience. Paul knew that Reggie was having some problems with the math.

"How do you know what time to set?" Reggie asked. He had been promoted to one of the unit's gun sections. He was responsible for the ammunition wagon and its horse team.

"Good question. There are a number of factors that we need to consider when setting the fuse. The first is having an accurate distance to the target. Ideally, we will have a known landmark and the distance to it. The second is the terrain. Are we firing level, downhill, or uphill? This needs to be considered in our calculations. A shell will land shorter uphill and longer downhill.

"The third is atmospheric conditions such as ..." He pointed to the drumming on the tent roof. "Also, a strong wind at your back or in your face can have the same impact as firing uphill or downhill. And a crosswind will push the shells slightly off target. That's why it is critical that the observers relay to the command post accurate yardages so that we can make fire adjustments. We want to make sure that our barrages will have maximum impact on the enemy.

"So if the range is 2,800 yards on level ground how do we calculate the fuse times?" the captain asked Reggie. Paul could see that he was struggling. A slight frown appeared on the captain's face, and then he put his gaze on Paul. "Corporal Ryan, how would you determine the timing?"

"Me, sir?" croaked Paul. He felt uncomfortable being put on the spot, especially when all the men turn their heads toward him. A couple of men elbowed each other and whispered, "McGill."

Paul paused to consider the question then asked, "What is the speed of the artillery shell?"

"Very good, Corporal. Muzzle velocity is sixteen hundred feet per second."

"Hmm," said Paul as he mentally converted from feet to yards and came up with a figure of 533 yards per second. He then divided twenty-eight by five to come with 5.6 as his time. He knew velocity was not constant, since the shell would travel in an arc and the speed would drop, so he decided to add a second to be on the safe side.

"About 6.6 seconds, give or take," Paul said. He knew the number wasn't accurate, but it would be close.

The captain arched an eyebrow. "Is he correct?"

When no one said anything, he shook his head sadly. "We can check the fuse indicator attached to the shield." He walked over the metal plate fixed to the front of the gun and ran a finger across the ruler that was bolted to it. "It indicates for 2,800 yards, the time should be set at 7.8 seconds."

He turned to Paul with an impressed smile. "You're off by 1.2 seconds, but not bad, all things considering."

When the captain heard several men chuckling derisively, he silenced them with a glare.

"Tomorrow we will be having a live fire exercise, God willing! There will be four different schemes. The first target will be a mock four-gun enemy emplacement. The range will be twenty-four hundred to 3,000 yards. The second target will be a column of infantry, ten sections of fours. Range eighteen hundred to twenty-two hundred. The third will be a line of infantry; forty-five kneeling dummies at one yard apart will be set up. The final scheme will be firing from a concealed emplacement. Is that understood?"

"Yes, Captain," shouted the men back to him.

"I want a good showing tomorrow. General Alderson and other senior Imperial Officers will be in attendance. Do I make myself clear?"

"Yes, Captain!"

"Good. First section, front and centre," he ordered.

Paul watched as six men of the first section took their places around the 18-pounder. The other four stood where the limber and ammunition would be placed. They began their drill of finding the range, setting the fuse, loading, firing, and ejecting the dummy shell.

He was turning to leave when Captain Masterley waved him over.

"Well, Corporal Ryan, are you enjoying working the remount depot?"

"Yes, Captain, very much," he replied cautiously. He didn't know where this was heading.

"Hmm. I have the request from Captain Fuller to make the transfer permanent," the captain said with deliberate casualness.

"You have?" Paul said in alarm.

"You didn't know that you were on secondment?" Secondment meant that his unit could, at any time, demand that he be returned to them.

"Not really, sir."

"Valuable skills?"

"Yes, Captain. I can type."

"Really! That's interesting," he replied with a thoughtful nod.

Oh shit! thought Ryan. *Oh shit!*

CHAPTER 29

DECEMBER 6, 1914
NO. 2 CANADIAN STATIONARY HOSPITAL,
LE TOUQUET, FRANCE

Samantha jumped when she heard artillery fire that seemed rather close.

A couple of British soldiers laughed and then one said, "They're a bit distant." He cocked his head to listen to the roar again. "Fifteen miles, I'd say."

He turned his head toward his companion, who nodded and replied, "Definitely fifteen."

She wasn't about to question the two men, seeing as they were lying on stretchers before the main entrance to the Hotel du Golf. For men who had been recently wounded in the fighting at the front, they seemed rather cheerful. They also seemed rather amused by the lieutenant's stars on her uniform.

"You're one of the nursing sisters here?" the man asked as a couple of stretcher-bearers picked him up. He was rather thin, with dirty blond hair and a couple of days' growth on his cheeks. A bottle of blood was strapped to his stretcher. His companion, a large man with brown hair, had his feet wrapped in bandages.

"Good! I hope to see you inside," he remarked after she nodded. He winked. "Onward, James," he directed the orderly.

"It's Frank," muttered the man as he carried the stretcher through the entrance.

Samantha glanced at the lineup of ambulances that were beginning to disembark patients. The No. 2 Canadian Stationary Hospital was now open for business. It had been nearly three weeks since she and the other nursing sisters had marched from the West Down North camp to the Lavington train station. At Paddington Station in London they were bused to the military hospital at Hampstead. The voluntary aid detachment nurses were kind enough to make room for them for the night. They were exhausted when they finally reached Boulogne on the 20th after taking a train to Southampton then a ship across to Le Havre, where they spent another night at the No. 1 Rest Camp. That was false advertising, as they didn't get any rest. Then they were unceremoniously shipped to Boulogne, where they spent a delightful week or so doing very little while the senior brass tried to figure out what to do with them.

She knew that she was being rather harsh on Colonel Shillington, the unit's commanding officer, and her matron, Captain Riley. They were all relieved when they were ordered to set up their hospital in Le Touquet.

When they arrived, they needed a week to convert the upscale resort. It included an eighteen-hole championship golf course. A couple of the doctors were excited when they found out that in July the French Open was held here. The unknown James Edgar had beaten the British Open champ Harry Vadon by six shots. She listened politely, as she didn't know anything about the sport. What she had learned of the game so far it seemed rather boring.

The clubhouse now housed the NCOs, orderlies, stretcher-bearers, and the ambulance drivers. She and the other nurses were situated in the Villa Tino. She liked the whitewashed villa, which had sufficient room for them all. From the decor, especially the dining room with its wood-beamed ceiling and open feeling, it had been designed for the upper crust. The senior officers were sleeping in the Robinson Villa.

The hotel itself was a three-storey building set upon a raised basement. The exterior was red brick with white accents and had a red clay roof. The conversion resulted in ten wards, named after the nine provinces and the Yukon territory as the tenth ward, with a 320-bed capacity. It included a surgery, a lab, and an X-ray machine. When looking for suitable accommodations for medical services, hotels, schools, and other public buildings that contained commercial kitchens and cleaning facilities were the most desirable.

When Samantha entered the grandiose main hall, she ran into Matron Riley, who glanced at the small watch that was attached to her blouse. The matron was thirty-six years old, with light ash-coloured hair bunched under her white veil.

"Good afternoon, Matron," Samantha said as he skidded to a stop on the gleaming marble floor. She felt somewhat nervous, wondering if she had arrived late for her shift.

"Yes, it is, Miss Lonsdale," she said. "I'm glad that I ran into you. We need some help in the Alberta Ward." The initial ward assignments were based on the nurse's home province. Samantha had been assigned to the Ontario ward. The matron herself came from Belleville, Ontario. However, the nurses were reassigned where they were needed.

"The patients are finally arriving," she stated. They had been warned

262

to expect a hundred or so in the next few days.

"Did they say what kind of injuries we could expect?" Samantha asked.

"They did," Riley answered with a slight amusement. "Most of the patients are suffering from swollen feet and frostbite. Some from minor gunshot wounds."

"Swollen feet and frost bite?" Samantha repeated, not sure that she had heard correctly.

"I'm afraid so," the matron answered. Her tone became serious. "For some, it is so bad that they need to have their toes amputated. In a few cases their entire foot."

"I didn't think it was that cold," said Samantha, perplexed. She had worn her overcoat to keep the chill off. The risk for frostbite when the temperature was between fourteen and sixteen degrees Fahrenheit was relatively low.

"Normally, yes," Riley said as she headed toward the grand staircase that led to the second floor. "We are not sure what exactly is happening. What we suspect is that the men are standing in pools of cold water in the trenches. It penetrates their boots. They freeze and then thaw in the morning."

"So we are to use the standard treatment of ice rubs or cool baths to return circulation back to normal?" asked Samantha.

"Yes. Our job is to help the men recover sufficiently so they can return to duty."

"Yes, ma'am."

"Good, I'll check up on you before I leave shift this evening," the matron said as she headed down the floor for an inspection tour of the other wards.

The Alberta ward that Samantha entered had high, ornately decorated ceilings and a bank of glass windows that provided plenty of light to the ten beds arranged below it.

A tall, thin soldier was hobbling on crutches from the direction of the bathroom. Samantha didn't say anything, but the poor man had forgotten to button up his fly. The men kept their uniforms, if they were still serviceable. When they first entered, their clothes were taken to be steam cleaned to remove lice and other critters, then were returned.

"Now, Mr. Henry, I would have been glad to help," said Claire. She was the duty nurse for the afternoon shift.

"I can go to the bathroom myself, thank you," he replied gruffly as he tugged at his blanket.

"Of course you can," Claire replied patiently.

After she had finished helping the man, she called Samantha to the small table set at the far wall that acted as a nurse's station.

"Is there anything that I need to do before you end your shift?" asked Samantha.

"Not much. Two of the men need sponge baths, and the patients in beds four and five need their bandages replaced. The evening meal will be coming up in about an hour's time. I've given them their medicines and ice bags at four, so you're good for now."

"Sounds good."

"The doctors haven't made their rounds yet, so they should be in soon."

"Okay," Samantha replied. "I wanted to ask, what did you think about the hospital at the casino?" She had been so busy that she hadn't found the time for a courtesy call to the nearby Red Cross Hospital.

Claire gave a dismissive wave. "I know they were trying to be helpful, but wearing tiaras and evening gowns to greet wounded soldiers. Really!"

"You saw that?"

"Well, no," Claire replied reluctantly. "But there are stories."

The Duchess of Westminster, at her Le Touquet villa, had established the No. 1 Red Cross Hospital so she and her aristocrat friends could help the wounded. They had thought that by dressing elegantly it would help the spirits of the wounded men. As the number of wounded grew, the hospital was moved to the casino building with an increase to 150 beds. Also, the management of the hospital was being put on a more professional basis by the hiring of trained nursing staff.

"This I have to see," said Samantha.

"Sure, when we get a few hours' leave. Well, I'm off. I need to get to bed, I'm exhausted. Have a good shift," Claire said as she left.

She was just beginning to read Claire's notes when she heard a stretcher being rolled into her ward.

"I have a patient for you. Which bed should I put him in?" Frank asked. Samantha pointed to the empty bed near her desk. "Okay, Peter. One, two, three," he said as he and the other orderly lifted the man, ensuring that the man's back remained straight as they lowered him gently into the bed.

"Here's his chart," Frank said as he hand it to her.

"Thanks, James," the man in the bed said to the departing orderly.

"It's Frank," he replied as he disappeared down the hall.

"So we meet again," said the blond man she had met at the front entrance. He looked rather handsome cleaned up, but he still needed a shave.

"Obviously," she replied with a smile. When she read the chart, she nearly gasped. She couldn't help her eyes darting to his face.

A shadow crossed his eyes and then a wry smile appeared. "It's a small wound. Nicked the spine. I didn't feel a thing."

DECEMBER 7, 1914
PRIVY COUNCIL OFFICE, EAST BLOCK,
PARLIAMENT HILL, OTTAWA

"Gentlemen, please!" Borden demanded as he slapped the table in the Privy Council Chamber. If he had a gavel, the wood would have had numerous dents and gouges.

"Son of a bitch!" was the least colourful invective Sam Hughes had used as he waved a scrunched sheet of paper in the air.

Thomas White had risen from his chair. He was leaning toward Hughes with his weight supported by his hands on the polished surface. The other men at the table were sitting back in their chairs with blank faces, keeping their mouths shut. They didn't want to get between the two men.

Borden knew what it said and who had written it. Last Friday, after he had left Ottawa to give speeches at the Canadian and Empire Clubs in Montreal and Toronto, the auditor-general had sent a memo to the Militia and Defence Department. When it landed on his brother's desk, John hadn't been too pleased when he read it. Their line of credit had been cancelled. All payments for military contracts were put on hold.

The auditor-general had examined the expenditure vouchers for the month of September and had discovered nearly a million dollars had not been approved by the cabinet. Hughes had spent the bulk of it, nearly half a million, on trucks, but also $90,000 were disbursed for medical supplies and $50,000 for acquiring field glasses. This was a clear violation of the protocol that had been negotiated by the deputy-ministers and John Fraser, the auditor-general, in White's office in August. All contracts above $5,000 were to be approved by the cabinet.

Obviously, this was a great concern for his finance minister, who was responsible for the state of the country's finances. White, like Borden, had been a Liberal, but he became a Conservative when he disagreed with some of Sir Wilfrid Laurier's fiscal policies. He had been appointed to the Leeds, Ontario, riding in the election, and Borden had quickly appointed the forty-four-year-old to the cabinet post with good reason. White had been a journalist before he got a law degree from Osgoode. While he never practiced law, his legal training was useful in his position as the vice-president of the National Trust Company. His financial expertise had been invaluable in dealing with the banking crisis that loomed shortly after the war was declared.

White had projected before the war that government revenues would be $145 million for 1914. Expenditures, however, were projected at $175 million, a $30 million deficit. The bulk of the government's revenues came from custom duties and excise taxes on alcohol and tobacco. The economy had slowed during the first half of the year, and government revenues had declined by $10 million. In August, they had raised the tariffs and the excise taxes to generate an additional $15 million to help finance the war.

With the first contingent in England, a second currently being recruited and trained, and the government preparing to announce a third contingent in late December, the financial drain would only increase. To plan for it, White needed Hughes' cooperation by following the contracting rules, and he wasn't getting it.

Borden was of the same mind. He glanced at Hazen sitting a couple of chairs over. Hazen had warned him that the militia department was a mineshaft. No one there knew what the minister was up to. Hughes was not a very good manager or an administrator, since he disliked delegating.

"Mr. Hughes," snapped Borden. This finally caught Hughes' attention, because he hadn't used his military title. Hughes was touchy that way. "The Honourable Mr. White wants to ensure that our men get the supplies and the equipment that they require in a timely manner. However, we have a responsibility that the taxpayer's money is spent wisely and that we pay fair prices. This why large expenditures require this cabinet's approval."

Borden didn't feel that it was an appropriate time to mention the rumours that were being whispered that there had been some price gouging on the contracts. The reports from Commissioner Sherwood and Inspector MacNutt of the Dominion Police concerning Colonel

Allison were alarming. He hadn't decided what action to take on that yet. One thing for certain was that he needed to start reining in his militia minister, if he could.

"That is also one of the reasons that I have discussed with you the candidates for the Inspection Service," stated Borden. They were considering Major-General Lessard and Major-General Sam Steele, of the North-West Mounted Police fame, to head the inspection department to ensure that the equipment and supplies that were acquired met the contract specifications.

"Of course, Prime Minister," replied Hughes defensively.

"If you comply with the August agreement, I'm certain that Mr. Fraser would be quite happy to reinstate the line of credit." Whoever worried about Fraser's independence as auditor-general had wasted their time.

"Agreed," muttered Hughes. But he still glared balefully at White.

When White retook his seat, Borden could see that he was somewhat mollified but still unhappy. He had to talk to him before he left for Nova Scotia. The main reason for the trip was that his mother was ailing and he wanted to visit her. There were some political events on his itinerary: handling the local Conservative supporters and reviewing an artillery battery named in his honour.

Damn, Borden thought, *every man has a breaking point.* He hoped that White hadn't reached the point where he would consider resigning. Borden would really hate to lose him.

DECEMBER 8, 1914
RADNOR HOUSE, SALISBURY

Lieutenant-General Alderson's boots crunched on the gravel path that led to Radnor House, the HQ for Southern Command, in Salisbury. The rectangular three-storey white stone building used to be the local jail, which explained its plain features and iron-barred windows. The War Office had leased the property from the current owners several years before. With the increase of the number of men training on the plain, new structures were being erected to accommodate the increase in administrative staff. It wasn't raining at the moment, but the workers were colourfully cursing as they could see the dark clouds on the horizon.

The officers at the main entrance made way for Alderson as an orderly sergeant greeted him and escorted him to Lieutenant-General William Pitcairn Campbell's office. When he entered, Campbell was signing an order. He indicated with his pen that Alderson should take a seat in front of him, and he continued to sign additional orders that were stacked up. Alderson observed his commanding officer to gauge his mood. At fifty-seven years old, Campbell had gained weight since his days as a commissioned officer in the King's Royal Rifle Corps. He had served in the Sudan and in the South African war. He had a number of successive commands, the 3rd Brigade in 1904, 5th Division in 1905, and finally the Southern Command. When he finished, he looked up at Alderson and said, "Coffee?"

"Thank you, sir, but I'm fine."

"Very well. There are several items that I would like to talk with you about concerning the Canadian Division," Campbell said while he stroked his grey moustache.

"They have come a long way in the past month. I wish that they would be further along. Unfortunately, the weather has hampered the training schedule."

"Things are quiet along the front at the moment. The French have been pressing Lord Kitchener to start moving some of his new armies to France. So far he has been delaying, informing General Foch that he would like his men to be fully trained before he commits them."

"I understand," replied Alderson. "My division is quite eager to go. When do you expect that orders will be received to dispatch us?"

"As far as I'm aware, the War Office has not decided. From the correspondence that I've seen, they don't want to put an untried division in the line until it has been seasoned. What they are considering is pairing new battalions with experienced ones in the trenches, where they can learn the ropes, so to speak. Once they've been given a taste and we see how they perform, they will be reconstituted."

When the lieutenant-general noticed Alderson's stiffness, he asked, "You have concerns?"

"The idea is sound, but I suspect that the Canadian government may not approve the scheme."

"Why not?" Campbell demanded.

"From the cables I've received from Ottawa and the discussions with my officers, they are sensitive about their contingent," replied Alderson. "They may perceive it as an attempt to break them up."

Campbell frowned. "Has the War Office not requested that all communications concerning your command be submitted to me first? They were put out when they received correspondence concerning the remount depot from you that bypassed the normal channels and that you were communicating directly with the Canadian authorities."

"I have no wish or desire to communicate with the Canadian government, except to minimize correspondence and facilitate obtaining equipment. My men were and still are in desperate need of boots, web equipment to replace their Oliver pattern, and spare parts for their wagons and lorries. Since much of their equipment is not of a British pattern or manufacture, I have no choice but to contact Ottawa for replacements.

"As well, I must inform you that I have received direct cables from the Canadian minister of Militia and Defence, as well as visits and enquiries by his personal representative ..."

"Personal representative?" Campbell interjected.

"Yes, Colonel Carson is Minister Hughes' personal representative based in London. As well, I received similar demands from George Perley, the Canadian High Commissioner. There have been a number of instances where the requests were duplications."

Seeing that Lieutenant-General Campbell was not fully aware of his situation, he said, "You did give me permission to contact the War Office on all matters that didn't relate to your command. If you would like to rescind your permission...?"

Campbell shook his head. "The Canadians appear to be somewhat challenging."

Alderson suppressed a smile. "Somewhat."

CHAPTER 30

When Llewellyn entered the wet canteen, he intended to talk to a friend who worked for Lieutenant-Colonel Currie before he reported for duty at his headquarters. He wanted to learn as much as he could about Currie so that he could make a good first impression. Well, at least a better second one than his first.

The canteen was crowded since the day's tactical exercise had been cancelled, again. That was the reason why the men's tempers were rather frayed, even though it was two o'clock and it had just opened. Some of the men downed their beers in a single gulp, which they immediately regretted. There was a limit on the number of beers they could order, a precaution against drunkenness. The men were rather inventive in the various means that they devised to skirt the rules. Llewellyn hoped that they would be that imaginative against the Germans.

He found his friend, Major Alfred Tennison, sitting at a table with two other captains who had their backs to Llewellyn. The beers in front of them were three-quarters full. A section of the canteen had been designated for officers. Llewellyn knew that an officer's mess and canteen were in the works. When the major spotted Llewellyn, he gave him a grin as he puffed on a briar pipe.

"She was a great fuck. A wildcat in bed," said a rather stocky captain with a battered nose.

"Yeah, right," said the other captain with watery blue eyes below a mop of thin, straw-coloured hair. "How much did you have to pay her?"

"Hey, I have the scratches to prove it. You want to see?" The stocky man moved as if to unbutton his jacket.

"No!" both Tennison and the straw-haired captain exclaimed.

"Take a seat, Captain." Tennison pointed to the seat on the wooden bench beside him with his pipe. When Llewellyn sat, he pushed his glass toward him. "Have a beer."

Llewellyn looked suspiciously at it. He had known Tennison off and on for the last ten years. In civilian life, he was a brewmaster. Considering the strength of the temperance movement, it was a career with limited prospects.

When the captain reached for the glass, the major noticed that his friend's hand was lightly bandaged. "What happened to your hand?" Llewellyn flexed his hand to show it still worked. "Nothing serious. Burned it when I was changing a Vickers gun barrel," he replied before he raised the amber liquid to his lips. He understood why Tennison was passing it on. It was thin and watery.

"Ah. I heard that you were sent to Hayling Island," said Tennison between puffs. Hayling Island, near Southampton, was just off the southern coast of England. It was where the British had a musketry and a machine gun school.

"You were on the machine gun course?" asked the watery-eyed captain eagerly. "I'm scheduled to go on it next week."

"That's Captain Henry, and the reprobate is Captain Griffiths. They command B and C companies. Captain Llewellyn, late of the Fusiliers," Tennison introduced them.

From the glances the captains gave each other, Llewellyn knew his reputation had proceeded him.

"It's a good course," he stated.

"What are the accommodations like, and the food?" Captain Henry asked.

"The Royal Hotel is rather bare, but comfortable, and army food is army food." That brought a grin from the two men. "You won't be spending a lot of time there. Most of it will be forced marches on the beach and at the ranges."

"Learn anything useful?" asked the major.

"Yes, don't stand in front of them."

Tennison gave him a wry smile. "And don't change hot gun barrels."

"That too."

"So what do you think about the Vickers?" asked Captain Griffiths.

"As far as I'm concerned, they are far better than the Maxim. I'm glad that we left those behind at Valcartier."

The Maxim was the first machine gun to use a recoil system to load and fire. It was considered obsolete because it was heavy and awkward to manoeuvre on the battlefield. The Vickers machine gun was its replacement. Introduced in 1912, the water-cooled weapon could fire 450 rounds per minute. A minimum of three men was required to operate it; however, the normal complement was six to eight men. It

271

was light enough that two men could carry it, one for the gun and one for the tripod. The rest of the men were needed to act as observers and to handle the belt feed ammunition.

"So when are we going to get them?" asked Griffiths.

Tennison waved his pipe hand. "I'm afraid that we're not going to get them anytime soon."

"Why not?" demanded Griffiths.

"I thought we had ordered fifty last April. We were supposed to get four for our unit," Henry interjected.

Tennison shrugged. "The War Office decided they needed every single one they could get their hands on. So we're getting the potato diggers instead."

"Aren't they a bit long in the tooth?" asked Llewellyn. He was familiar with the weapon that Tennison referred to. He had handled it during the Boer War. It was designed by the famed gun designer John Moses Browning and manufactured by the Colt Company. It was an air-cooled weapon capable of firing 400 rounds per minute. It was nicknamed the "potato digger" because of the unusual piston action below the breach. It required a certain amount of clearance, otherwise the piston would strike the ground every time it fired a round. It was lighter than the Vickers and required less maintenance. It was the standard machine gun in the Canadian militia's inventory.

"Don't forget they're prone to cook-offs," interjected Captain Henry. He shuddered. "It happened to me once. I had the finger off the trigger and the damn thing still continued firing until the belt was empty." Cook-offs usually happened when the gun barrel was so hot that the heat would ignite the gunpowder in the bullets.

"We're getting the 1914 model rather than the 1898. The barrel has been redesigned with cooling fins that are supposed to deal with the heating problem," Tennison informed them.

"Our new machine gun instructor will give us his assessment," said Captain Griffiths.

"Sure, no problem. As long as I'm behind it."

Major Tennison smiled as he took out a match to relight his pipe. "About that. I hope that you haven't unpacked."

Llewellyn looked at the major. "Why?"

"New orders. You're going to France in two days."

"Miss Lonsdale, it is a pleasure to see you again," said a deep male voice.

When she looked up from her tin plate filled with beef stew, she saw the greeting smile of Captain Llewellyn. She was momentarily speechless.

Samantha had been settling into the hospital's routine. Her twelve-hour shift started at seven, after she and the other nurses attended morning prayers in the chapel led by the unit's chaplain. The first thing she did when she entered the Alberta ward was to take the men's temperature. Depending on the number of beds that were filled, it took her from forty-five minutes to an hour to complete. After that she needed to change the bed linen, dust, and sweep. An orderly with a bucket of hot, soapy water and a mop would come in later to wash and disinfect the floor. Around nine she would take her fifteen-minute coffee break. Five minutes, actually, since it took her five to go down to the cafeteria to fill her mug in the first place. After that, she checked the patients' dressings and ordered any supplies that she needed. Between ten and twelve the senior medical officers made their rounds. She needed to be available to answer any questions they may have concerning any of her patients. Around noon, the meals for the patients who were not ambulatory were distributed. She needed to verify that they matched the diet sheets per the doctor's instructions. It was at 12:45, when the meal trays had been gathered, that she had left the ward while Claire covered for her as she had her lunch.

She was in the Hotel du Golf's dining room. It was now self-service, since the waiters were long gone. She was so worried about Claire that she hadn't noticed a group of senior officers on a tour of the hospital had entered the cafeteria. Since they shared a room, Samantha knew that she wasn't sleeping well.

"What are you doing here?" she blurted. When Llewellyn raised an inquiring eyebrow, she blushed. "Sorry, Captain. You're appearance was so unexpected that you startled me."

"The element of surprise is a military virtue," he said in an amused tone. "May I take a seat? If it is permissible?" he asked, putting a hand on the back of the empty white cane chair across from her.

"I'm not a VAD," she stated, which gave him permission to sit at her table. The Volunteer Aid Detachment nurses were not allowed to socialize with the opposite sex. She heard of one case where a VAD was not even permitted to see her father.

"Thanks," replied the captain as he removed his greatcoat. When he sat, he laid it across his knees. She noticed the slight healing burn mark on his hand and that he was no longer wearing the Fusiliers' insignia. She was not familiar enough with the man to ask what had happened in either case.

"So what are you doing here?"

"I was passing by and decided to drop in," he teased. "I'm with the advance party. We're here to prepare for the arrival of the Canadian Division."

This piqued her curiosity. "What does that entail, exactly?"

"It's a long list. We've taken tours of the trenches that we could be occupying, which will help us identify what equipment and supplies we will need. I've spoken with the various commanders who will be protecting our flanks there. We also have to look at where we're going to billet our men, locations for our supply depots and artillery, and how we will move the division there."

"Are the trenches as bad as everyone is saying?" she asked.

"Yes, it can be pretty bad," he confirmed.

"So most of the contingent will be arriving in mid-January then."

Llewellyn's face became blank. "Where did you hear that?"

It was Samantha's turn to be concerned. "Just rumours." She wasn't about to tell him that Emily had mentioned it in a recent letter.

"I would advise not spreading rumours like that," he stated flatly. He softened then changed the topic. "Is your shift starting or ending?"

"I'm on the morning shift. I have another six hours to go."

"Things are busy for you then?"

She shrugged. "No lack of patients, I'm afraid. I need to get back soon. The doctors usually make their second rounds around two o'clock to check on the patients. Then I have to prepare tea for them, give them their baths …"

"The men love that."

She blushed again but continued. "Prepare their medication, then take their temperatures. In between, I need to write notes for the night sister so that she can keep an eye on critical patients."

"Sorry I asked."

"To be honest, I enjoy my work very much." Samantha was afraid that she had rather shocked him with her statement.

"Don't take this the wrong way, Miss Lonsdale, but I don't have any intention of being under your tender care. You are much too efficient."

Samantha laughed. "I'm not that bad. I'm sure that you will survive."

"Whether or not it might be enjoyable is a different matter," he remarked.

When Llewellyn's focus shifted from her, Samantha turned and saw that Lieutenant-Colonel Currie, the 2nd Brigade commander, was approaching their table. Both of them were rising to their feet when the colonel said, "Don't get up on my account. We still have a few minutes before Colonel Shillington's briefing."

When she read the clock above the lieutenant-colonel's head, Samantha remained on her feet while Llewellyn fell back on his chair. "I'm afraid that I have to go, otherwise I'm going to be late for my shift."

"By all means, we can't have that, can we?" replied Currie in amusement.

"It is a pleasure to meet you, sir," said as she saluted Currie. She glanced at her tray then at the exit.

"I'll take care of the tray for you." Currie raised an eyebrow when he heard Llewellyn's offer.

"Thank you," she said as she gave Llewellyn her hand. When he took it, she liked his firm grip and held it a trifle longer than maybe she should have.

"You're going to be late. Are you not?" he stated.

She quickly released her hand. Her heart was already beating rapidly as she walked briskly out of the cafeteria.

CHAPTER 31

It was a rather sad Christmas, Samantha thought as she ran a brush through Claire's hair. Claire didn't complain when Samantha used a bit of extra pressure when the brush got caught in a couple of tangles. Her eyes were closed and her hands were folded neatly on her unmoving chest. Claire had passed away during the night. Her death was caused by pneumonia.

The chaplain was waiting outside with the rest of the off-duty nurses and medical staff. They were going to escort her to the nearby cemetery, where she would be laid to rest.

"She's done," Samantha said. The men beside her nodded and then slid a board of plain pine in position and nailed it close. When they were done, six sisters lifted the casket by the metal handles and carried her out of the villa to the truck. Waiting beside the vehicle were Matron Riley and Lieutenant-Colonel Shillington. The casket was slid gently into the back and then the driver locked the gate into place.

Samantha, the matron, and the lieutenant-colonel stepped into the staff car to follow the truck to the nearby cemetery.

"How are you doing?" asked the matron with concern.

"I'm fine," Samantha replied.

"If you want, you can have leave for the rest of the day," she suggested.

"I'd rather work," Samantha said as she watched the truck in front. She was going to miss Claire's gentle snoring.

DECEMBER 24, 1914
TRAIN STATION, AMESBURY

"Jesus!" exclaimed Captain Llewellyn as a truck mirror barely missed his nose. He hadn't been paying attention. He had looked to his Canadian left rather than his British right for traffic. It would have been an inglorious death being run over on High Street in front of the Amesbury train station.

He had taken a few days' leave in London with Captains Griffiths and Henry, but he had decided to call it short and return to Salisbury. He hadn't gotten much sleep since the two men had found some bedmates. He didn't have a problem paying, per se, but none of the ladies he had met appealed to him, for one reason or another. Besides, he got bored after the third day, and he was itching to get back and plough through the intelligence reports that were piling up on his desk.

As the truck screeched to a halt, he saw that it belong to the CEF. The steering wheel was on the left. The driver poked his head out and Llewellyn recognized the Fusiliers' cap badge when the driver shouted out, "You okay, buddy?"

"Why the hell are you driving a truck?" he demanded when he saw the face under the cap. "You damn nearly took my head off."

"I wouldn't have done that, Captain," said Corporal Duval with a hurt expression. "I like you, sir."

"How the hell did you get a driver's license?" To drive a military vehicle, you needed a military driver's license.

"License, sir?"

"Right," the captain said slowly.

"Need a lift back to camp?"

Llewellyn paused to calculate the odds of getting there in one piece. "What the hell! Sure, why not. You can only live once."

"Toss your bag in the back and get in."

The captain lifted the canvas cloth that covered the gate and was surprised to see it was packed with boxes and parcels of various shapes and sizes. When he shoved his bag in, he made sure that it was secure so it wouldn't fall out. This time he kept an eye on the traffic as he made his way to the passenger door. Duval's partner in crime, Private Dack, made room as the captain squeezed into the seat. When he slammed the door shut, he was surprised how smoothly Duval engaged the clutch.

"Congratulations on the promotion, Corporal Duval," said Llewellyn when he noticed the freshly sewn stripes on the man's sleeves.

"Things have gone to hell in a handbasket since you left, Captain," said Dack with a guffaw.

"I can see that. What's with the parcels in the back?"

Both men grinned sheepishly. "We're Santa's helpers," replied the corporal.

"You're what?" he said incredulously. The two men looked as far from being Santa's helpers as he could imagine.

"You wouldn't believe the number of packages that have been coming in for the men from Canada, the States, and from all over England," said Duval.

"I should know. My back's been sore for the last few days. Chaplain Stoat has been working us to the bone. I should have taken that offer in Wiltshire," stated the private. "A warm heart, good food, and a comfortable bed."

"The farmer's daughter would have something to say about that," said Duval.

"True, true," replied Dack. Llewellyn had read the orders that had been transmitted by General Alderson. Many British families had offered to take in Canadian soldiers for the holidays.

"No rest for the wicked. The chaplain also wants to donate what the men don't need to the local workhouse," Dack continued. The workhouse was where the poor and destitute were offered accommodation and employment.

"What I really need is some Christmas cheer," stated Duval.

"Not while you're driving," snapped Dack.

"Scrooge."

Dack turned to Llewellyn and said, "You're invited, Captain. The mess cooks have outdone themselves with fine victuals."

"I'd like that," replied the captain. He was actually looking forward to it. The paperwork could wait.

DECEMBER 24, 1914
BULFORD MANOR, BULFORD,
SALISBURY PLAIN

"Did you lose another horse?"

Paul Ryan looked up from the beer that his friends had bought him. His remount depot section had selected the Heart and Crown to have a Christmas party and to celebrate his leaving the unit. Standing before him, being leered at by a couple of his envious buddies, was a girl in her late teens dressed in a smart white blouse, an amber-coloured gored shirt, and a matching jacket.

"No," replied Paul. "I haven't. But your mother did threaten to turn more lost horses into glue."

Her cheeks dimpled in exactly the same way as the last time he saw her a few months back, when he had gone to her family's farm to retrieve a lost Canadian horse.

"What's with the long face?" she asked over the loud buzzing background noise of conversation and Christmas carols. "It's Christmas, you know."

"Yes, it is," Paul replied. He wasn't about to tell her that his worst fears had been realized. He received orders this morning, transferring him from his cushy job at the depot back to C Battery. He was going to back to being called McGill again, and he might even lose his acting corporal rank. Captain Fuller wasn't very happy about it, either, but he was somewhat mollified when Captain Masterley had agreed to exchange Reggie to replace him. It was part of Paul's doldrums. The other was the fact that his mother had not responded to his numerous letters. He had received Christmas letters from his brother and sister, as well as a long letter from his father, but nothing from his mom.

The girl looked at him for a moment with disapproval, then at the barely touched beer on the bar. She said, "Why don't you come for Christmas dinner tomorrow?"

"Excuse me?" replied Paul. He wasn't sure that he heard her correctly. He glimpsed a couple of friends enviously nudging each other with their elbows.

"We've invited some soldiers over, and I'm inviting you."

"I don't know," said Paul. He didn't want to appear eager. "What will your mother say?"

"If you can't face my mom, how will your face the Boche?" she pointed out. "By the way, what's your name?"

"Paul. Paul Ryan," he said, offering her his hand.

She shook it with a firm grip. "I'm Addy."

"Nice to meet you, Miss Addy."

"Be there at twelve sharp."

"Yes, ma'am," he replied. He was surprised by the lightness in his tone. His mood improved considerably when she gave him another over-the-shoulder dimpled smile before she disappeared in the crowded bar.

Paperwork! And more paperwork! sighed Prime Minister Borden as he put his signature on a standard letter to the Canadian Steel Company in reply to their request to be considered for the ship-building contracts that his government was considering. They had probably heard that the general manager of the Electric Boat Co. had met with him, John Hazen, and Admiral Kingsmill two weeks ago to discuss obtaining ten 602-type submarines similar to the ones that Premier McBride had bought in August. The proposal was interesting, and Kingsmill had forwarded it to the Admiralty in London for consideration.

Most of his day was like this. He had sent messages to George Perley, to the British prime minister, to the colonial secretary in London. He also had sent personal Christmas greetings to the provincial premiers, as well as to the prime ministers of the other British colonies: Newfoundland, South Africa, Australia, and New Zealand. He did have an hour and half respite when he met with his cabinet to discuss army boots.

When he glanced at the small clock on his desk, he grimaced. The black hands read six thirty. Laura was going to be upset with him for being late for supper. She also wanted him to take a nap before they attended midnight Mass at the All Saints Church. It was going to be cold, a forecast of minus fifteen. She was going to be even more displeased when he informed her that he needed to come in to the office on Christmas day. There were mailbags in the outer office that needed his attention.

He was looking forward to the hymns this evening. The choir was quite good. The one thing he planned on doing was to offer a prayer for the men and women that had been placed in harm's way.

CHAPTER 32

Matron Macdonald was pursing her lips as she read the memo. She was not pleased for a number of reasons, and she was deciding how to deal with the problem. It seemed that some colonel in the War Office had complained that he had seen a couple of her nurses dressed inappropriately while out riding over the weekend. The question was whether or not it was one of her nurses. That was yet to be determined. Still, she was reissuing a directive informing her people what was and was not appropriate to wear. She needed to protect their reputation.

"Matron," said Brenda Lowe. Her assistant stood in her office's entrance. She was in her late twenties, with a solid figure and black hair. She had worked at the general hospital before volunteering. Macdonald had taken her on because of the mountain of paperwork that was accumulating, and Brenda had shown some administrative ability.

"What is it, Brenda?" she asked. She could tell from Brenda's tense shoulders that it was bad news.

"We lost nursing sister, Claire Chapman," Brenda blurted as she handed her a telegram. Macdonald took it and read the details of the nurse's passing. It hurt that she lost one of her people so soon. She knew it was going to happen, but she hoped it would be later rather than sooner.

Macdonald raised an eyebrow when she saw the time stamp and looked up at Brenda.

Brenda flushed. "With Christmas yesterday, I didn't get to the grams until this morning," she replied.

"Let's not let this happen again," stated the matron. "Pull her file and make a note of the date of death. On her attestation papers, she should have indicated her next of kin. I'll write a letter to them offering my condolences. We'll have to send them a notification of her passing. Contact the pay office to inform them that she has deceased. All monies that she is entitled will be sent to her estate. Also, check to see if she had lodged a will. It she has, it will provide guidance on how her estate will be distributed."

"Yes, ma'am," Brenda acknowledged.

"Also, inform Matron Newman at Salisbury of her death. She can tell Claire's friends of her passing. On Sunday we'll have a memorial Mass in her memory, here in London and on Salisbury Plain. I expect that all nurses not on duty to attend."

"Is that everything, Matron?"

"Yes," she said. As she glanced at the telegram, another thought occurred to her. "Wait, send a gram to La Touquet asking them if they need a replacement."

As Brenda hurried off to perform her tasks, Margaret rose from her desk and crossed the hall. She knocked on the heavy oak-panelled door with the brass plaque and black lettering that read, *Director, Canadian Medical Army Corps.*

"Come in," said a muffled voice.

When she opened the door, she saw two officers sitting in front of Colonel Jones's desk.

"I'm sorry. I didn't realize that you were currently engaged in a meeting," she said as she started to back out of the room.

"No! No! Do come in," Jones said as he waved her in. "You may provide a valuable point of view to our discussion." He noticed that she was somewhat tense. "Something happened?"

"Yes, Colonel," she replied, "I regret to inform you that we lost a nurse."

The colonel winced at the news. "How?"

"Nurse Chapman died the day before Christmas in La Touquet due to pneumonia."

The officer with the colonel tabs and the Royal Medical Army Corps insignia offered his condolences. "Sorry for your loss."

"Thank you, Colonel."

"Excuse my manners. This is Colonel Cunningham from the War Office, and you know Major Shaw." The matron acknowledged the major, who was Colonel Jones's adjutant, with a brief nod.

"Major, if you can be so kind, please grab a chair from her office."

"Of course. Please have my seat," he offered as he rose to his feet.

By the time she was seated comfortably, the major had returned with a chair with a red velvet seat and back cushions. He then sat near the door, slightly out of the line of vision of Colonel Cunningham and the matron.

"We have been discussing the cerebrospinal meningitis outbreak among the men at Salisbury Plain," stated Colonel Jones.

"Of course. I've been reading the reports. They indicated that we've

282

had seven cases since we've been on the plain," she replied. Cerebrospinal meningitis was an infection that caused inflammation of the spinal cord and the lining covering the brain. If diagnosed early enough and given serums, the chances of the patient recovering were quite good. Otherwise, the disease was fatal. There were always sporadic cases, but epidemics occurred every three to four years, usually during the winter months.

"The War Office is of the opinion that we brought a new strain of the disease," stated the colonel in a flat tone.

"Really?" said Macdonald with a raised eyebrow.

"We have been informed that there was one case at Valcartier and three cases during your voyage to England," said Colonel Cunningham.

"One of those cases was a seaman. Not a member of the contingent," she pointed out. She noticed that the colonel didn't like being corrected by her.

"True," conceded Cunningham reluctantly. "However, there have been seven more cases confirmed among the Canadians. And the latest returns we have received indicate that several new cases are waiting for confirmation."

"Unfortunately, that is correct," replied the colonel. "From our analysis, it seems the disease is more prevalent among the men in the huts than those still under canvas. We have not been able to determine the cause or how exactly it is being spread."

"One theory suggests that fatigue could be a factor," interjected Major Shaw.

"There isn't sufficient evidence to support that at present," said Cunningham.

"The men have been complaining about their food rations," stated Macdonald.

"They are always complaining about the food," replied Colonel Cunningham.

"True. In this case, it is not about the quality but about the quantity," answered the matron. "Which could increase the men's fatigue."

"Aren't they getting the standard imperial rations?" asked Cunningham.

"From our observations, our men seemed to be slightly taller and larger than the regular imperial troops," indicated Colonel Jones.

The colonel was somewhat taken aback from that statement. "Aren't most of your men of British stock?"

"Yes," stated Matron Macdonald. "We're not sure exactly why."

"Diet," interjected the major.

The matron and the colonels turned to the major. "I don't have sufficient evidence to prove it, but I believe that our diet has had an impact."

"How?" asked Cunningham.

"I've noticed that red meat here in England is expensive. You import most of your beef from us, the States, and Australia. In Canada, the same meats are considerably cheaper, and they could get better cuts for the same price. If a man immigrated when he was in his teens or younger, the red meat plus the milk we drink would add an inch or two of growth to his size. If he moved to Canada in his twenties, he could be bigger around the waist, but his overall size would not be different."

"An interesting theory," said the colonel skeptically. "I'll talk with the War Office about increasing your men's rations. As for the cerebrospinal meningitis, we are setting up a committee to investigate the subject. We ask that you appoint a delegate to present your views on the matter," he said as he rose to his feet, calling the meeting to an end.

When Cunningham left the room, Colonel Jones looked at his two subordinates then asked, "What do you think?"

"I think that we're going to be blamed for a meningitis outbreak," said Matron Macdonald.

"I agree," said the major.

"But I think we'll have to prove that's not the case," she said.

Colonel Jones nodded. "I'll talk with Colonel Adami and have him investigate it. Major, send a telegram to Ottawa. Ask them to contact the provincial medical authorities for details on any reported cases," he ordered.

"Yes, Colonel," said the major as he rose to take the borrowed chair with him.

"Again, I'm sorry to hear about the lost of your nursing sister," said Jones.

"Thank you, Guy. But it does bring up something to consider. We may need to set up a convalescent home to treat my nurses if they get sick or ill. Especially if the war is going to be a long one."

"We may need one for our medical staff as well," the colonel agreed. "I'll pass that on to Ottawa and see if we can get authorization. Now, if you have a few minutes, I have some administrative details to discuss. What I would like ..."

"Good morning, William," said Major-General Gwatkin as he entered his adjutant-general's office. "How are you settling in?"

Brigadier-General William Egerton Hodgins grinned at his boss. "Getting there. The staff here has been quite helpful. I'm staying at the Roxborough Apartments while my wife is bringing our things from London."

Hodgins had just been appointed acting adjutant-general to replace Colonel Denison, who was given command of an infantry brigade with the second contingent. Actually, the position still belonged to Colonel Williams, who was in France attached to General French's staff. To take the position, he had to give up command of the No. 1 Military District, which was headquartered in London, Ontario. One of the enticements was that it would eventually be permanent. A former lawyer with the Justice Department, he had resigned in 1903 to become an officer in the permanent force. He was promoted earlier in the year to his current rank. He was another Boer War veteran.

"Can I help you with anything?" Hodgins asked as he shifted a stack of red-striped manila folders to the corner of his desk. It was obvious he wanted to rearrange the office to his liking.

"We have a meeting this afternoon concerning how we will start recruiting the third contingent."

"Have we received word when the second contingent will sail?"

Gwatkin shook his head. "The War Office has requested that we hold off sending them for now. They don't have room for them at the moment."

"When the first contingent goes to France, that should free up some space."

"It will. It also gives us more time to train the men," Gwatkin replied. He didn't bother to say that the War Office was not happy with the CEF. They had been led to believe that the men were fully trained. Kitchener was notorious for not deploying troops until he felt that they were ready.

"The training syllabus that General Alderson was able to share with us, plus the reports and intelligence summaries, were quite useful," stated Hodgins. "We incorporated as much as we could in the No. 1 District's lesson plan for the men."

"Good," replied a pleased Gwatkin.

"I wanted to ask about the Ross rifle production. It took too long to equip the second contingent. We were still using the Mk II. I hope that it will improve with the third contingent."

"I know. Demand is exceeding production, even though they have been ramping it up. As for the third contingent, we want to modify the recruitment."

Hodgins nodded. "I've read the proposal. You want to spark local interest, especially among the native-born Canadians. The general feeling is that we've exhausted those who were British-born."

"The plan is the local regiments will provide the recruits with basic drill. The more advance training will be done at the battalion HQs. It's our hope it will increase recruitment rates."

"So the current plan for the third contingent will be three battalions of infantry and two squadrons of cavalry from the 2nd military district."

Gwatkin pointed to the pile of folders on Hodgins' desk. "You will find a return there of the surplus officers from the first contingent. They just recently disembarked at Halifax. I want you to go through the list and select those who you feel are good officers."

"Won't the minister want to have a say in the matter?" asked Hodgins.

Gwatkin shrugged and said, "He'll want to have a say in the senior commanders. My main concern is the junior officers. It is important that we find good lieutenants and captains, as they will be in the thick of it."

"I agree. If the war continues, we may have to establish an officer school in England."

"We may have to do that. In that pile you will also find a recommendation from General Alderson that a remount base be established at Salisbury Plain."

Hodgins frowned. "Don't they already have one?"

"It's advance depot. It's too small to meet our needs. He wants one that can accommodate nearly 5,000 horses. Based on his report he states that it will cost nearly $400,000 to construct the base. Most of the money will go into constructing storage, stables, barracks, and mess halls. For staff it would require about thirty-six officers, 2,000 enlisted men, and four veterinarians."

Hodgins grimaced at the mention of the veterinarians. "Getting qualified horse doctors is going to be a problem. They are in short supply." He had to look into finding suitable candidates to take care of the cavalry horses for the No. 1 Military District. According to the last census, there were only 1,200 veterinarians in Canada, and they were in heavy demand. In 1910, the militia establish the Army Veterinary Corps to provide appropriate care of the various animals in service. It had two branches: the Canadian Permanent Army Veterinary Corps was the permanent force component, while the Canadian Army Veterinary Corps took care of the mounted corps of the Militia. It was from these organizations that the veterinarians for the first two contingents were drawn upon. He would have to talk with the director as to what his needs were.

"And we'll have to talk with Sir Beck at the Remount Commission as well. Getting suitable cavalry mounts have been an issue," stated Hodgins. Sir Adam Beck headed the special committee on remounts. Sir Beck was a prominent Ontario Conservative who once headed the Hydro-Electric Commission of Ontario, where he was a strong proponent of public electrical power. He was also a prominent horse breeder and racer.

"I've seen the reports on the difficulties that he has been having," stated Gwatkin. "Considering that there are nearly 2.6 million horses in Canada, I'm somewhat surprised."

"Finding the animals we need is a bit of a challenge considering we want them between five to nine years of age and at reasonable prices," pointed out Hodgins. "Most of the working animals are needed by farmers to raise crops. The British Remount Commission is also competing for horses. Even though they are buying most of them from the States."

Led by Sir William Frederick Benson, nine British officers had arrived in August to supply remounts to the British Army.

Gwatkin looked thoughtfully. "We may have to look at the motorized vehicles to take up the slack."

"We may have to."

"Let's discuss at this afternoon's meeting then. It's at 1:30 sharp," stated Gwatkin as he turned to leave.

"Yes, sir. I'll be there," replied Hodgins as he returned to reorganizing his office.

DECEMBER 29, 1914
MINISTER OF MILITIA AND DEFENCE,
WOODS BUILDING, OTTAWA

"That's my report on the conditions at Salisbury Plain," concluded Colonel Carson as he leaned back in the chair.

"I didn't realize that the mud was that bad," said Colonel E.W. Wilson, the commanding officer of Montreal's No. 4 Military District.

"I wore long rubber boots the entire time that I was there," stated Carson. "Even then the mud was so deep it came of the top of them. The water will not drain away, and with all the traffic, the plain has become a bog." There was a tone of disgust in the man's voice.

"How have my boys been holding up?" asked Sam Hughes. All three men were sitting in his office in the Woods Building. A brisk wind buffeted the window that had frost at the edges. The muted rumble of streetcars and traffic was heard on occasion.

"Like I said in my letter to you at the beginning of December, they have been enduring the conditions with little complaint so far. They are all anxious to do something. Rumours have been flying around that the War Office needed troops in Egypt. When I spoke with Lord Kitchener, he said that the Australian contingent was sufficient for the moment and there was no need for more. From what he indicated, he might not be able to use us until February."

"Damn it, the war could be over by then," exclaimed Hughes. The two men didn't contradict the minister, since they were of the opinion it was going to last longer than that.

"The only troops that have been deployed have been the No. 2 Stationary Hospital and the Princess Patricia's, who arrived in the Havre on the 22nd."

Hughes turned sour when the Princess Patricia's were mentioned. "Against my better judgement, I allowed them to go. Because of that I have to now squash rumours that our boys will go as separate battalions and they will be merged with British divisions. And I had to answer questions as to why they were re-equipped with Lee-Enfields." Both men were well aware of the complicated relationship that the minister had with Lieutenant-Colonel Francis Farquhar. Some of that was coloured by the fact that Farquhar had been the Duke of Connaught's military secretary. Also, the colonel was a British professional soldier who had seen service in the South African and Somalia campaigns.

"That's one of the reasons that I've asked you here, Colonel Wilson. Since they are now in France sooner or later they will need reinforcements. I would like you to supply them from your command."

"Of course, General," replied Wilson. "Would about 120 to 130 men be sufficient?"

"At the moment, yes," replied Hughes.

288

"I don't think that it will be a problem when I ask for volunteers," said Wilson with a smile. Colonel Wilson had once been the CO of the Victoria Rifles stationed in Montreal. In 1907 he had resigned his position and moved to the reserve list. The reason he had given at the time was that he wanted to make room for the younger officers. Since August, he was promoted to full colonel and was made commander of the No. 4 Military District. "When I get a list, I'll forward them to your office."

"Good," said Hughes. When another brisk gust rattled the window, it broke Hughes' train of thought for a moment. "How many men do we still have under canvas?"

"About 11 to 12,000," replied Carson. "We would have had nearly all of them in suitable housing if General Alderson hadn't blocked my efforts. Lord Kitchener had agreed to make room by moving some of the imperial troops out after I had brought it to his attention. I was not happy, to say the least."

"I wasn't happy with him either, when he countermanded my orders concerning the canteens," answered Hughes. "There have been rumours in the papers that he is considering resigning his post. When I telegrammed the War Office to confirm, they have assured me that the rumours are false. So for the moment he has my full support."

He then pointed to Carson. "I want you back in England as soon as possible. I'm pushing through an order-in-council that will make you my representative. You will be rated as a general staff officer and be responsible for equipment and supplies for our forces there."

"Yes, minister," replied Carson. Hughes' message was quite clear. He was to keep an eye on General Alderson.

Hughes nodded. "Now, I've have been looking at the contingent, and I've made the decision that the four extra battalions at Salisbury will be used as infantry reinforcements. The 6th Mounted Battalion will reinforce the other mounted units. To complete the second Canadian Division, we will need to raise four more battalions, in addition to the ones that we are currently recruiting. The fourth infantry brigade will be made up of units from London, Toronto, and Kingston, while the sixth will be formed from the Vancouver, Winnipeg, and Calgary regiments.

"The 5th Brigade will include units from your command," Major-General Hughes said as he looked at Wilson, who stiffened in anticipation. "It will be comprised of the French-Canadian Battalion, the 22nd, and your 24th. The 25th from Halifax and the 26th from St. John will be added. We haven't made a final decisions, but we may add Quebec City's 23rd Battalion to the brigade."

"I appreciate the confidence, General," replied Wilson. "I have good men under my command."

"I'm sure that they will give a good account for themselves. Whenever we can get to the front," replied Hughes. "Now, I want to discuss some of the senior commanders for the various units and what your opinions are …"

CHAPTER 33

As Colonel Williams was giving a lecture, Llewellyn noticed that from time to time he would adjust the sling that held his broken arm. The captain could imagine that the white cast was itching, and he couldn't get to the spot to scratch it.

The former Valcartier camp commander had broken his arm on the 24th when he and three other colonels suffered a traffic accident on their way back from Southampton. The initial report was that no one survived. The next Llewellyn heard about the colonels was that Williams suffered a broken arm, Turner a broken collarbone and two fractured ribs, and Burling a sprained wrist. His commander, Lieutenant-Colonel Currie, was unscathed.

Captain Llewellyn was sitting in the middle row of benches with the other senior offices of Lieutenant-Colonel Currie's command.

Everyone was paying attention to Williams as he continued his briefing. "During our visit, we have been informed that willow and poplar tree stumps resemble a crouching soldier. A branch sticking out can be mistaken as a gun. Patrols have been lost when they fired on them, betraying their positions."

He turned a page with one hand then continued. "The Germans are quite adept at misdirecting our artillery. One of the popular contraptions they use is a Maltese cart with a wine or water barrel strapped to it. From a distance it resembles a German 42-centimetre gun when the barrel is tilted skyward. The artillery officers have stated they have wasted a fair amount of ammunition firing at them.

"I'm well aware that a popular topic is the state of the trenches that we will soon occupy." There was a slight rustling of anticipation that Williams might now announce the date they would be shipped to France. "I'm sorry to say that the trenches in France are in the same conditions that we face here. The communication trenches are the most problematic. With the record rains, units have lost men while marching through them.

"One item that I have observed is that the trenches are well protected by barbed wire. We are currently deficient in wire cutters. The quartermaster is currently looking into acquiring suitable supplies. When they become available, we'll distribute them to the appropriate units. What is of interest is that the French have developed a crossbow that launches hooks into the barbwire. They will then pull on the hooked wires, hoping to drag them down. I've put a request to see if we can examine the device and determine its usefulness.

"Also, the commanders that I have spoken with have been quite firm about drunkenness in the trenches. Several have stated summary executions have been dealt out to men who have been drunk on duty. Inform the men quite firmly that alcohol and drunkenness in the trenches will not be tolerated.

"A significant number of losses have been due to enemy pinking our men. It is important to instil that they do not expose themselves. Most of the losses have been due to carelessness as they move through the trenches and communication lines.

"Are there any questions?" the colonel asked. When no one raised their hand, he continued. "We received orders that on Sunday, January 3, there will be special intercession services. All men are urged to attend the religious parades. All churches in the Empire will be offering prayers for the welfare of the Empire.

"On a personal note, I wish you all a safe and productive New Year," he said as he closed the leather folio that held his speech, indicating that the men were dismissed.

"Well, that was a cherry lecture to welcome the New Year," said Captain Henry in a dry tone. "You were there with the advance party. What do you think?"

"It's what I've been saying," replied Llewellyn. He had spent the same three days and nights that Colonel Williams had. The one thing that he had to admit was that he had a difficult time not putting his head up over the trenches to take a look. But his escorts refused to allow him to except through special binoculars that permitted the sentries to view the enemy trenches without putting themselves in danger.

"The one thing is that the barbed wire is not that thick at the moment, and only two or three feet high."

Captain Griffiths frowned. "It doesn't seem to be much of an obstacle."

Llewellyn cocked an eyebrow in amusement. "Really! You should try it some time." Griffiths' face flushed when he realized he had said something stupid. "And what the colonel said about the sharpshooters is accurate. I didn't see them when I was in the line, but they told me stories about a captain walking in the trenches. The Germans would fire just behind him to speed him up. At one point he stopped to smoke a pipe."

"Did he survive?" asked Griffiths.

"No! As he lit his pipe he was hit in the head."

Both captains winced. "That's what we have to look forward to!"

As they exited the tent, they watched a company slough through the muddy field at the back of the Ye Old Bustard. The air was crisp and there was a ray of sunshine that lingered around the thin wisps of clouds. The mess kitchens were working at full tilt as they were preparing a hot meal for the men. Actually, they were preparing a special meal of turkey with all the trimmings for their New Year's meal. The canteens had opened earlier, but they would be closed earlier as well. After supper, the YMCA tents would be filled with men and guests to celebrate the new year. He and the other officers were attending.

When Llewellyn saw the bandages and plasters on the men's hands, he knew that they were coming from bayonet practice. It was easy to tell because their left hands were bleeding. Some were still bright red. The left hand held the gunstock and was nearest the bayonet. The men's sweaty hands combined with the gun oil on the stock that hand that had a tendency to slip and jam against the foresight and against the metal ring for the leather sling. In some cases, they'd sliced their hands on the bayonet's sharp edge.

As Griffiths, Henry, and Llewellyn headed toward their transport back to their camp, they passed a group of men who were re-bandaging their hands after the men were ordered to fall out.

Captain Llewellyn grinned when he heard one of the soldiers saying, "I'm getting tired of this shit."

"Yeah," said the other, who then yelped when the bandaged was tightened. "Hey, take it easy! I need that fucking hand, you know!"

As the man loosened the bandage, he said sourly, "Ever since I volunteered in August, all I've been doing is fucking drill."

"Yeah! When the fuck are we going to France?" the soldier demanded as his companion retightened the bandage on his bloody hand.

The story continues in

HAMMERING THE BLADE

The Canadians are being hammered on two fronts.

On the home front, Sir Robert Borden's government is being rocked by scandals. First it was the soldiers' bad boots, then charges of graft and corruption in the militia department's contracts, followed by the shell crisis. With an election in the air and the opposition pounding his minister of Militia and Defence, Major-General Sam Hughes, Borden is fighting desperately to save his government.

On the western front, after six months of constant harsh training, the CEF finally enter the trenches in France. Infantry Captain Llewellyn struggles to keep his men alive as snipers take their toll, and the Ross rifle fails its first combat test. Nothing prepares him for the chlorine gas attack at Ypres. A frustrated Gunner Paul Ryan watches helplessly as his comrades-in-arms suffer. He can't help, since artillery shells are in short supply. As the battles rage, nursing sister Samantha Lonsdale is nearly overwhelmed as she cares for the sick, the wounded, and the dying.

As the hammer blows fall, the blade is being tempered into cold steel.

To be released in late 2016.

For latest news and updates visit
www.sambiasebooks.ca